KU-204-128

FEAR

DON'T BE TOO AFRAID ANNIE!

MICHAEL GRANT

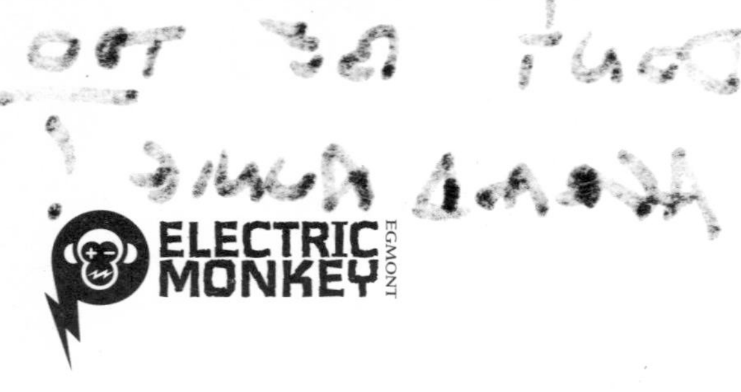

First published in Great Britain 2012
by Egmont UK Limited
239 Kensington High Street
London W8 6SA
First published in the USA 2012
by HarperTeen

Published by arrangement
with HarperTeen
a division of HarperCollins Publishers, Inc.
1350 Avenue of the Americas, New York,
New York 10019, USA

Text copyright © 2012 Michael Grant

The moral rights of the author have been asserted

ISBN 978 1 4052 5761 9

3 5 7 9 10 8 6 4

www.egmont.co.uk

A CIP catalogue record for this title is available from the British Library

Typeset by Avon DataSet Ltd, Bidford on Avon, Warwickshire
Printed and bound in Great Britain by Clays Ltd, St Ives plc

47252/5

All rights reserved. No part of this publication may be reproduced, stored in a retrieval system, or transmitted, in any form or by any means, electronic, mechanical, photocopying, recording or otherwise, without the prior permission of the publisher and copyright owner.

EGMONT

Our story began over a century ago, when seventeen-year-old Egmont Harald Petersen found a coin in the street. He was on his way to buy a flyswatter, a small hand-operated printing machine that he then set up in his tiny apartment.

The coin brought him such good luck that today Egmont has offices in over 30 countries around the world. And that lucky coin is still kept at the company's head offices in Denmark.

For Katherine, Jake, and Julia

O LORD, my God, I call for help by day;
I cry out in the night before thee . . .
Thou hast put me in the depths of the Pit,
in the regions dark and deep.
Thy wrath lies heavy upon me, and thou dost overwhelm
me with all thy waves.
Thou hast caused my companions to shun me;
thou hast made me a thing of horror to them.
I am shut in so that I cannot escape;
my eye grows dim through sorrow . . .
Afflicted and close to death from my youth up,
I suffer thy terrors; I am helpless.
Thy wrath has swept over me; thy dread assaults destroy me . . .
Thou hast caused lover and friend to shun me;
my companions are in darkness.

– Psalm 88: 1, 6–9, 15–16, 18
(Revised Standard Version)

OUTSIDE

ONE MINUTE NURSE Connie Temple had been updating her journal on her little laptop. And the next minute she was gone.

There.

Gone.

No 'poof'. No flash of light. No explosion.

Connie Temple had found herself on the beach. On her back. In the sand. She'd been sitting when it happened and so she had sat down suddenly on the sand and had fallen on to her back, with her knees drawn up.

All around her lay others. People she didn't know. Some she recognised as faces in town.

Some were standing, some were sitting, some sat as though they were still holding on to a steering wheel. Some were in workout clothing and seemed to have arrived on the beach, on the highway, still running.

A man Connie recognised as a teacher at Sam's school stood

blinking, hand raised, like he'd been writing something on a chalkboard.

Connie had stood slowly, dazed, not believing any of it was real. Wondering if she'd had a stroke. Wondering if this was some hallucination. Wondering if this was the end of the world. Or the end of her life.

And then she had seen it: a blank, grey, featureless wall. It was incredibly tall and seemed to curve away.

It extended out into the ocean. It cut the highway. It cut Clifftop, a posh hotel, in half. It extended inland, far out of sight, cutting through everything in its way.

Only later would they learn that it was a sphere twenty miles across. Aerial shots soon popped up all over the internet.

Only later, after days of disbelief and denial, did the world accept that none of the children had been transported. Every single person under the age of fifteen was gone.

Of the population of Perdido Beach, California, and some of the surrounding area, not a single adult had been killed, though some were injured when they found themselves suddenly in the desert, suddenly in the water, suddenly tumbling down a hillside. One woman found herself suddenly in another person's home. One man had appeared wet, wearing a bathing suit and standing in the middle of the highway with cars swerving like crazy to avoid him.

But in the end there had been only one death: a salesman

from San Luis Obispo on his way down to talk about insurance with a couple in Perdido Beach. He hadn't seen the barrier across the road up in the Stefano Rey National Park and his Hyundai hit it going seventy miles an hour.

Connie couldn't remember his name now.

A lot of names had come and gone in her life since then.

With an effort she pulled herself out of the memory of that day. Something important was being said.

'The energy signature has changed.'

'The what?' Connie Temple glanced at Abana Baidoo. They had become good friends over these long, terrible months. Abana usually had a better grasp of the scientific details than Connie. But now she just shrugged.

George Zellicoe, the third of the family spokespersons, had checked out mentally a long time ago. He still came to the briefings, but he'd fallen silent. Connie and Abana had both tried to reach out to him, but he was lost now. Depression had claimed him and now there wasn't much left of the once energetic, opinionated man.

'The energy signature,' Colonel Matteu said. 'What we've started calling the J wave.'

'What does that mean, exactly?' Connie asked.

The colonel didn't look much like a colonel. He had the flawlessly pressed army uniform, of course, and the neatly trimmed hair, but he tended to slouch inside that uniform, leaving the impression that either it was a size too big or he had shrunk since buying it.

He was the third officer to be assigned to command the forces at the Bowl. The Bowl. The Perdido Beach Blister. He was the first to be able to answer a simple question honestly.

'We don't know. All we know is that right from the start we got this energy signature and it was one-way. And now it's shifting.'

'But you don't know what that means,' Abana said. She had a way of talking that turned every question into an incredulous challenge.

'No, ma'am. We don't know.'

Connie heard the slight overemphasis on the word 'know'.

'What is it they suspect?' Connie asked.

The colonel sighed. 'I preface this by reminding all of us that we've been through a dozen – a hundred – different theories. Nothing has been right so far. We had one set of theories when the twins appeared safe and sound. And then, when Francis . . .'

No one needed to be reminded of Francis. What had emerged of Francis had been a horror caught on camera, live, and rebroadcast again and again to a sickened world. Seventy million plays on YouTube.

Soon after that, there had been Mary. That, mercifully, had not been filmed. They'd found her and removed what was left of the girl to a facility where she was kept alive. If you could call it life.

The air-conditioning suddenly came alive. The trailers tended to be hot, even on cool days like this one, with the ocean breeze blowing.

'We know by now not to believe everything we hear,' Abana said mordantly.

The colonel nodded. 'They think there may be a . . . a softening, they're calling it.' He held up a hand, cutting off the quick reaction. 'No, they still can't penetrate the barrier. But in the past when they've tried bombarding portions of the barrier with X-rays or gamma rays the barrier has acted as a perfect mirror, bouncing back a hundred per cent of the energy that struck it.'

'That's changed?'

'The last test showed ninety-eight-point-four per cent refraction. It doesn't sound like much. And it may not mean anything. But it's been a hundred per cent since day one. And a hundred per cent every day since. And now it's not a hundred per cent.'

'It's weakening,' Abana said.

'Maybe.'

The three of them, Connie, Abana, and George (the parents of Sam, Dahra, and E.Z.) left the trailer. The California National Guard's grandly named Camp Camino Real stood on the landward side of the highway, in a vacant stretch of land just a quarter mile from the southern boundary of the Bowl. It was an array of two dozen trailers and sheds laid out with military precision. More permanent buildings – a barracks, a motor pool, a maintenance building – were under construction.

When Camp Camino Real had first gone up it was all alone on the lovely, windswept heights above the beach. But since then the Courtyard by Marriott had been completed, as had the Carl's Jr. The Del Taco had just sold its first burrito a few days ago, and the Holiday Inn Express had opened one wing while construction continued on the rest.

There were only two media satellite trucks left, parked by the side of the highway. But they rarely got any on-air time any more: the country and the world had largely lost interest, although about two thousand tourists a day still made the trip up the highway to the viewing area, parking all along the highway for a mile or more.

A handful of souvenir vendors still made a living from canvas-awninged stalls.

George climbed into his car and drove off without a word. Connie and Abana lived here now, sharing a Winnebago with a privileged parking spot overlooking the Pacific. They had a nice gas barbecue donated by Home Depot, and every Friday evening she and Abana would have a cookout – burgers or ribs – with the media people and whatever Guardsmen or soldiers or highway patrolmen happened to be around and off duty.

The two women walked across the highway from Camp Camino Real and sat in lawn chairs turned towards the ocean. Connie made coffee and brought a cup to Abana.

'Do we hold a conference call on this?' Abana asked.

Connie sighed. 'The families will want to know.'

The families. That was the term settled on by the media. At first they had referred to them as 'the survivors'. But that had implied the others, the children, had died. Even at the start, the mothers and fathers, brothers and sisters, had rejected that idea.

Out at sea a coastguard cutter rode on gentle waves, guarding the watery perimeter of the anomaly. A grief-crazed family member had driven a boatload of explosives into the side of the dome months earlier. The resulting explosion had had no effect on the Bowl, of course.

'I was just getting to the point . . .' Connie began.

Abana waited and sipped her coffee.

'I was getting to the point where I was starting to think I needed to get back to something else. You know? Like maybe it was time to move on.'

Her friend nodded. 'And now this. This weakening. This one-point-six per cent change.'

'And now, and now, and now,' Connie said wearily. 'Hope is cruel.'

'Some guy, some physicist at Stanford, says if the barrier ever does come down it could be catastrophic.'

'He's not the first to say that.'

'Yeah, well, maybe not. But he's the first to have a Nobel Prize. He thinks the barrier is some form of protective coating over an antimatter sphere. He's worried it could set off an explosion big enough to annihilate the western half of the United States.'

Connie made a dismissive snort. 'Theory number eight thousand, seven hundred, and forty-two.'

'Yeah,' Abana agreed. But she looked worried.

'That's not going to happen,' Connie said firmly. 'Because what's going to happen is that the barrier is going to come down. And my son Sam and your daughter, Dahra, are going to come walking down that road.'

Abana smiled. She finished their long-worn joke. 'And walk right past us to get a burger at Carl's.'

Connie reached for her hand. 'That's right. That's what's going to happen. It'll be, "Hey, Mom, see you later: I'm going to go grab a burger."'

They were quiet for a while. Both women closed their eyes and lifted their faces to the sun.

'If only there had been some warning,' Abana said.

She'd said it before: she regretted having argued with her daughter the morning before the event.

And as usual the response was on the tip of Connie's tongue: *I did have warning.*

I had a warning.

But this time, as every time, Connie Temple said nothing.

ONE

65 HOURS 11 MINUTES

SHE WORE A pair of jeans and a plaid flannel shirt over a black T-shirt several sizes too big.

A leather belt made two turns around her waist. It was a man's belt, and a big man at that. But it was sturdy and bore the weight of the .38 revolver, the machete, and her water bottle.

Her backpack was dirty and the seams were all frayed, but it sat comfortably on her thin shoulders. In the pack she had three precious vacuum packs of dehydrated macaroni liberated from distant campsites. Just add water. She also had most of a cooked pigeon in a Tupperware container, a dozen wild green onions, a bottle of vitamins – she allowed herself one every three days – as well as pencil and paper, three books, a small bag of pot and a little pipe, needle and thread, two Bic lighters, and a spare water bottle. There was also a medicine pouch: a few Band-Aids, a mostly used tube of Neosporin and a dozen precious Tylenol, and infinitely more precious tampons.

Astrid Ellison had changed.

Her blonde hair was short, hacked off crudely with a knife and without benefit of a mirror. Her face was deeply tanned. Her hands were calloused and scarred from the innumerable small cuts she'd got from prying open mussels. One fingernail had been torn completely off when she slipped down an abrupt hill and ended up saving herself only by clawing madly at rocks and shrubs.

Astrid swung the pack off her shoulders, loosened the drawstring, and extracted a pair of heavy gloves sized for a grown man.

She surveyed the blackberry bramble for ripe berries. They didn't all ripen at once, and she never allowed herself to take any before they were fully developed. This was her blackberry patch, the only one she'd located, and she was determined not to be greedy.

Astrid's stomach rumbled as she dealt with the incredibly sharp thorns – so sharp they sometimes went right through the gloves – and pried berries loose. She took two dozen: dessert for later.

She was at the northern edge of the FAYZ, up where the barrier cut through the Stefano Rey National Park. Here the trees – redwoods, black oak, quaking aspen, ash – grew tall. Some were cut through by the barrier. In places branches went into the barrier. She wondered if they came out the other side.

She wasn't far inland, just a quarter mile or maybe a little more from the shore, where she often searched for oysters, clams, mussels, and crabs no bigger than large roaches.

Astrid was usually hungry. But she wasn't starving.

Water was a bigger concern. She'd found a water tank at the ranger station, and she'd found a tiny stream of what seemed like clean, fresh water fed from some underground aquifer, but neither was close to her camp. And since water weighed a lot to carry, she had to watch every drop and –

A sound.

Astrid crouched, swung her shotgun off her shoulder, raised it, sighted along the barrels, all in one fluid, long-practised move.

She listened. Listened hard. She heard her heart pounding and willed it to slow, slow, quiet so she could listen.

Her breath was ragged but she calmed it a little, at least.

She scanned slowly, turning her upper body left to right, then back, covering the trees where she thought the sound had come from. She listened hard in all directions.

Nothing.

Sound!

Dry leaves and damp earth. Not heavy, whatever it was. It wasn't a heavy sound. Not a Drake sound. Not even a coyote.

Astrid relaxed a little. Her shoulders were tight. She rolled them, hoping to avoid a cramp.

Something small scuttled away. Probably a possum or a skunk.

Not Drake.

Not the monster with the tentacle for an arm. Not the sadist. The psychopath.

The murderer, Whip Hand.

Astrid stood all the way up and slipped the shotgun back into place.

How many times each day did she endure this same fear? How many hundreds of times had she peered into the trees or bushes or rocks searching for that narrow, dead-eyed face? Day and night. As she dressed. As she cooked. As she used the slit trench. When she slept. How many times? And how many times had she imagined firing both barrels of the shotgun straight into his face, obliterating his features, blood spraying . . . and knowing that he would still come after her?

She would pump round after round into him and still she would be the one running and gasping for air, tripping through the forest, crying, and knowing that nothing she could do would stop him.

The evil that could not be killed.

The evil that sooner or later would take her.

With her berries safely tucked away in her backpack Astrid headed back towards her camp.

Camp was two tents: one – buff coloured – she slept in, and one – green with tan lining – she used for storage of non-food items scavenged from the various campgrounds, ranger offices, and trash heaps in the Stefano Rey.

Once home Astrid unloaded her berries and the rest of the food she'd brought with her into a red-and-white plastic cooler. She'd dug a hole right up against the barrier, and the cooler fit perfectly into that hole.

She'd learned many things in the four months since she had left everyone and everything behind and gone off into the woods. One thing she had learned was that animals avoided the barrier. Even the insects stayed a few feet back. So storing her food right up against that eye-tricking, pearly grey wall kept it safe.

It also helped to keep her safe. Camping here, this close to the barrier, and right at the cliff's edge, meant there were fewer ways a predator could come at her.

She had strung a wire in a perimeter around the camp. The wire was hung with bottles containing marbles, and rusty cans. Anything that hit the wire would make a racket.

She couldn't say she felt safe. A world where Drake was presumably still alive would never be safe. But she felt as safe here as anywhere in the FAYZ.

Astrid flopped into her nylon sling chair, propped her weary feet up on a second chair, and opened a book. Life now was an almost constant search for food, and without any lamp she had only an hour of light at sunset to read.

It was a beautiful location atop a sheer bluff by the ocean. But she turned her back to the setting sun to catch the red rays on the page of her book.

The book was *Heart of Darkness.*

I tried to break the spell – the heavy, mute spell of the wilderness – that seemed to draw him to its pitiless breast by the awakening of forgotten and brutal instincts, by the memory of gratified and monstrous passions. This alone, I was convinced, had driven him out to the edge of the forest, to the bush, towards the gleam of fires, the throb of drums, the drone of weird incantations; this alone had beguiled his unlawful soul beyond the bounds of permitted aspirations.

Astrid looked up at the trees. Her camp was in a small clearing, but the trees pressed close on two sides. They weren't as towering here close to the shore as they were farther inland. These seemed friendlier trees than the ones deeper into the forest.

"'The heavy, mute spell of the wilderness,'" Astrid read aloud.

For her the spell was about forgetfulness. The harsh life she now lived was less harsh than the reality she had left behind in Perdido Beach. That was the true wilderness. But there she had awakened forgotten and brutal instincts.

Here it was only nature trying to starve her, break her bones, cut and poison her. Nature was relentless but it was free of malice. Nature did not hate her.

It was not nature that had driven her to sacrifice her brother's life.

Astrid closed her eyes and then the book, and tried to calm the rush of emotion inside her. Guilt was a fascinating thing: it seemed not to weaken over time. If anything it grew stronger as the circumstances faded from memory, as the fear and the necessity became abstract. And only her own actions stood out with crystal clarity.

She had hurled her sick, strange little brother to the huge, appalling creatures that threatened her and threatened every human in the FAYZ.

Her brother had disappeared.

So had the creatures.

The sacrifice had worked.

Then God said, 'Take your son, your only son, Isaac, whom you love, and go to the region of Moriah. Sacrifice him there as a burnt offering on one of the mountains I will tell you about.'

Only no loving God, seeing her faith, had intervened to stop the killing.

For the excellent reason that there was no loving God.

That it had taken her so long to realise this was an embarrassment to her. She was Astrid the Genius, after all. The name she had carried for years. And yet Sam, with his shoulder-shrugging indifference to all matters religious, had been so much closer to the truth.

What kind of a fool looked at the world as it was – and this terrible world of the FAYZ especially – and believed in God? A God actually paying attention, let alone caring about his creations?

She had murdered Little Pete.

Murdered. She didn't want to dress it up with any nice word. She wanted it harsh. She wanted the word to be sandpaper dragged across her raw conscience. She wanted to use that awful word to obliterate whatever was left of Astrid the Genius.

It was a good thing to have decided there was no God, because if there were then she would be damned to eternal hell.

Astrid's hands shook. She laid the book flat on her lap. From her backpack she retrieved the bag of pot. She rationalized the drug on the grounds that it was the only way she could fall asleep. If this were the normal world, she might have a prescription for a sleeping pill. And that wouldn't be wrong, would it?

Well, she needed to sleep. Hunting and fishing were early morning activities and she needed to sleep.

She flicked the lighter and brought it to the bowl of the pipe. Two hits: that was her rule. Just two.

Then she hesitated. A memory twinge. Something nagging at her consciousness, warning her that she had seen something important and missed it.

Astrid frowned, tracing back her actions. She set aside the pot and the book and walked back to her buried pantry. She hauled up the cooler. It was too dark to see into the hole, so she made the decision to use a few precious seconds of battery life and flicked on a small flashlight.

She knelt down and yes, there it was. Three sides of the hole were dirt; the fourth was the barrier. Nothing ever stuck to the barrier – nothing. And yet, a few small clumps of dirt now did exactly that.

Astrid drew her knife and poked at the dirt, which fell away.

Was it her imagination? The barrier down in the hole looked different. It no longer seemed to glow softly. It was darker. The illusion of translucency was gone. Now it seemed opaque. Black.

She drew the sharp point of her knife along the barrier, from above the hole down.

It was subtle, almost imperceptible. But the knifepoint glided with no resistance whatsoever until it reached the darker colour and then the point dragged. Not much. Not much at all. Just as if it had gone from polished glass to burnished steel.

She flicked off the light and took a deep, shaky breath.

The barrier was changing.

Astrid closed her eyes and stood there for a long moment, swaying slightly.

She put the cooler back into the hole. She would have to await sunrise to see more. But she already knew what she had seen. The beginning of the endgame. And she still didn't know what the game was.

Astrid lit the pipe, took a deep lungful, then, after a few minutes, another. She felt her emotions go fuzzy and indistinct. The guilt faded. And within half an hour sleep drew her to her tent, where she crawled into her sleeping bag and lay with her arms curled around the shotgun.

Astrid giggled. So, she thought: she wouldn't have to go to hell. Hell was coming to her.

When that final night came, the demon Drake would find her.

She would run. But never fast enough.

TWO

64 HOURS 57 MINUTES

'**PATRICK,** YOUR GENIUS is showing!' Terry cried in a high falsetto voice.

'It iiiiis?' Philip asked in a low, very dumb voice. He covered himself with his hands and a wave of laughter rose from the assembled audience.

It was Friday Fun Fest at Lake Tramonto. Every Friday the kids rewarded themselves with an evening of entertainment. In this case, Terry and Philip were doing a re-creation of a *SpongeBob* episode. Terry had a yellow T-shirt painted with spongelike holes, and Phil wore an arguably pink T-shirt for the role of Patrick Star.

The 'stage' was the top deck of a big houseboat that had been shoved out into the water so that it wallowed a few dozen feet off the dock. Becca, who played Sandy Cheeks, and Darryl, who did a very good Squidward, were in the cabin below waiting for their cues.

Sam Temple watched from the marina office, a narrow,

two-storey, grey-sided tower that afforded him a clear view over the heads of the crowd below. Normally the houseboat was his, but not when there was a show to put on.

The crowd in question was 103 kids, ranging from one year old to fifteen. But, he thought ruefully, no audience of kids had ever looked quite like this.

No one over the age of five went unarmed. There were knives, machetes, baseball bats, sticks with big spikes driven through them, chains, and guns.

No one was fashionably dressed. At least, not by any of the normal standards. Kids wore disintegrating shirts and jeans in sizes way too large. Some wore ponchos made of blankets. Many went barefoot. Some had decorated themselves with feathers stuck in their hair, big diamond rings made to fit with tape, painted faces, plastic flowers, all manner of bandannas, ties, and criss-cross belts.

But they were clean, at least. Much cleaner than they'd been back in Perdido Beach. The move to Lake Tramonto had given them a seemingly endless supply of fresh water. Soap was long gone, as was detergent, but fresh water did wonders all by itself. It was possible to be in a group of kids now without gagging on the stink.

Here and there, as the sun sank and the shadows grew, Sam could make out the flare of cigarette butts. And despite all they'd tried to do there were still bottles of booze – either original or moonshine – being passed around the small gaggles of kids. And probably, if he'd bothered, he could have caught a whiff of marijuana.

But mostly things were better. Between the food they grew and the fish they caught in the lake, and the food they traded for from Perdido Beach, no one was starving. This was an accomplishment of epic proportions.

And then there was the Sinder project, which had amazing potential.

So why did he have this itchy feeling that something was wrong? And more than just a feeling. It was like something half-seen. Less than that. Like a feeling that there was something he should have seen, would have seen if he just turned around quickly enough.

It was like that. Like something that stood just outside the range of his peripheral vision. When he turned to look it was still in his peripheral vision.

It was looking at him.

It was doing it right now.

'Paranoia,' Sam muttered. 'You're going slowly nuts, dude. Or maybe not so slowly, since you're talking to yourself.'

He sighed and shook his head and formed a grin he hoped would spread from without to within. He just wasn't used to so much . . . peace. Four months of it. Sam heard footsteps on the rickety stairs. The door opened. He glanced back.

'Diana,' he said. He stood up and offered her his chair.

'Really not necessary,' Diana said. 'I'm pregnant, not crippled.' But she took the chair anyway.

'How are you doing?'

'My boobs are swollen and they hurt,' she said. She cocked her head sideways and looked at him with a degree of affection. 'Really? That makes you blush?'

'I'm not blushing. It's . . .' He couldn't really think of what else it might be.

'Well, then, I'll spare you some of the more disturbing things going on with my body right now. On the good side, I no longer throw up every morning.'

'Yes. That is good,' Sam said.

'On the downside, I have to pee more or less all the time.'

'Ah.' This conversation was definitely making him uncomfortable. In fact, even looking at Diana made him uncomfortable. She had a definite, noticeable bulge beneath her T-shirt. And yet she was no less beautiful than she'd ever been and still had the same knowing, challenging smirk.

'Shall we discuss the darkening of areolae?' she teased.

'Please, I'm begging you: no.'

'The thing is, it's early for some of this,' Diana said. She tried to make it sound casual. But she failed.

'Uh-huh.'

'I shouldn't be this big. I have all the books on pregnancy, and they all say I shouldn't be this big. Not at four months.'

'You look OK,' Sam said with a certain desperate edge in his voice. 'I mean good. You look good. Better than good. I mean, you know, beautiful.'

'Seriously? You're hitting on me?'

'No!' Sam cried. 'No. No, no, no. No. Not that . . .' He let that trail off and bit his lip.

Diana laughed delightedly. 'You are so easy to mess with.' Then she grew serious. 'Have you ever heard of the quickening?'

'Like for taxes?'

'No. No, Sam, that would be "quicken". The quickening is when the fetus starts to move.'

'Oh. Yeah. That.'

'Give me your hand,' Diana said.

He was absolutely sure he did not want to give her his hand. He had a terrible premonition what she would do with his hand. But he could not think of a way to refuse.

Diana looked at him with an innocent expression. 'Come on, Sam, you're the one who can always find a way out of a life-or-death crisis. Can't you think of a way to refuse?'

That forced a smile from him. 'I was trying. Brain freeze.'

'OK, then, give me your hand.'

He did and she placed his palm against her belly.

'Yep, that's a, um, a definite belly,' he said.

'Yeah, I was hoping you'd agree that that is a belly. I needed a second opinion. Just wait . . . There!'

He had felt it. A small movement in her tight-stretched bulge.

He made a sickly smile and withdrew his hand. 'So, quickening, huh?'

'Yes,' Diana said, no longer kidding. 'But here's the thing, Sam: human babies all grow at basically the same rate. It's clockwork. And human babies do not start kicking at thirteen weeks.'

Sam hesitated, not sure if he should acknowledge the use of that word, 'human'. Whatever Diana feared or suspected or even was just imagining, he didn't want it to be his problem.

He had plenty of problems already. Distant problems: down on a deserted stretch of beach there was a container-load of shoulder-fired missiles. As far as he knew his brother, Caine, had not found them. If Sam tried to move them and Caine found out, it would likely start a war with Perdido Beach.

And Sam had problems nearer to his heart: Brianna had discovered Astrid's haunt in the Stefano Rey. Sam had known Astrid was still alive. He'd had reports of her staying near the power plant for a few days after the great bug battle and the Big Split that had separated the kids of the FAYZ into Perdido Beach and Lake Tramonto groups.

He'd also learned that she had slept for a while in an overturned Winnebago on a back road in the farm country. He had waited patiently for her to come back. But she never had, and he'd heard nothing about her for the last three months.

Now, just yesterday morning, Brianna had located her. Brianna's super-speed made her an effective searcher on roads, but it had taken her longer to thread her way through the forest; it was not a good idea to trip over a tree root at seventy miles an hour.

Of course, searching for Astrid was not Brianna's main mission. Her main mission was to find the Drake-Brittney creature. Nothing had been seen or heard of Drake, but no one believed he was dead. Not truly dead.

Sam came reluctantly back to the problem of Diana. 'What's your reading on the baby?'

'The baby is a three bar,' Diana said. 'The first time I read? Two bar. So, still growing.'

Sam was shocked. 'Three bar?'

'Yes, Sam. He, she or it, is a mutant. A powerful one. Growing more powerful.'

'Have you told anyone else?'

Diana shook her head. 'I'm not stupid, Sam. Caine would come after it if he knew. He would kill us both if he had to.'

'His own child?' Sam had a hard time believing that even Caine would be that depraved.

'Maybe not,' Diana said. 'He made it very clear when I told him that he wanted nothing to do with it. I would say the idea sickened him. But a powerful mutant? Very different story. He might just take us. Caine might want to control the baby, or he might want to kill it, but for him there's no third choice. Anything else would be . . .' She searched his face as if the right word might be written there. '. . . Humiliating.'

Sam felt his stomach churning. They'd had four months of peace. In that time Sam, Edilio, and Dekka had taken on the job of setting up a sort of half-aquatic town. Well, mostly Edilio. They had parcelled out the houseboats, sailboats, motorboats, campers, and tents. They'd arranged for a septic tank to be dug, well away from the lake to avoid disease. Just to be safe they had set up a system of hauling water from halfway down the shore to the east in what they called the lowlands, and forbidden anyone to drink the water where they bathed and swam.

It had been amazing to watch the quiet authority Edilio brought to the job. Sam was nominally in charge, but it never would have occurred to Sam to worry so much about sanitation.

Fishing boats, with crews trained by Quinn down in Perdido Beach, brought in a decent haul every day. They had planted carrots, tomatoes, and squash in the low patch up by the barrier, and under Sinder's care they were growing very nicely.

They had locked up their precious stash of Nutella, Cup-a-Noodles, and Pepsi, using those as currency to buy additional fish, clams, and mussels from the ocean, where Quinn's crews still fished.

They also had negotiated control over some of the farmlands, so artichokes, cabbage, and the occasional melon could still be had.

In truth Albert managed all the trade between the lake and PB, as they called it, but the day-to-day management of the lake was up to Sam. Which meant Edilio.

Almost from the beginning of the FAYZ, Sam had lived with fantasies of a sort of personal judgment day. He pictured himself standing before judges who would peer down at him and demand he justify every single thing he had done.

Justify every failure.

Justify every mistake.

Justify every body buried in the town plaza in Perdido Beach.

These last few months he had begun to have those imaginary conversations less frequently. He'd started thinking maybe, on balance, they would see that he had done some things right.

'Don't tell anyone,' Sam cautioned Diana. Then he said, 'Have you thought about . . . Well, I guess we don't know what the baby's powers might be.'

Diana showed her ironic smirk. 'You mean have I thought about what might happen if the baby can burn things like you can, Sam? Or has his father's telekinetic power? Or any number of other abilities? No, Sam, no, I haven't even thought about what happens when he, she, or it has a bad day and burns a hole in me from the inside out.'

Sam sighed. 'He or she, Diana. Not it.'

He expected a wisecrack answer. Instead Diana's carefully controlled expression collapsed. 'Its father is evil. So is its mother,' she whispered. She twisted her fingers together, too hard, so hard it must be painful. 'How can it not be the same?'

'Before I pass judgment,' Caine said, 'does anyone have anything to say for Cigar?'

Caine did not refer to his chair as a throne. That would have been too laughable, even though he styled himself 'King Caine'.

It was a heavy wooden chair of dark wood grabbed from an empty house. He believed the style was called Moorish. It sat a few feet back from the top stair of stone steps that led up to the ruined church.

Not a throne in name, but a throne in fact. He sat upright. Not stiff, but regal. He wore a purple polo shirt, jeans, and square-toed black cowboy boots. One boot rested on a low, upholstered footstool.

On Caine's left stood Penny. Lana, the Healer, had fixed her shattered legs. Penny wore a sundress that hung limply from her narrow shoulders. She was barefoot. For some reason she refused to ever wear shoes since regaining use of her legs.

On his left stood Turk, supposedly Caine's security, though it was impossible to imagine a situation Caine couldn't deal with on his own. The truth was that Caine could levitate Turk and use him as a club if he chose. But it was important for a king to have people who served him. It made one look more kingly.

Turk was a sullen, stupid punk with a sawed-off double-barrelled shotgun over his shoulder and a big pipe wrench hanging from a loop on his straining belt.

Turk was guarding Cigar, a sweet-faced thirteen-year-old with the hard hands, strong back, and tanned face of a fisherman.

About twenty-five kids stood at the foot of the stairs. In theory everyone was supposed to show up for court, but Albert had suggested – a suggestion that had the force of a decree – that those who had work to do could blow it off. Work came first in Albert's world, and Caine knew that he was king only so long as Albert kept everyone fed and watered.

At some time in the night a fight had broken out between a boy named Jaden and the boy everyone called Cigar because he had once smoked a cigar and got spectacularly sick.

Both Jaden and Cigar had been drinking some of Howard's illegal booze, and no one was exactly clear what the fight had been about. But what was clear – witnessed by three kids – was that the fight had gone from angry words to fists to weapons in a heartbeat.

Jaden had swung a lead pipe at Cigar and missed. Cigar had swung a heavy oak table leg studded with big nails and he had not missed.

No one believed Cigar – who was a good kid, one of Quinn's hardworking fishermen – had meant to kill Jaden. But Jaden's brains had ended up on the sidewalk just the same.

There were four punishments in King Caine's Perdido Beach: fine, lock-up, Penny, or death.

A small infraction – for example, failing to show proper respect to the king, or blowing off work, or cheating someone in a deal – merited a fine. It could be a day's food, two days' unpaid labour, or the surrender of some valuable object.

Lock-up was a room in town hall that had last imprisoned a boy named Roscoe until the bugs had eaten him from the inside out. Lock-up meant two or more days with just water in that room. Fighting or vandalism would get you lock-up.

Caine had handed out many fines and several lock-ups.

Only once had he imposed a sentence of Penny.

Penny was a mutant with the power to create illusions so real it was impossible not to believe them. She had a sick, disturbed imagination. The girl who had earned thirty minutes of Penny had lost control of her bodily functions and ended up screaming and beating at her own flesh. Two days later she had still not been able to work.

The ultimate penalty was death. And Caine had never yet had to face imposing that.

'I'll speak for Cigar.'

Quinn, of course. Once upon a time Quinn had been Sam's

closest friend, his surfer-dude buddy. He'd been a weak, vacillating, insecure boy, one of those who had not handled the FAYZ very well.

But Quinn had come into his own as the head of the fishing crews. Muscles bunched in his neck and shoulders and back from pulling at the oars for long hours. He was the colour of mahogany now.

'Cigar has never been any kind of trouble,' Quinn said. 'He shows up for work on time and he never shirks. He's a good guy and he's a very good fisherman. When Alice fell in and was knocked out from hitting an oar, he was the one who jumped in and pulled her out.'

Caine nodded thoughtfully. He was going for a look of stern wisdom. But he was deeply agitated beneath the surface. On the one hand, Cigar had killed Jaden. That wasn't some random act of vandalism or small-bore theft. If Caine didn't impose the death penalty in this case, when was he ever going to?

He sort of wanted to . . . In fact, yes, he definitely wanted to impose the death penalty. Maybe not on Cigar, but on someone. It would be a test of his power. It would send a message.

On the other hand, Quinn was not someone to pick a fight with. Quinn could decide to go on strike and people would get hungry in a hurry.

And then there was Albert. Quinn worked for Albert.

It was fine to call yourself king, Caine thought. But not when the real power was held by some skinny, owlish black kid with a ledger book.

'It's murder,' Caine said, stalling.

'No one's saying Cigar shouldn't be punished,' Quinn said. 'He screwed up. Shouldn't have been drinking. He knows better.'

Cigar hung his head.

'Jaden was a good guy, too,' a girl with the improbable name of Alpha Wong said. She sobbed. 'He didn't deserve to be killed.'

Caine gritted his teeth. Great. A girlfriend.

No point stalling any longer. He had to decide. It was far worse to piss off Quinn and possibly Albert than Alpha.

Caine raised his hand. 'I promised as your king to deliver justice,' he said. 'If this had been deliberate murder I'd have no choice but the death penalty. But Cigar has been a good worker. And he didn't set out to kill poor Jaden. The next penalty is Penny time. Usually it's a half hour. But that's just not enough for something this serious. So here is my royal verdict.'

He turned to Penny, who was already quivering with anticipation.

'Penny will have Cigar from sunrise to sunset. Tomorrow when the sun rises clear of the hills it begins. And when the sun touches the horizon over the ocean, it ends.'

Caine saw reluctant acceptance in Quinn's eyes. The crowd murmured approvingly. Caine breathed a silent sigh. Even Cigar looked relieved. But then, Caine thought, neither Quinn nor Cigar had any idea just how far down into madness Penny had sunk since her long, pain-racked ordeal. The girl had always been a cruel creature. But pain and power had made her a monster.

His monster.

For now.

Turk hauled Cigar off to the lock-up. The crowd began to disperse.

'You can do this, Cigar,' Quinn called out.

'Yeah,' Cigar said. 'No problem.'

Penny laughed.

THREE

53 HOURS 52 MINUTES

DRAKE HAD GOT used to the dark, to seeing only by the faint green light of his master, the gaiaphage.

They were ten miles below ground. The heat was intense. It probably should have killed him – intense heat, no water, not that much air. But Drake wasn't alive in the usual way. It was hard to kill what was not quite alive.

Time had passed. He was aware of that. But how much time? It might be days or years. There was no day or night down here.

There was only the eternal awareness of the angry, frustrated mind of the gaiaphage. In the time he'd been down here Drake had become intimately familiar with that mind. It was a constant presence in Drake's consciousness. A nagging hunger. A need. A pressing, constant, unwavering need.

The gaiaphage needed Nemesis.

Bring me Nemesis.

And Nemesis – Peter Ellison – was nowhere to be found.

Drake had reported to the gaiaphage that Little Pete was

dead. Gone. His sister, Astrid, had tossed him to the bugs and in a panic Little Pete had not only caused the nearest, most threatening of the huge insects to disappear: he had eliminated the entire species.

It was a shocking demonstration of Little Pete's power.

A five-year-old, severely autistic little snot-nosed brat was the most powerful creature in this huge bubble. The only thing that limited him was his own strange, distorted brain. Little Pete was powerful but did not know it. Could not plan, could not understand, could only react.

React with incredible, unimaginable power. Like a toddler with his finger on a nuclear bomb.

Nemesis frightened the gaiaphage. And yet he was somehow necessary to the gaiaphage.

Once Drake had asked. 'Why, master?'

I must be born.

And then the gaiaphage had tortured him with shafts of bright pain, punishing Drake for having the presumption to question.

The answer had bothered Drake more than the pain. *I must be born.* There was a raw, ragged edge to that. A need that went beyond simple desire and drilled down into fear.

His god was not all-powerful. It was a shock to Drake. It meant the gaiaphage might still fail. And then what would become of Drake?

Had he sworn allegiance to a dying god?

Drake tried to hide his own fear. The gaiaphage might sense it if his attention was turned Drake's way.

But as the uncounted days had gone by, as he had listened night and day to the gaiaphage's desperation and impotent rage, he had begun to doubt. What place did Drake have in a universe where there was no gaiaphage? Would he still be unkillable? Would the gaiaphage's failure mean his own destruction?

Drake wished he could talk about it with Brittney. But in the nature of things he could never do that. Brittney emerged from time to time, writhing from Drake's melting flesh to take over for a while.

During those times Drake ceased to see or hear or feel.

During those times Drake drifted in a world even darker than the gaiaphage's subterranean lair. It was a world so tight it smothered Drake's soul.

It went on like this – the pressure of the gaiaphage's need, Drake's inability to comprehend what he could or should do, and periods of nonexistence in the void.

Drake filled his time with wondrous fantasies. He replayed the memories of pain he had caused. The whipping of Sam. And he worked through in elaborate detail the pain he would yet cause. To Astrid. To Diana. Those two especially, but also to Brianna, who he hated.

The deep lair changed. Weeks ago the floor – the very bottom limit of the barrier – had changed. It was no longer pearly grey. It had turned black. He noticed that the black-stained barrier under his feet felt different, not as smooth.

And he noticed that the parts of the gaiaphage that rested on the barrier were also becoming stained black. So far the stain had spread only a little into the gaiaphage, like the gaiaphage was some sort of spread-out, radioactive green sponge and the stain was spilled black coffee.

Drake had wondered what it meant, but he had not asked.

Suddenly Drake felt the gaiaphage's mind jolt. Like someone had shocked him.

I feel . . .

'Nemesis, master?' Drake asked the green-glowing cave walls.

Lay your arm upon me.

Drake recoiled. He had touched the gaiaphage a few times. It was never a pleasant experience.

But Drake lacked the will to refuse. He unwrapped the ten-foot-long tentacle from around his waist. He moved to a large clump of the seething green mass, a part he couldn't help but picture as the centre, the head of that centreless, headless creature. He laid his tentacle gingerly across it.

'Ahhh!' The pain was sharp and sudden and knocked him to his knees. His eyes flew open, strained to open wider still, until he felt like he was peeling his own face back.

Images exploded in his mind.

Images of a garden.

Images of a lake with boats floating calmly.

Images of a beautiful girl with dark hair and a wry half smile.

Bring her to me!

Drake had spoken little in months. His throat was dry, his tongue awkward in his mouth. The name came out in a harsh whisper.

'Diana.'

Quinn was not happy as he pulled at the oars, heading away from shore with his back to the dark horizon and his worried gaze on the mountains where the sun would soon appear.

None of his crews were happy. Normally there was good-natured grumbling, old jokes, and teasing. Usually the boats would call out cheerful insults to one another, mocking one another's rowing technique or prospects or looks.

Today there was no teasing. The only sounds were the grunts of effort, the creak of oars in the oarlocks, the musical trickle of water along the sides and the lap, lap, lap of tiny wavelets slapping the bow.

Quinn knew the crews were angry about Cigar. All agreed that Cigar had screwed up in a monumental way. But what was Quinn supposed to do? The other kid had swung first. If Cigar hadn't struck back, Jaden might well have killed him.

They were prepared to see Cigar pay a fine, endure some

lock-up, maybe even a few minutes of Penny to teach the boy to take it easy in the future.

But a whole day under mental assault from that creepy girl . . . That was too much. Cigar had all the fears any normal kid had, and given a whole day to work her evil Penny would find them all.

Quinn wondered if he should say something. It distressed him, this sullenness, this worry. But what could he say? What words of his were going to make these kids stop worrying for Cigar?

He was worried, too. And he shared some of their anger at himself and at Albert. He had hoped Albert would step in. Albert could have if he'd chosen to. Everyone knew that Caine could call himself king but Albert was the emperor.

The boats moved away from one another as the pole fishers went one way and the net casters went towards the barrier. A school of blue bats had been seen there the day before, skimming along a hundred yards from the barrier.

Quinn signalled a halt and motioned to Elise to ready the nets. His boat crew today was Elise, Jonas, and Annie. Elise and Annie were weaker on the oars than Quinn and Jonas, but they were nimble with the nets, casting them out in perfect circles, and sensing when the weights had dragged the net down before closing the trap.

Quinn sat at the stern now, using an oar and the rudder to

keep the boat stable while the girls and Jonas hauled in two blue bats and a nondescript seven-inch fish.

It was wearying work, but Quinn was used to it, and he handled the oar and rudder on automatic. He gazed off to see the other boats take up their own positions.

Then, hearing a splash, he turned towards the barrier to see a flying fish – not great eating, but not inedible – take a short hop.

But that wasn't what made him narrow his eyes and squint in the faint morning light.

Elise and Annie were getting ready to cast again.

'Hold up,' Quinn said.

'What?' Elise demanded. She was cranky in the morning. Crankier still on this morning.

'Jonas, grab an oar,' Quinn said.

While Elise neatened her net, pulling out bits of seaweed, the boat crept towards the barrier. Twenty feet away they shipped oars.

'What is that?' Jonas asked.

The four of them stared at the barrier. Up above it became an illusion of sky. But straight ahead it was pearly grey. As always. As it had been since the coming of the FAYZ.

But just above the waterline the barrier was not grey but black. The black shadow rose in an irregular pattern. Like a rollercoaster's curves.

Quinn glanced away to see the sun just peeking over the mountains. The whole sea went from dark to light in a few swift minutes. He waited until the sunlight touched the water between him and the barrier.

'It's changed,' Quinn said.

He pulled his shirt over his head and dropped it on to the bench. He fumbled in the locker for a face mask, spit into it, wiped the spit around with his fingers, slipped it on his head, and without another word dived off the side. The water was cold and instantly blew the last of the morning cobwebs out of his head.

He swam gingerly to the barrier, careful not to touch it. Six feet down the barrier was black.

Quinn surfaced, took a deep breath, and went down again. He wished he had fins; it wasn't easy pushing his buoyant body downward. He reached maybe twenty feet before letting himself float back up.

He climbed back into the boat with an assist from Jonas.

'It's like that all the way down as far as I can tell,' Quinn said.

The four of them looked at one another.

'So?' Elise asked. 'We have work to do. The fish won't catch themselves.'

Quinn considered. He should tell someone. Caine? Albert? He didn't really want to have to deal with either of them. And they had blue bats right under the boat just waiting to be caught.

Either Caine or Albert might easily tear into him for sloughing off on work just to report something that might be meaningless.

Not for the first time he wished it was still Sam he had to report to, not the other two. In fact, if there was anyone he really wished he could tell, it was Astrid. Too bad no one had seen her. She might well be dead. But Astrid was the only one who would look at this and actually try to figure out what it meant.

'OK, let's get back to work,' Quinn said. 'We'll keep an eye on it, see if it changes by the end of the day.'

FOUR

50 HOURS

FOR ALL OF his five years Pete Ellison had lived inside a twisted, distorted brain. No longer.

He had destroyed his dying, diseased, fever-racked body.

Poof.

All gone.

And now he was . . . where? He didn't have a word for it. He had been freed from the brain that had made colours scream and turned every sound into a hammering cymbal.

He drifted now in a silent, blissful place. No loud noises. No too-bright colours. No brain-frying complexity of overwrought sensation. No blonde sister with her bright yellow hair and stabbing blue eyes.

But the Darkness was still there.

Still looking for him.

Still whispering to him. *Come to me. Come to me.*

Without the cacophony of his brain Pete could see the Darkness more clearly. It was a glowing blob at the bottom of a ball.

Pete's ball.

That realisation surprised him. But yes, now he remembered: such noise, people screaming, his own father in panic, all of it like hot lava poured into Pete's skull.

He had not understood what was happening, but he could see clearly the cause of all the panic. A green tendril had reached for and touched long glowing rods, caressed them with a greedy, hungry touch. And then that arm of the Darkness had reached for minds – weak, malleable minds – and demanded to be fed the energy that flowed from those rods.

It would have meant a release of every sort of light, and everyone except the Darkness would have been burned up.

Meltdown. That was the word for it. And it had already begun and it was too late to stop it by the time Pete's father was rushing around and Pete was moaning and rocking.

Too late to stop the reaction and the meltdown. By normal means.

So Pete had made the ball.

Had he known what he was doing? No. He looked back at it now with a feeling of wonder. It had been an impulse, a panic reaction.

He had never meant a lot of things to happen.

He was like that guy Astrid used to have in the stories she read to him. The one called God. The one who said, 'Poof, make everything!'

Pete's world was full of pain and disease and sadness. But hadn't the old world been that way, too?

He no longer had his handheld game. He no longer had his body. He no longer had his old, miswired brain. He no longer balanced atop the sheet of glass.

Pete missed his old game. It had been all he had.

He floated in a sort of haze, a world of vapours and disconnected images and dreams. It was quiet, and Pete liked quiet. And in this place no one ever came to tell him it was time to do this or do that or go here or hurry there.

No sister's loud yellow hair and stabbing blue eyes.

But as time passed – and he was sure it must be passing, somewhere if not here – he could picture his sister without feeling the mere image overwhelming.

It surprised Pete. He could look back at that day in the power plant and almost look on the confusion and screeching sirens and panic without feeling panic himself. It still all seemed like too much, way too much, but no longer so much that he would lose all self-control.

Was it that memories were quieter? Or that something had changed in him?

It had to be that second thing, because Pete's mind no longer felt the same. For one thing he felt as if he could think about himself for the first time in his jangled life. He could wonder where he was and even who he was.

The one thing he knew was that he was bored with this disconnected existence. For most of his life the only peace and pleasure he had found had been within his handheld game. But he had no game to play here.

He had wished for a game.

He had gone looking for a game, but there was nothing like his old handheld. Just avatars that seemed to drift by. Avatars, symbols with curlicues inside. They formed into groups or clusters. Or sometimes they went off alone.

He sensed there might be a game, but with no controls, how could the game be played? Many times he had watched the shapes, and sometimes it almost seemed they were looking at him.

He peered closer at the avatars. They were interesting. Little geometric shapes but with so much twisted and coiled inside them so that he had the impression that he could fall into any one of those avatars and see a whole world within.

He wondered if it was one of those games you just . . . touched. It felt wrong and dangerous. But Pete was bored.

So he touched one of the avatars.

His name was Terrel Jones, but no one called him anything but Jonesie. He was just seven, but he was a big seven.

He was a picker working an artichoke field. It was hard, hard work. Jonesie spent six hours a day walking down the rows of chest-high artichoke plants with a knife in his gloved right hand and a backpack on his back.

The larger artichokes were higher up on the plant. Smaller ones lower down. The up-chokes – picker slang for the higher ones – had to be a minimum of five inches across. The ankle-chokes – the lower ones – had to be at least three inches. This was to make sure the pickers didn't wipe out the whole crop at once.

No one was exactly sure if this rule made sense, but Jonesie didn't see any reason to argue. He just moved along the row cutting with practiced ease and tossing the chokes over his shoulder to drop into the backpack. Up one row and down the next was all it would take to fill his pack. Then he would sling it off and dump it into the old wagon – a big, ramshackle wooden thing that rested on four bald car tyres.

And that was all Jonesie had to worry about. Except that right now he was finding it more and more tiring. He felt as if he couldn't catch his breath.

He reached the end of the row carrying no more than the usual weight of chokes, but staggered to the wagon. Jamilla, the wagon tender, had that relatively soft job because she was only eight years old and small. All she had to do was pick up the stray chokes that might fall to the ground, and carefully rake the chokes in the wagon into an even layer, and check in each backpack load on a sheet of paper for Albert so that the daily harvest could be accounted for.

'Jonesie!' Jamilla cried angrily when he failed to heft his bag high enough and it slipped from his hands, spilling chokes everywhere.

Jonesie started to say something but his voice was gone. Just not there.

He tried to suck in breath to cry out, but air did not flow through his mouth and into his lungs. Instead he felt a sudden, searing pain, like a cut, like a knife was drawn across his throat from ear to ear.

'Jonesie!' Jamilla screamed as Jonesie fell to the ground, facedown.

His mouth gulped helplessly at the air. He tried to touch his throat but his arms didn't move.

Jamilla had jumped down from the wagon. Jonesie could see a misty, distant, distorted image of her above him. A face, mouth wide, all the way open, screaming silently.

And behind her a shape. It was transparent but not invisible. A huge hand with one finger extended. That finger reached through his body. He couldn't feel it.

And then he couldn't feel anything.

Jamilla's scream brought Eduardo and Turbo from the adjacent fields. They came at a run from different directions, but Jamilla hardly noticed them at first. She stared and screamed and screamed . . .

And then she spun away and started running. Turbo caught her in his arms. He had to lift her up off the ground to get her to stop running.

'What is it? Is it zekes?'

Zekes were the carnivorous worms that inhabited many of the fields and had to be bribed with payments of blue bats and junk fish.

Jamilla went still. Turbo was there, and now so was Eduardo. They were her friends, her co-workers.

Jamilla steeled herself to try to explain what had just happened. But before she could gain control of her raw voice, Eduardo said, 'What is that?'

Jamilla felt Turbo crane to see past her. He set her down. She no longer felt like running. Or screaming. Turbo left her and walked the ten steps to join Eduardo.

'What is that thing?' Turbo asked. 'Is that what scared you, Jammy?'

'Looks like some kind of weird fish or something.'

'Big. And weird,' Turbo repeated. 'I worked a couple of days filling in with Quinn and I never saw anything like that.'

'Like a fish with, like, armour. But what's it doing here in the middle of a choke field?'

Jamilla did not dare to come any closer. But her voice was her own again.

'It's Jonesie,' she said.

The two boys turned slowly to look at her. 'Say what?'

'He was . . . Something touched him. And his whole body . . .' She made a writhing movement with her hands. Twisting the fingers together as somehow the pieces of Jonesie had been twisted together, turned inside out, and formed this . . . thing.

They stared at her. Probably glad to have any excuse not to stare at the thing she was calling Jonesie.

'Something touched him? What touched him?'

'God,' Jamilla said. 'God's hand.'

Turk brought Cigar in with his hands tied behind his back.

'Untie him,' Penny said.

Cigar was nervous. Penny smiled at him. He seemed to relax a little.

'I don't think I'll have any problems with Cigar,' Penny said to Turk. 'He's basically a good kid.'

Cigar swallowed hard and nodded.

Plywood had been nailed up over the windows. The room was bare. Before leaving town Sam had left a small Sammy sun burning in one corner. It provided the only light and added a lugubrious quality, casting dark green shadows in the corners. It was dawn but you'd never know it in this room. Not even high noon would penetrate here.

'I'm really sorry,' Cigar said. 'About what happened, I mean.

You're right, actually; I mean, I'm not bad.'

'No, of course you're not bad,' Penny said. 'Just a murderer.'

Cigar's face went pale. His left hand started shaking. He didn't know why. Why just his left hand? He fought the urge to grab it and hold it still. He stuck it in his pocket and tried not to breathe too loud.

'What do you like, Cigar?' Penny asked.

'What do I like?'

Penny shrugged. She was moving around him, her bare feet silent. 'What kind of stuff do you miss? From the old days, I mean. From before.'

Cigar shifted uncomfortably. He wasn't stupid. He could sense there was a cat-and-mouse game being played. He knew Penny's reputation. He'd heard about her. And the way she would walk almost past him, then back up to send him a searching, penetrating look made him queasy.

He decided on an innocuous answer. 'Candy.'

'Like candy bars?'

'Like Skittles. Or Red Vines. Anything, I guess.'

Penny smiled. 'Look in your pocket.'

Cigar felt in the front pocket of his jeans. He felt a packet of something that hadn't been there before. He pulled it out and stared in amazement at a fresh pack of Skittles.

'Go on. Have some,' Penny said.

'They're not real. Are they?'

Penny shrugged. She twined her hands behind her back. 'Try them. You tell me.'

He tore the package open with trembling fingers. He spilled a half dozen of the bright pellets on the floor before catching the next few. He popped them in his mouth.

Cigar had never tasted anything half so wonderful. 'Where . . . Where did you get these?'

Penny stopped. She leaned in close to him and jabbed suddenly at his head with her finger. It hurt, but just a little. 'In there. From inside your head.'

Cigar looked doubtfully at the Skittles still in the pack. His mouth watered. Sugar was almost a forgotten memory. But he was pretty sure the candies had never been this good. These were crazy good. He could eat a million of these, and maybe they weren't real, but they felt real in his hand and tasted better than real in his mouth.

'Good, huh?' Penny asked. She was still way too close.

'Yeah. Really good.'

'People think because things aren't real that the pleasure wouldn't be as great. I used to think that, too. But things that are in your head can be pure, you know? Realer than real.'

Cigar realised he'd finished the whole pack. He wanted more. He had never wanted anything half as much as he wanted more Skittles.

'Can I have more?' he asked.

'Maybe if you asked me nicely.'

'Please? Please can I have more?'

She put her lips close to his ear and whispered, 'On your knees.'

He barely hesitated. The longer he went without more of the candy the more he wanted it. The need was incredibly urgent. It took his breath away, he needed the candy so badly.

Cigar dropped to his knees. 'Can I have more?'

'You're easy to train,' Penny smirked.

Suddenly there was a handful of Skittles in Cigar's palm. He tossed them into his mouth. 'Please, more?'

'How about some Red Vines?'

'Yeah, yeah!'

'Lick my foot. No, not the top, you idiot.'

She held her foot up so he could lick the dirty sole and Red Vines sprouted in his hand. He rolled on to his back and gobbled them up and licked her foot again and got more, and his head was swimming, swirling, the taste of candy overwhelming, like nothing he'd ever had, like nothing could ever have been, but so good. He needed more, desperately.

The Red Vines were in his hand and somehow hard to get. Like they had melted into his skin and he had to dig at them with his fingernails, and he did and sucked on the ends as soon as he had freed them.

And then, with a sickening lurch, the Red Vines weren't

candies any more. They were the veins in his wrists.

'Ahhhh, ahha, ahhh!' Cigar cried in horror.

Penny clapped her hands together. 'Oh, ho-ho, Cigar, we are going to have a lot of fun together.'

FIVE

44 HOURS 12 MINUTES

ASTRID PACKED ALL her perishable food into her backpack. It wasn't much, but she might be gone for a while, and she couldn't tolerate the idea of letting anything go to waste.

She checked her shotgun. She had four shells loaded and five more in her pack.

Nine shotgun shells would kill just about anything.

Except Drake.

Drake scared her deep down. He had been the first person in her life to hit her. To this day she could remember the sting and force of his slap. She could remember the certainty that he would quickly escalate to closed-fist punches. That he would beat her and that the beating would give him pleasure so that nothing she could ever say would stop him.

He had forced her to insult Little Pete. To betray him.

It hadn't bothered Petey, of course. But it had eaten at her insides. It seemed almost quaint now when she recalled that guilt. She'd had no way of knowing then that she would someday do far, far worse.

Fear of that psychopath was part of the reason she had needed to manipulate Sam. She had needed Sam's protection for herself and even more for Little Pete. Drake wasn't Caine. Caine was a heartless, ruthless sociopath who would do anything to increase his own power. But Caine didn't revel in pain and violence and fear. However amoral, Caine was rational.

To Caine's eyes Astrid was just another pawn on the chessboard. To Drake she was a victim waiting to be destroyed for the sheer pleasure it would bring him.

Astrid knew she couldn't kill Drake with the shotgun. She could blow his head off his shoulders and still not kill him.

But that image brought her some sense of reassurance.

She slung the gun over her shoulder. The gun's weight and length, along with the pack that was loaded down with water bottles, made her a bit slower and more awkward than when she was running free down the familiar trail.

Astrid had never measured the distance from her camp to Lake Tramonto, but she guessed it was six or seven miles. And if she was going to follow the barrier so as to avoid getting lost, it would mean traveling over rough terrain, up steep hills. She'd have to keep up a pretty good pace to get there before night and see Sam.

Sam.

The name made her stomach tense. He would have questions. He would make accusations. He would be angry. He would resent her. She could deal with all of that. She was strong.

But what if he wasn't mad or sullen? What if he smiled at her? What if he put his arms around her?

What if Sam told Astrid he still loved her?

She was far less prepared to deal with that.

She had changed. The sanctimonious girl with so many certainties in her head had died with Little Pete. She had done the unforgivable. And she had seen the person she truly was: selfish, manipulative, ruthless.

She was not a person Sam could love. She was not a person who could love him back.

Probably it was a mistake going to him now. But whatever her failures and foolishness, she still had her brain. She was still, in some attenuated way, Astrid the Genius.

'Yeah. Right. Genius,' she muttered. That was why she was living in the woods with flea-bites in her armpits, smelling of smoke and carrion, hands a mass of calluses and scars, eyes darting warily to identify every sound in the woods around her, tense, practising the smooth unlimbering of a shotgun. Because that was definitely the life of a genius.

The trail led closer to the barrier now. She knew this trail well; it would disappear through the barrier. There would be some rough terrain for half a mile before another trail would appear. Or maybe it was the same trail doubling back; who could tell.

Here, suddenly, she noticed that the dark part of the barrier had crept higher. Two tall spikes of black on the barrier, like fingers reaching up out of the earth. The taller of the two stretched up for maybe fifteen or twenty feet.

Astrid steeled herself for a necessary experiment. She stuck out one finger and touched the black portion of the barrier.

'Ahhh!' She cursed under her breath. It still hurt to touch. That hadn't changed.

As she threaded her way through dense bushes and emerged into a blessed clearing, she considered the problem of measuring the advance of the stain. Here, too, she saw rising fingers of darkness, not as high as the others she'd seen, and thinner. She watched one of the stains closely for half an hour, anxious at wasting time but wanting to have some kind of observation. The scientifically inclined part of her brain had survived intact where other aspects had diminished or disappeared.

It was growing. At first she missed it because she'd been waiting for the stain to rise higher and instead it had thickened.

'Still remember how to calculate the surface area of a sphere?' Astrid asked herself.

She did the maths in her head as she walked. 'One thousand two hundred and sixty square miles. Of course, half that is underground or underwater, so six hundred and thirty square miles of dome.

'It's all a question of how fast the stain is spreading,' Astrid told herself, taking pleasure from the precision of numbers.

How long until the dome was dark? Astrid wondered.

Because Astrid had very little doubt that the stain would continue spreading.

Into her head came a memory from long ago: Sam admitting to her that he was afraid of the dark. It was in his room, in his former home, the place he'd shared with his mother. It was perhaps the reason that in a sudden panic he had created the first of what would come to be known as Sammy suns.

Sam had many more terrible things to be scared of now. Surely he was over that ancient terror.

She hoped so. Because she had a terrible feeling that a very long night was coming.

The baby would not look at her. Diana looked at him even though doing so filled her with sick dread.

He could already walk. But this was a dream, so of course things didn't have to make sense. It was a dream; she knew that for sure because she knew the baby was not able to walk.

It was inside of her. A living thing inside of her own body. A body within a body. She could picture it in there with its eyes closed, all twisted so that its tiny legs were drawn up to its barrel chest.

Inside her body.

But now in her head, too. In her dream. Refusing to look at her.

You don't want to show me your eyes, she said.

He was holding something now. Tiny, webbed fetus fingers clutched a doll.

The doll was black and white.

No, Diana begged.

The doll had a pouting, dissatisfied mouth. A small red mouth.

No, Diana begged again, and she was afraid.

The baby seemed to hear her voice and it held the doll out to her. Like it wanted her to take it. But Diana couldn't take it, because her arms were like lead and so terribly heavy.

Noooo, she moaned.

I don't want to see it.

But the baby wanted her to look; it insisted she look, and she couldn't stop herself, couldn't look away, could not move or turn or run and oh, God, she wanted to run.

What is it, Mommy? The voice had no character, just words, not a voice, not a sound, like someone was typing them on to a keyboard so that she could kind of hear but also see the words in letters, *bam, bam, bam,* each letter thudding in her brain.

What is it, Mommy?

The baby held the black-and-white plush toy in her face and asked again, *What is it, Mommy?*

She had to answer. No choice now. She had to answer.

Panda, she said, and with that word the full deluge of sadness and self-loathing burst in her mind.

Panda, the baby said, and smiled without teeth, smiled with the panda's own red mouth.

Diana woke. Opened her eyes.

Tears blurred her vision. She rolled out of the bed. The trailer was tiny, but she kept it clean and neat. She was lucky: the only person other than Sam at the lake to have a place without a room-mate.

Panda.

The baby knew. It knew she had eaten part of a boy with the nickname Panda. Her soul was bare to the baby. It could see inside her.

Oh, God, how was she going to be a mother carrying that terrible crime in her soul?

She deserved hell. And she had the terrible suspicion that the baby inside her was the demon sent to conduct her there.

'I don't like the idea of leaving those missiles just lying there,' Sam said.

Edilio said nothing. He just shifted uneasily and glanced

back at the dock to make sure no one was standing around listening for gossip.

Sam, Edilio, Dekka, and Mohamed Kadeer were on the top deck of the houseboat everyone called the White Houseboat. It wasn't white, exactly, more of a dirty pink actually. And it looked nothing like the real White House. But it was where the leaders met, up on the open top deck. So White Houseboat it was.

It was also Sam's home, a home he shared with Dekka, Sinder, Jezzie, and Mohamed.

Mohamed was a non-voting member of the Lake Tramonto Council. But more important, he was Albert's liaison at Lake Tramonto.

Some said 'liaison'. Some said 'spy'. There wasn't much difference. Sam had decided early on not to try to keep secrets from Albert. Albert had to know what was going on. In any case he would find out: Albert was the FAYZ's closest thing to a billionaire, although his wealth was measured in 'Bertos, McDonald's game pieces, food and jobs.

On the White Houseboat there were two cabins aft, each with a single bunk above a double bed. Sinder and Jezzie shared one of those cabins; Mohamed and Dekka shared the other. Sam had the relatively roomy bow cabin to himself.

'If Caine's people find out . . .' Dekka said.

'Then we may have a problem,' Sam said, nodding. 'But we

won't ever use the things. We'll just be making sure Caine doesn't use them, either.'

'Yeah, and Caine will buy that explanation because he's so trusting,' Dekka said mordantly.

The missiles had been part of a desperate ploy to get from the Evanston Air National Guard base to the coast. Dekka had been able to use the crate as a platform that, cut off from gravity by Dekka's power, would scrape along the barrier.

The plan was decidedly imperfect. It had almost worked. Kind of worked. Worked just well enough. But it had also moved the weapons into a place where they might be found.

Found and used.

The fifth person on the deck was not a part of the council. He was a boy called Toto. Toto had been found in a desert facility – or part of a facility, with the rest beyond the barrier – that had kept him imprisoned in order to study the mutations occurring in the Perdido Beach area.

The facility had been set up before the coming of the FAYZ. The government had known of, or at least suspected, the very odd things beginning to occur in the months before the barrier.

Toto was probably close to being clinically insane. He'd been alone – all alone – for seven months. He still had a tendency to talk to Spider-Man. No longer his old Styrofoam Spider-Man bust – which Sam had incinerated in a moment of irritation – but the ghost of that former bust. Which was decidedly crazy. But crazy or not, he had the power to instantly determine truth from lie.

Even when it was inconvenient.

Now Toto said, 'Sam is not telling the truth.'

'I have no intention of using the missiles,' Sam said heatedly.

'True,' Toto said blandly. 'But not true when you said you won't ever use them.' Then, in a furtive aside, he added, 'Sam thinks he may have to use them.'

Sam gritted his teeth. Toto was extremely useful. Except when he wasn't.

'I think we might have all guessed that, Toto,' Dekka said.

Dekka had recovered her strength after the shocking ordeal she'd endured from the infestation of bugs. She had not entirely recovered from what she'd thought was her deathbed confession to Brianna. Even now the two girls could barely be in the same room together without awkwardness.

Dekka had never told Sam exactly what she'd whispered into Brianna's ear. But he was pretty sure he knew. Dekka was in love with Brianna. And Brianna had evidently not felt the same way.

'Yes, she might have guessed it,' Toto said, speaking now to his sleeve.

'Mohamed, what is Albert's feeling about this?'

Mohamed had a habit of taking a long pause before

answering any question. Even 'How are you?' It was probably one of the things that endeared him to Albert, who had grown suspicious, some might even say paranoid, about secrecy.

'Albert has never spoken to me about this. I don't know whether he knows about these missiles or not.'

'Uh-huh,' Dekka said, and rolled her eyes. She held her palm out to Toto. 'Don't even bother, Toto; we all know that's baloney.'

But Toto said, 'He's telling the truth.'

Mohamed took another long pause. He was a good-looking kid with the barest beginning of whiskers on his upper lip. 'But, of course, now that I know, I'll have to tell him.'

'If we leave them where they are, sooner or later someone's going to find them,' Sam said.

Edilio said, 'Dude, all due respect, you're trying to talk yourself into this.'

'Why would I do that?' Sam demanded, and sat forward in his chair and widened his stance, sending the message that he had nothing to hide.

Edilio smiled affectionately. 'Because we've had four months of peace, my friend. And you're bored.'

'That's not –' Sam began, but with a glance at Toto fell silent.

'Still, if the missiles have to be somewhere, better with us,' Edilio said reluctantly.

Sam felt a little embarrassed by how eager he was to grab on to that rationale. OK: so he was bored. It still made sense to secure those weapons.

'OK,' Sam said. 'We grab them. Dekka, it'll be on you and Jack to move them. We'll have Brianna check out the area, make sure no one's around. They're just inside Caine's borders. We'll need to get them across our line as quick as possible. Get them loaded on to a pickup.'

'Burn gas?' Mohamed asked.

'It's worth the gas,' Sam said.

Mohamed spread his hands apologetically. 'Gas is under Albert's control.'

'Look, if Albert gives us the gas he's supporting us,' Sam said. 'So how about just this once we just do it? It won't be more than a couple of gallons. We'll skim from several different tanks so it won't show on your books.'

Mohamed took an even longer pause than normal. 'You never said that, and I never heard you.'

'That's not true,' Toto said.

'Yeah,' Dekka said, rolling her eyes, 'we know.'

'OK. Tonight,' Sam said. 'Breeze out front; Dekka, Jack, and me in the truck. We park the truck and the three of us head to the beach. Hopefully we're back by morning.'

'What about me, boss?' Edilio asked.

'Deputy mayor is a heavy burden sometimes, dude. But someone's got to stay and keep everyone else out of trouble.'

Sam smiled. He felt a rush from the idea of a daring night-time mission. Edilio was right: running the lake had been boring after the first frantic month. Sam basically hated handling all the little details and decisions. Most of his day was taken up dealing with stupid fights over nothing – kids arguing over ownership of a toy or some food, people slacking off on work they owed to the town, crazy ideas for getting out of the FAYZ, unhappiness over accommodations, violations of sanitation rules. Increasingly – not without a feeling of guilt – he had turned most of it over to Edilio.

It had been months since Sam had been involved in any serious craziness. And this mission had just enough craziness without any real danger.

The meeting broke up. Sam stood up, stretched, and noticed Sinder and Jezzie running along the shore from the eastern end, where they had been tending a small, irrigated plot of vegetables.

Something about their body language spelled trouble.

'Sam!' Sinder gasped. She was in her modified Goth stage – it was hard to find make-up, but she could still manage to find black clothing.

'T'sup, Sinder? Hi, Jezzie.'

Sinder gathered her wits, took a steadying breath, and said, 'This is going to sound crazy, but the wall . . . It's changing.'

'We were weeding the carrots,' Jezzie said.

'And then we noticed this, like, black stain on the barrier.'

'What?' Sam said.

'The barrier,' Sinder said. 'It's changing colour.'

SIX

43 HOURS 17 MINUTES

QUINN LEFT HIS crews to unload the catch at the dock. Normally he went straight to Albert to report the day's haul, but he had a more pressing concern today. He wanted to check on Cigar.

It was still an hour or so to sundown. He wanted to at least yell some encouragement to his friend and crewman.

The plaza was empty. The town was mostly empty – the pickers were in the fields still.

Turk lounged on the steps of the town hall. He was asleep with a baseball cap pulled down over his eyes and his rifle between his crossed legs.

A girl walked across the square with hurried steps. She glanced fearfully towards the town hall. Quinn knew her a little, so he gave a small wave. But she glanced at him, shook her head, and scurried off.

Feeling worried now, Quinn headed into the building. He climbed the stairs to the detention room where Cigar would be.

He found the door easily enough. He listened and heard nothing from inside. 'Cigar? You in there?'

The door opened, revealing Penny. She was still wearing a summer dress, and she was still barefoot. She blocked the door.

'It's not time yet,' Penny said.

There was blood on her dress.

Blood on her narrow feet.

Her eyes were feverish. Lit up. Ecstatic.

Quinn took it all in at a glance. 'Get out of my way,' Quinn said.

Penny looked at him. Like she was trying to see something inside his head. Considering. Measuring.

Anticipating.

'What have you done, you witch?' Quinn demanded. His breath was coming short. His heart was pounding. The skin on his sunburned arms was cracking, turning deathly white and cracking like dried mud. Deep cracks.

'You're not threatening me, are you, Quinn?'

The eruption on Quinn's arm stopped, reversed itself, and his skin was back to what it should be.

'I want to see Cigar,' Quinn said, swallowing his fear.

Penny nodded. 'OK. OK, Quinn. Come on in.'

Quinn pushed past her.

Cigar was in a corner. He seemed at first to be asleep. But his shirt was soaked with blood.

'Cigar, man. You OK?'

Cigar did not move. Quinn knelt by him and raised his head. It took Quinn a few terrible seconds to make sense of what he was seeing.

Cigar's eyes were gone. Two black-and-red holes stared from the front of Cigar's face.

Then Cigar screamed.

Quinn jumped back.

'What have you done? What have you done?'

'I never touched him,' Penny said with a happy laugh. 'Look at his fingers! Look at his wrists! He did it all himself. It was funny to watch.'

Quinn's fist was drawn back before he knew it. Penny's nose exploded. Her head snapped back hard and she fell on her behind.

Quinn grabbed Cigar's bloody forearm in a strong grip. Over Cigar's screams, Quinn said, 'We're going to Lana.'

Penny snarled and all at once Quinn's flesh caught fire. He bellowed in terror. The flames quickly burned away his clothing and ate at his flesh.

Quinn knew it wasn't real. He knew it. But he couldn't believe it. He could not refuse to feel the agony of the illusion. He could not help but smell the smoke of burning, popping flesh and –

He aimed a desperate kick.

His sneaker caught Penny in the side of her head.

The fire went out instantly.

Penny rolled over, got to her feet, trying to get control of her scattered mind, but Quinn was behind her now and had his powerful arm around her neck.

'I will snap your neck, Penny. I swear to God, I will snap your neck. Nothing you can do will stop me.'

Penny went limp. 'You think the king will let you get away with this, Quinn?' she hissed.

'Anyone messes with me, Penny, you or anyone else, and I go on strike. See how well you enjoy life without me and my crews. Without food.'

Quinn shoved her away and took Cigar's arm again.

Some jobs were tougher than others. Blake and Bonnie had the worst job you could have: maintaining the septic tank. Also known as the Pit.

Dekka had used her powers to help dig the pit, although it had still taken twenty other kids to clear the levitated dirt away. The result was a hole in the ground ten feet deep, twelve feet long, and three feet across. Give or take: no one had exactly used a tape measure.

It was basically one long slit trench. The trench had been covered with an entire side of one of the Nutella train's steel boxcars. Sam had cut it free and Dekka and Orc had hauled it the miles from the train crash site.

Sam had then burned five two-foot holes in the steel.

And that was where Blake and Bonnie came in. Alone neither of them had any special talent for building, but somehow the two of them joined had a strange sort of genius, recognised by Edilio, their direct supervisor. Together (with some help from Edilio) they had taken on the job of creating five outhouses perched above those holes. This they had done by taking shipping crates, removing the top, and sawing out a sort of doorway. The end result was an open-topped wooden crate with a narrow door covered with a shower curtain to provide some privacy.

The open top had the disadvantage that the heads of tall people could be seen. The advantage, however, was that the smell of the septic tank wasn't trapped in a closed space.

The individual outhouses had benches made of desk tops brought from the Air National Guard base. Sam had burned holes in each of these, and Blake and Bonnie had thoughtfully attached actual toilet seats to them.

There was something pleasant – once you got used to it – about relieving yourself under the stars or sun. Except for the lack of toilet paper.

Blake and Bonnie solved this problem – partly – by selling various leaves, official reports and records from the Air National Guard facility, and out-of-date reference books.

And, of course, the two Bs were responsible for keeping the facility clean. This wasn't terribly hard usually, because Bonnie in particular had no reluctance to call someone out for making a mess.

And the hours weren't bad. Since absolutely no one wanted their jobs, Blake and Bonnie were given plenty of time off. And since they were seven and six years old, respectively, they spent their time off swimming, collecting rocks, and playing a more or less continuous game of war that involved various action figures, the severed heads of Bratz dolls and interesting insects.

That was what they were doing, playing war in the sandpit they'd excavated a hundred feet or so away from the Pit. In fact, they were arguing over whether a battered Bratz head had or had not got the drop on a group of three mismatched beetles.

Two of the outhouses were occupied: number one by Pat and number four by Diana. Diana was there frequently as a consequence of being pregnant.

Blake grabbed the Bratz doll head angrily and said, 'OK, if you won't play by the rules –' This happened about six times a day. There weren't really any rules.

Bonnie was just about to hotly deny that she was cheating, when her face smeared. Like it was a still-wet painting and someone had dragged a brush through it.

Blake stared at the most familiar face in his world and saw it flatten, like it was suddenly just two-dimensional. And something that was transparent, but not somehow invisible, pierced her through.

Bonnie jerked to her feet like a puppet on a string. Her eyes went wide and her face smeared again as her mouth dripped down her chin.

A finger made of air, as big as a tree, swept over her, came back to touch her, and then disappeared.

Bonnie gave a single terrible spasm, then stopped moving, fell over, and landed atop her army.

Blake stood staring at something that was no longer Bonnie. No longer anything he had ever seen before. What lay there in the dirt had one arm and half a face, and the rest – no more than two feet long – looked exactly like a rotted dead log.

Blake started screaming and Diana and Pat moved as fast as they could, but Blake was not one to just stand and scream; he took action. He grabbed the log with half a human face by its one arm and threw it as hard as he could towards the Pit.

It didn't go far, so he grabbed it again, screaming all the while at the top of his lungs, and dragged it towards the number five as Diana and Pat both shouted for him to stop, stop, stop, but he couldn't stop; he had to get rid of it, this thing, this monster that had replaced his friend.

Diana almost reached him. But not quite.

Blake threw the thing into the hole of the number five outhouse.

'What is going on?' Pat demanded, rushing up.

Blake was silent.

'He had some kind of . . .' Diana began. She made a face, then added, 'I don't know what it was.'

'It was a monster,' Blake said.

'Jeez, dude, you scared me half to death,' Patrick said. 'I mean, enjoy your game or whatever, but don't be screaming when I'm doing my business.' He stomped off down the hill towards the lake.

Diana didn't yell at Blake. 'Where's the other one of you? What's her name? The girl?'

Blake shook his head dully. A veil went down over his eyes. 'I don't know,' he said. 'I guess she's gone.'

Orc sat reading.

That fact, the sight of Orc sitting on a rock with a book in his hands, was still inexplicable to Howard.

Orc and Howard had gone with Sam to Lake Tramonto during the Big Split. Sam was a pain in the butt, but he wasn't likely to decide to throw you through a wall, like Caine might.

The only problem with the lake was that most of the drinking and drugging population had stayed in Perdido Beach. Howard operated a whiskey still at Coates, but travelling from Coates to the lake was not exactly an easy trip. And Howard couldn't do it with more than about a dozen bottles in a backpack.

Orc could carry far more, of course. But Orc wasn't helping any more. Orc was reading. He was reading the Bible.

Orc drunk was depressed, dangerous, unpredictable, and occasionally murderous. But Orc sober was just useless. Useless.

Orc had been given the job of guarding Sinder's little farm. Mostly this involved sitting on a rock outcropping and reading.

Sinder's farm wasn't much bigger than a good-size backyard, a wedge-shaped piece of land that had once been a streambed back when rain still fell in the mountains and sent streams to replenish the lake. Orc had helped them dig a web of shallow canals that brought lake water in to water the neat rows.

Sinder and Jezzie spent all day, every day, planting and tending. Orc spent just as much time there. In fact, he had set up a little tent just beside the rock and he slept there most nights.

Howard had spent a couple of nights there as well, trying to keep alive his friendship with Orc, trying to get Orc past this whole newfound sobriety thing.

It wasn't that Howard liked Orc drunk. (Orc had no money, so whatever he drank came straight out of Howard's profits.) It was just that sober, Bible-reading Orc was useless to Howard. Useless for intimidation and debt collection, and useless for hauling booze.

'What's "meek" mean?' Orc asked Howard. Then he spelled it, because he wasn't sure if he was saying it right. 'M-E-E-K.'

'I know how to spell "meek",' Howard snapped. 'It means

wimpy. Weak. Pathetic. Pitiful. A sucker. A victim. A stupid, Bible-reading, monster-looking fool, that's what it means.'

'Well, it says here they're blessed.'

'Yeah,' Howard said savagely, 'because that's the way it always works out: wimps always win.'

'They're gonna inherit the earth,' Orc said. But he seemed doubtful about it. 'What's that mean, "inherit"?'

'You are sucking the life right out of me; you know that, Orc?'

Orc shifted and turned his book to get better light. The sun was going down.

'Where are the girls? Farmer Goth and Farmer Emo?'

'Went to get Sam,' Orc grunted.

'Sam? Why didn't you tell me, dude?' Howard glanced around for a place to hide his backpack. He was on a delivery run. And while Sam didn't go out of his way to try to shut down Howard's business, he could get it into his head to confiscate Howard's product.

'I think "inherit" means take over, like,' Orc said.

Howard slung his pack behind a bush and stepped back to see if it was still visible. 'Yep. Take over. The meek. Just like rabbits take over from coyotes. Don't be an idiot, Orc.'

Howard would never have insulted Orc back in the old days. Back when Orc was Orc. Even now he saw Orc's eyes narrow – they were one of the few remaining human parts of him. Orc was a slag heap of living gravel with a patch of human skin where his mouth and part of one cheek were.

Howard almost wished Orc would get up and pound him. At least he'd be Orc again. Instead Orc narrowed his eyes and said, 'You know, there's a lot more rabbits than there are coyotes.'

'Why are the girls getting Sam?' Howard glanced back towards the marina, the centre of life at the lake. Sure enough, Sam, Jezzie, and Sinder were coming along at a quick walk.

'"Blessed are they who hunger and thirst for justice,"' Orc read in his slow, laborious way.

'You want to ask me what that means, Orc?' Howard snapped. 'Because I think justice may not be something you want to see so much.'

Orc's face wasn't capable of showing much emotion. But Howard could see that the shot had hit home. In a drunken rage Orc had accidentally killed a kid back in Perdido Beach. No one but Howard knew about it.

'What's that?' Howard asked, pointing. He had just noticed a discolouration of the dome behind Orc.

'That's why they went for Sam.'

At that moment Sam and the girls came up. Sam nodded to Howard and said, 'Orc, how's it going?'

Sam went straight to the barrier and stood looking at the black peak thrusting up behind Orc's rock.

'Have you seen this anywhere else?' Sam asked Sinder.

'We never go anywhere else,' Sinder said.

'I appreciate the time you put in,' Sam said. But he wasn't paying any attention to Sinder or Jezzie. He walked along the barrier towards the lake.

Howard fell in beside him, relieved that Sam hadn't spotted his backpack.

'What do you think it is?' Howard asked.

'There. Another one.' Sam pointed at a much smaller dark bump rising from the dirt. He marched on and they reached the lake's edge. Here again was a low, undulating ridge of black stain.

'What the . . .' Sam muttered. 'You see anything like this, Howard?'

Howard shrugged. 'I probably wouldn't notice it. Anyway, I don't walk by the barrier that much.'

'No,' Sam agreed. 'You just go back and forth to your still at Coates.'

Howard felt a sudden chill.

'Of course I know about your still,' Sam said. 'You know it's on the other side of the line. It's Caine's territory. He catches you over there, you won't like it, unless you're sharing your profits with him.'

Howard winced and decided to say nothing.

Sam stood looking at the stain. 'It's growing. I just saw it grow. Just now.'

'I saw it, too,' Sinder said. She looked to Sam for reassurance.

Weird, Howard realised: he, too, was looking to Sam for reassurance. As much as he and Sam had been enemies at times, and still were, more or less, he wanted Sam to have some quick answer to this stain thing.

The troubled look on Sam's face was not reassuring.

'What is it?' Howard asked again.

Sam shook his head slowly. His tanned face looked suddenly so much older than his barely fifteen years. Howard had a vision of Sam as an old man, hair grey and thin, face creased with deep worry lines. It was a face marked by all the pain and worry Sam had endured.

Howard had the sudden, ridiculous urge to offer Sam a drink. He looked like he could use it.

SEVEN

36 HOURS 19 MINUTES

ASTRID STOOD GAZING down at the lake from the heights to the west. The barrier went straight into the lake, of course, cutting it roughly in half. The lake's shoreline bulged out so that she could no longer keep following the barrier without going out of her way. Anyway, it was getting too dark to see the stain now. Time to turn towards the human habitations.

The sun was down and a small, far-off bonfire was burning in a circle of tents and trailers. Astrid couldn't see the kids around the fire, but she could see shapes occasionally crossing in front of the flames.

Now that she was here she could no longer even pretend to suppress her emotions. She was going to see Sam. Others, too, and she would no doubt have to endure stares and greetings and probably insults.

All that she could handle. But she was going to see Sam. That was the thing. Sam.

Sam, Sam, Sam.

'Stop it,' she told herself.

A crisis was coming. She had a duty to help her friends understand it.

'Weak,' she muttered.

The suspicion had been growing in her head that she was just coming up with an excuse to see Sam. At the same time she suspected that she was looking for an excuse to back off and avoid her duty to help.

It occurred to Astrid that in days gone by she might have prayed for guidance. It brought a wistful smile to her lips. What had happened to that Astrid? Where had she gone to? Astrid hadn't prayed since . . .

Put aside childish things, she quoted mentally. A Bible quote, which was ironic, she supposed. She shifted her pack and slipped her shotgun off her sore right shoulder on to her left. She started towards the fire.

On the way she worked out a simple method for measuring the spread of the dark stain on the barrier. If someone had a functioning digital camera it would be easy enough. She ran the maths in her head. Maybe five sample locations. Calculate the progression day by day and she would have pretty good data.

Numbers still gave her pleasure. That was the great thing about numbers: it required no faith to believe that two plus two equalled four. And maths never, ever condemned you for your thoughts and desires.

'Who's there?' a voice cried from the shadows.

'Take it easy,' Astrid said.

'Who is it or I shoot,' the voice said.

'It's Astrid.'

'No way.'

A boy, probably no older than ten, stepped out from behind a bush. He had a rifle levelled, with his finger near but not directly on the trigger.

'Is that you, Tim?' Astrid asked.

'Whoa. It is you,' the boy said. 'I thought you were dead.'

'You know what Mark Twain said? "Reports of my death have been greatly exaggerated."'

'Yep. That's you, all right.' Tim shouldered his weapon. 'I guess you're OK to go on in. I'm not supposed to let anyone pass unless I know them. But I know you.'

'Thanks. Good to see you well. Last time I saw you, you had the flu.'

'Flu's all gone now. Hope it doesn't ever come back.'

Astrid walked on, and now the trail was clearer and easier to follow, even as the night fell.

She passed a few tents. An old-fashioned Airstream trailer. Then she reached the circle of tents and trailers that ringed the bonfire. She heard kids laughing.

She approached nervously. The first to see her was a little girl, who nudged the older girl beside her. Astrid instantly recognised Diana.

Diana looked at her without showing the least surprise and said, 'Well, hello, Astrid. Where have you been?'

Conversation and laughter died, and thirty or more faces, each lit orange and gold, turned to look.

'I've been . . . away,' Astrid said.

Diana stood up and Astrid realised with a shock that she was pregnant.

Diana saw the look on Astrid's face, smirked, and said, 'Yes, all kinds of interesting things have happened while you were away.'

'I need to see Sam,' Astrid said.

That drew a laugh from Diana. 'No doubt,' she said. 'I'll take you.'

Diana led the way to the houseboat. She still moved with unselfconscious grace despite the bulge. Astrid wished she moved like that.

'By the way, you didn't happen to see a kid, a girl, on your way here, did you? Her name is Bonnie. About seven, I think.'

'No. Is someone missing?'

Edilio was sitting in a folding chair on the top deck, keeping watch over the scattered tents, trailers, Winnebagos, and boats. He had an automatic rifle on his lap.

'Hi, Edilio,' Astrid said.

Edilio jumped up and clambered down to the dock. He swung his rifle out of the way and threw his arms around Astrid. 'Thank God. It's about time.'

Astrid felt tears forming. 'Missed you,' she admitted.

'I guess you're here to see Sam.'

'Yes.'

Edilio nodded to Diana, dismissing her. He drew Astrid up on to the boat and then into the empty cabin. 'There's a little problem with that,' Edilio said in a whisper.

'He doesn't want to see me?'

'He's, um . . . He's out.'

Astrid laughed. 'I assume from your conspiratorial look you mean he's up to something dangerous?'

Edilio grinned and shrugged. 'He's still Sam. He should be back by morning. Come on; let's get you something to eat and drink. You can sleep here tonight.'

The pickup truck crept down the road. Crept for many reasons: First, it saved gas. Second, they were driving with the lights out because headlights would be visible a long way off.

Third, the road from the lake down to the highway was narrow and only sketchily paved.

And fourth: Sam had never really learned to drive.

Sam was behind the wheel. Dekka was beside him. Computer Jack was in the cramped space behind the front seat, wedged in and not happy.

'No offence, Sam, but you're going off the road. Off the road! Sam! You're going off the road!'

'No, I'm not; shut up,' Sam snapped as he guided the huge truck back on to the road, narrowly avoiding overturning in the ditch.

'This is how I'm going to die,' Jack said. 'Crammed in like this in a ditch.'

'Oh, please,' Sam said. 'You're strong enough to tear your way out even if we did crash.'

'Do me a favour and rescue me, too,' Dekka said.

'We're fine. I have this down now,' Sam said.

'Coyotes will totally eat us,' Jack said. 'Tear our guts open and . . .' He fell silent.

Sam glanced in the rearview mirror and saw Jack mouth the word 'sorry'.

Dekka sighed. 'I hate when you guys do that. Stop treating me like I'm going to fall apart. Not helpful.'

Saving Dekka's life from the infestation of bugs had meant cutting her open. Lana had been there to heal her, but Dekka had not come through unscathed. She put on a good act, but Dekka was no longer the fearless, indestructible girl she had once seemed to be.

That and Brianna's obvious rejection of her had left her withdrawn, defeated. Hopeless.

'I hope Brianna's OK,' Jack said. 'She shouldn't be running around in the dark.'

'As long as she sticks to the road and takes it slow she'll be all right,' Sam said, hoping to forestall any further conversation about Brianna. Jack was extremely intelligent in areas having to do with technology. But he could be clueless when it came to humans.

Sure enough, he stepped right in it.

'Brianna's been weird lately,' Jack said. 'Ever since we came up to the lake. She's like, all . . .'

Sam refused to ask him to continue.

Dekka shot a sidelong look at Sam and said, 'She's like all what, Jack?'

'Like all . . . I don't know. Like she wants to . . . you know . . .'

'No, I don't know,' Dekka growled. 'So if you've got something to say, spit it out.'

'I don't know. Like, be friendly with me. Like, she made out with me the other day.'

'Poor you,' Dekka said in a voice that would have frozen a more sensitive person into a block of ice.

Jack spread his hands. 'I was busy. She could see I was busy.'

At that point Sam decided it might be a good idea to weave off the road and knock into a fence post.

'Sam! Sam, Sam, Sam!' Jack yelled. He jerked in fear, which, because of his ridiculous strength, pushed the seat so hard Sam was smacked into the wheel.

'Ow!' Sam stepped on the brake. 'OK, that's enough. Do either of you two want to drive? No? Then shut up. Jeez, my head is bleeding.'

The truck moved again and soon the wheels went from gravel to the smooth pavement of the highway. Sam drove a quarter mile down the highway, spotted a landmark, and parked on the shoulder of the road.

'Cut across here. Right?' Sam asked.

Dekka peered out, nodded. 'Yeah, this looks right.'

They climbed out and stretched. It was still half a mile to the shore. Half a mile across a zeke field.

The zekes hadn't bothered anyone since the humans and the worms had worked out the arrangement of tossing blue bats and other inedible animals – to humans – into the fields to feed the worms. But just in case, Dekka had some baggies of fish entrails and bits and pieces of raccoon and deer tendons and the like in a pack. She emptied one of these out at her feet and instantly the zekes seethed up out of the ground and swarmed over the food. But left the three of them unharmed.

'The stuff we get used to,' Jack said, and shook his head.

Sam said, 'Listen, guys, you'll hear about it soon enough: there's something hinky going on with the barrier.'

'Kinky?'

'No, hinky. Weird.' Sam told them what he had seen.

'Maybe it's Sinder's powers causing it,' Jack suggested.

Sam nodded. 'Possible. So tomorrow we're going to have to explore a bit, see if the same thing is going on anywhere else.'

They had crossed the fields and now had to make it through a strip of weeds and sea grasses that ran along the top of the bluff.

It had been a while since Sam had seen the ocean. Not since they'd gone to the lake. It was black, painted with only the faintest glimmers of starlight. The moon was not out yet. The sound of the ocean had long been muted: there were no real waves in the FAYZ. But even the soft *shush . . . shush . . . shush* of water lapping on gritty sand touched something in Sam's heart.

They had miscalculated their location by a few hundred yards and had to walk north along the sand in order to find the crushed container. The steel box – a shipping container with 'Maersk' written down the side – had fallen from a great height when Dekka lost control of it hundreds of feet in the air.

The contents – long, heavily constructed crates – had spilled out on to the sand. One of the crates had popped open. Sam decided to use a bit of battery power and flicked on a flashlight. Tail fins were clearly visible.

He flicked the light off. Paused.

Something not right.

'No one move,' Sam said. He played the light around on the sand. 'Someone smoothed the sand.'

'Say what?' Jack asked.

'Look how flat and neat the sand is here. It's like when they drag the beaches at night and in the morning all the footprints and everything are gone.'

'You're right,' Dekka said. 'Someone's been here and then covered their tracks.'

No one spoke for a few minutes as each thought through the implications.

'Caine could easily lift these things and move them,' Sam said.

'So why are they still here?' Jack asked. Then he answered his own question. 'Maybe they took the other missiles and just left this one. We should check the seals.'

Sam took slow, cautious steps closer. He aimed the light's beam at bright yellow tape that sealed each crate. The tape had been carefully sliced and then pressed back into place.

'They're gone,' Sam said flatly. 'Caine has them.'

'Then why leave the one?' Jack asked.

Sam took a shallow breath. 'Booby trap.'

EIGHT

36 HOURS 10 MINUTES

'YOU CAN'T LET him get away with this!' Penny shrieked.

Caine wasn't having it. 'You stupid witch,' he yelled back. 'No one told you to let it go that far!'

'He was mine for the day,' Penny hissed. She pressed a rag to her nose, which had started bleeding again.

'He tore his own eyes out. What did you think Quinn would do? What do you think Albert will do now?' He bit savagely at his thumb, a nervous habit.

'I thought you were the king!'

Caine reacted without thinking. He swung a hard backhand at her face. The blow did not connect, but the thought did. Penny flew backwards like she'd been hit by a bus. She smacked hard against the wall of the office.

The blow stunned her, and Caine was in her face before she could clear her thoughts.

Turk came bursting in, his gun levelled. 'What's happening?'

'Penny tripped,' Caine said.

Penny's freckled face was white with fury.

'Don't,' Caine warned. He tightened an invisible grip around her head and twisted it back at an impossible angle.

Then Caine released her.

Penny panted and glared. But no nightmare seized Caine's mind. 'You'd better hope Lana can fix that boy, Penny.'

'You're getting soft.' Penny choked out the words.

'Being king isn't about being a sick creep,' Caine said. 'People need someone in charge. People are sheep and they need a big sheepdog telling them what to do and where to go. But it doesn't work if you start killing the sheep.'

'You're scared of Albert.' Penny followed it with a mocking laugh.

'I'm scared of no one,' Caine said. 'Least of all you, Penny. You live because I let you live. Remember that. The kids out there?' He waved his hand towards the window, vaguely indicating the population of Perdido Beach. 'Those kids out there hate you. You don't have a single friend. Now get out of here. I don't want to see you back here in my presence until you're ready to crawl to me and beg my forgiveness.'

Penny said two words, the second of which was 'you'.

Caine laughed. 'I think you meant "– you, *Your Highness*".'

He lifted Penny up with a slight motion of one hand and tossed her out through the open door and into the hallway.

'She could be trouble, Your Highness,' Turk said.

'She's already trouble,' Caine said. 'First Drake, now Penny. I'm surrounded by psychos and idiots.'

Turk looked hurt.

'One thing, Turk. You ever see me freaking out, like Penny is pulling something on me? You shoot the witch. We clear on that?'

'Absolutely,' Turk said. 'Your Highness.'

'You get that you're the idiot, right, Turk?'

'Um . . .'

Caine stormed off, muttering, 'I miss Diana.'

Quinn was still vibrating with rage by the time he made his way to Clifftop. Rage. But fear, too. In getting Cigar out of Penny's grip he had made a very dangerous enemy. Maybe two. Or even three, depending on where Albert came down.

Walking through the carpeted hall, feeling his way in the dark, Quinn realised with surprise that he was hearing voices. From a room at the far end of the hall from Lana's oceanfront room he heard children playing.

He stopped and listened.

'You lose; you totally lose, Peace.'

'Because you cheated, you little thief!'

'Guys, keep it down, huh?' That last voice Quinn recognised as Virtue, who was often called Choo.

Sanjit had moved his siblings into Clifftop? When had that

happened? The whole bunch of them, all the island kids, had moved to the lake with Lana. But after a few days they'd returned. Clifftop had become a part of Lana. It was where she felt safe.

Quinn realised with a stab of jealousy that Lana had OKed the island kids moving in here. No one argued with Lana. And until now she had placed an absolute ban on anyone sharing even a tiny corner of her Clifftop redoubt.

He knew that Lana was sort of seeing Sanjit, the new kid. But letting him move his whole family into Clifftop?

There had been a time when Quinn thought Lana and he might . . . But then events and realities had killed that daydream. Quinn was just a working guy, a fisherman. Lana was the Healer. As such she was the most protected, respected, even revered person in the FAYZ. Not even Caine would dream of messing with Lana.

And as intimidating as all that was, there was more: Lana was as tough as a spiked baseball bat.

She had seemed far, far above Quinn.

Patrick heard him and set up a loud and sustained barking.

Quinn knocked even though it seemed superfluous. The peephole went dark. The door was opened by Sanjit.

'It's Quinn,' he yelled over his shoulder. 'Come on in, man.'

Quinn stepped in. In the weird glow of a small Sammy sun the transformation of Lana's room was shocking: it was clean.

Really clean. With the bed made and the coffee table clear. The usual overflowing ashtray was nowhere to be seen – or smelled.

Even Patrick looked as if he'd been bathed and brushed. He ran over and began rubbing himself against Quinn, probably looking to pick up some pleasant fish smell to replace all the odours that had been rudely shampooed away.

Sanjit, a slim Indian-looking kid with an infectious smile and long black hair, noticed Quinn's surprise but said nothing.

Lana came in from the balcony. She at least had not changed much. She still had a huge semi-automatic pistol stuck in a thick belt. She still had the same pretty but not beautiful looks. And her expression was still somewhere between vulnerable and forbidding, like she might just as easily break down in tears or shoot you in the stomach.

'Hi, Quinn, what is it?'

There was nothing embarrassed or ill at ease in her tone. If she knew that Quinn was feeling jealous she gave no sign of it.

Not what I'm here for, Quinn told himself, feeling guilty to be letting his own feelings gain any hold when the picture of poor Cigar was still so fresh in his mind.

'It's Cigar,' Quinn said. 'He's at Dahra's.' He quickly told her what had happened.

Lana nodded and grabbed her backpack. 'Don't wait up,' she told Sanjit.

Quinn swallowed hard on that. He was actually living with Lana? In the same room? Was he misunderstanding this? Because that was sure what it sounded like.

Patrick fell in beside Lana, sensing an adventure.

Down the hallway, then down the stairs to ground level, Lana led the way through the pitch-black lobby and out into the night, bright by contrast.

'So,' Quinn said, letting the word hang there between them.

'I got lonely,' Lana said. 'I get nightmares. It helps having someone there sometimes.'

'It's not my business,' Quinn muttered.

Lana stopped and faced him. 'Yeah, it's your business, Quinn. You and I . . .' She didn't quite know how to finish that, so she just shifted to a gruffer tone and said, 'But it's no one else's business.'

They walked on quickly.

'Who would I tell?' Quinn asked rhetorically.

'You ought to have someone to tell,' Lana said. 'I know. Sounds weird coming from me.'

'A little bit.' Quinn was trying to nurture his resentment, but the truth was, he liked Lana. Had for a long time. He couldn't stay mad at her. Anyway, she deserved some peace in her life.

'It still reaches me sometimes,' Lana said.

Quinn knew she meant the Darkness, the thing that named itself the gaiaphage.

'What does it want from you?' Quinn asked. Even talking about the gaiaphage cast a shadow on him, made his breathing heavy and his heartbeat too loud.

'It wants Nemesis. It's looking for him.'

'Nemesis?'

'Man, you don't get any of the good gossip, do you?'

'I'm mostly hanging with my crews.'

'Little Pete,' Lana explained. 'Nemesis. It wants him night and day, and sometimes it's like that voice is screaming in my head. Sometimes it's bad. Then I need someone to, you know, bring me back.'

'But Little Pete's dead and gone,' Quinn said.

Lana laughed a hard, pitiless laugh. 'Yeah? Tell the voice in my head, Quinn. The voice in my head is scared. The gaiaphage is scared.'

'That's probably a good thing. Right?'

Lana shook her head. 'Doesn't feel good, Quinn. Something big is happening. Something definitely not good.'

'I saw . . .' He winced; he should be telling Albert first. Too late. 'The barrier. It seems like it's changing colour.'

'Changing colour? Changing to what colour?' Lana asked.

'Black. It may be turning black.'

NINE

35 HOURS 25 MINUTES

SO FAR PETE had experimented only a little with his new game. It was a very complicated game with so many pieces. So much he could do.

There were avatars, about three hundred of them, which was a lot. They hadn't seemed particularly interesting until he looked very close at them and saw that each one was a complex spiral, like two long ladders joined together, then twisted and compressed so that if you looked at the avatar from a distance you didn't see anything but a symbol.

He had touched a couple of the avatars, but when he did that they blurred and broke and disappeared. So maybe that wasn't the right thing to do.

But the real question was: what was the point of the game? He didn't see any score.

All he knew was that it was all inside the ball. The game did not see outside the ball. It was all inside, and there was the Darkness glowing at the bottom, and the ball itself, and neither of them was affected by the game. He had tried to move the Darkness but his controls had no effect on it.

In some ways it really wasn't a very good game.

Pete picked an avatar at random, and zoomed in on it until he could see the spirals inside spirals. They were beautiful, really. Delicate. No wonder his earlier moves had destroyed the avatars; he had just been scrambling up the intricate latticework.

This time he would try something different. And there, flitting magically from place to place, was the perfect avatar.

Taylor was enjoying the best of both worlds. Using her power she could 'bounce' from the island to the town to the lake. All in all it was the most useful power imaginable. Brianna could keep her super-speed and her worn-out sneakers and the broken wrists she got when she fell, and the rest of it.

Taylor just had to picture a place where she'd been, and pop! There she was. In the flesh. So once Caine had arranged for Taylor to visit the island – San Francisco de Sales Island, formerly owned by Jennifer Brattle and Todd Chance – she could bounce back anytime.

Which meant that Taylor slept in a fabulous bedroom in a fabulous mansion. She could have also worn Jennifer Brattle's amazing wardrobe, but she was too small in a number of dimensions.

But if she ever got lonely, she could just picture Perdido Beach and be there.

It made her very useful. Which was how she ended up working for both King Caine and Albert. Caine wanted information on Sam and what was happening at the lake. And Albert wanted some of that, plus information on Caine.

Taylor owned the gossip of the FAYZ. She was the TMZ of the FAYZ.

Or maybe the CIA of the FAYZ.

But either way, life was good for a smart girl with the power to simply pop from place to place. And just as important: pop right back out.

At the moment she was lying in her bed. The room she was in had been called the Amazon Room because of the leafy green colour of the walls and the jaguar-print bedclothes. There were a lot of bedrooms in the mansion, and amazingly some still had clean sheets.

Clean sheets! The equivalent of living in a palace compared to life in the rest of the miserable FAYZ, where you were lucky to have a mattress no one had peed on recently.

She was in bed munching on slightly stale saltines – she had to be careful about raiding the pantry; Albert had inventoried it – and watching an old *Hey Arnold*! on DVD. The fuel for the generator, too, was controlled and very limited, but occasional electricity was part of her salary.

Suddenly Taylor had the feeling someone else was in the room. It made the hairs on the back of her neck stand up. 'OK, who is there?'

No answer. Could it be Bug? She would know if Bug had been brought out to the island.

Nothing. She was letting her imagination –

Something moved. Right in front of her. For just a second the TV screen had blurred. Like something transparent but distorting had moved in front of it.

'Hey!' She was poised, ready to bounce out of here in a heartbeat. She listened to the room. Nothing. Whatever had been there was gone now. Or maybe had never been there to begin with; that was most likely. She was imagining things.

Taylor reached for the remote control and saw that her skin was gold. Her first reaction was that it was a trick of the light from the cartoon. But after a few seconds she decided, no. No, this was weird.

Taylor climbed out of bed and went to the window. In the moonlight her skin was still gold.

Crazy. Not real.

She searched in the dark and found a candle. She clumsily thumbed a lighter and brought fire to the wick.

Yes. Her skin was gold.

Carrying the candle, she went to the bathroom to look at herself in the mirror.

She was gold. From head to toe. Her black hair was still black, but every square inch of her skin was the colour of actual yellow gold.

Then she leaned close to look at the reflection of her own eyes. And that was when she screamed, because the irises were an even deeper gold.

'Oh, my God,' she whispered.

Shaking, she switched out of her bed shirt into jeans and a T-shirt. Because maybe she was just hallucinating, so she needed to have someone else look at her.

Taylor pictured Lana's hotel, the hallway.

She bounced.

The pain was instant and unbearable. Like nothing she had ever felt or imagined. Her left hand and the outer meat of her left calf felt as if they were pressed against red-hot steel.

Taylor screamed and thrashed and the pain only grew worse. She was hanging from her hand and her leg, just hanging, not standing on anything, just hanging from . . . She screamed again as she realised she was not at Clifftop. She was in the forest, hanging from a tall tree. Her left hand and the outer edge of her left calf had materialised in the tree.

In the tree.

She dangled, screaming, right arm and left arm reaching, grabbing, wild and out of control. Her golden flesh shining dully in the moonlight.

And the pain!

It had to be a dream. This couldn't be real. She hadn't bounced here. No, it was just a horrible nightmare. She had to bounce away, even if it was a dream, bounce back to her bedroom.

Taylor strained to visualise her room. Pushed back the pain for just a second . . . just . . .

Taylor bounced.

The hand was gone. Neatly cut off at the wrist. No blood, just a sudden ending. Taylor could not see her calf. Nor could she feel it.

She was not in her bedroom. She was on a car in the driveway of Clifftop.

On the car. Both of her legs were in the car, but she was on it, on the dusty roof of a Lexus. She had materialised with her legs sticking through the roof.

Taylor bellowed in pain and terror.

Her flailing caused her to topple over. The stumps of her legs didn't do a very good job of holding her in place. She rolled once, fell the four feet to the pavement, landed on her chest.

Shaking with fear, she fumbled for and reached the door handle and used it to pull herself up into a seated position. Her legs ended in neat stumps, just above the knees. Just like her left hand.

No blood.

But so much pain.

Taylor screamed and fell back and lost consciousness.

Astrid had found the sight of a visibly pregnant Diana disturbing.

It was strange enough to see a fifteen-year-old girl pregnant in any context. In the FAYZ it was far more jarring. The FAYZ was a trap, a prison, a purgatory maybe. But a nursery?

Each week that had gone by from that first day, the number of kids alive in the FAYZ had gone down. Always down, never up. The FAYZ was a place of sudden, horrifying death. Not a place of life.

And who had changed all that? A cruel, sharp-tongued girl and a boy who had never been anything but evil.

Astrid had taken a life. Diana was bringing one into the world.

Astrid sat on the sticky plastic cushions around the houseboat's tiny dining table. She put her elbows on the table and held her head in her hands.

Edilio came in, nodded at Astrid, and poured himself a glass of water from the jug on the counter. He was being discreet, not asking her questions, not wanting, probably, to scare her off.

'You like irony, Edilio?' Astrid asked him.

For a moment she thought she'd embarrassed him by using a word he didn't understand. But after a long, reflective pause

Edilio said, 'You mean like the irony of an illegal from Honduras ending up being what I am?'

Astrid smiled. 'Yeah. Like that.'

Edilio gave her a shrewd look. 'Or maybe like Diana having a baby?'

That forced a laugh from Astrid. She shook her head ruefully. 'You are the most underestimated person in the FAYZ.'

'It's my superpower,' Edilio said dryly.

Astrid invited him to sit down. He laid his gun down carefully and slid into a seat opposite her.

'Who would you say are the ten most powerful people in the FAYZ, Edilio?'

Edilio raised a skeptical eyebrow. 'Really?'

'Yes.'

'Number one is Albert,' Edilio said. 'Then Caine. Sam. Lana.' He thought about it for a moment longer and said, 'Quinn. Drake, unfortunately. Dekka. You. Me. Diana.'

Astrid folded her arms in front of her. 'Not Brianna? Or Orc?'

'They're both powerful, sure. But they don't have the kind of power that moves other people, you know? Brianna's cool, but she's not someone who other people follow. Same with Jack. More so with Orc.'

'You notice something about the ten people you named?' Astrid asked. Then she answered her own question. 'Four of the ten have no powers or mutations.'

'Irony?'

'And Diana's importance isn't about her power. It's about her baby. Diana Ladris: mother.'

'She's changed,' Edilio said. 'So have you.'

'Yeah, I'm a bit more tanned,' Astrid said evasively.

'I think it's more than that,' Edilio said. 'The old Astrid would never have just disappeared like you did. Wouldn't have stayed out there all on her own.'

'True,' Astrid acknowledged. 'I was . . . I was doing penance.'

Edilio smiled affectionately. 'Old-school, huh? Like a hermit. Or a monk. Holy men . . . women, too, I guess . . . going off to the wilderness to make peace with God.'

'I'm not a holy anything.'

'But you made peace?'

Astrid took a deep breath. 'I've changed.'

'Ah. Like that?' Her silence was confirmation. 'Lots of people, they go through bad times, they lose their faith. But they come back to it.'

'I didn't lose my faith, Edilio. I killed it. I held it up to the light and I stared right at it and for the first time I didn't hide behind something I'd read somewhere, or something I'd heard. I didn't worry about what anyone would think. I didn't worry about looking like a fool. I was all alone and I had no one to be right to. Except me. So I just looked. And when I looked . . .' She made a gesture with her fingers, like things blowing away, scattering in the wind. '. . . There was nothing there.'

Edilio looked very sad.

'Edilio,' she said, 'you have to believe what's right for you, what you feel. But so do I. It's hard for someone who has had to carry the nickname "Astrid the Genius" to admit she was wrong.' She made a wry smile. 'But I found out that I was . . . not happier, maybe; that's not the right word . . . It's not about happy. But . . . honest. Honest with myself.'

'So you think I'm lying to myself?' Edilio asked softly.

Astrid shook her head. 'Never. But I was.'

Edilio stood up. 'I have to get back out there.' He came to stand beside her, put his arms around her shoulders, and she hugged him, too.

'It's good to have you back, Astrid. You should get some sleep.' He nodded. 'Use Sam's bunk.'

Astrid felt weariness rise up and almost close her eyes where she sat. A nap. Just a brief one. She made her way to Sam's bunk and flopped down.

The bed smelled of Sam.

She wondered who he had found to be with. Surely someone by now. Well, good. Good. Sam needed someone to take care of him, and she hoped he'd found that.

She felt around, looking for a pillow. She hadn't had a pillow in a long, long time, and now the idea of one seemed incredibly luxurious.

Instead of a pillow her hand touched sheer, silky fabric. She pulled it to her and ran the fabric against her cheek. She knew it. It was her old nightgown, the filmy white thing she used to wear back in the days when she didn't need to sleep with her clothes on and a shotgun nestled to her breast.

Her old nightgown. Sam kept it with him, in his bed.

TEN

34 HOURS 31 MINUTES

'I'M GOING TO risk some light,' Sam said.

'I think some light would be a great idea,' Dekka said.

Sam raised his hands, and a ball of light, like a pale greenish sun, began to form in mid-air. It created more shadows than illumination. So he leaned to his right as far as he could without moving his feet and hung a second light in mid-air. The two lights banished some of the shadows.

'OK, everyone kneel down real slowly and check all around your feet,' Sam instructed.

'Aaahh!' Jack yelled.

'Don't move!'

'I'm not moving, I'm not moving, my foot is underneath a wire, I'm not moving, Oh, God, I'm going to die!'

Sam formed a third light down by Jack's feet. Now he could easily see the taut wire crossing the toe of Jack's boot.

'Dekka, are you clear?' Sam asked.

'I think so. Anyway, I can see where the wire runs now.'

'OK, then move back to a safe distance.'

'Any idea what a safe distance would be?'

'Far,' Sam said. 'OK, Jack, just stand still. I'm going to scoop the sand out from under your foot. That'll take the pressure off the wire.'

Sam used his two index fingers to begin very, very delicately scooping sand. Then he used two fingers from each hand.

Jack's shoe dropped half an inch. Then a bit more.

'OK, now just move your foot back.'

'You sure?'

'I'm right here next to you, aren't I?' Sam snapped.

Jack moved his foot. Nothing blew up.

'Now we all just back away.'

'Hey, what are you guys doing?' It was Brianna atop the bluff. 'What's with all the light? I thought we were being all –'

'Stay right there!' Dekka yelled.

'OK, jeez, you don't have to yell.'

Sam explained what was going on. 'We can't leave this thing booby-trapped. Some innocent person could stumble across this place. We either have to disarm it or blow it up.'

'Since I'm the tech guy, and disarming a booby trap is a sort of tech problem,' Jack said, 'I vote we blow it up from a safe distance.'

'Oh, come on, Jack, don't be a wimp,' Dekka teased.

'Breeze,' Sam called up to her. 'Find us a rope or a long string.'

Brianna blurred out of view.

'OK, let's all go down to the water,' Sam said.

They did not have to wait long. In five minutes Brianna was vibrating to a stop next to them.

'I don't guess you can outrun an explosion, right?' Sam asked doubtfully.

Jack rolled his eyes and sighed his condescending geek sigh. 'Seriously? Brianna runs in miles per hour. Explosions happen in feet per second. Don't believe what you see in movies.'

'Yeah, Sam,' Dekka said.

'In the old days I always had Astrid around to humiliate me when I asked a stupid question,' Sam said. 'It's good to have Jack to take over that job.'

He'd said it lightheartedly, but the mention of Astrid left an awkward hole in the conversation.

Brianna said, 'I can't outrun an explosion, but I'll tie the string around the wire.'

She zipped over to the wire and zipped back holding the loose end. 'Who gets to yank the string?'

'She who ties the string pulls it,' Sam said. 'But first –'

BOOOOM!

The containers, the sand, pieces of driftwood, bushes on the bluff all erupted in a fireball. Sam felt a blast of heat on his face. His ears rang. His eyes scrunched on sand.

Debris seemed to take a long time to fall back down to earth.

In the eventual silence Sam said, 'I was going to say first we should all lie flat so we didn't get blown up. But I guess that was good, too, Breeze.'

He looked towards the south. From where he was standing he couldn't exactly see Perdido Beach. There were no lights except for his eternal Sammy suns, and they would be behind curtains at night.

Down there in town his brother, Caine, was . . . doing what exactly? That was the question. Had this been Caine's idea, this booby trap? Had he heard or seen the explosion and was he now rejoicing, believing Sam had been killed?

What would Caine do if he thought Sam was dead? Would he come against the lake? Could Albert stop him?

Caine wouldn't dare attack the lake as long as Sam was alive. As long as Sam was alive and could join forces with Albert, Caine would be careful.

But he wondered how long it would be before Caine moved against Albert and Sam. Would Caine really let Diana have his child and stay with Sam?

It did occur to Sam for just a fleeting moment that Caine might not be the one who had taken the missiles. But there was really only one other possibility. A ridiculous possibility.

Ridiculous.

No, Caine had the missiles. Which meant the four-month-long peace was coming to an end. It was dark, and no one was looking at him, so Sam didn't feel too guilty about the fact that he was smiling.

Cigar felt hands touching him.

Maybe. Maybe hands. Maybe the paws of a monster who would sink terrible claws into him and rip the flesh from his arm.

He screamed.

Maybe. He couldn't be sure. Had he ever stopped screaming?

He heard a far-off wail, a hopeless, helpless sound. Was it coming from him?

'I've never been able to grow an organ back,' Lana's voice said. 'Last time I tried . . . Let's just hope you don't end up with whip eyes.'

He knew her voice. He knew she was there beside him. Yes. That was her touch on him. Unless she was the creature that smiled before chewing your fingers off and then ate its way up your arms, blood spurting around its grinning, needle-toothed mouth, laughing at his pain, chewing him, ripping until he screamed and screamed and his screaming throat became a roaring animal, a lion's mouth roaring out of his throat . . .

'Look! Something's happening.'

Cigar didn't recognise that voice. A boy's voice, wasn't it?

'Who are you?' Cigar cried out.

'It's Lana.'

'Who are yoooooou?'

'I think he means me. It's me, Sanjit. Lana sent for me to help hold you . . . to help.'

There were snakes in Cigar's dried-blood eye sockets. He could feel them. They were writhing like mad.

'Nerves,' Sanjit said.

'You might be feeling something,' Lana said.

'Aaaaahhhhhh!' Cigar cried. He tried to claw at his eyes but his hands were pinned. Helpless. He'd had his arms chewed off, hadn't he? He didn't have arms any more. So how had he clawed the roaches out of his eyes if he had no arms? Answer that, Bradley. His real name, Bradley.

Answer that.

And if you don't have arms how did you light those cigars, those big fat cigars and puff until the ends were glowing red and so hot and then plunge those red-hot tips into the empty holes of your eye and then shriek in agony and beg God, 'Kill me, kill me, kill me'?

'The nerves are regrowing. Unbelievable,' Sanjit said.

'He's trying to claw his eyes again,' Lana said.

'Yeah,' Sanjit agreed. 'This can't ever happen again. That witch has to be stopped.'

'It was Caine's doing,' Lana said angrily. 'He knows what Penny is like. She's a mental case. She's evil. She was always twisted, but after her injuries . . . something snapped in that girl.'

'My eyes!' Cigar screamed.

Something. A bar of faint, distant light. Like the earliest hints of sunrise, like the blackness was just a little bit less black.

'Something is happening,' Sanjit said. 'Look! Look!'

'My eyes!'

'Not yet, dude, but something is growing. Little white balls, no bigger than BBs right now.' Sanjit put his hand on Cigar's chest and dug his ripping, tearing, stiletto fingers into Cigar's heart and . . .

No. No. That wasn't real. That wasn't real.

The light bar, that faint glow was growing. Cigar stared at it, willing it to be real. He needed something to be real. He needed something to not be a nightmare.

'Cigar,' Sanjit said in a kind voice. 'It looks like the gouging and the cuts are healing up. And it seems like tiny little eyes are forming.'

But then Lana's more astringent voice said, 'Don't get your hopes up too much.'

Her hands. On his temples. On his brow. Slowly, slowly she probed towards the black sockets.

'No, no, no, nooooooooo!' he wailed.

Lana's fingers slid back.

Lana was real. Her touch was real. The light he could see was real. He tried so very hard to hold on to that.

'We're going to cover your eyes with a cloth, OK?' Sanjit

said. 'Your eyeballs are jerking around and it may be that the light from the Sammy sun bothers them.'

An eternity, during which he slid in and out of consciousness, in and out of screaming nightmares. At times he was on fire. At times his skin crisped like bacon. At times scorpions burrowed into his flesh.

All the while, Lana kept her hands on his face.

'Listen to me,' Lana said at last. 'Can you hear me?'

How much time had passed? The madness was not past, but it was diluted, weakened. The screams still threatened to tear his throat, but he could hold them off; he could mount some resistance, at least.

'We've been here all night,' Lana said. 'So whatever you've got is what you've got. I can't do any more.'

'I'm here, too, brother. It's me, Quinn.' Quinn laid his calloused hand on Cigar's shoulder and it made him want to cry. 'Listen, dude, however it turns out, you've got a place with your crew. You're one of us.'

'We're going to take the cloth off now,' Sanjit said.

Cigar felt the cloth slide away.

Quinn gasped.

Cigar saw something that looked very much like Quinn. But a Quinn with a storm of purple-and-red light around his head. Quinn enveloped in what looked like the beginning of a tornado.

Cigar saw Sanjit behind him. He glowed softly, a steady silvery light.

Then he saw Lana. Her eyes were beautiful. Shifting rainbows. Sudden, piercing shafts like bright moonlight. She outshone both Quinn and Sanjit. She was a moon to their stars.

But wrapped around her was a sickly green tendril, like an infinitely long snake that writhed and probed at her, seeking a way into her head.

And that was all that Cigar saw. Because everything around the three kids was blank, empty darkness.

There was no teasing or even conversation on the trip back to the lake. Sam drove slowly. Jack slept, snoring from time to time, but not so loud that it bothered Sam.

Dekka stared out of the window. They had waited until dawn – no point risking another drive through the dark. After all, the need for secrecy was long gone.

Sam had no doubt that Caine had the missiles.

No real doubt. Despite the nagging voice in the back of his head that told him that if Caine had the missiles he'd have long since used them to move against the lake.

No. That was stupid. Caine was just biding his time. Waiting.

Brianna came running up alongside the truck and made the signal for, *Roll down your window.*

'You need me any more?' Brianna asked. 'Otherwise I'll go catch some z's.'

'No, I'm good, Breeze.'

But she didn't zoom off; she kept pace. The truck was moving at no more than twenty to thirty miles an hour, so it was a pleasant walking speed for Brianna.

'You're not letting Caine keep those things, are you?' Brianna asked.

'Not tonight, huh? I'm really beat. I don't want to think about it. I just want to crawl into my bunk and pull the covers over my head.'

Brianna looked as if she was going to argue, but then she gave a theatrical sigh, winked at Sam like she had already read his inner thoughts, and zoomed away down the road.

Sam noticed that Dekka refused to look at her. He thought of talking to her about it, but he was talked out. He could barely keep his eyes open.

And yet, there it was again, that feeling of not quite seeing something. He felt eyes on him. Something watching him from out there in the black desert night.

'Coyotes,' he muttered. And he almost believed it.

They got back to the lake just as the faintest light of dawn shone from the false sun of the FAYZ. They got nice sunrises on the lake – if you could get past the fact that the 'sun' was an illusion crawling up a barrier that was no more than half a mile away across the water.

Sam was stiff and tired. He crept on to the houseboat, careful not to wake anyone, and sidled down the narrow passage to his bunk. The shades were drawn and of course there were no lights, so he felt his way to the edge of his bed and crawled across it on hands and knees to find his pillow.

He collapsed on his back.

But even at the edge of sleep he was aware of something different about the bed.

Then he felt soft breath on his cheek.

He turned and her lips were on his. Not gentle. Not soft. She kissed him hard, and it was like he'd been awakened by an electric power line.

She kissed him and slid on top of him.

Their bodies did the rest.

At some point in the hours that followed he said, 'Astrid?'

'Don't you think you should have made sure of that about three times ago?' Astrid said in her familiar, slightly condescending tone.

They said many things to each other after that, but nothing that involved words.

OUTSIDE

MARY TERRAFINO HAD come through the barrier four months ago. She had leaped from a cliff inside the FAYZ at the exact moment of her fifteenth birthday.

She had landed. Not on the sand and rocks beneath the cliff, but two miles away from the barrier. She had appeared in a dry gulch and would have died but for the two dirt-bikers who were racing across bumps and drops, yelling and roaring along and definitely not looking for what they found.

The bikers had not called for an ambulance. They had called animal control. Because what they thought they had seen was a terribly mangled animal. It was an understandable mistake.

Mary was in a special ward at the UCLA hospital down in Los Angeles. The ward had two patients: Mary and a boy named Francis.

The doctor in charge was a woman named Chandiramani. She was forty-eight and wore her white coat over a traditional sari. Dr Chandiramani had a tense but proper relationship with Major Onyx. The major was supposedly the liaison with the Pentagon. In theory he was there only to offer Dr Chandiramani and her team any necessary support.

In reality the major clearly thought he was in charge of the ward. He and the doctors often clashed.

It was all very polite, with never a raised voice. But the Pentagon's priorities were somewhat different from those of the doctors. The doctors wanted to keep their two horribly damaged patients alive and comfortable. The soldiers needed answers.

Major Onyx had arranged to have equipment installed in the room, and in both adjacent rooms, that definitely had nothing to do with Mary's medical condition. Dr Chandiramani had pretended not to understand any of it, but the doctor had not always confined her studies to medicine. In earlier life she had made a serious start at studying physics. And she knew a mass spectrometer when she saw one. She knew that this room, and Francis's room, were effectively inside of a sort of super-sensitive mass spectrometer. What other instruments the major had packed into the walls and ceiling and floor she could only guess.

Francis was alive. But no way had yet been found to communicate with him. There were brain waves. So he was conscious. But he had no mouth or eyes. He had one appendage that might be an arm, but it was in a continuous state of spasm, so even if the fingers had not been oddly jointed claws he would not have been able to use either a keyboard or a pencil.

Mary had somewhat more potential. She had a mouth and it appeared to have some limited functionality in terms of speech. They'd had to remove some of the grotesque teeth that had grown through her cheeks. And they had performed other surgeries to repair her tongue and mouth and throat to the best of their abilities.

The result was that Mary could speak.

Unfortunately she had only screamed and leaked tears out of the smear that was her only eye.

But now they had found the right mix of sedatives and anti-seizure meds, and Dr Chandiramani had finally agreed to allow Major Onyx and an army psychologist to question the girl.

The first questions were overly broad.

'What can you tell us about conditions inside?'

'Mom?' she had asked in a voice that was barely a whisper.

'Your mother will come later,' the psychologist said in a soothing voice. 'I am Dr Greene. With me is Major Onyx. And Dr Chandiramani, who has been taking care of you these last months since you escaped.'

'Hello, Mary,' Dr Chandiramani said.

'The littles?' Mary asked.

'What does that mean?' Dr Greene asked.

'The littles. My kids.'

Major Onyx had close-cut black hair, a dark tan, and intense blue eyes. 'The twins told us that she took care of the little children.'

Dr Greene leaned closer, but Dr Chandiramani could see him fighting the nausea that people always felt seeing Mary. 'Do you mean the little children you took care of?'

'I killed them,' Mary said. Tears flowed from her one tear duct and ran down the seared, boiled, lobster-red skin.

'Surely not,' Dr Greene said.

Mary cried aloud, a sound of keening despair.

'Change topic,' Dr Chandiramani said, watching the monitor.

'Mary, this is very important. Does anyone know how this all started?'

Nothing.

'Who did it, Mary?' Dr Chandiramani asked. 'Who created the anom – the place you called the FAYZ?'

'Little Pete. The Darkness.'

The two doctors and the soldier looked at one another, puzzled.

The major frowned and whipped out his iPhone. He tapped it a few times. 'FAYZ Wiki,' he explained. 'We have two "Pete" or "Peter"s listed.'

'What are the ages?' Dr Chandiramani asked.

'One is twelve; one is four. No, sorry, he would have turned five.'

'Do you have children, Major? I do. No twelve-year-old would be happy to be called "Little Pete". It must be the five-year-old she's talking about.'

'Delusional,' Dr Greene said. 'A five-year-old did not create the anomaly.' He frowned thoughtfully and scribbled a note. 'Darkness. Maybe she's afraid of the dark.'

'Everyone's afraid of the dark,' Dr Chandiramani said. Greene was getting on her nerves. So were the major and his horrified stare.

The monitor above Mary's bed suddenly beeped urgently.

Dr Chandiramani reached for the call panel and yelled, 'Code blue, code blue,' but it was unnecessary, because nurses were already rushing in through the door.

At the same time Major Onyx's phone began chiming. He didn't answer it, but he did open an app of some sort.

A tall, thin doctor in green scrubs swept in behind the nurses. He glanced at the monitor. He put his stethoscope in his ears and asked, 'Where is her heart?'

Dr Chandiramani pointed to the unlikely place. But she knew it was useless. All lines on the monitor had gone flat. All at the same time. Which was not how it happened. Heart, brain, everything suddenly and irreversibly dead.

'You'll find the other one's gone, too,' Major Onyx said calmly, consulting his phone. 'Francis. Something pulled his plug, as well.'

'Are you going to tell me what you're talking about?' Dr Chandiramani snapped.

The major jerked his head, indicating that the other doctor and the nurses should get out. They didn't argue.

Major Onyx closed the app and put his phone away. 'The people who were ejected when the dome was created? They came out clean. So did the twins. The rest, the ones who've appeared since? They've always had a sort of . . . umbilical cord . . . connecting them to the dome. J waves, that's what we call them. But don't ask me what they are, because we don't know. We can detect them, but they are not something encountered in nature.'

'What does "J wave" stand for?' the doctor asked.

Major Onyx barked out a laugh. 'Some smart-ass physicist at CERN called them "Jehovah waves". According to him they might as well come from God, because we sure don't know what they do or where they come from. The name stuck.'

'So what just changed? Did something happen with these J waves?'

The major started to answer but, with a visible effort, and a last appalled look at Mary, stopped himself. 'The conversation we just had? Never happened.'

He left and Dr Chandiramani was alone with her patient.

Four months after her ghastly appearance, Mary Terrafino was dead.

ELEVEN

26 HOURS 45 MINUTES

SAM WOKE TO a feeling of utter, profound, incredible relief.

He closed his eyes as soon as he opened them, afraid that being awake would just invite something terrible to appear.

Astrid was back. And she was asleep with her head on his arm. His arm was asleep, completely numb, but as long as that blonde head was right there his arm could stay numb.

She smelled like pine trees and campfire smoke.

He opened his eyes, cautious, almost flinching, because the FAYZ didn't make a habit of allowing him pure, undiluted happiness. The FAYZ made a habit of stomping on anything that looked even a little bit like happiness. And this level of happiness was surely tempting retaliation. From this high up the fall could be a long, long one.

Just yesterday he'd been bored and longing for conflict. The memory shocked him. Had that really been him grinning in the dark at the prospect of war with Caine?

Surely not. He wasn't that guy. Was he?

If he was that guy, how could he suddenly do a 180 and now feel so different? Because of Astrid? Because she was in his bed?

Without moving he could see the top of her head – her hair looked as if someone had cut it with a weed whacker – part of her right cheek, her eyelashes, the end of her nose, and farther down a long, shapely, much-scarred and bruised leg entwined with his own leg.

One of her hands was on his chest, just over his heart, which was starting to beat faster, so fast and so insistently he was afraid the vibration might wake her. Her breath tickled.

Sam's mind was happy to let this go on forever. His body had a different idea. He swallowed hard.

Her eyelid flickered. Her breathing changed. She said, 'How long can we go before we have to talk?'

'A while longer,' he said.

The while longer eventually came to an end. Astrid finally pulled away and sat up. Their eyes met.

Sam didn't know what he expected to see in her eyes. Maybe guilt. Remorse. Loathing. He saw none of those things.

'I forget,' Astrid said, 'why was I so against doing that?'

Sam smiled. 'I'm not about to remind you.'

She looked at him with a frankness that embarrassed him. Like she was taking inventory. Like she was storing images away in memory.

'Are you back?' Sam asked.

Astrid's gaze flicked away, evasive. Then she seemed to think better of it, and she met his gaze squarely. 'I have an idea. How about if I just tell you the truth?'

'That would be good.'

'Don't be so sure,' she said. 'But I'm out of practice lying. I guess living alone kind of made me intolerant of BS. Especially my own.'

Sam sat up. 'OK. Let's talk. First, let's jump in the lake for a minute.'

They made their way on deck and plunged off into the chilly water.

'People will see us,' Astrid said, smoothing her hair back and revealing the tan line on her forehead. 'Are you ready for that?'

'Astrid, by now not only everyone at the lake, but everyone in Perdido Beach and probably whoever is out on the island knows all about it. Taylor's probably been here and gone; most likely Bug, too.'

She laughed. 'You're suggesting gossip actually moves at speeds that are impossible.'

'Gossip this juicy? The speed of light is nothing compared to the speed this will move at.'

'Move at?' she mocked. 'Your participle is dangling.'

Several bits and pieces of leering jokes came to Sam's mind, but Astrid had got there quicker and she shook her head and said, 'No. Don't. That kind of joke would be beneath even you.'

It was good to have her back.

They climbed aboard and towelled off. They dressed and came out on to the top deck with breakfast: carrots, yesterday's grilled fish, and water.

Astrid got down to business. 'I came back because the dome is changing.'

'The stain?'

'You've seen it?'

'Yeah, but we thought maybe it was because of what Sinder's doing.'

Astrid's eyebrows rose. 'What is Sinder doing?'

'She's developed a power. She can make things grow at an accelerated rate. She has a little garden right up against the barrier. We're experimenting a little, eating just a little of the vegetables, seeing if there's any kind of . . . you know, effect.'

'Very scientific of you,' Astrid said.

He shrugged. 'Well, my scientist girlfriend was off in the woods. I had to do my best.'

Had she just reacted to the word "girlfriend"?

'Sorry,' he said quickly. 'I didn't mean to . . .' He wasn't sure what he hadn't meant to do.

'It wasn't the word "girlfriend",' Astrid said. 'It was the possessive. The "my". But I realised that was stupid of me. There's no better way to say it. It's just that I haven't been thinking of myself as anyone's anything.'

'No girl is an island.'

'Seriously? You're misquoting John Donne? To me?'

'Hey, maybe I've spent the last four months reading poetry. You don't know.'

Astrid laughed. He loved that laugh. Then she grew serious. 'The stain is everywhere I looked, Sam. I travelled along the barrier. It's everywhere, sometimes just a few inches visible, but I saw areas where it rose maybe twenty feet or so.'

'You think it's growing?'

She shrugged. 'I know it's growing; I just don't know how fast. I'd like to try to measure it.'

'What do you think it is?' he asked.

She shook her head slowly, side to side. 'I don't know.'

He felt as if a hand was squeezing his heart. The FAYZ punished happiness. He had made the mistake of being happy.

'Do you think . . .' he began, but he couldn't quite get the words out. He changed it to, 'What if it keeps growing?'

'The barrier has always been a kind of optical illusion. Look straight at it in front of you and you see a blank, non-reflective grey surface. A nullity. Look higher up and you see an illusion of sky. Day sky, night sky – but never a plane. The sun and moon wax and wane as they should. It's an illusion but they're also our only sources of light.' She was thinking aloud. The way she sometimes did. The way he had missed.

'I don't know, but this seems like some kind of breakdown.

You know how sometimes a movie projector – like the one we had at school, remember? – will get dimmer and dimmer until pretty soon you're squinting to see anything?'

'You're talking about it going completely dark?' He was relieved that his voice did not betray him with a tremor.

Astrid started to reach to touch his leg and stopped herself. Then she twined her fingers together, giving them something else to do. She wasn't meeting his gaze but looking slightly past him, first to his left, then to his right.

'It's possible,' she said. 'I guess, yes. I mean, that was my first thought. That it's going dark.'

Sam took a deep breath. He wasn't going to freak out; he was sure of that. But the only reason he was confident was that he, himself, had the power to create light. Pitiful little Sammy suns and blinding beams, not bright yellow suns or even moons. But he himself would have light. He wouldn't have to be completely in the dark.

He couldn't be in the dark. Not in the total dark.

He realised his palms were damp and he wiped them on his shorts. When he glanced up he knew Astrid had seen, and that she knew what he was feeling.

He tried out a wry grin. 'Stupid, huh? All we've been through? And I'm still scared of the dark?'

'Everyone's afraid of something,' Astrid said.

'Like I'm a little kid.'

'Like you're a human being.'

Sam looked around at the lake, at the sun sparkling on the water. Some kids were laughing, little kids playing at the water's edge.

'Complete darkness.' Sam said it to hear it, to see if he could accept it. 'Nothing will grow. We won't be able to fish. We'll . . . We'll wander in the dark until we die of hunger. Kids will figure that out. They'll panic.'

'Maybe the stain will stop,' Astrid said.

But Sam wasn't listening. 'It's the endgame.'

Sanjit and Virtue found Taylor that morning when they went outside for some exercise: Sanjit running back and forth, circling around a huffing and puffing Virtue, who was definitely not much of a runner.

'Come on, Choo, this is good for you.'

'I know,' Virtue said through gritted teeth. 'But that doesn't mean I have to enjoy it.'

'Hey, we have a nice view of the beach and the –' Sanjit stopped because Virtue had disappeared behind a car. He doubled back and saw his brother bent over something, and then he saw the something he was bent over.

'What the . . . Oh, God, what happened to her?'

Sanjit knelt next to Virtue. Neither of them touched her. The girl with skin the colour of a gold bar and both lower legs and one hand simply gone. Cut off.

Virtue held his breath and put his ear close to Taylor's mouth. 'I think she's still alive.'

'I'll get Lana!' Sanjit raced back inside, down the hallway to the room he shared with Lana. He burst inside yelling, 'Lana! Lana!'

He found himself staring at the bad end of her pistol. 'Sanjit, how many times do I have to tell you not to surprise me!' Lana raged.

He said nothing, just took her hand and drew her along with him.

'She's definitely breathing,' Virtue said as they ran up. 'And I found a pulse in her neck.'

Sanjit looked at Lana as though she might understand what this meant. A girl with golden skin suddenly minus a hand and both legs. But Lana was just staring with the same horror he felt.

Then he saw the flash of suspicion, the hard, angry look she got when she felt the distant touch of the gaiaphage. Followed, as it usually was, by her jaw tightening, muscles clenching.

Moved by a grim instinct, Sanjit peered through the dirty windows of the car. 'I found her legs.'

'Get them,' Lana said. 'Virtue? You and I can carry her inside.'

* * *

'We're still going out? After what they did to Cigar?' Phil was outraged. He wasn't the only one.

Quinn said nothing. He didn't trust himself to say anything. There was a volcano inside him. His head was buzzing from lack of sleep. The sight of Cigar, with those creepy, frightening marble-size eyeballs hanging from snakelike tendrils of nerve inside black crater eye sockets . . .

He had clawed his own eyes out.

He's one of mine, Quinn thought, and the phrase went over and over in his head. *One of mine.*

Cigar had done wrong – a terrible wrong. He deserved punishment. But not to be tortured. Not to be driven insane. Not to be made into a monstrous creature that no one would be able to look at without stifling a scream.

Quinn climbed into his boat. His three crew members hesitated, looked at one another, and climbed in after him. The other three boats all did likewise.

They cast off and shipped oars and began to make their way out to sea.

Two hundred yards out, a distance where people onshore could still easily see them, Quinn gave a quiet order.

'Oars in,' he said.

'But there's no fish this close in,' Phil objected.

Quinn said nothing. The oars came in. The boats rocked almost imperceptibly on the faint swell.

Quinn watched the dock and the beach. It wouldn't be long before someone reported to Albert and/or Caine to tell them the fishing fleet was not fishing.

He wondered who would react first.

Would it be Albert or Caine?

He closed his eyes and pulled his hat down low. 'I'm going to get some sleep,' he said. 'Use the oars only to keep us in position if needed. Let me know if anyone comes.'

'You got it, boss.'

Albert heard about Quinn first. Both Caine and Albert had spies – sometimes the same kids – but Albert paid better.

Albert had around-the-clock bodyguards now. He had come very, very close to dying after the remains of the Human Crew had broken into his house, robbed and shot him.

Caine had executed one of the villains, a kid named Lance. Another one, Turk, had been reprieved and now worked for Caine. It was a message from Caine to Albert, his keeping Turk around. It was a threat.

Albert's previous bodyguard had been killed by Drake.

Now he hired a total of four. They each worked an eight-hour shift, seven days a week. The fourth guard was on call, living at Albert's new compound. Whenever Albert stepped outside of the gate he would have whichever guard was on duty, plus the on-call guard. Two tough kids, both heavily armed.

But even that wasn't enough for Albert's security. He had taken to carrying a gun himself. Just a pistol, not a long gun, but it was a nine-millimetre in a brown leather holster, a serious, dangerous gun. He had learned how to shoot it, too.

And as a final line of security Albert had made sure that everyone knew he would pay whoever brought proof of a plot against him. It would always pay better to side with Albert.

Unfortunately that still left Caine. The self-anointed king.

Albert knew he could never take Caine on in a fight. So he made sure he knew exactly what Caine was up to. Someone very close to Caine worked secretly for Albert.

And yet, despite all this preparation, Albert had let this new problem sneak up on him.

It was a good long walk from Albert's edge-of-town compound to the marina. He hurried. He had to resolve this before Caine did. Caine had a temper. People with tempers were bad for business.

What Albert saw from the end of the dock was not good. Four boats and fifteen kids doing nothing. In his head Albert ran the numbers: maybe three days' worth of food, just two days' worth of blue bats. If the bat supply stopped then there was no safe way to harvest the worm-infested fields.

'Quinn!' Albert shouted.

He was furious to see that three kids were on the beach, eavesdropping. Didn't they have anything better to do?

'Hi, Albert,' Quinn called back. He seemed distracted. And Albert was sure that he'd seen Quinn motion for someone to stay down.

'How long is this supposed to go on?' Albert asked.

'Until we get justice,' Quinn said.

'Justice? People have been waiting for justice since the dinosaurs.'

Quinn said nothing and Albert cursed himself for indulging in sarcasm. 'What is it you want, Quinn. I mean in practical terms.'

'We want Penny gone,' Quinn said.

'I can't afford to pay you any more,' Albert shouted back.

'I didn't say anything about money,' Quinn said, sounding puzzled.

'Yeah, I know: justice. Usually what people really want is money. So why don't we get down to it?'

'Penny,' Quinn said. 'She leaves town. She stays gone. When that happens we fish. Until it happens, we sit.' He sat down as if to emphasise his point.

Albert bit his lip in extreme frustration. 'Quinn, don't you know that if you don't work this out with me you'll be dealing with Caine?'

'We don't think his powers reach this far,' Quinn said. He

seemed, if not smug, then at least determined. 'And we kind of think he likes to eat, too.'

Albert considered. He did some more quick calculations. 'OK, look, Quinn. I can up your share by five per cent. But that's as much as I can do.' He made a hand-washing gesture, signalling that it was a take-it-or-leave-it.

Quinn sat back down in the boat, pulled his hat – nearly unrecognisable as having once been a fedora but now stained, cut, scratched, torn, and twisted – down over his eyes and kicked his feet up on the gunwale.

Albert watched him for a while. No, there would be no bribing Quinn.

He took a deep breath and blew it out, releasing his frustration. Caine had created a problem that could bring everything crashing down. Everything Albert had built.

No Quinn, no fish; no fish, no crops. Simple maths. Caine would not give in – he wasn't the type. And Quinn, who had once been such a reliable coward, had grown and matured and become what he was now: useful.

One of them had to go, and if the choice was between Caine and Quinn the answer was simple.

The tricky part was in delivering the news to Caine. The trap he had long since laid for King Caine was ready and waiting. Albert only wished there was some way to get Penny at the same time. Enough with both of them, they were both pains in his butt: Albert was trying to run a business.

Maybe it was time to tell Caine that some very interesting toys were sitting in crates on an unfrequented beach.

It might just be time to kill the king.

In the interests of business.

25 HOURS 8 MINUTES

CAINE.

I'm writing this because I don't really have a choice. You'll probably figure I'm up to something. So when I'm done writing this I will read it out loud in front of Toto and Mohamed. Mo will be able to tell you that Toto testifies I'm telling the truth.

Something is happening to the barrier. It is turning black. We're calling it the stain. We're trying to figure out how fast this stain is spreading. No information yet. But it's possible this thing will just keep growing. It's possible the whole barrier will go dark. And we will all be in total darkness.

I'm sure you can figure out just how bad that will be if it happens.

If the FAYZ is going dark, I'll do my best to hang Sammy suns around. They aren't very bright but they'll hopefully keep people from going completely nuts until we can figure out –

Sorry, I had to stop myself there. I was starting to sound like I had a plan. I don't. If you do I'd like to hear it.

In the meantime I'm sending a copy of this to Albert and asking if the two of you will allow me to go to Perdido Beach to create at least a few lights.

– Sam Temple

He read the letter aloud, as he had promised to do. Toto muttered, 'That's true,' a couple of times. Mohamed waited while Sam wrote out a copy for Albert. He took both and stuck them in his jeans pocket.

'Listen, Mo, one more thing. Tell Caine – tell my brother – that I was expecting him to use those missiles of his against us. And I was ready for a war. But we are past that now.'

'OK.'

'Toto, have I written and spoken the truth?'

Toto nodded, then added, 'He believes it, Spidey.'

'Good enough, Mo?'

Mohamed nodded.

'Walk fast,' Sam said. Then in a mordant tone he added, 'Enjoy the sunshine.'

'Get me a knife,' Lana said when they had what was left of Taylor laid out in an unoccupied hotel room.

Sanjit had carried her legs, one in each hand, and laid them on the bed beside her.

'Knife?' It was just Lana and Sanjit now; Virtue was watching the rest of the family. He had no stomach for this. And no one wanted the little kids to come in and see this horror.

Lana didn't explain, so Sanjit handed her his knife. She looked at the blade for a moment, then at Taylor, who was now breathing a little more audibly, a thready, uncertain sound. Lana pushed Taylor's shirt up a little and drew the blade across her abdomen. The cut was shallow and bled only a little.

'What's that for?' Sanjit didn't doubt Lana, but he wanted to know, and to keep up a flow of conversation to keep from thinking about Taylor.

'I tried to regrow eyeballs and got BBs. The time before that when I tried to regrow an entire limb I didn't get quite what I expected,' Lana said.

'Drake?'

'Drake. I just want to test my powers on Taylor before . . .' She fell silent as she touched the wound she had made.

The wound was not closing. Instead it was bubbling, like someone had poured peroxide into it.

Lana drew back. 'Something is not right.'

Sanjit saw her brow furrow deeply. She seemed almost to be cringing away from Taylor. 'The Darkness?' Sanjit guessed.

Lana shook her head. 'No. Something . . . something else. Something wrong.' She closed her eyes and rocked back slowly on her heels. Then, like she was trying to surprise someone, she twisted her head to look behind her.

'I would tell you if someone was sneaking up behind you.'

'It's not the Darkness,' Lana said. 'Not this. But I can feel . . . something.'

Sanjit was inclined by his nature to be sceptical. But Lana had told him everything about her desperate battles with the gaiaphage. He could understand how even now she could feel the creature's mind reaching for hers, its voice calling to her. Things that he'd have dismissed as impossible in the old world – things that *were* impossible – happened here.

But this was something different, or so she said. And her eyes were not filled with the barely suppressed rage and fear she showed when the Darkness reached her. Now she seemed puzzled.

Suddenly Lana grabbed Sanjit's arm, yanked him closer, and felt his forehead with her palm. Then she released him and placed her palm on Taylor's forehead.

'She's cold,' Lana said, eyes gleaming.

'She's lost a lot of blood,' Sanjit said.

'Has she? Because it looks to me as if all her injuries are sealed off.'

'Then what would make her so cold?' Because now Sanjit had noticed it, too. He touched the severed legs, then Taylor's forehead, then his own. Taylor's legs were the same temperature as her torso.

Room temperature.

'Sanjit, turn away,' Lana said. She was already pushing Taylor's T-shirt up and Sanjit hastily looked away.

Next he heard Lana unzipping Taylor's jeans.

'OK,' Lana said. 'Nothing you shouldn't see.'

Sanjit turned back and gasped. 'She's . . . OK, I don't know what she is.'

'I forget exactly what all the signs are of a mammal,' Lana said, voice level. 'But there was something about giving birth to babies and then nursing them. And being warm-blooded. Taylor no longer has any of that . . . those . . .' She shook her head, trying to clear her thoughts. 'Taylor's not a mammal any more.'

'Hair,' Sanjit said. 'Mammals have hair.' He touched Taylor's hair. It felt like a sheet of rolled-out Play-Doh.

'So she's a freak?' Sanjit suggested.

'She was already a freak,' Lana said. 'And none of the freaks have ever developed a second power. Or stopped being human. Even Orc seems to be human beneath that armour of his.'

'So the rules are changing,' Sanjit said.

'Or being changed,' Lana said.

'What do we do with her? She's still alive.'

Lana didn't answer. She seemed to be staring at the space a few inches in front of her face. Sanjit reached for her, to touch her arm, remind her she wasn't alone. But he stopped himself. Lana's wall of solitude was going up, shutting her off in the world she shared with forces Sanjit could not understand.

He let her be, just kept his position close by. It made him feel very isolated. His gaze was drawn irresistibly to the monstrous parody of Taylor.

Taylor's mouth snapped open. A long, dark green, forked tongue flicked out, seemed to taste the air and withdraw. Her eyes remained blessedly closed.

Sanjit felt himself back on the streets of Bangkok. One of the beggars he'd known back then had a two-legged dog he kept on a leash. And the beggar himself was legless and his hands were formed into two thick fingers and a stub of thumb.

Other street kids had called him a two-headed monster, as if the man and the dog were a single malformed creature. Sometimes they would throw rocks at the beggar. He was a freak, a monster. He made them afraid.

It's not the monsters who are so completely different that are scary, Sanjit reflected. *It's the ones who are too human. They carry with them the warning that what happened to them might happen to you, too.*

A part of Sanjit was telling him to kill this monstrous body. There was no way to help her. It would be an act of charity. Taylor, after all, was just one manifestation of a consciousness that would go on forever. Samsara. Taylor's karma would determine her next incarnation, and Sanjit would earn good karma for a charitable deed.

But he'd also heard people of his religion who would say, *No, you can never take a life because if you do you interrupt the proper cycle of rebirth.*

'Do you ever have feelings you can't really explain?' Lana asked.

Sanjit was startled out of his own thoughts. 'Yes. But what do you mean?'

'Like . . . Like feeling that a storm is coming. Or that you'd better not get on a plane. Or that if you turn the wrong corner at the wrong time you'll come face-to-face with something awful.'

Sanjit did take her hand now and she didn't refuse him. 'Once I was to see a friend in the market. And it was as if my feet were refusing to move. Like they were telling me, 'No. Don't walk.''

'And?'

'And a car bomb went off.'

'In the market where you didn't want to go?'

'No. Ten feet away from the place where I was standing when my feet told me not to move. I ignored my feet. I went to the market.' Sanjit shrugged. 'Intuition was telling me something. Just not what I thought it was telling me.'

Lana nodded. Her face was very grim. 'It's happening.'

'What's happening?'

She fidgeted and dropped his hand. Then she smiled wryly

and took his hand back, holding it between hers. 'Kinda feels like a war is coming. It's been coming for a long time.'

Sanjit broke out a grin. 'Oh, is that all? In that case all we have to do is figure out how to survive. Haven't I told you what 'Sanjit' means? It's Sanskrit for 'invincible'.'

Lana actually smiled, something so rare it broke Sanjit's heart. 'I remember: you can't be vinced.'

'No one vinces me, baby.'

'Darkness is coming,' Lana said, her smile fading.

'You can't tell the future,' Sanjit said firmly. 'No one can. Not even in this place. So: what do we do with Taylor?'

Lana sighed. 'Get her a room.'

THIRTEEN

25 HOURS

IT WASN'T POSSIBLE to draw on or mark the surface of the dome. So Astrid gave Sam a plan and Sam asked Roger – he liked to be called the Artful Roger – to build ten identical wooden frameworks. Like picture frames exactly two feet by two feet.

The frameworks were mounted on poles, each exactly five feet high.

Then Astrid, with Edilio for security, and Roger to help carry, walked along the barrier from west to east. They paced off distances of three hundred paces. Then, using a long tape measure, they measured off a hundred feet from the base of the barrier. There they dug a hole and set up the first frame. Another three hundred paces, then another carefully measured hundred feet, and another frame.

It took the whole day. At each frame Astrid stepped back to a precisely measured ten paces. She took a photograph through each frame, carefully thumbing in the day and time and approximately how much of the area inside the frame appeared to be covered by the stain.

This was why Astrid had come back. Because Jack might be smart enough to think of measuring the stain, but then again he might not think of it.

It was not that Astrid was lonely. It was not that she was just looking for an excuse to go to Sam.

And yet, look what had happened when she did, finally, go to Sam.

Astrid smiled and turned away so Edilio wouldn't see it and be embarrassed.

Had this been her desire all along? To find some excuse to go running back to Sam and to throw herself on him? It was the kind of question that would have preoccupied Astrid in the old days. The old Astrid would have been very concerned with her own motives, very much needing to be able to justify herself. She had always needed some kind of moral and ethical framework, some abstract standard to judge herself by.

And, of course, she had judged other people the same way. Then, when it had come down to survival, to doing whatever it took to end the horror, she had done the ruthless thing. Yes, there was a certain crude morality at work there: she had sacrificed Little Pete for the greater good. But that was the excuse of every tyrant or evildoer in history: sacrifice one or ten or a million for some notion of the common good.

What she had done was immoral. It was wrong. Astrid had set aside her religious faith, but good was still good, and evil was still evil, and throwing her brother into the literal jaws of death . . .

It wasn't that she doubted she had done wrong. It wasn't that she doubted she deserved punishment. In fact, it was the very idea of forgiveness that made her rebel. She didn't want forgiveness. She didn't want to be washed clean of her sin. She wanted to own it and wear it like a scar, because it was real, and it happened, and it couldn't be made to unhappen.

She had done something terrible. That fact would be part of her forever.

'As it should be,' she whispered. 'As it should be.'

How strange, Astrid thought, that owning your own sins, refusing forgiveness, but vowing not to repeat them, could make you feel stronger.

'When do we check back?' Edilio asked her when they were finished installing.

Astrid shrugged. 'Probably better come back tomorrow, just in case the stain is moving faster than it appears to be.'

'What do we do about it?' Edilio asked.

'We measure it. We see how much it advances in the first twenty-four hours. Then we see how much it advances in the second and third twenty-four-hour periods. We see how fast it grows and whether it's accelerating.'

'And then what do we do about it?' Edilio asked.

Astrid shook her head. 'I don't know.'

'I guess I'll pray,' Edilio said.

'Couldn't hurt,' Astrid allowed.

A sound.

The three of them spun towards it. Edilio had his submachine gun off his shoulder, cocked and the safety off in a heartbeat. Roger sort of slid behind Edilio.

'It's a coyote,' Astrid hissed. She had not brought her shotgun, since she was carrying half of the measuring frames. But she had her revolver and drew it.

It was almost immediately clear that the coyote was not a threat. First, it was alone. Second, it was barely able to walk. Its gait was shuffling and it seemed lopsided.

And something was wrong with its head.

Something so wrong that Astrid could hardly encompass it. She stared and blinked. Shook her head and stared again.

Her first thought was that the coyote had a child's head in its mouth.

No.

That. Wasn't. It.

'*Madre de Dios*,' Edilio sobbed. The creature was now just twenty feet away and so terribly visible. Roger put a comforting hand on Edilio's shoulder, but he looked sick, too.

Astrid stood rooted in place.

'It's Bonnie,' Edilio said, his voice shrill. 'It's her. It's her face. 'No,' he moaned, a long, drawn-out wail.

The creature ignored Edilio, just kept walking on two coyote front legs, and twisted furless legs – bent human legs – in the back. Kept walking as though those empty, blue, human eyes were blind, and those shell-like pink human ears were deaf.

Edilio wept as it kept moving.

Astrid aimed her revolver at the creature's heart, just behind the shoulder, and fired. The gun kicked in her hand and a small, round, red hole appeared and began leaking red.

She fired again, hitting the creature in its canine neck.

It fell over. Blood pumped from the thing's neck and formed a pool in the sand.

Once again, the avatar broke apart.

Pete had tried to play with the bouncy avatar and it had broken apart, changed colour and shape, and stopped.

He had tried to play with another avatar and it had melted into something different.

Was this the game?

It wasn't very fun.

And he was beginning to feel bad when the avatars fell apart. Like he was doing a bad-boy thing.

So he had imagined the avatars all back the way they started.

Nothing happened. But things always happened when Pete

wanted them really hard. He had wanted the terrible sirens and screams to stop and the world not to burn up and he had created the ball he now lived in.

He had wanted other things and they had happened. If he wanted something badly enough it happened. Didn't it?

Well, now he was feeling sick inside and he wanted the avatars to go back and be right again. But they didn't.

No, Pete corrected himself. He'd always been afraid when the big sudden things happened. He couldn't just wish them and make them happen. He'd always been scared. Panicked. Screaming inside his overloaded brain.

He wasn't afraid now. The frenzy that used to take him over couldn't touch him now. That was the old Pete. The new Pete wasn't scared of noises and colours and things that moved too fast.

The new Pete was just bored.

An avatar floated by and Pete knew it. Even without the stabbing bright blue eyes, without the shrieking voice. He knew her. His sister, Astrid. A pattern, a shape, a coil of strings.

He felt very lonely.

Had he ever felt lonely before?

He felt it now. And he longed to reach out, and with just the smallest touch, to let her know he was here.

But, oh, so delicate, those avatars. And his fingers were all thumbs.

FEAR

The joke made him laugh.
Had he ever laughed before?
He laughed now. And that was enough for a while, at least.

FOURTEEN

24 HOURS 57 MINUTES

ALBERT HAD MADE the decision early on to play Caine's ridiculous game of royalty. If Caine wanted to call himself king, and if he wanted people to call him 'Your Highness', well, that didn't cost Albert a single 'Berto.

The truth was, Caine did keep the peace. He enforced rules, and Albert liked and needed rules.

There had been very little shoplifting at the mall, the ironically named stalls and card tables that were the market outside the school.

There had been fewer fights. Fewer threats. Albert had even seen a decline in the number of weapons being carried. Not much of a decline, but every now and then you could actually see a kid forgetting to carry his nail-studded baseball bat or machete.

Those were good signs.

Best of all, kids showed up for work and they put in a full day.

King Caine scared kids. And Albert paid them. And between

the threat and the reward, things were running more smoothly than they ever had under Sam or Astrid.

So if Caine wanted to be called king . . .

'Your Highness, I'm here with my report,' Albert said.

He stood patiently while Caine, seated at his desk, pretended to be absorbed in reading something.

Finally, Caine looked up, affecting an expression of unconcern.

'Go ahead, Albert,' Caine said.

'The good news: water continues to flow from the cloud. The stream is clean – most of the dirt and debris and old oil and so on has been washed away. So it's probably drinkable down at the beach reservoir as well as directly from the rain. Flow rate is twenty gallons an hour. Four hundred and eighty gallons a day, which is more than we need for drinking, with enough left over to water gardens and so on.'

The cloud had been created by Astrid's autistic brother Little Pete, to cool him down while he was suffering from the flu. Albert had arranged for the gutters to be carefully blocked so that the stream could run all the way down and out through a gap in the wall to form a pool in the sand of the beach.

'Washing?'

Albert shook his head. 'No. And we can't have kids showering in the rain as it falls, either. Kids are washing their butts in what will end up being drinking water once we open the reservoir.'

'I'll make a proclamation,' Caine said.

There were times Albert almost couldn't resist the impulse to laugh. Proclamation. But he kept a straight, impassive face.

'Food is not as good,' Albert went on. 'I made a graph.' He drew a nine-by-twelve poster board from his briefcase and held it so Caine could see it.

'Here's food production over the last week. Good and steady. You see a drop today because we have nothing from the fishing crews. And this dotted line is the food supply over the next week, projected.'

Caine's face darkened. He bit at his thumbnail, then stopped himself.

'As you know Cai – Your Highness . . . sixty per cent of our vegetables and fruit comes from worm-infested fields. Eighty per cent of our protein comes from the sea. Without Quinn we have nothing to feed the worms. Which means picking and planting basically stop. To make matters worse, there's a crazy story going around about one of the artichoke pickers being turned into a fish.'

'What?'

'It's just a crazy rumour, but right now no one is harvesting artichokes.'

Caine cursed and shook his head slowly.

Albert put away the graph and said, 'In three days we'll have major hunger. A week from now kids will start dying.

I don't have to tell you how dangerous things get when kids get hungry.'

'We can replace Quinn. Get other kids out in other boats,' Caine said.

Albert shook his head. 'There's a learning curve. It took Quinn a long time to get to be as good and efficient as he is. Plus he has the best boats, and he has all the nets and poles. If we decided to replace him it would be probably five weeks before we would get production back up to non-starvation levels.'

'Then we'd better get started,' Caine snapped.

'No,' Albert said. Then added, 'Your Highness.'

Caine slammed his fist down on the desk. 'I'm not giving in to Quinn! Quinn is not the king! I am! Me!'

'I offered him more money. He isn't looking for more money,' Albert said.

Caine jumped up from his chair. 'Of course not. Not everyone is you, Albert. Not everyone is a money-grubbing . . .' He decided against finishing that thought, but kept ranting. 'It's power he wants. He wants to bring me down. He and Sam Temple are friends from way, way back. I should have never let him stay. I should have made him go with Sam!'

'He fishes in the ocean, and we're on the ocean,' Albert pointed out. This kind of outburst irritated Albert. It was a waste of time.

Caine seemed not to have heard. 'Meanwhile Sam's sitting

up there with that lake stocked with fish, and his own fields, and somehow he has Nutella and Pepsi and Cup-a-Noodles, and what do you think happens if kids here start thinking we have no food?' Caine was red in the face. Furious. Albert reminded himself that Caine, while an out-of-control egomaniac, was also extremely powerful and dangerous. He decided against answering the question.

'We both know what happens,' Caine said bitterly. 'Kids leave town and head for the lake.' He glared at Albert as if it was all Albert's fault. 'This is why it's no good having two different towns. Kids can just go where they want.'

Caine threw himself back in his chair but banged his knee on the desk. With an angry sweep of his hand he threw the desk crashing into the wall. The impact was hard enough to knock the ancient pictures down, all those ego shots of the original mayor. The desk left a long, triangular dent in the wall.

Caine sat chewing his thumbnail and Albert stood thinking of all the more useful things he could be doing. At last Caine used his powers to scoot the desk back into place. He seemed to need something to lean on in a dramatic fashion, because that was what he did, placing his elbows on the table, forming his fingers into a steeple, an almost prayerful position, and tapping the fingertips thoughtfully against his forehead.

'You're my adviser, Albert,' Caine said. 'What do you advise?'

Since when had Albert become an adviser? But he said, 'OK,

since you ask, I think you should send Penny away.' When Caine started to object, Albert, finally evincing his impatience, raised his hand. 'First, because Penny is a sick, unstable person. She was bound to cause problems, and she'll cause more. Second, because what happened to Cigar turns everyone against you. It's not just Quinn: everyone thinks it's wrong. And third: if you don't, and if Quinn stands firm, this town will empty out.'

And if you don't, Albert added silently, *I will suddenly learn about a cache of missiles up the coast. And you, King Caine, will go to take them.*

Caine's prayerful hands fell flat on the desk. 'If I give in everyone will think . . .' He took a shaky breath. 'I'm the king. They'll think I can be beaten.'

Albert was actually surprised. 'Of course you can be beaten, Your Highness. Everyone can be beaten.'

'Except for you, right, Albert?' Caine said bitterly.

Albert knew he shouldn't let himself be baited. But the cheap shot rankled. 'Turk and Lance shot me,' he said, with his hand on the doorknob. 'I'm only alive because of luck and Lana. Believe me: I stopped thinking I was unbeatable.'

And made plans, he thought, but did not say.

FIFTEEN

24 HOURS 29 MINUTES

THEY WATCHED MOHAMED leave.

Then, when she was sure Sam had at least a couple of minutes to think clearly, Astrid told him what they had found in the desert. 'Edilio's bringing it in so we can take a look at it. I came straight back. When they get it here I'll see what I can learn.'

Sam seemed barely to pay attention. His eyes were drawn towards the barrier. He wasn't alone. The stain was clearly visible to kids as they worked. The kids out in the fields probably wouldn't notice, but the ones still here in the town around the marina couldn't avoid seeing it.

They came in ones or twos or threes to ask Sam what it meant. And he would say, 'Get back to work. If you need to worry I'll let you know.'

Each time he said it – and it must have been two dozen times – he used the same gruff but ultimately reassuring voice.

But Astrid knew better. She could feel the tension bleeding

from his every pore. She saw the way the corners of his mouth tugged downward, the way his forehead formed twin vertical worry lines between his eyes.

He didn't need some new thing to worry about. So the awful freak monster thing she and Edilio had found, that would have to wait. Because all Sam had time for right now was the mesmerising advance of the stain. His imagination was torturing him. She could see it in the way his hands would form into fists, tighten and then release, but the release was forced, conscious, and accompanied each time by a deliberate exhalation.

He was seeing a world of total darkness.

So was Astrid. And though it made no sense she worried about her tents. The ropes needed tightening periodically or they would start to sag. And the fabric of the tent itself needed checking, because small tears got bigger fast, and beetles and ants were very good at finding such openings.

She recalled once waking up in the tent to find a steady stream of ants crossing right over her face and picking at a morsel of food she'd let fall. She had jumped up and run for the water, but not before the ants panicked at her panic and bit her a dozen times.

She could smile at the memory now. At the time it had made her cry at the weirdness and sadness of her stupid life.

But she had learned from that. And there had never again

been so much as a crumb of anything edible in her tent.

And what about the time she found a snake in her boot? Lesson learned there, too.

If no one picked her blackberries, the birds would get them.

She went on this way for a while, fully aware of the fact that she was nostalgic over things that had usually been pretty miserable, realising that she was as trapped as Sam in waiting, waiting, waiting for doom.

The image of the coyote with the human face and legs came suddenly to mind. It knocked the breath out of her.

BANG. BANG. She could hear the sound of the gun better in memory than she had at the time. At the time she'd been numb. Now she recalled, too, the way the gun bucked. The way the abomination bled out in the sand.

The way the little girl's face relaxed in death and the blind eyes filmed over.

What terrible thing was happening? Why couldn't she figure it out? Why couldn't she help Sam to pull off one more impossible victory?

One of the great reliefs about living on her own had been the fact that she had no expectations to meet. She didn't have to be Astrid the Genius, or Astrid the Mayor, or Astrid Sam's girlfriend, or Why-won't-she-shut-up Astrid.

All she'd had to do was get enough food to eat each day. A huge accomplishment that was all hers.

Sam had binoculars to his eyes. He checked the barrier. Then swung them inland.

'Mo's on his way,' he said. He shifted slightly. 'So is Howard, out in front of him by a quarter mile. He's just . . . OK, now I can't see him.' He lowered the binoculars. 'Figures. Howard's heading to his still to bring back one more shipment of booze.'

Astrid made a wry smile. 'Life goes on, I guess.'

Sam frowned. 'You were telling me something. Earlier.'

'Get back to work. If I need you to worry, I'll let you know.'

'Very funny.' He almost smiled.

He looked suddenly very young. Well, he was, Astrid supposed. So was she. But they'd forgotten about all that in this world where they were the elders. He looked like a kid, a teenager, a boy who ought to be yelling happily as he ran into the surf with his board.

That image made her hurt. A tear welled. She pretended to have a speck of dust in her eye and wiped it away.

He wasn't fooled. He put his arms around her and drew her close. She couldn't look at him for fear of crying. She couldn't see the fear in him and not want to just hold him like he was a little boy.

'No,' he whispered. 'You have to open your eyes, Astrid. I don't know how many more times I'll see them.'

Her cheek was wet when she pressed it to his.

'I want to make love to you again,' he said.

'I want to make love to you, Sam,' she answered. 'We're scared.'

He nodded and she saw his jaw clench. 'Inappropriate, I guess.'

'Human,' she said. 'Most of human history people huddled, scared in the dark. Living in little huts with their animals. Believing the woods around them were haunted by spirits. Wolves and werewolves. Terrors. People would hold on to each other. So that they wouldn't be so afraid.'

'I have to ask you to do something dangerous,' Sam said.

'You want me to go back out and check the measurements.'

'I know we were thinking tomorrow morning . . .'

She nodded. 'I think it's growing faster than that. I think you're right. I think we need to know whether we'll have a sunrise tomorrow.'

His face was bleak. He wasn't looking at her, but past her. He looked like he wanted to cry but knew it was futile.

Once again she saw him as he must have been once upon a time, long, long ago. A big, good-looking boy out in the waves, trading jokes with Quinn, giddy that they were skipping school. Happy and carefree.

She imagined him drawing strength from the sun beating down on his brown shoulders.

The FAYZ had finally found the way to beat Sam Temple. Without light he would not survive. When the final night came with no prospect of dawn, he would be done.

She kissed him. He did not kiss her back, just gazed at the growing stain.

Once upon a time, long, long ago, Sinder had been very fond of black. She had painted her fingernails black. Dyed her brown hair jet-black. Donned clothing that was either black, or some secondary colour chosen to accentuate the black.

Now her colour was green. She loved green. Carrots were orange and tomatoes were red, but each lived within green. The green turned light into food.

'How cool is photosynthesis?' Sinder called to Jezzie, who was half a dozen rows away, down on her knees, searching with deadly focus for weeds, bugs, or disease that might endanger her beloved plants. An overprotective mother had nothing on Jezzie. The girl hated weeds with a burning passion.

Jezzie didn't answer – she frequently didn't when Sinder turned loquacious. 'I mean, I remember learning about it in school, but, man, who cared? Right? Photo-wuh? But I mean, it turns light into food. Light becomes energy becomes food and becomes energy again when we eat it. It's like . . . You know . . .'

'It's a miracle,' Orc rumbled.

'No,' Jezzie said, 'it would be a miracle if it didn't also work for weeds. Then it would be a miracle.' She'd found a root of something she didn't like and was pulling on it, grunting with the effort.

'I could pull that for you,' Orc said.

'No, no, no!' both girls cried. 'But thanks, Orc.'

Orc did not wear shoes, but if he had they'd probably have been size twenty. Extra, extra, extra wide. When he stepped into the garden things had a tendency to be crushed.

Sinder liked to get down low and look at her plants from close up. From one side she would see the miraculous leaves outlined against the backdrop of the lake and the marina area. From the other side she would see them almost like mounted specimens against the pearly grey blankness of the barrier.

Now she was looking at the feathery structure of a carrot top against the blank black of the stain. It had the odd effect of making the leaf seem like a work of abstract art.

She looked up from the plant and saw the stain suddenly shoot upwards. What had been a ragged, undulating wave of black extending only a dozen or so feet above her head blossomed like one of her charges to become a terrible black bloom thirty, fifty, a hundred feet high before it slowed and stopped.

She hoped Jezzie hadn't seen it. But when her friend stood up there were tears running down her cheeks.

'I feel bad inside,' Jezzie said simply.

Sinder nodded. She glanced at Orc, but he was absorbed in

reading. 'Me, too, Jez. Like . . .' She didn't have the words for what it was like. So she just shook her head.

Jezzie wiped dirt from her brow and managed to actually transfer more dirt there. She was looking down towards the marina. Sinder followed her gaze and saw Sam and Astrid holding each other close on the top deck of the White Houseboat.

Jezzie said, 'At first when I heard she was back I thought it was a good thing. I thought Sam would be happy. You know: he's been lonely.'

It was a fact of life in the FAYZ that kids cut off from TMZ and Facebook and the ins and outs of Hollywood and reality shows focused much of their gossip hunger on the closest thing they had to celebrities: Sam, who most people liked and everyone worried about; Diana, who most people didn't like but whose baby everyone worried about; the baby itself, in particular betting about its gender and possible powers; news of Caine from Perdido Beach; affectionate speculation about Edilio and the nature of his friendship with the Artful Roger; theories about Astrid with passionate disagreement as to whether she was a good person and good for Sam, or alternately a sort of Jadis, the White Witch from Narnia; and, of course, the whispered-about, much-speculated-about relationship (or lack of same) between Brianna and Jack and/or Brianna and Dekka.

But with Sam it was different. Every person at the lake felt his or her own fate was all too closely tied to Sam Temple.

'He doesn't look good,' Jezzie said. Sam was a tiny, distant figure from where she stood. And Sinder might have pointed that out on some other day. But the truth was that something about the way Sam held Astrid was wrong.

Sinder looked out across her garden, the plants she knew as individuals, many with names she and Jezzie had given them. And she saw the line of stain push slowly now, slowly but relentlessly, towards the sky.

Drake found the light almost unbearable. The setting sun stabbed his eyes with jagged pain. How long since he had seen the sun? Weeks? Months?

There was no time down in the gaiaphage's lair, no rising or setting moon, no mealtime, bath time, wake-up time.

The coyotes that had survived the infestation of bugs were waiting for him in the ghost town below the mine entrance. Pack Leader – well, the current Pack Leader, if not the original – licked a scab on his right front paw.

'Take me to the lake,' Drake said.

Pack Leader stared at him with yellow eyes. 'Pack hungry.'

'Too bad. Take me.'

Pack Leader bared his teeth. The coyotes of the FAYZ were not the runts that coyotes had been back before the FAYZ. They weren't as big as wolves, but they were big. But it was easy to see that they were not well. Their fur was mangy. There were bare patches on all of them where scraped grey-and-red flesh showed through. Their eyes were dull. Their heads hung low and the tails dragged.

'Humans take all prey,' Pack Leader said. 'Darkness says don't kill humans. Darkness does not feed pack.'

Drake frowned and counted the pack. He saw seven, all adults, no pups.

As if reading Drake's mind, Pack Leader said, 'Many die. Killed by Bright Hands. Killed by Swift Girl. Killed by bugs. No prey. No food for pack. Pack serves Darkness and pack goes hungry.'

Drake barked out a disbelieving laugh. 'Are you bitching out the gaiaphage? I'll whip the skin off you!'

Drake unwrapped his tentacle arm, which had been wound around his torso.

Pack Leader retreated a few dozen feet. The pack might be weak with hunger but they were still far too quick for Drake to catch. He felt uneasy. The gaiaphage would not listen to excuses. Drake had a mission. He had been to the lake before, but never alone. He knew he could follow the barrier, but the barrier itself was a long way off. If he wandered around lost he might be spotted. The success of his mission lay in stealth and surprise.

And then there was the problem of Brittney. Had the gaipahage told her what to do? Would she do it? Would she know how to find the way without the coyotes as guides?

'How am I supposed to feed you?' Drake demanded.

'Darkness say to coyote: don't kill human. Did not say don't eat dead human.'

Drake laughed with a certain delight. This Pack Leader was definitely a smarter animal than his predecessors. The gaiaphage had ordered the beasts not to kill humans for fear they might unknowingly kill someone useful: Lana, or even Nemesis. But Drake knew which humans were expendable.

'You know where I can find a human?' Drake asked.

'Pack Leader knows,' Pack Leader said.

'OK, then. Let's get you boys some dinner. Then we go get Diana.'

Astrid found Edilio just coming back down from the Pit. The Artful Roger, and Justin, the little kid Roger looked after, were with him, but Edilio sent them both away when he spotted Astrid.

'I got that thing, that . . . whatever it was. Up under a tarp. You want to look at it now?' Edilio asked.

'No. I'm sorry you had to do that. It couldn't have been very pleasant.'

'It wasn't,' Edilio said flatly.

'Listen, it looks like the stain is accelerating. Sam wants me to check the frames early.'

'I saw it growing. Faster. A lot faster,' Edilio said. 'But I understand if Sam wants more information.' He blew out a weary breath and drank from a water bottle.

'Don't come yourself,' Astrid said. 'Just send one of your guys.'

Edilio made an incredulous face. 'And tell Sam something happened to you because I wasn't there?'

Astrid treated it as a joke and laughed.

But Edilio didn't join in. 'Sam's all we've got. You're all Sam's got. Come on, it'll be a quick, easy walk without having to carry those frames.'

The plan had been to allow twenty-four hours before checking the frames. The idea had been that a frame that was 10 per cent stain might grow to 20 per cent stain and that then Astrid could calculate the rate of growth.

Only a few hours had passed. But the plan was revealed as absurdly optimistic. All the frames were 100 per cent filled with black. There was no chance of an accurate calculation: it had grown too far, grown too fast. And the rate of acceleration could only be increasing geometrically.

She stood looking up, craning her neck to see the tallest black finger yet. It stretched three hundred feet up the side of the dome.

As she watched, it grew. She could see it moving.

Then, from a low point in the stain, a new black tendril shot up as fast as a car on the freeway. It just seemed to explode upwards. Up and up, and she tilted her head back to see it, and up farther and farther.

The stain crossed the line between blank pearly grey and sunlight. Then it slowed. But that slim black finger violated the sky like graffiti on the Mona Lisa. It was vandalism. It was ugliness.

It was the future written clearly for Astrid to see.

SIXTEEN

22 HOURS 16 MINUTES

MOHAMED HAD SET out from the lake on the tedious walk to Perdido Beach as soon as he could get a water bottle and a little food in his belly.

He carried a pistol and a knife, but he wasn't really worried. Everyone knew he was under Albert's protection. And no one messed with Albert's people.

For most of the time since the coming of the FAYZ, Mohamed had lain low, stayed out of the way of all the big wheels who were busy killing and being killed.

As crazy as things were in the FAYZ, the smart move was to just do the minimum to get food and shelter. And not even shelter some of the time.

He was thirteen, a man. He was thin and starting to get taller, a growth spurt that had left his shorts too short and his shoes too tight. His family had just moved to Perdido Beach when his mother got a job at the power plant. The school was supposed to be better than the one he'd been at in King City.

His dad still worked there, working ten hours a day at the family's Circle K, selling gas and cigarettes and milk to a mostly Hispanic population. It was a really long commute, and some nights his dad hadn't come home, which made everyone feel strange and abandoned.

But that was the way it was, his father had explained. A man worked. A man did what he had to do to take care of his family. Even if it meant he saw less of them.

Sometimes Moomaw – Mohamed's paternal grandmother – would talk about going back to Syria. But Mohamed's father would shut that down right away. He had left Syria when he was twenty-two and didn't miss it at all, not even a little, no, sir. Yes, he'd been a medical student there and sold hot dogs to farmhands now, but it was still better.

Was it tough sometimes being the only Muslim at the Perdido Beach school? Yeah. He'd been pushed around by Orc a few times. Kids made fun of him for praying. For refusing the pepperoni pizza at lunch. But pretty soon Orc had lost interest and most kids didn't even think twice about where his parents came from or how he prayed.

Fortunately Mohamed's family had never been all that strict about the dietary laws. He hadn't eaten pork since the coming of the FAYZ, but he would have in a heartbeat if anyone had some. He'd eaten rat, cat, dog, birds and fish and slimy things he didn't have a name for. He'd have jumped all over a pepperoni pizza if anyone had one. Staying alive was not a sin: Allah saw all; Allah understood all.

Someday this would all end; Mohamed was sure of that. Or tried to be. Someday the barrier would come down and his father and mother and brothers and sister would be waiting for him.

How would he get along with his brothers? They would ask him all the questions his parents wouldn't. They'd ask him what he had done. They'd ask him if he represented. They'd ask him if he had stood up or wimped out. That was what brothers were like, at least his.

Whenever the barrier came down there would be all kinds of people talking to the media and telling all kinds of stories. And pretty quick people would realise they hadn't just all sat around catching up on their homework.

People would realise it had been more like a war. And then all those questions. Were you scared, Mohamed? Were you picked on? Did you ever run into all these insane freaks we hear about on TV?

Did you ever kill anyone? What was it like?

He hadn't killed anyone. He'd had a couple of fights; one of them was pretty bad. He'd had a nail driven into his butt cheek and broken his wrist.

Mohamed figured he'd change that story a little. Nail in the butt sounded funny. It hadn't been, but if he ever got out, yeah, he'd change that story.

As for freaks, the only one he'd spent any time with was Lana. She had healed his butt and his wrist.

So, yeah, don't diss all the freaks, not to Mohamed.

When it came time for the Big Split, Mohamed had been forced to commit, one way or the other. He had gone to Albert and asked his advice. Until then Mohamed had stuck to working in the fields, but Albert had seen something in him.

Albert had liked him for the fact that he had no real friends. No family inside the FAYZ. He liked the way Mohamed had managed to stay under the radar. All those things – plus Mohamed's basic intelligence – made him just right for the job Albert had for him: representing Alberco at the lake.

Mohamed still had no friends. But he had a job. An important one. Albert would want to know details of Astrid's return. He'd want to know that she was measuring some kind of stain on the dome. Maybe he'd want to know about some weird, mutant animal Astrid had supposedly killed. And he would definitely want to hear what Mohamed knew about the secret mission Sam and Dekka had gone out on.

Mohamed walked down the familiar, dusty road.

He walked alone.

Howard was already en route to Coates. He had a long day of work ahead of him. Hopefully his contractors would have run some corn and assorted other vegetables and fruits up to Coates and locked them in the rat-proof steel cupboards in the kitchen.

Howard would have to chop the produce up as small as he had patience for, then carry it to the still. He had a little firewood in place, hopefully enough to get the cooker started. Then while the batch was cooking he would have to hack around the woods looking for fallen trees, which he would then have to cut.

All of this used to be Orc's job. Orc could haul a lot of bottles. Orc could haul a lot of firewood. Orc swinging an axe was a whole different story from Howard doing it. Orc was like two swings and, snap, the log would be cut through. For Howard the same job could take fifteen minutes.

This bootlegging thing was getting to be a lot less fun. It was a lot more like real work. In fact, Howard realised with a sudden shock, he was now working harder than just about anyone else. Kids picking veggies in the fields didn't even work like Howard did.

'Gotta get Orc to be normal again,' Howard muttered to the bushes. 'Boy needs to take a drink or six and start feeling it again.'

After all, Orc and him were friends.

Drake stood atop the rise. He'd just returned after a Brittney episode and was surprised to find that she had kept moving along with the coyotes.

'Human,' Pack Leader said.

Drake followed the direction of the animal's intense gaze. A kid – Drake couldn't tell who it was – was down below, walking steadily along the dirt-and-gravel road.

'Yep,' Drake said. 'There's your lunch.'

SEVENTEEN

22 HOURS 5 MINUTES

'**SO**. WHAT IS it?' Sam asked.

The 'it' in question had been carried to a picnic table not far from the Pit. A plastic tarp had been spread out over and under it – after all, kids still used these tables sometimes. The picnic area was inconveniently far from town but still had a nice view of the lake.

'It's a coyote, mostly,' Astrid said. 'With a human face. And back legs.'

He glanced at her to see if she was really as calm as she seemed. No. She was not calm, but Astrid could do that, seem totally in control when she was freaking out inside.

She'd managed to seem calm when she came back from her quick trip with Edilio. She'd been calm when she said, 'The sun may come out tomorrow. But it may not. And unless something changes that will be the last sunrise.'

And he had put on a pretty good show of looking calm himself. He'd given Edilio orders to come up with a list of places where he could hang a Sammy sun. They'd had a very calm discussion of other ways to prepare: start food rationing, test the effect of Sammy suns on growing plants – after all, maybe his own personal light could trigger photosynthesis. Move to more use of nets for fishing; maybe a hovering Sammy sun would bring fish to the surface.

Plans they all knew were bull.

Plans that were about nothing but prolonging the agony.

Plans that would fall apart as soon as the kids in Perdido Beach realised the only light they were likely to see was up here at the lake.

Sam was going through the motions. Pretending. Putting on a brave face to delay the inevitable total social meltdown.

In the back of his mind the gears spun like mad. Solution. Solution. Solution. What was it?

Astrid had laid out a large chef's knife, a meat cleaver – borrowed from a seven-year-old who carried it for protection – and an X-Acto knife with a less-than-perfect blade.

'It's beyond creepy,' Sam said.

'You don't have to be here, Sam.'

'No, I love watching autopsies of disgusting mutant monsters,' Sam said. He felt like throwing up and she hadn't even started.

Solution. Solution. Solution.

Astrid was wearing pink Playtex gloves. She rolled the

creature on to its back. 'You can see the line where the human face stops and the fur starts. There's no human hair, just coyote. And look at the legs. There's no blurring. It's a clean line. But the bones inside? Those are coyote bones. It's articulated like a coyote leg covered with human skin and probably muscle, too.'

Sam had run out of useful things to say or energy to say them. He was fighting the surge of bile into his throat, hoping not to puke. A sudden gust of wind bringing the smell of the Pit did not help. Plus the creature itself smelled. Like wet dog and urine and sticky-sweet decay.

And throughout it all: solution. Where was the solution? Where was the answer?

Astrid took the cleaver and slammed it into the creature's exposed belly. It made a six-inch cut. There was no bleeding; dead things didn't bleed.

Sam braced himself to burn anything that suddenly emerged, *Alien*-like, from the cut. But nothing popped or squirmed out. He had terrible memories of what he'd had to do with Dekka. He'd burned her open to get the bugs out of her. It had been the most gruesome thing he'd ever done. And now, as Astrid used the big knife to saw away and widen the cut, it was all coming back.

Astrid turned away from the smell to compose herself. She pulled out a rag and tied it over her mouth and nose. Like that would help. She looked like a very pretty bandit.

Incredibly a second line of thinking was forcing its way into his consciousness. He wanted her. Not here, not now, but soon. Soon. The endless, hopeless brain merry-go-round that sang the solution song sang a much nicer tune, too. Why couldn't he just crawl into his bunk with Astrid and let someone else break his soul searching for a non-existent solution?

Astrid now cut vertically, opening the animal up along its length. 'Look at this.'

'Do I have to?'

'You can see organs attached to each other that just don't fit. It's bizarre. The stomach is the wrong size for the large intestine. It's like a really bad plumber tried to attach different-size pipes together. I can't believe this thing lived as long as it did.'

'So it's a mutant?' Sam asked, anxious to reach some kind of conclusion and then bury the carcass and do his best to forget about it and get back to the twin thought streams of 'solution' and 'sex'.

Astrid didn't answer. Her silent staring went on and on. At last she said, 'Every mutant so far has been survivable. You shoot light out of your hands and never get burned. Brianna runs at a hundred miles an hour but her knees don't break. The mutations haven't harmed anyone yet. In fact, the mutations have been survival tools, really. Like the goal was to build a stronger, more capable human being. No. No, this is something different.'

'OK. What?'

She shrugged, pulled off her gloves, and tossed them on to the open wound. 'This is bits of human – probably the missing girl – and coyote. Mix and match. Like someone just randomly took parts from one and swapped them for parts from the other.'

'Why would –' Sam began.

But Astrid was still talking, to herself more than to him. 'Like someone tossed two different DNAs into a hat and drew out this and that and tried to fit them together. It's . . . It's stupid, really.'

'Stupid?'

'Yeah. Stupid.' She looked at him as if she was surprised to be talking to him now. 'I mean, it's something that makes no sense. It serves no purpose. It's obvious it wouldn't work. Only an idiot would think you could just randomly plug pieces of human into a coyote.'

'Wait a minute. You're acting like this is someone doing it. A person. How do you know it isn't just something natural?' He thought about that for a moment, sighed, and added, 'Or at least what passes for natural in the FAYZ.'

Astrid shrugged. 'What's happened so far? Coyotes evolved limited powers of speech. Worms developed teeth and became aggressive and territorial. Snakes grew wings and developed a new form of metamorphosis. Some of us developed powers. So far there's been a lot of strange, but not a lot of stupid. This, though. This –' she aimed her finger at the carcass of the monstrosity '– is just stupid.'

'The gaiaphage?' Sam asked, feeling in his gut it was the wrong answer.

Astrid held his gaze for a moment but her brain was somewhere else. 'Not stupid,' she said.

'You just said it was –'

'I was wrong. It's not about stupid. It's ignorant. Clueless.'

'Is there –' He wasn't surprised when she interrupted him as if he hadn't even been talking.

'Unbelievable power,' Astrid said. 'And absolute ignorance.'

'What does that mean?' Sam asked.

Astrid wasn't listening. She was slowly turning her head, eyes aimed all the way to the right, as if she thought someone was sneaking up on her.

It was so compelling that Sam followed the direction of her gaze. Nothing. But he recognised the movement: how many times in the last months had he done the same himself? A sort of paranoid, sidelong glance at something that wasn't there?

Astrid shook her head slowly. 'I'm . . . I have to go. I'm not feeling well.'

He watched her walk away. It was irritating, to put it mildly. Infuriating.

In the old days he'd have called her out on it, demanded to know what she was thinking.

But he sensed that what he had with Astrid was fragile. She was back, but not all the way back. He didn't want to start a battle with her. There was a war coming, no time for battles with someone he loved.

But her abrupt departure had the effect of leaving him with only one thread to follow, one thing to think about: the solution.

The solution that did not exist.

Penny lived alone in a small house on the eastern edge of town. From her upstairs bedroom window she could see just a narrow slice of the ocean and she liked that.

She wanted to move into Clifftop. But Caine had denied that request. Clifftop was Lana's to do with as she pleased. Even when Lana had moved to the lake – temporarily, as it turned out – Clifftop had remained a no-go zone.

'No one messes with Lana,' Caine had decreed.

Lana, Lana, Lana. Everyone just loved Lana.

Penny had spent some time with her when Lana fixed her shattered legs. It had taken a long time, in fact, because there were so many breaks in the bones. Penny found Lana stuck-up. It was certainly a relief to have her legs fixed, and it was very nice not to have that pain, but that didn't mean Lana had a right to act all high-and-mighty and above it all.

And have an entire massive hotel all to herself. Deciding who could come or go.

It bothered Penny that Lana had that kind of respect. Because Penny knew she could leave Lana crawling and crying and tearing her eyes out like Cigar had done.

Oh, yeah. Oh, yeah. Five minutes alone with Little Miss Healer. See how she liked it. See how high-and-mighty she was then.

The only problem was that Caine would kill Penny. Caine felt nothing for Penny. She had hoped after Diana took off . . . But no, there was no disguising Caine's look of contempt whenever he saw Penny.

Even now, even with all Penny's power, Caine was still the big man, the popular guy, the good-looking guy who would spit on someone like Penny, with her scraggly hair and awkward, bony arms and flat-as-a-board chest. Even now life was all about who was hot and who was not.

But Caine wasn't the only boy around.

There was a soft knock at the back door. Penny opened it for Turk.

'Were you careful?' she asked.

'I went way out of the way. Then I jumped a couple of fences.' He was breathing hard and sweating. She believed him.

'All that just to see me?' Penny asked.

He didn't answer. He flopped down in one of the easy chairs, sending up a cloud of dust. He leaned his gun against the side of the chair. Then he pulled off his boots, making himself comfortable.

Suddenly a scorpion crawled on to his arm. He yelled, swatted at it frantically, jumped out of his chair.

Then he saw the smile on her face.

'Hey, don't do that to me!' Turk cried.

'Then don't ignore me,' she said. She hated the pleading sound in her own voice.

'I wasn't ignoring you.' He sat back down, carefully inspecting for scorpions – as if it had been real.

Turk wasn't the smartest guy, Penny acknowledged with a sigh. He was no Caine. Or Sam. Or even Quinn. Maybe they could ignore Penny, and not even treat her like a girl, and curl their lips in disgust at her, but not Turk. Turk was just a dumb punk.

Penny felt a surge of fury so strong she had to turn away to hide it. Overlooked, ignored, forgotten Penny.

She was the middle of three girls in her family. Her older sister was named Dahlia. Her younger sister was named Rose. Two pretty flower names. And a plain old Penny in between.

Dahlia was a beauty. As early as Penny could remember her family had all loved Dahlia. So Penny had put bleach in Dahlia's cereal, just to see how pretty she would be with her throat burned out. And then Penny was shipped off to Coates.

In two years at Coates she had not heard from her sisters.

Her mother had written to her once, an incoherent, self-pitying Christmas card.

Penny was as ignored at Coates as she had always been. Until she began to develop her power. It came late to her. After the first big battle in Perdido Beach, when Caine had walked off into the wilderness with Pack Leader.

When he returned at last, ranting and seemingly insane, Penny kept her secret to herself. She knew better than to show Drake. Drake was ruthless: he would have killed her. Caine was softer, smarter than Drake. When at last Caine came back to something like sanity, Penny started to show him what she could do.

And still she was ignored in favour of Drake and, worst of all, that witch Diana. Diana, who never loved Caine, who always criticised him, had even betrayed him and fought with him.

In that terrible moment standing at the edge of the cliff on San Francisco de Sales Island, when Caine could save only one of them, Diana or Penny, he had made his choice.

Penny had endured pain like nothing she could have ever imagined. But it cleared her mind. It strengthened her. It obliterated what faint echoes of pity were still left in her.

Penny was no longer ignored.

She was hated.

Feared.

No longer ignored.

'You have anything to drink?' Turk asked.

'You mean water?'

'Don't be stupid; you know I don't mean water.'

Penny fetched a bottle from her kitchen. It was half-full of whatever vile liquid Howard brewed. It smelled like a dead animal, but Turk took a long, long drink.

'Want to make out?' Turk asked.

She slinked towards him.

Turk made a face. 'Not like that. Not like you.'

Penny felt it like slap in the face.

'Like you were the other time. You know, in my head. Make it like the other time.'

'Oh, like that,' she said flatly. Penny had the power to send horrifying visions. But she also had the power to create beautiful illusions. They were one and the same. It was one of the ways she had driven Cigar over the edge. She'd found a picture of his mother and made him see her . . .

Now, for Turk, she made a vision of Diana.

And a while later she spoke, using the vision of Diana still to say, 'Turk, the time has come.'

'Mmm?'

'Caine humiliated me,' Penny said with Diana's voice.

'What?'

'He's the only one who can stop me,' Penny said. 'He's the only one who can humiliate me like that.'

Turk was dumb but not that dumb. He pushed her away.

She became herself again.

'One of these days he'll kill you, Turk,' Penny said. 'Remember what he did to your friend Lance?' She drew a long arc in the air and punctuated it with a 'Splat!'

Turk looked nervously around. 'Yeah, I remember; that's why I am totally loyal to the king. He's the king and I don't mess with him.'

Penny smiled. 'No, you just fantasise about his girlfriend.'

Turk's eyes widened. He swallowed anxiously. 'Yeah, well, what about you?'

Penny shrugged.

'Anyway, she's not even his girlfriend any more,' Turk said.

She stayed silent, waiting, knowing he was so very weak, so very fearful.

'What are you even talking about, Penny?' Turk cried. 'You're crazy.'

Penny laughed. 'We're all crazy, Turk. The only difference is, I know I'm crazy. I know all about me. You know why? Because sitting there with my legs broken and wanting to scream every single minute, eating the scraps Diana brought me, that kind of clears out your mind and you start seeing things the way they are.'

'I'm out of here,' Turk yelled, and jumped up. He made it two feet before Caine was standing right in his path. Turk stepped back, one leg collapsing, barely catching himself from falling.

The Caine illusion disappeared.

'Just let me go, Penny,' Turk said shakily. 'I'll never tell anyone. Just let me go. You and Caine . . . whatever, OK?'

'I think you'll end up doing what I want you to do,' Penny said. 'I'm done being ignored and I'm all done being humiliated.'

'I'm not going to kill Caine. No matter what you say.'

'Kill? Kill him?' Penny shook her head. 'Who said kill? No, no, no. No killing.' She pulled a prescription bottle from her pocket, twisted it open, and shook six small, pale, oval pills into her palm. 'Sleeping pills.'

She slid the pills back into the bottle and closed it again.

'I got the pills from Howard. He's very useful. I told him I was having a hard time sleeping and I paid him with . . . Well, let's just say that Howard has his own fantasies. Which, by the way, you would not believe.'

'Sleeping pills?' Turk said in a shrill, desperate voice. 'You think you're going to take Caine down with sleeping pills?'

'Sleeping pills,' Penny said, and nodded with satisfaction. 'Sleeping pills. And cement.'

Turk's face was drained of colour.

'Find a way to get him here. To me, Turk. Bring him to me. Then it will be just the three of us running things.'

'What do you mean, three?'

Penny smiled and with Diana's lips said, 'You, me, and Diana.'

Howard smelled them before he saw them. The coyotes smelled of rotten meat.

He quelled the urge to run in panic when Pack Leader slouched on to the road ahead of him. He couldn't outrun a coyote. But the coyotes hadn't attacked anyone in a long time. The rumour was that they had been warned off by Sam. That was what people said, that Sam had laid down the law and threatened to go medieval on the whole coyote population if they messed with anyone.

The coyotes were scared of Bright Hands. Everyone knew that.

'Hey,' Howard said with all the bluster he could summon, 'I'm a good friend of Bright Hands. You know who I mean? Sam. So I'm just going to walk on.'

'Pack hungry,' the coyote said in his slurred, high-pitched, mangled speech.

'Hah, very funny,' Howard said. His mouth was dry. His heart was pounding. He swung his heavy pack down. 'I don't have much food, just a boiled artichoke. You can have that.'

He reached into the pack, fumbling noisily among empty bottles, searching for the feel of metal. He found it, closed his hand around the heavy knife, and pulled it out. He waved it in front of him and yelled, 'Don't do anything stupid!'

'Coyote not kill human,' Pack Leader said.

'Yeah. Yeah, you'd better not. My boy Bright Hands will burn you mangy dogs down!'

'Coyote eat. Not kill.'

Howard tried a couple of times to speak but the words would not come. His bowels were suddenly watery. His legs were shaking so hard he feared they would collapse. 'You can't eat me without killing me,' he said finally.

'Pack leader not kill. He kill.'

'He?'

Howard felt a prickling on the back of his neck. Slowly, horror draining the strength from his muscles, he turned.

'Drake,' he whispered.

'Yeah. Hi, there, Howard. How's it going?'

'Drake.'

'Yeah, we did that already.' Drake unwrapped the whip hand. He looked more wolfish than the coyotes that now emerged from cover to form a circle around Howard.

'Drake, man, no, no. No, no, no. You don't want to do this, Drake, man.'

'It'll only hurt for a while,' Drake said.

His whip snapped. It was like fire on Howard's neck.

He turned and ran in sheer panic, but Drake's whip caught his leg and sent him facedown into the dirt. He looked up to see one of the coyotes looking at him with greedy intensity and licking his muzzle.

'I'm useful!' Howard cried. 'You must be up to something; I can help you!'

Drake straddled him and slowly, almost gently wrapped his tentacle arm around Howard's throat and started squeezing.

'You might be useful,' Drake allowed. 'But my dogs gotta eat.'

Howard's eyes bulged. His whole head felt like it would explode from the pressure of blood. His lungs sucked on nothing.

Mohamed saw the circle of coyotes.

He ducked quickly behind a scruffy bush that wouldn't really hide him if anyone was looking. But it was all the cover he could find. He had come across a slight rise in the road and, reaching the top, was practically on the coyotes before he saw them.

Then he realised he was seeing more than just coyotes. Drake.

Mohamed took a sharp breath, and the ears of the closest coyote – maybe a hundred yards away – flicked.

There was something . . . no, someone . . . on the ground. Drake had his whip hand around someone's neck. Mohamed couldn't see who it was.

Mohamed had a pistol. And a knife. But everyone knew

Drake couldn't be killed with a gun. If he tried to play hero, he would just get himself killed, too.

There was no right answer. No way to stop what he was witnessing. There was only surviving.

Mohamed backed away, crawling like a crab on hands and knees. Once he was out of sight he got to his feet and ran back towards the lake.

He ran and ran without stopping. He had never run so far or so fast in his life. He reached the blessed, blessed lake, pushed past kids who said a pleasant, 'How's it going?' and ran for the houseboat.

Sam was on the deck, sitting with Astrid. Mohamed registered the fact that he had set out to tell Albert she was here and realised how completely he didn't care about telling Albert anything.

He leaped aboard the boat, spun as though half-convinced the coyotes had followed him, and fell panting and gasping on the deck. Sam and Astrid both came to him. Astrid pressed a water bottle to his parched lips.

'What is it, Mo?' Sam asked.

Mohamed couldn't answer at first. His thoughts were a tangle of images and emotions. He knew he should think about controlling the situation, at least find some kind of way to put himself in a better light, but he didn't have the heart for it.

Edilio emerged on deck.

'Drake.' Mohamed gasped. 'Coyotes.'

Sam was suddenly very still. His voice dropped in volume and register. 'Where?'

'I was . . . on the road towards PB.'

'Drake and the coyotes?' Astrid prompted.

'They were . . . They had someone. On the ground. I couldn't see who. I wanted to stop them!' Mohamed said this last in a pleading voice. 'I had a gun. But . . . I . . .'

Mohamed looked at Sam, tried to meet his gaze, looking for something: Understanding? Forgiveness?

But Sam wasn't looking at him. Sam's face was like stone.

'You would have just got yourself killed,' Astrid said.

Mohamed grabbed Sam's wrist. 'But I didn't even try.'

Sam looked at him as if he had just remembered Mohamed was there. His cold gaze flickered and became human again.

'This isn't your fault, Mo. You couldn't have stopped Drake. The only one who could have stopped him is me.'

EIGHTEEN

20 HOURS 19 MINUTES

'**SOUND** THE ALARM,' Sam ordered.

The alarm was a big brass bell they'd taken from one of the boats and mounted atop the two-story marina office.

Edilio ran to the tower, climbed up and up, and began ringing the bell.

A part of Sam's mind was curious how well everyone would behave. They had practiced this three times before. When the bell rang certain kids were to run to the fields and alert kids there.

Each tent or trailer had an assigned boat to go to – either to the houseboats or sailboats, or on to smaller boats, anything bigger than a rowboat.

Edilio rang the bell and the few kids standing nearby looked around baffled.

'Hey!' Sam yelled. 'This is not a drill; this is the real thing! Do it the way Edilio taught you!'

Brianna appeared in her usual startling way. 'What's up?'

'Drake,' Sam said. 'But before you worry about him, make sure we're getting everyone back from the fields. Go!'

Dekka came at a run. Slower than Brianna. 'What is it?'

'Drake.'

Something electric passed between them and Sam had to stop himself from laughing out loud. Drake. Something definite. Something real. An actual, tangible enemy. Not some vague process or mysterious force.

Drake. He could picture him clearly in his mind's eye.

He knew that Dekka was doing the same.

'He's been seen with a pack of coyotes. It looks like they killed someone. Howard, most likely.'

'You think he's on his way here?'

'Probably.'

'How soon?' Dekka asked.

'Don't know. Don't even know for sure he's coming this way. As soon as Brianna's free I'll send her to scout.'

'No mercy this time,' Dekka said.

'None,' Sam agreed. 'Do your thing.'

Dekka's 'thing' was basically being Dekka. She was respected to the point of awe by younger kids. Everyone knew she had been right up close with the most gruesome kind of death. She'd also been the one who saved the littles when Mary took the poof. And, of course, everyone knew how highly Sam thought of her.

So her place during the drills had been standing by the dock while everyone rushed to the boats. She was the anti-panic presence. You just could not freak out when Dekka was eyeballing you.

Kids were just beginning to stream in from the fields, trotting along with all the food they could carry, watched over by a flitting Brianna.

The kids who had been in camp were already emptied out of the trailers and tents and had begun to take their places on the boats at the dock.

As soon as the boats had all their assigned passengers they cast off and rowed or poled or just drifted out on to the lake.

Orc came into view accompanying Sinder and Jezzie, all three weighed down with vegetables. Sam debated sharing his suspicions with Orc and decided against it. He might need Orc's strength and near indestructibility. He couldn't have the boy-monster charging off on his own.

In thirty minutes most of the population was in the motley collection of sailboats, motorboats, cabin cruisers, and houseboats that formed the Lake Tramonto armada.

In an hour all eighty-three kids were in seventeen different craft.

Sam looked out at the lake with some satisfaction. They had planned for this day, and amazingly enough, the plan had worked. All his people were on the water. The water they were on was drinkable, so there was no question of thirst. The lake provided a reasonable amount of fish, and all their stores of food were likewise in the boats.

And the kids could quite easily survive out there on the boats for a good week, maybe even two, without much problem.

If you ignored the fact that accidents would happen. And stupidity would happen.

And if you ignored the fact that the whole world might be dark very soon.

And that something was scrambling kids and coyotes together like they were making an omelette.

The only boat that didn't pull out was the White Houseboat. Sam, Astrid, Dekka, Brianna, Toto, and Edilio met on deck, out where anxious kids peering from the surrounding mismatched watercraft could see them. (Sinder, Jezzie, and Mohamed had been packed off to other boats.) It was important to send the signal that they had things under control. Sam wondered how long that illusion would last.

'OK, first things first,' Sam said looking at Brianna.

'I got it,' she said. She had her runner's backpack. The one with a sawed-off double-barrelled shotgun sticking through the bottom, turning the pack into a holster.

'Wait!' Sam yelled before she could disappear. 'Find. Look.' He pointed his finger at her and leaned forward, making sure she heard. 'And come back.'

Brianna made a fake wounded expression and said, 'What, you think I would go and pick a fight? Me?'

That earned a laugh from everyone but Dekka, and the sound of that laugh was reassuring to the scared kids in the boats.

Brianna blurred out and Sam heard a cheer go up from multiple boats.

'Go, Breeze!'

'Yeah, the Breeze!'

'Breeze versus Whip Hand!'

Sam looked at Edilio and said, 'Just what Brianna needs: a boost for her ego.' Then he said, 'Anyone have any idea who was killed? Who's missing?'

Edilio shrugged. He stood up, went to the side, and yelled to the boats. 'Hey! Listen up. Is anyone missing?'

For a while no one had any suggestions. Then Orc, on the bow of a sailboat, and so heavy that the entire boat was two feet lower in the water at the front than at the back, said, 'I haven't seen Howard. But he's always . . . you know . . . going off by himself.'

Sam met Edilio's gaze. Both of them had already guessed it was Howard.

Sam saw Orc stand up, shifting the entire boat and in the process scaring Roger, Justin, and Diana, who were out there with him. He went below.

'It's good you're back,' Sam said to Astrid. 'Orc trusts you. Maybe later . . .'

'I don't think Orc and I –' she began.

'I don't care. I may need Orc. So you may have to talk to him,' Sam snapped.

'Yes, sir,' she said with only a trace of sarcasm.

'Where's Jack?' Edilio asked, looking peevish. 'He's supposed to check in.'

'On his way,' Dekka answered, and pointed with her chin. 'I see him. He's just dawdling.'

'Jack!' Sam bellowed.

Jack was a hundred yards away. His head jerked up. Sam stuck his fists on his waist and glared impatience. Jack started running in his powerful, bounding way.

As soon as he reached the dock Edilio demanded to know what he thought he was doing. 'You're supposed to be armed and you're supposed to be at the Pit.'

'What's going on?' Jack asked sheepishly. 'I was asleep.'

'Brianna didn't wake you up?' Sam asked.

Jack looked uncomfortable. 'We're not talking.'

Sam pointed angrily at the boats bobbing on the lake. 'I got five-year-olds getting two-year-olds where they're supposed to be, but one of my two certified geniuses is asleep?'

'Sorry,' Jack said.

'He is,' Toto confirmed.

Sam ignored him. He was pumped full of adrenaline. Ready to forget about the disgusting mutation under the tarp. Ready to forget, for the moment, at least, that this might be the last real day they had. Ready to forget his worries about Caine and the missiles. Ready to push all those intractable problems and unanswerable questions aside, because now – now, finally – he had a straight-up fight.

Astrid took his shoulder and pulled him aside. He didn't want a conference with Astrid: he had things to do. But he couldn't quite say no. Not without listening first.

'Sam. This means your letter isn't getting to Caine or Albert.'

'Yeah. So?'

'So?' Her incredulity was so sharp it made him take a step back. 'So? So the lights are still going out, Sam. And we're still facing a possible disaster. And you don't know what Caine or Albert might do.'

'That's for another day,' he said, chopping the air with his hand to cut off debate. 'We have a slight emergency here.'

'Where is that ninny Taylor, anyway?' Astrid said angrily. 'If she doesn't show up, then send Brianna to get that note to Caine and Albert.'

'Brianna? Pull her off hunting for Drake? Good luck.'

'Then send Edilio and a couple of his –'

'Not now, Astrid. Priorities.'

'You're choosing the priority, Sam. You're doing the

easy thing instead of the smart thing.'

That stung. 'The easy thing? Drake suddenly shows up after being off the radar for four months? Don't you think maybe it's all one thing? Drake, the stain, whatever your "ignorant" force is?'

'Of course I suspect it's all one thing,' Astrid said through gritted teeth. 'That's why I want you to get some help.'

He held up one fist and began running down a list, raising a finger with each bullet point.

'One, Breeze locates him. Two, Dekka, Jack, and I converge. Three, whether he is Drake or Brittney, we cut him up, burn him in detail, piece by piece, and sink any ashes into the lake inside a locked, weighted metal box.' He closed his fingers back into a fist. 'We're putting an end to Drake once and for all.'

Drake heard the pealing of the bell. It was a distant sound but edgy and penetrating. He felt the urgency behind it. He guessed what it meant.

He cursed the coyotes, and not quietly, either. 'They found the mess you left back on the road. Now they'll be ready for us.'

Pack Leader offered no comment.

How soon before they sent Brianna after him? Soon. If she found them she would take out the coyotes in a few bloody seconds. And then she would keep him from advancing.

He had fought the Breeze before. She couldn't kill him, but

she could slow him down. She had chopped limbs from him. That kind of damage took time to repair.

And, of course, she would bring Sam. Sam and his little helpers. This time maybe Sam wouldn't be put off by the emergence of Brittney. Maybe this time Sam would burn him inch by inch, as he had started to do once –

'Aaaarrrgh!' Drake shouted. He raised his tentacle and snapped it down, making a loud crack.

The coyotes watched impassively.

'I need to hide,' Drake said. It was a shameful thing to admit. 'I have to hide until night comes.'

Pack Leader tilted his head and in his mangled speech said, 'Human hunter sees. Does not smell or hear.'

'Brilliant observation, there, Marmaduke.' It was true: Brianna was not a coyote. She couldn't smell him or even hear him unless he was pretty loud. He just needed a way to stay out of sight. 'OK, get me a place where I won't be seen until dark.'

'High place with deep cracks.'

'Let's make it quick, before they get around to sending your friend Swift Girl after us.'

The coyotes did not dawdle. They took off at a quick lope, moving with a sort of relentless fluidity around obstacles. It was uphill at first until they topped a rise. There Drake saw the barrier within a quarter mile.

He stopped and stared.

It was as if his master was reaching up from far underground with black claws. Like he was reaching to grab and then envelop this unnatural world with thousands of fingers.

It should have been inspiring. But it made Drake uneasy. This was the same black stain he had seen begin to spread into the gaiaphage itself.

It was a reminder that maybe not everything was right with the Darkness. It was a reminder that this mission was not born out of the gaiaphage's ambition alone, but out of fear.

'Move,' Pack Leader urged anxiously. They were partially silhouetted atop the bluff. Drake ducked low. He could see the lake spread out below. If he could see, he could also be seen.

Drake hurried along behind Pack Leader, disappearing quickly amidst a maze of fallen rock and rain-etched bluff.

He had to suck in his breath to squeeze through the crack they'd found for him. One of the advantages of hanging out with coyotes: no one knew the terrain better.

There was no room to sit, barely room to stand. But Brianna wouldn't find him; he was confident of that.

And he could see a narrow slice of the lake, a few boats, and a sliver of the sky.

Night was coming on.

OUTSIDE

NURSE CONNIE TEMPLE swallowed the Zoloft. It worked better than Prozac for her, left her less tired.

She chased it with most of a glass of red wine. Which would make her feel tired.

She turned on the TV and clicked without any real interest through the movies on demand. She wasn't in her trailer. She was at the Avania Inn in Santa Barbara. It was where she regularly met Sergeant Darius Ashton.

They had started going out months earlier. He had shown up at one of the Friday cookouts. And soon after that they had realised they would need to keep their relationship secret.

Connie heard the familiar knock. She let Darius in. He was short, only a couple of inches taller than she was herself. But he had a thick, hard body decorated with tattoos and scars he'd brought home from Afghanistan.

He had a six-pack of beer in one hand and a sheepish grin. Connie liked him. She liked the fact that he was smart enough to know that part of the reason she was with him – not all, just part – was that she was using him for information. He had lost most of the sight in one eye, so Darius was never going back to combat. His current assignment was to Camp Camino Real. He had been assigned to maintenance. He had no direct access to anything classified, but he heard things. He saw things. He hated his job, and if he couldn't be a combat soldier he was determined to leave the service when his enlistment was up.

Basically Sergeant Darius Ashton was killing time. He liked killing that time with Connie.

Connie sat on the bed drinking red wine. Darius drank his third beer and flopped in the chair with his feet up on the end of the bed, toes occasionally playing with hers.

'Something is up,' he said without preamble. 'I hear the colonel threatened to resign.'

'Why?'

Darius shrugged.

'Is he out?' Connie asked.

'Nah. The general choppered in. They had a chat that could be heard from some distance. Then the general choppered out, and that was that.'

'And you have no idea what it was about?'

He shook his head slowly. He hesitated before he went on, and Connie knew there was something big coming. Something he was leery of telling her.

'My sons are in there,' Connie said.

'Sons? Plural?' He looked sharply at her. 'I've only heard you talk about your boy, Sam.'

She took a deep pull at the wine. 'I want you to trust me,' she said. 'So I'm telling you the truth. That's how trust works. Right?'

'That's what I hear,' he said dryly.

'I had twins. Sam and David. I guess I liked the biblical names back then.'

'Good strong names,' Darius said.

'They were fraternal, not identical. Sam was a few minutes older. He was the smaller one, though, by seven ounces.'

She started again and was surprised to find that her voice betrayed her with a wobble. She powered through it, determined not to get weepy. 'I had postpartum depression. Pretty bad. You know what that is?'

He didn't answer but she saw that he did not.

'Sometimes a woman, after she gives birth, her hormones go seriously off-kilter. I knew this. After all, I'm a nurse, although not much lately.'

'So there are pills and all,' Darius suggested.

'There are,' she confirmed. 'And I kept it together. But early on I formed this . . . this fantasy, I suppose. That something was wrong with David.'

'Wrong?'

'Yes. Wrong. I don't mean physically. He was a beautiful little baby. And smart. It was so strange, because I worried that I would prefer him to Sam because he was bigger and so alert and so beautiful.'

Darius set aside his now-empty beer. He popped another.

'Then the accident. The meteor.'

'Heard about that,' Darius said with interest. 'Like, twenty years ago, though, wasn't it?'

'Thirteen years ago.'

'Must have been something to see. A meteor smashes a nuclear power plant? People must have freaked.'

'You could say that,' Connie said dryly. 'You know they still call Perdido Beach "Fallout Alley". Naturally they told us everything was fine . . . Well, they didn't tell me that. In fact, what they told me was that my husband, the father of my two little boys, was the only person killed.'

Darius sat up, tilting his head, and leaned in. 'The fallout?'

'No, the actual impact. He never suffered. Never even knew what was coming. He was just in the wrong place at the wrong time.'

'Killed by a meteor.' Darius shook his head. Connie knew he had seen death in Afghanistan.

'After that the depression came back. Worse than ever. And with it this conviction, this powerful belief that there was something wrong with David. Something very, very wrong.'

The memory of those days swept over her, making it impossible to speak. The madness had been so real. What had begun as a symptom of postpartum depression came to be something like a psychotic symptom. Like there was a voice in her head, whispering, whispering that David was dangerous. That he was evil.

'I was afraid I might harm him,' Connie said.

'Harsh.'

'Yeah. Harsh. I loved him. But I was afraid of him. Afraid of what I would do to him. So.' She took a deep, shaky breath. 'I gave him up. He was adopted immediately. And for a long time he disappeared from my life. I gave all my attention to Sam and told myself I had done the right thing.'

Darius frowned. 'I've read through the Wiki. There's no David Temple. I would have noticed because of the last name.'

Connie smiled slightly. 'I never knew who had adopted him. I never knew where he was. Until one day I was at work, at Coates. I wasn't even employed there at the time; I was filling in while their regular nurse was on maternity leave. And this boy was brought in. I knew immediately. Never any doubt. I asked him his name. He said he was Caine.'

'How had he turned out? I mean, you had this idea he was going bad . . .'

Connie lowered her head. 'He was still beautiful. And very

smart. And so charming. You should have seen the girls flock to him.'

'He got his looks from his mom,' Darius said, trying to be gallant.

'He was also cruel. Manipulative. Ruthless.' She spoke the words with great care, considering each one. 'He scared me. And he was one of the first to begin the mutation. The same time as Sam, actually, but Sam was a totally different person. Sam lashed out with his power, lost control of himself, and was devastated by it. But Caine? He used his power without the slightest concern for anyone but himself.'

'Same mother, same father, and so different?'

'Same mother,' Connie said, her voice flat. 'I was having an affair. I never had a DNA test, but it is possible that they had different fathers.'

She could see that this shocked Darius. He didn't approve. Well, why should he? She didn't approve of herself.

The room suddenly felt cold.

'I'd better get going,' Darius said. 'You cooking some ribs on Friday?'

'Darius. I told you my secret,' Connie said. 'I gave you everything. What is it you aren't telling me?'

Darius stopped at the door. Connie wondered if he would ever come back. He'd seen a side of her he had never expected.

'I can't tell you anything,' Darius said. 'Except that the military loves acronyms. Just saw a new one the other day I didn't recognise on some vehicles that came into camp. NEST. Sounds innocent, huh?'

'What's NEST?'

'Look it up. See you Friday if I can.'

He left.

Connie opened her laptop and tied into the hotel's wi-fi. She opened Google and typed in NEST. It took a few seconds to find that NEST stood for Nuclear Emergency Support Team.

They were the scientists, technicians, and engineers who were called in to deal with a nuclear incident.

A nuclear response team.

And the colonel threatening to quit.

Something was going on. Maybe some controversial new experiment. Something dangerous. Something involving a possible radiation spill.

Which may have been how this whole thing started to begin with.

NINETEEN

18 HOURS 55 MINUTES

FULL NIGHT.

Sam had recalled Brianna when the sun went down. The darkness was deadly to her. One stumble and she'd be a bag of broken bones.

Brianna raged and demanded to be turned loose again. But she knew better. Sam sent her below to take one of the unused bunks and get some sleep. Mere seconds later he heard her snoring.

The guards were changed. Edilio sat blinking sleep away. Dekka brooded. He hadn't seen Astrid in a while. He assumed she was down in his bunk. Maybe she was mad at him. Probably. And maybe he deserved it. He'd been curt with her.

He wanted to go down there and be with her. But he knew if he gave in to that need, if he found peace and forgetfulness, he might not have the strength to come out again.

The light was dying. But the moon – or an illusion of it – was rising. This was not yet true darkness. But it was coming.

'Where is he?' Sam wondered for the millionth time. He scanned the beach, already dark. He scanned the woods and the bluff. Drake could be in either place. Beneath those dark trees. Or somewhere up in those rocks.

He sank into a canvas chair.

'You awake enough to keep your eyes open?' he asked Dekka.

'Catch some z's, Sam.'

'Yeah,' he said, and yawned.

Astrid was waiting for him.

He said, 'Sorry, I snapped at you before.'

She didn't say anything but kissed him, holding his face with her hands. They made love slowly, silently, and when they were finished, Sam drifted into sleep.

When Cigar looked at Sanjit he saw a dancing, twirling, happy creature that looked like a greyhound walking erect. The one called Choo looked like a sleepy gorilla with a slow-beating red valentine of a heart.

Cigar knew he wasn't seeing what other people saw. He just didn't know whether what he was seeing was a result of having his new eyes, or whether it was madness that turned everything so strange and incredible.

Strange eyes. Strange brain. Some combination of the two?

Even objects – the beds, the tables, the steps at Clifftop –

had an eerie glow, a vibration, a streaming light as though, rather than being fixed in place, they were moving.

Mad eyes, mad brain.

Memories that made the screams rise in his raw throat.

When that happened Sanjit or Choo or the little one, Bowie, who looked like a spectral white kitten, would come to him and speak soothing words. At those times he seemed to see something like dust in a strong beam of sunlight, and that . . . that . . . he didn't know what to call it, but that . . . stuff . . . would calm the panic.

Until the next panic.

There was another thing, very different from the sparkly sunlit dust, that reached tendrils through the air, passing through objects, rising sometimes like smoke from the floor, and other times like a slow, pale green whip.

When Lana came the green whip would follow her, reaching to touch her, sliding away, reaching again, insistent.

And sometimes Cigar felt it was looking for him. It had no eyes. It couldn't see him. But it sensed something . . . something that interested it.

When it came close to him he would have visions of Penny. He would have visions of himself doing terrible, sickening things to her.

Making her suffer.

He wondered if the rising smoke, the slow green whip, this

stuff, could give him power over Penny. He wondered if he said yes – yes, reach me; here I am – if then he would be able to get revenge on Penny.

But Cigar's thoughts never lasted for very long. He would put together pictures in his head; then they would fly apart like an exploding jigsaw puzzle.

At times the little boy would come.

It wasn't easy to see the little boy. The little boy always stayed just to the side. Cigar would sense his presence and look towards him, but no matter how quickly he moved his head, Cigar could never see the little boy clearly. It was like seeing someone through a narrow opening in a door. It was a glimpse, and then the little boy would be gone.

More madness.

If you had inhuman eyes and a shattered mind, how could you ever know what was real and what was not?

Cigar realised he had to stop trying. It didn't matter, did it? Did anyone ever really see what was there around them? Were regular eyes so perfect or normal minds so clear? Who was to say that what Cigar saw wasn't as real as what he had seen in the old days?

Weren't regular eyes blind to all sorts of things? To X-rays and radiation and colours off beyond the visible spectrum?

The little boy had put that thought in his head.

There he was now, Cigar realised. Just outside of view. A

suggestion of a presence. Right there where even Cigar could not see.

Cigar's thoughts fell to pieces again.

He stood up and made his way to the door that vibrated and pulsed and called to him.

There was a knock on Penny's door.

Penny did not fear a knock at the door. She opened it without even checking the peephole.

Caine stood framed by silvery moonlight in the door.

'We have to talk,' Caine said.

'It's the middle of the night.'

He came in without waiting for an invitation. 'First things first: if I see anything I don't like, even so much as a flea, anything that comes from your sick imagination, Penny, I won't hesitate. I'll throw you through the nearest wall. And then I'll drop the wall on top of you.'

'Hello to you, too. Your Highness.' She closed the door.

He was already sitting, flopping down in her favourite chair. Like he owned the place. He had brought a candle. He lit it with a Bic and set it on the table. So very Caine: he would arrange to be dramatically lit, even though candles were rarer than diamonds in the FAYZ.

King Caine.

Penny swallowed the rage that threatened to boil over. She

would make him crawl. Make him scream and scream!

She said, 'I know why you're here.'

'Turk said you were ready to get real, Penny. He said you wanted to negotiate some terms. Fair enough. So spit it out.'

'Look,' Penny said, 'I screwed up with Cigar. And I know what happens if the food supply dries up. I'm not as pretty as Diana, but that doesn't mean I'm stupid.'

'OK,' he said cautiously.

'So, like I told Turk to tell you, I'm going to leave town. I already packed a few things.' She gestured to a backpack lying in one corner. 'I just don't think it should look like you made me go, because then it's like Quinn won. I think I should make it be like I just chose on my own to leave.'

Caine stared at her, obviously trying to figure out what she was up to.

Penny showed a little anger then. 'Hey, I'm not happy about it, all right? But I'll get by. Believe it or not I can survive without you, King Caine.'

'Take all the food you want,' he said.

'How generous of you,' she snapped. 'The deal is I leave, but you have to make sure I don't starve. Once a week I'll meet Bug out on the highway, right by the overturned FedEx truck. If I need something he brings it. That's my demand for leaving and making it easy for you.'

Caine relaxed a bit. He tilted his head sideways and looked at her, considering. 'Fair enough.'

'But we have to talk about how to make it look good. Let's face it, Caine: you and I can still be useful to each other in the future, right? So I need you to stay in charge. Better than the alternative.'

'What do you have in mind?'

She sighed. 'Right now I have in mind some hot cocoa. Taylor brought me some from the island. Have a cup with me and we'll work something out.'

Caine didn't ask why Taylor would have brought her something as precious as cocoa from the island. Taylor no doubt used Penny's fantasy-making powers for something.

Penny saw the look of distaste on his face as he worked it out. She went to the kitchen, to the little Sterno stove she used to heat the water and the cocoa.

She lit the Sterno.

Caine did not follow her into the kitchen.

He was still sitting there with a puzzled look on his face when she handed him the cup.

They each sipped.

'So I guess if I'm leaving and making it look like it's not your fault, we should maybe act like we're fighting,' Penny said.

'It would have to be where people can overhear. But not right out in public, because that'll look phony,' Caine said. And sipped again at his cocoa. 'Kind of bitter,' he said, grimacing at the cup.

'I have a little sugar I could add.'

'You have sugar?'

She fetched it. Two sugar cubes, and she plopped them into his cup. He swirled it around to stir the sugar in.

'You're right about one thing, Penny,' he said. 'You're useful. Crazy, but useful. No one has sugar, but you do.'

She shrugged modestly. 'People like to get away, you know? Think about something more fun than just life and work and all.'

'Yeah. Still: actual sugar? That's worth a lot.'

'I guess you know I have a crush on you,' Penny said.

'Yeah, well, no offence, but it doesn't go both ways,' he said.

It took all her self-control not to lash out at him, to cause his skin to burn and bubble.

'Too bad,' Penny said. 'Because I can be anyone . . . in your imagination.'

'Do me a favour; don't give me any details,' he said. 'Now . . .' He yawned. 'Let's lay plans here. I've had a long couple of days, and I want to get this over with.'

So Penny made a suggestion.

And Caine countered with another.

And she smiled and made a small objection.

And he yawned. A long, long yawn.

'You look tired, Caine. Why don't you close your eyes and rest a few minutes.'

'I can't . . .' He started to say, but yawned again. 'Talk later. In the morning.'

He tried to stand up. He barely rose, then sagged back. He blinked and stared at her.

She could practically see the wheels turning slowly, slowly in his brain. He frowned. Forced his eyes open and said, 'Did you . . . ?'

She didn't bother answering. She was bored with the game and sick of playing nice.

'I'll kill you,' he said. He raised one hand, but it wavered in the air. She got up quickly and stepped aside. She came around behind him.

He tried to turn but he couldn't do it. Could not get his body to respond.

'Don't worry, Your Highness. In fact, I don't think you'll be able to worry at all pretty soon. In addition to the Ambien I mixed in some Valium.'

'I'll . . . k . . .' he said, and breathed heavily, unable to go on.

'Nighty-night,' Penny said. She picked up a heavy snow globe from the knick-knack shelf, where it had no doubt been a prized possession of whoever had owned this house. The snow globe had a little Harrah's casino inside. A tacky keepsake.

She smashed the globe against the back of Caine's head. He slumped forward.

The glass shattered, lacerating his scalp but also slicing her thumb.

She looked at the blood on her hand.

'Worth it,' she snarled.

She wrapped a towel around the cut on her hand, then brought in a large wooden salad bowl and a pitcher of water.

Then she dragged the heavy bag of cement from the closet.

TWENTY

17 HOURS 37 MINUTES

SILENT AS A shadow Astrid crept from the bunk. It was so hard to leave the warmth of his body. He was a magnet and she was an iron filing, drawn almost irresistibly back to him.

Almost irresistibly.

She crept out into the hallway. Brianna was snoring. It almost made Astrid giggle to realise that she snored at normal speed, like anyone else.

She found her old clothes. She dressed in the shadows. T-shirt, multiply-patched jeans. Boots. She checked her backpack. Shotgun shells still there. She would refill her water bottle from the lake. Some food would be good, but Astrid had long since adjusted to extended periods of hunger.

Hopefully this trip wouldn't take too long. If nothing happened she could make the walk to Perdido Beach in what, five hours? She sighed. Walk to Perdido Beach through the night or crawl back into bed with Sam and let him wrap his strong arms around her and entwine her legs with his and . . .

'Now or never,' she whispered.

She had the letters. The ones Mohamed had failed to deliver. She folded them and stuck them into her front pocket, where they couldn't possibly fall out or be dropped.

The whole plan rested on what she found when she went up on deck. The houseboat was still moored at the dock – a symbolic defiance – but someone would be on watch.

She emerged on the dock side. Maybe whoever was on the top deck wouldn't notice. Maybe she could just walk away.

'Freeze,' a voice said. Dekka.

Astrid cursed under her breath. She had made it about six feet down the dock. She was well within Dekka's range, which meant Astrid had zero chance of getting away. Dekka would cancel the gravity beneath her feet, and it was hard to run while floating in the air.

Dekka stepped to the edge of the top deck and then off into space. She cancelled gravity for a split second, just enough to allow her to make the drop silently.

'Heading out for a snack run?' Dekka asked dryly. 'Pick me up a pack of Ho Hos.'

'I'm going to Perdido Beach,' Astrid said.

'Ah. You're going to be the big hero and deliver Sam's letter.'

'Minus the 'big hero' snark, yes.'

Dekka jerked her thumb towards the land. 'Drake's out there. And the same coyotes that ate Howard for lunch. No offence, honey, but you're the brains, not the muscle.'

'I've learned a few things,' Astrid said. Without taking her eyes off Dekka's she swung the butt of her shotgun up and sideways. The wood stock caught Dekka on the side of her face. Not enough to knock her out, but enough to make her drop to her knees.

Astrid moved quickly to get behind Dekka and take advantage of her momentary weakness. She shoved Dekka facedown on the rough planks.

'Sorry, Dekka,' she said, and wrapped a length of rope around her wrists. She stuffed an old sock in Dekka's mouth. 'Listen to me, Dekka. We need Caine; Caine needs us. So this has to happen. And I'm not necessary here.'

Dekka was already straining against the rope and starting to spit the gag out of her mouth.

'If you wake Sam up, he'll send Brianna after me.'

That quieted Dekka's struggles.

'I know this sucks, and later you can punch me back,' Astrid said. 'Give me twenty minutes before you get Sam. Tell him you were knocked out. You'll have a nice bruise to show him. He'll believe you.'

Astrid stood back. Dekka wasn't struggling. 'Tell Sam I said I need to do this. Tell him I won't stop until I get it done.'

Dekka had managed to spit out the gag. She could yell now and all would be lost. Instead she said, 'Cut into the woods; stay away from the bluff. For my money Drake's in those caves and cracks in the bluff. Breeze cleared the woods pretty well.'

'Thanks.'

'Anything else you want me to tell Sam?'

Astrid knew what she was asking. 'He knows I love him.' Then with a sigh she said, 'OK: tell him I love him with all my heart. But tell him also that this battle isn't on him alone. I'm in this, too.'

'All right, blondie. Good luck. And hey: shoot first; think about it later, huh?'

Astrid nodded. 'Yeah.'

She walked quickly away. A part of her was cruelly disappointed that she'd been able to get past Dekka. If she'd been stopped, she would have got some credit for making a brave effort. And she'd be back with Sam instead of walking, tense and fearful, towards the line of the woods.

Diana hadn't thought she'd be able to sleep out on a sailboat. It wasn't like there were waves, but she still had powerful memories of the days of morning sickness. And she was not happy about anything that might upset the delicate peace she'd achieved with her stomach.

But she had fallen asleep on one of the narrow, cushioned bench seats in the stern of the sailboat.

On the boat were Roger and Justin and one of Justin's

friends, a little girl with the interesting name of Atria. They were asleep. Or at least they were quiet, which, from Diana's point of view, was just as good.

Diana had watched Roger earlier with the two littles. She wondered if she would ever manage that kind of patience and playfulness. Roger had found some chalk somewhere and had kept the kids calm by drawing funny characters on the deck. Justin and Atria seemed to think it was all a sort of picnic.

The other occupant of the boat was Orc. He had decided his place was up on the front deck, the bow or whatever they called it. His weight lifted the stern so it was at an angle that threatened to spill her out of her seat. But she wrapped one arm around a chrome upright and the other arm uncomfortably around a cleat, tucked a blanket up close to her chin, and sure enough she fell asleep.

But it was one of those strange sleeps. Not complete unconsciousness, but a sort of drifting, smiling, pleasantly cloudy sleep that hovered right on the edge of consciousness.

She could hear voices, but she didn't understand them or want to.

She could feel the lift and fall of the boat when Orc moved, or when another drifting boat jostled theirs.

It was in this state that Diana heard the voice. It was a voice at once new and familiar. It resonated up from her belly.

She knew it was a dream. At this point the baby – even if it was a little advanced for its age – didn't have a functioning brain, let alone the power to formulate words and thoughts and sentences.

Baby was warm . . .

Baby was in the dark . . .

Baby was safe . . .

A dream, a pleasant fantasy invented by her subconscious. She smiled.

What are you? her dreaming mind asked.

Baby . . .

No, silly, I mean are you a boy or a girl?

Diana felt confusion coming from the dreamed baby. Well, of course, that would make sense. After all, this was a dream, and this conversation was a fantasy, with both voices coming from her own subconscious, and since she didn't know the –

He wants me . . .

Diana's hazy dream suddenly filled with storm clouds. The smile was gone. Her jaw muscles clenched.

He whispers to me . . .

Who? Who whispers to you?

My father . . .

Diana's heart skipped beats, then thudded hard to make it up.

Do you mean Caine?

My father says I must come to him . . .

I asked you a question: do you mean Caine?

'Do you mean Caine?' Diana was awake. Her skin was goose pimpled. 'Do you mean Caine?'

She was breathing hard. Drops of sweat stood on her forehead. She felt clammy all over.

Other kids were staring at her. She could see white eyes in the almost pitch-black.

She had been shouting.

'I had a dream,' she whispered. Then, 'Sorry. Go back to sleep.'

She couldn't look at them. She couldn't have them looking at her.

'Do you mean Caine?' Diana whispered.

No voice answered. But it didn't matter. Diana had felt the answer. Had known the answer all along.

No . . .

Diana pulled her ratty blanket around her and went up on deck. She needed fresh air as an antidote to her overactive imagination. Probably hormones were to blame. Her body was all weird now.

She saw Orc. He sat with his back to her. His few remaining human characteristics were invisible from this angle. But there was still something human in the slump of his massive gravel shoulders. His head hung so low it was barely a bump.

'Aren't you cold out here?' Diana asked. Stupid question. She wasn't even sure Orc could feel cold.

Orc didn't answer. Diana took a few steps closer. 'I'm sorry about Howard,' she said. She searched for something kind to say about that thief and drug dealer. It took too long, so she said nothing.

Diana wondered if Orc had been drinking. Orc drunk could be dangerous. But when he spoke at last his words were clearly enunciated. 'I looked in the book and didn't find nothing.'

'The book?'

'It don't say blessed are the weaselly little guys.'

Oh, that book. She had nothing to say and now she was regretting starting things with Orc. Her cot was suddenly seeming attractive. And she had to pee.

'Howard was . . . unique, I guess,' she said, wondering what she meant even as she spoke the words.

'He liked me,' Orc said. 'Took care of me.'

Yeah, Diana thought, *made sure you stayed drunk. Used you.* But she kept that to herself.

As if Orc had read her thoughts he said, 'Not saying he wasn't a bad person a lot of times. But so am I. We all do bad stuff. Me worse than most.' Diana flashed on memories of her own. Things she'd done and now couldn't bear to think about. 'Well, maybe like people say, he's in a better place.'

That sounded stupid to her. But wasn't that what people said? Anyway, where exactly was a place worse than this? The news had gone round the flotilla that Howard had been choked to death and then had the flesh gnawed from his bones.

'I worry because maybe he's in hell,' Orc said. The words sounded tortured.

Diana cursed softly, under her breath. How had she got herself into this? Really: had to pee. 'Orc, God is supposed to be forgiving, right? So probably he forgave Howard. I mean, that's his job, right? Forgiving?'

'If you do bad stuff and don't repent you go to hell,' Orc said, like he was begging for a refutation.

'Yeah, well, you know what? If Howard's in hell, I guess we can all have a big get-together soon enough.' She turned to go.

'He liked me,' Orc said.

'I'm sure he did,' Diana snapped, wearying of the conversation. 'You're a big, lovable teddy bear, Orc.' *Plus a thug and a murderer*, she added silently.

'I don't want to start up drinking again,' Orc said.

'Then don't,' Diana said.

'But I ain't ever killed anyone sober.'

Diana had run out of time. She raced down the stairs, found the pot they were all sharing, squatted, and sighed with relief.

The boat rocked wildly. One of the kids yelled a sleepy, 'Hey!'

Diana went back up on deck and saw that Orc was gone. The small rowboat that had been tied to one of the boat's cleats was thirty yards away, moving swiftly towards shore, driven by superhumanly powerful thrusts of the oars.

* * *

Caine was still asleep. Penny wasn't sure how long it would take him to wake up. But she was in no hurry.

No hurry at all. Not now.

She sat watching him. He was in a very uncomfortable position, really. He sat slumped forward on the couch. His hands were wrist-deep in the bowl. The cement had dried pretty quickly.

King Caine.

He wouldn't be clawing at his eyes, at least. Not with five gallons of cement on his hands. He would barely be able to stand up.

She considered him. The big-deal four bar. The most powerful freak in Perdido Beach, one of just two four bars.

Helpless.

Brought down, all the way down, by bony, unattractive little Penny.

She fetched scissors from the kitchen. He shifted a little and moaned something as she cut the shirt apart and removed it.

Much better. A much more vulnerable look. After all he had been through, he still had a very nice chest. The muscles stood out in his flat stomach.

But before she could show him off, he needed one more thing. The idea she had in mind made her laugh with delight.

There was a roll of aluminum foil in the kitchen. She found it, rolled it out, and set to work by candlelight.

Drake had watched everything from the high ground out past Sinder's garden. It made him happy to see that Sam and all his little charges were cowering in boats. It was a testament to Drake's power.

But unfortunately it made it very hard to get to Diana. There was no way even to know where she was. She could be on any of dozens of boats.

All during the morning he had cowered up here as every half an hour or so a whirlwind blew past. Brianna.

Each time Drake would sink back against the rocks. The coyotes would turn their ears towards the sound and lie perfectly still. They feared Swift Girl.

But Brianna had not seen them. And now it was deepest night, and Swift Girl wasn't so swift in the dark.

And then Drake had had some luck. Diana herself, wrapped in a shawl or something, had stepped into view on one of the boats. The one with Orc sitting in the bow.

Even by dim starlight he knew her. No one else moved like Diana.

Of course. He should have thought of that. Sam would make sure she had a strong protector, so of course she would be on the boat with Orc.

The sight of her made his whip twitch. He unwrapped it from his waist. He wanted to feel the power in it as he gazed down at her.

She would be brave at first. Say what he might about Diana, she was not soft or weak. But the whip would change her attitude. Nothing that would harm the baby. But that still left Drake plenty of possibilities.

If he could just figure out how to get to her. And past Brianna. And Orc.

He glanced at the big houseboat, the only thing still attached to the dock. It was farther away, and the angle was bad for seeing anything other than the top deck. Dekka had been on watch there. Now she was gone. But Drake knew perfectly well the houseboat had been left there as a lure for him. They wanted him to be stupid enough to attack.

He felt a sudden flash of rage. Sam, oh, so very clever, moving all his vulnerable people out on to the boats. He hadn't seemed so clever when Drake had whipped the flesh from him and Sam had cried out in pain and tears had streamed from his eyes . . .

A low growl of pleasure came from Drake's lips. It made the coyotes nervous.

Then two things happened: Orc climbed heavily down into a comically small rowboat.

Perfect! Let Orc bring the boat in. Drake would wait until

the behemoth was clear and then he could take the boat out to collect Diana.

The only problem was the second thing that was happening: Drake was feeling the queasy sensation he got when Brittney emerged.

He snapped his whip in frustration. But that whip had already shrivelled to a third of its usual length.

Drake quickly bit his index finger, drawing blood. He found a flat surface of rock and in the few seconds he had left he scrawled the word 'sailbo –'

TWENTY ONE

17 HOURS 20 MINUTES

SAM WOKE SUDDENLY and knew something had happened.

He lay amid the twisted blanket for a few seconds trying to gather together the threads of unconscious perception. Movements, sounds, hazy notions of murmured conversation.

Then he got quickly to his feet. He pulled on his clothing and stepped out into the main hallway. He was heading for the stairs when he stopped, turned, and saw confirmation: Astrid's backpack was gone.

He pushed back a sliding closet door. Her shotgun was gone as well.

At that moment Dekka came down the stairs. She was startled to see him up. He was sure he saw a guilty look cross her face before being suppressed.

'She took the letters,' Sam said flatly.

'She knocked me out,' Dekka said. She pointed at the bruise on the side of her head and turned her face so he could see it by the light of the small Sammy sun.

Sam's lips curled into a feral snarl. 'Right. Astrid. Knocked you out.'

'She popped me with the butt of her shotgun.'

'I can see that. I also know what it takes to beat you down, Dekka.'

She flared angrily, but he knew it was the truth, and she knew that he knew.

'I'm sending Brianna after her.'

'Astrid's right: we need PB to know what's happening, and we need to work together with them. Someone needs to take that letter to Albert and Caine.'

'Not Astrid,' Sam snapped. He started to push past her to where Brianna lay snoring, blissfully unaware.

Dekka stepped in front of him. 'No, Sam.'

Sam stepped up to her, so close they almost touched. 'You don't tell me no, Dekka.'

'If you send Brianna after her, one of two things: Breeze finds her and drags her back. And Astrid will hate you for it. Or Breeze hits a rock at seventy miles an hour and ends up dead or busted up.'

Sam started to say something angry. Instead his voice broke. 'Drake's out there!' He tried to say more but the words couldn't get past the lump in his throat, so he pointed, jabbing his finger furiously towards the land.

'She's doing the right thing,' Dekka said. 'And you can't

send the girl I love to die in order to rescue the girl you love.'

Sam felt his lip quiver. He wanted to be furious, but raw emotion was making him weak. He swallowed hard and shook his head once, angrily shaking off the upwelling fear and loss. 'I'll go after her. I'll bring her back.'

'No, boss.' It was Edilio. He stepped out from behind Dekka. 'Kids wake up tomorrow morning and see you gone without even an explanation, that's it, man. You gotta look strong and stay strong. You have the light, Sam, and that's all that will keep people together.'

'You don't understand,' Sam pleaded. 'Drake is sick. He hates Astrid. You don't know what he can do.'

'Drake hates everyone,' Edilio said.

Suddenly Sam found his anger. 'You don't understand a damned thing, Edilio; you don't have anyone, you don't have anyone you need or love or care about, it's just you.'

He regretted the words as soon as he spoke them. But it was too late.

Edilio's usually warm, sad eyes narrowed and went cold. He pushed his way around Dekka and stood face-to-face with Sam. He stabbed his finger in Sam's face. 'There's a lot you don't know, Sam. There's a lot I don't tell you. I know who I am,' he said with a ferocity to match Sam's own anger. 'I know what I do, and what I am to this place. I know what I am to you, and how much you depend on me. You may be the symbol, and you may be the one everyone turns to when something goes bad, and you are the big badass, but I'm the guy doing the day-in, day-out work of running things. So I don't make this about me.'

He practically spat the word 'me'.

'I don't live my life so everyone pays attention to me. I do my job without making me the story, and without people having to wonder what's going on with me.'

Sam blinked. He felt awash in feelings, none of which made any sense together. In the tornado of fear and fury he felt shame. Everything Edilio had said was true.

Edilio wasn't finished. It was as if he'd held way too much inside and now that the dam had burst it was going to come out. 'You and Astrid, you're making a spectacle of yourselves. Kids are scared to death and what they're seeing is you and Astrid having a great time. I'm not judging what you're doing, that's not my business, but you're putting your personal life first and you can't do that: you are Sam Temple. All these people look to us, to you and Dekka and me – and Astrid now that she's back – and what do they see? You and Astrid rocking the houseboat every time you get a chance, and Dekka snapping at everyone because Brianna isn't a lesbian and doesn't want to be her girlfriend. The only one keeping his personal business personal is me. And you're going to get nasty about it?'

He turned away and angrily shouldered Dekka aside.

'You two get it together, because we got problems enough,' Edilio said, and stomped away.

Brianna continued to snore.

Moonlight picked Orc out of a pile of jumbled rock. Astrid wondered if Sam knew that Orc had gone ashore. She wondered if she needed to send word.

No. This was the more important mission. She had to get to Perdido Beach. Maybe Caine and Albert knew what was coming. But maybe not. If the kids in town weren't prepared they would panic and then they would all be lost.

An image came to mind, unbidden, unwelcome: a picture of kids in absolute darkness walking lost in the desert. They would walk until a hungry zeke, or a coyote, or Drake caught them. And those would be the luckier ones. Most would die an excruciating death of hunger and thirst.

Astrid steered clear of Orc. He was searching for someone or something. It had to be Drake, which could only be a good thing from her point of view.

She tried to think of something other than the image her mind had conjured of slow death by starvation in absolute darkness.

She needed to think.

Darkness wasn't the end state, was it? Surely something was causing the barrier to darken. The stain had a reason if not a purpose. It meant something. But what?

Most likely it was linked to the gaiaphage, that unknowable evil. The FAYZ's own personal Satan.

No one knew much about it. Lana didn't like to talk about it. Little Pete had been in contact with it, manipulated by it. The chimera that called itself Nerezza had been its creature. It had co-opted Caine at one point, or so the story went, but Caine had broken free.

Astrid began to jog, careful to watch the path beneath her feet. As soon as she was well away from the lake she planned to stay just off the gravel road. She wasn't sure if that was the smart thing to do or very stupid. But she reasoned that anyone looking for her would first check the main roads.

It would take her longer this way. But no one would expect her – of all people – to go overland through rough terrain.

Well, they didn't know her. In the last four months she had become quite comfortable with rough terrain.

She loped along, glorying in the sense of power from overcoming fear. Yes, it was dark. Yes, evil forces were on the loose. But she would outrun them or out-think them or if necessary outfight them.

If she couldn't do any of those, then she would endure.

A pang of guilt stabbed her without warning. She should have made her case to Sam and tried to get him to agree. She shouldn't have just run off on her own.

He would never have agreed.

She was doing the right thing. For once she was deciding to act. Not to manipulate or convince. But to act.

With luck she would reach Perdido Beach by morning.

And with a bit more luck she would be back with Sam by tomorrow night.

Brittney knew what she was to do. Mostly. The god that named itself gaiaphage had told her what she and Drake were to do. But the gaiaphage had not given her the power to keep Drake's memories as her own. Each time she emerged it was into a situation that might be totally unexpected.

In this case she recognised the crack in the bluff and knew she was hiding from Brianna. But now it was night and that was a surprise.

Almost as big a surprise as the fact that when she peered out she saw Orc looming huge no more than fifty feet away from the opening.

Brittney froze. The coyotes were already as quiet and still as statues.

Orc was slowly labouring up the hill, searching as he went in a steady, methodical way that was like nothing she'd ever seen from her former jailer.

He was meticulously scanning the ground, stomping through bushes, shoving boulders aside. Orc would not find them anytime soon, and the coyotes would show Brittney another hiding place if need be, but there was something disturbing in the way Orc was searching. Methodical. Calm. Dangerous.

The coyotes would be no use against Orc. And Brittney would be helpless. Orc was powerful. He could rip her into pieces. Those massive gravel hands could tear her apart as easily as she might tear a piece of bread.

He couldn't kill her, or Drake, so it seemed. But even now, as far from her old life as it was possible to get, Brittney felt sick with dread at what Orc could do. She might not feel pain like she once had. But she would feel something.

Orc moved on, lumbering past, a starlit beast. She did not understand why he wanted her, or wanted Drake, but she was sure that was his purpose.

Her hand brushed against a smooth rock face and she felt something wet.

'Whip Hand made blood,' Pack Leader said.

'It's too dark to see,' Brittney said. 'Do you –' No, that was stupid. Pack Leader did not read. But still, he might know something. She didn't have to ask.

'Rock That Lives came from there.' Pack Leader couldn't point, but he could aim his eyes. Through the gap in the rock Brittney could see what might be a small rowboat. She inched forward, silent, afraid of a massive stone hand reaching down from above. Inch by inch, until she was standing outside the cave. She stood perfectly still. Listened. She heard the monster moving rocks, but the sound was not close at hand.

The moon shone down on the forlorn rowboat. It had painted trim – possibly green, impossible to tell for sure.

She scanned the boats at anchor, bobbing gently at the end of ropes or in some cases seemingly just drifting randomly. A sailboat caught her eye. It had trim that was very much like that on the rowboat.

'We must go,' Brittney told Pack Leader. 'I'll take Orc's – Rock That Lives's – boat. You'll wait on shore to fight off anyone who comes along.'

Pack Leader's soulless, intelligent eyes stared at her. 'Pack hide from Swift Girl and Rock That Lives.'

'No,' Brittney said. 'We cannot hide any longer.'

'Swift Girl kills many coyotes.'

'You'll have to take your chances. The Darkness commands.'

Pack Leader's tail flicked. 'Bright Hands is there.' He pointed his muzzle at the houseboat. 'Rock That Lives is close. Pack Leader does not see Whip Hand. Does not see Darkness.'

Brittney gritted her teeth. So that was it. The coyotes were calculating the odds and not liking what they saw. Cowards.

'Are you dogs?' Brittney taunted.

But Pack Leader was unmoved. 'Pack almost gone. And only three pups.'

'If Drake was here he would whip the fur off you!'

'Whip Hand is not here,' Pack Leader said placidly.

'Fine. Then wait here. I'll go alone.'

Pack Leader did not argue. Neither did he agree.

Brittney began to pick her way quietly, cautiously down towards the shore. She stayed under the cover of rocks when she could, and hunched down low when she had no choice but to cover open ground.

She kept a sharp eye on the houseboat. She didn't need Drake's memories to know that was where Sam would be. And she listened carefully for Orc.

The last fifty yards there was no cover, nothing she could do to hide as she crossed the pebbly shore to the rowboat. She crouched and looked hard at the houseboat. She saw no one on the top deck. That didn't mean eyes weren't watching from the houseboat's windows. But if she could only barely see them it stood to reason they could see her only if they were staring in her direction.

Once the boat started moving . . .

She rushed to the rowboat and crouched in its shadow, eyes on the houseboat. If she tried to move the boat she would be caught. Maybe Drake could have done it, moving swiftly in a way that she could not. But she had no idea how to row a boat and was likely to make noise.

If she tried to swim it would be even worse. She knew how to swim, but she knew only the crawl, and the splashing would draw every ear in the small fleet.

Then Sam and his people would hear and they would catch her and Sam would burn her to ashes.

She would fail Drake. She would fail the gaiaphage.

Then: a flash of genius. Brittney almost laughed out loud.

She breathed, but she did not need to breathe.

Brittney began picking up small rocks and stuffing them in her pockets. She tied off the bottom of her shirt, as tight as she could make it, then dropped more rocks down the front of her shirt, using her arms to hold them all in like a pregnant woman's belly.

Weighed down, she walked into the water. As the water rose around her she kept her gaze on the sailboat. She walked directly towards it, fixing the direction in her mind.

The water rose over her waist, over her chest, to her mouth and nose. And then it closed over her head.

She was almost completely sightless in the water. The only light was from the moon, and it seemed to reach only a few feet into the lake.

Brittney focused all her energy on walking in a straight line. The rocks controlled her buoyancy, but still she tended to float just a little, which made holding to a straight line very hard.

Freezing water filled her lungs. She could tell that it was cold, but the cold did not bother her. What did bother her was the certainty that she was off course. How many steps should she take? How far out was the sailboat? It had seemed like perhaps two hundred steps, but she had lost count after stumbling and losing some of the rocks that held her down.

No choice now but to surface. She opened the bottom of her shirt and let the rocks fall free. Her feet came up off the stony lake bottom and she floated upwards.

It took a very long time. She was not very buoyant.

All the while she looked around and saw nothing until she was near the surface. Then she saw a rope slanting down into the darkness below.

She swam underwater, silent, no bubbles issuing from her mouth. She gripped the rope and began to pull herself upwards, careful not to yank on that line.

She came up face-first. The twisted wires of her braces glinted with moonlight. A boat – a boat with a tall mast and what might be green trim – was directly above her.

Brittney wasn't sure whether it was proper to say a prayer of thanks to the gaiaphage. Maybe that was just for her old god. But she smiled in the renewed belief that she had purpose, and that she was serving her master well.

TWENTY TWO

15 HOURS 12 MINUTES

ASTRID'S PLAN WOULD have been brilliant.

Except that in distancing herself from the road for safety she managed to get lost.

This quasi-desert was not her familiar woods. And the funny thing about a road was that from a distance you couldn't actually see it at night unless you were seeing streetlights or car lights.

The FAYZ had neither.

So the gravel road disappeared from view, and although she was sure she was paralleling it, she seemed now to be in much less austere countryside than that which the road passed through.

The moon had set and the stars provided far too little light to see by. So she had gone slower and slower. And then she had tried to turn a sharp right angle to intersect the road. But the road was not there. Or if it was there it was much farther off than she had imagined.

'Stupid,' she told herself. So much for the newly competent Astrid. She'd managed to lose herself in just a couple of hours.

As much as she hated to admit it, the only wise movement now was to stand still and wait for dawn. If dawn came. That thought sent a thrill of fear through her stomach. Even by starlight she was helpless. In total darkness she could wander forever. Or more accurately, wander until thirst and hunger killed her.

She wondered which would do it first. People assumed it was thirst. But she'd read in a book somewhere that hunger –

'Not helpful,' she said aloud, just for the reassurance of hearing her own voice. 'If . . . when . . . the sun comes up I'll be able to locate the ridges and hills and maybe even see a bit of ocean.'

So she found a patch of ground with some tall grass and sat down carefully.

'Bad start,' she admitted. Lost in the wilderness. How long had Moses and the Hebrews managed to stay lost on the Sinai Peninsula before stumbling into the land they were to reconquer? Forty years?

'A pillar of smoke by day and a pillar of fire by night. And they still couldn't find their way out of the Sinai,' Astrid muttered. 'I'll settle for one last day of sunlight.'

At some point sleep carried her off to unsettling dreams.

And when she woke at last she knew that her one wish was not to be granted.

Looking up, she could make out a circle of deepest, darkest blue just beginning to lighten on the eastern edge and push the stars away.

Beneath that midnight blue was black. Not the black of night with stars and the Milky Way and distant galaxies, but the absolute blank, flat black of the stain.

The sky no longer stretched from horizon to horizon. The sky was a hole in the top of an upended bowl. The sky was the circle at the top of a well. And before the day was done the sky would be altogether gone.

Caine woke. His head was pounding. A headache so painful he thought he might pass out from the sudden onslaught of pain.

Then he felt something else. It felt like cuts. Itchy and sharp at once, all around his head.

He reached to touch it. But his hands would not move.

Caine's eyes opened.

He saw the grey cement block, shaped like a bowl. It rested on the coffee table. His hands were in the block up to the wrists.

Fear struck. Panic.

He fought to control it but he couldn't. He cried out.

'No, no, no, no!'

He tried to pull back, tried to free his hands, but they were absolutely held fast by the concrete, which itched and squeezed his skin. He had done this to people; he had ordered this done and he knew the results; he knew what it did; he knew the cement could not just be broken off; he knew he was trapped, powerless.

Powerless!

He jumped to his feet but the cement block weighed him down so that he stumbled forward and banged his knee against the sharp edge of the concrete. Pain in his knee, but nothing next to the panic, nothing compared to the awful pain in his head.

He whimpered like a scared child.

With all his strength he lifted the cement block. It banged against his thighs, but yes, he could lift it; he could carry it.

But not far. He set it down but missed the table, so that it slammed on to the floor, bending him over into an upside-down 'U'.

Had to get a grip. Had to not panic.

Had to figure out . . .

He was at Penny's house.

Penny.

No.

Sick, terrible dread filled him.

He looked up as well as he could and there she was, walking towards him. She stopped just inches from his bowed head. He was staring at her feet.

'Do you like it?' Penny asked.

She held an oval mirror out so that he could look at it and see his face. His head. The streams of dried blood that had run from the crown she'd made of aluminum foil and then stapled to his head.

'Can't be a king without a crown,' she said. 'Your Highness.'

'I'll kill you, you sick, twisted maggot.'

'Funny you should mention maggots,' she said.

He saw one then. A maggot. Just one. It was squirming up out of the concrete block. Only it wasn't coming from the cement; it was coming from the skin of his wrist.

He stared at it. She'd put maggots in with his hands!

A second one was coming out now. No bigger than a grain of rice. Eating its way through his skin, coming out of . . .

No, no, it was one of her illusions. She was making him see this.

They would burrow into his flesh and –

No! No! Don't believe it!

It wasn't real. The cement was real, nothing else, but he could feel them now, not one or two, but hundreds, hundreds of them eating into his hands.

'Stop it! Stop it!' he cried. There were tears in his eyes.

'Of course, Your Highness.'

The maggots were gone. The feeling of them digging into

him was gone. But the memory persisted. And even though he knew absolutely that they were not real, the sense memory was powerful. Impossible to dismiss.

'Now we're going on a walk,' Penny said.

'What?'

'Don't be shy. Let's show off that washboard stomach of yours. Let's let everyone see your crown.'

'I'm not going anywhere,' Caine snapped.

But then something dropped on to his left eyelash. He couldn't bring it into focus. But it was small and white. And it writhed.

His resistance crumbled.

In the space of minutes he had gone from king – the most powerful person in Perdido Beach – to slave.

With a desperate heave he lifted the block and staggered towards the door.

Penny opened it and her step faltered.

'It's still night,' Caine said.

Penny shook her head slowly. 'No. I have a clock. It's morning.' She threw him a haunted, troubled look, as if she suspected him of some trick.

'You look scared, Penny,' he said.

That brought the hard look back to her face. 'Get going, King Caine. I'm not afraid of anything.' She laughed, suddenly delighted. 'I don't have fear. I am fear!'

She liked it so much she repeated it, cackling like a mad creature. 'I am fear!'

Diana stood on the deck of the sailboat. One hand was on her belly, rubbing it absentmindedly.

She saw the leaders – Sam, Edilio, Dekka – all standing on the White Houseboat looking at the place where the rising sun should be.

My baby.

That was her thought. My baby.

She didn't even know what it meant. She didn't understand why it filled her mind and simply shoved aside every other thought.

But as she gazed in growing horror at that dark sky all Diana could think was, My baby.

My baby.

My baby.

Cigar wandered, not really knowing where he was. Nothing looked like it should look. In his world, things – houses, curbs, street signs, abandoned cars – were merest shadows. He could make out their edges, enough to avoid walking into them.

But living things were twisty phantasms of light. A palm tree became a narrow, silent tornado funnel. Bushes beside the road were a thousand crooked fingers twisting together like the hands of a cartoon miser. A seagull floated overhead looking like a small, pale hand waving goodbye.

Was any of it real?

How was he to know?

Cigar had memories of days when he was Bradley. He could see things in his memory that were so different: people who looked flat and two-dimensional. Like they were pictures in an aged magazine. Places that were so brightly lit the colours were all washed out.

Bradley. Have you cleaned your room yet?

His room. His stuff. His Wii. The controller was in the messed-up covers of his bed.

We have to get going, Bradley, so do me a favour and just clean up your room, OK? Don't make me have to yell at you. I don't want to have that kind of day.

I'm doing it! Jeez! I said I'd do it!

Ahead of him, someone who looked like a fox. Funny-looking. Moving faster than him, moving away, looking back with sharp fox eyes and then running away.

Cigar followed the fox.

More people. Wow. It was like a parade of angels and prancing devils and dogs walking erect, and ooh, even a walking fish with gossamer fins.

Red dust floated up from them, thickening as more of the

kids came together. The red dust began to pulse, like a heart, like a slow strobe.

Cigar felt fear squeeze his heart.

Oh, God, oh, no, no, no. Fear. The red dust, it was fear, and look, it was coming from him, too, and when he looked close it wasn't particles of dust; it was hundreds and thousands of tiny, twisty worms.

Oh, no, no, this wasn't real. This was one of Penny's visions. But the red dust flowed over the heads and sank down into the mouths and ears and eyes of all the prancing, twirling, skipping, running, mad assembly.

Then Cigar felt its presence. The little boy.

He turned to see it but it wasn't behind him. Or in front. Or on either side. It was somewhere no eye could turn to. The little boy was there, though, in the space just to the side, just not quite where his eyes could see, in that sliver of reality that was not where you could see.

But could feel.

The little boy was really not so little. Maybe he was vast. Maybe he could reach down with one giant finger and twist Cigar inside out.

But maybe the little boy was as suspect as everything else Cigar saw.

Cigar followed the crowd that was heading towards the plaza.

* * *

Lana stood on her balcony. There was just enough light to see the stain that had painted most of the sky black. The sky high overhead was actually beginning to turn blue now. Sky blue. The dome was like an eyeball seen from the inside: where it should be white was opaque black, but with a blue iris up above.

It filled her with rage. It was mockery. A fake light in a fake sky as darkness closed in to shut off the last of the light.

She had had the chance to destroy it. The Darkness. She was convinced of it. And every evil thing that later had flowed from that monstrous entity was on her shoulders.

It had beaten her. It had overpowered her by sheer force of will.

She had crawled to it on hands and knees.

It had used her. Made her a part of it. Made its words come from her mouth. Made her point a gun at a friend and pull the trigger.

Her hand strayed to the pistol in her belt.

She closed her eyes and could almost see the green tendril reaching to touch her mind and invade her soul. Taking a shaky breath she lowered the wall of resistance she had built around herself. She wanted to tell it that she was not beaten yet, that she was not scared. And she wanted it to hear her.

Now again, as had happened from time to time recently, she felt the hunger, the need of the gaiaphage. But she felt something else, too.

Fear.

The bringer of fear was afraid.

Lana's eyes had closed. They snapped open now. A chill went down her spine.

'Afraid, are you?' she whispered.

It needed something. Needed it desperately.

Lana squeezed her eyes tight again, willing herself to do what she had refused to do before: to try to reach back across the void and touch the gaiaphage.

What is it you want so terribly, you monster?

What is it you need?

Tell me so I can kill it and you at the same time.

A voice – Lana could have sworn it was a real voice, a girl's voice – whispered, *My baby.*

Albert watched the crowd of kids, all pushing into the plaza. He could feel the fear. He could feel their desperation.

No crops would be picked. The market would never open.

It was the end. And time was short.

Kids brushed past him, stopped, realised who they had bumped into, and one of them said, 'What's going to happen, Albert?'

'What does this mean?'

'What are we supposed to do?'

Be afraid, Albert thought. *Be afraid, because there's nothing left to do now. So be afraid and then panic, and then spread violence and destruction.*

He felt sick inside.

Within hours everything he had built would be gone. He could see it too clearly.

'But you always knew it would come to a bad end,' he whispered.

'What?'

'What did he say?'

He stared at the kids. There was a crowd around him now. Crowds were dangerous. He had to keep them calm long enough to make his own escape.

He raised a disapproving eyebrow. 'You can start by not freaking out. The king will handle it.' Then, with his trademark cool arrogance, he added, 'And if he doesn't, I will.'

He turned and walked away. Behind him he heard a couple of uncertain cheers, and some encouraging words.

They'd bought it for now.

Idiots.

As he walked he went over a list in his head. His maid, Leslie-Ann, because she had saved his life. And Alicia, because she could handle a gun but wasn't ambitious. And she was cute. One of his security guys? No. Any one of them might turn on him. No, he'd get that girl they called Pug: she was very strong and too dumb to make trouble.

Just the four of them would take the boat to the island.

That would be enough to keep watch and man the missiles he'd arranged to smuggle on to the island. And to blow anyone else who arrived, uninvited, out of the water.

TWENTY THREE

14 HOURS 44 MINUTES

'COME ALONG, KING Caine,' Penny taunted.

Caine dragged the stone between his legs, bent over. The blood from the staples in his head had dried, but from time to time the tiny wounds would start bleeding again. And then the blood would run into his right eye and all he would see was red until he could blink it away.

He would gather his strength sometimes and heft the stone and walk painfully forward. But he couldn't hold it for long.

It was a long, slow, infinitely painful and humiliating walk/crawl to the plaza.

He was exhausted beyond belief. His mouth and throat were parched.

And for a long time he thought it must still be night. The street was dark, but with an eerie quality that wasn't like moonlight. Light seemed to be shining down faintly from above. Like a dull flashlight.

Shadows were eerie. They were the narrow shadows of high

noon, but dim. The air itself seemed to have taken on a sepia colour, as if he was looking at an old photograph.

Caine noticed Penny craning her neck and staring up at the sky. He blinked the blood out of his eyes and painfully twisted his neck back to see.

The dome was black. The sky was a blue hole in a black sphere.

Caine began to notice kids in the street, all walking towards the plaza. Their voices had that giddy, jumpy sound kids got when they were scared. He watched the backs of heads as they craned to look up at the sky.

People were walking hunched over, like they thought the sky might fall on them.

It was a while longer before the first person noticed Penny and Caine. That kid's cries turned every eye towards Caine.

He didn't know what to expect. Outrage? Joy?

What he got was silence. Kids would be talking, then turn to see him dragging his cement block, and the words would die in their mouths. Their eyes would widen. If there was any pleasure there it was very well concealed.

'What's happening to the sky?' Penny demanded, finally noticing something beyond herself. She glared at the nearest kids. 'Answer me or I'll make you wish you were dead!'

Shrugs. Shakes of the head. Backing away quickly.

'Keep moving,' she snarled at Caine.

They were in the plaza now and Penny shoved Caine in the direction of town hall.

'I need water,' Caine rasped.

'Get up the stairs,' Penny said.

'Drop dead.'

And instantly a pair of rabid dogs, their necks bearing massive iron collars, their teeth glowing pink from behind mouths full of foam, attacked him from behind.

He could feel their teeth sinking into his buttocks.

The pain – no, no, he told himself, the illusion, the illusion. But it was too real; it was impossible not to believe it as the dogs ripped at him and he cried out in agony and rage and dragged his burden away, up the first step.

The dogs fell back, but snarled and foamed and barked so loud he felt he might go deaf.

Caine dragged his burden up one step after the next.

At the top, in the very place where he had often addressed crowds as king, he collapsed, shaking with fatigue. He fell on to his imprisoned hands.

After a while someone pushed his head back and he felt a jar touch his lips. He drank the water, gulping it down, choking but not caring.

Caine opened his eyes and saw that the crowd had grown. And it had edged forward. Their faces wore expressions of horror and fear.

He had made enemies during his four months in charge. But what was happening now obliterated all of that. Right now this crowd was scared. Deep-down scared. Eyes went skyward again and again, checking to see if there was still any light, any light at all.

Caine searched the crowd through bleary eyes. He had one hope: Albert.

Albert would not let this stand. Albert had armed guards. He was probably figuring out right now how to save Caine.

But another part of Caine's mind was yammering that there was no way to escape the concrete. He knew: he had inflicted this on freaks early on. And the only reason any of them had been able to escape was that Little Pete had intervened.

Caine hadn't known at the time that it was Little Pete's doing. He had been deaf, dumb, blind, and stupid not to realise the little autistic creep was the real power. And now Little Pete was dead and gone.

Which left breaking the concrete chip by chip with a sledgehammer.

The pain would be unbearable. It would break every bone in his hands. Lana might be able to help, but first would come the pain.

As soon as Albert dealt with Penny.

'Here's your king!' Penny cried in a gloating voice. 'See? See the crown I gave him? Do you like it?'

No one answered.

'I said, don't you like it?' Penny screeched.

A couple of the kids nodded or muttered, 'Yeah.'

'OK,' Penny said. 'OK, then.' She sounded unsure what to do next. Her fantasy hadn't gone any farther than this. And now, Caine knew, she was trying to figure out how to enjoy her victory.

Her temporary victory.

'I know!' Penny said. 'Let's see if King Caine can dance. How about that?'

Again, the stunned and traumatised audience didn't know how to respond.

'Dance!' Penny roared in a voice that disappeared into a squeak. 'Dance, dance, dance!'

And suddenly the limestone beneath Caine's feet burst into flames. The pain was instant and unbearable.

'Dance, dance, dance!' Penny cried, jumping up and down. She was waving her awkward arms at the kids, urging them to chant along with her.

As the flames crisped the flesh on his legs Caine kicked and jerked madly in a bizarre parody of dancing.

The flames stopped.

Caine panted, waiting for the next assault.

But now Penny seemed to be out of steam. She slumped a little and looked at him. Their eyes met and he burned hatred at her. But it had no effect. Caine knew she was deranged. He'd known all along that she was a psycho, but psychos could be useful.

But this wasn't as simple as Drake's evil ruthlessness. This was madness. He was looking at eyes that were no longer partaking of reality.

She was insane.

He had helped to drive her mad.

And now all her rage, all her jealousy, all the hate that Caine had used for his own purposes was being turned against him.

He was a powerless toy in the hands of a lunatic with the power to make him as crazy as she was herself.

The FAYZ, Caine thought dully. *I always knew it would end in madness or death.*

For the first time, literally the first time, his thoughts went to the baby inside Diana. His own son or daughter. All that would be left of him when Penny was finished.

It might have gone either way for Penny at that moment. The crowd was nervous and unsure.

'Now I am the queen, and I am the boss in charge,' Penny announced. 'And I don't have to tell any of you what I can do. Do I?'

No response. Cautious silence.

Then a voice from the back. 'Let him go. We need him!'

Caine didn't recognise the voice. Neither, apparently, did Penny.

'Who said that?'

Silence.

Caine could hear Penny panting. She was in a very excited state. Mostly she didn't know what to do next. She had expected . . . something. But she had not expected to be completely overshadowed by this terrible darkness.

'Where is Albert?' Penny demanded petulantly. 'I want him here so I can tell him how it is now.'

No answer.

'I said, bring me Albert!' she screamed. 'Albert! Albert! Come out, you coward!'

Nothing.

But now the crowd was moving from fearful to mad. They didn't like this. They were scared and they had come seeking reassurance. What they were getting instead was a shrieking girl who had disabled the most powerful person in town precisely when they desperately needed someone to do something about the fact that the light was dying.

'Let him go, you stupid witch!'

Caine appreciated that, but the cold, calculating part of his mind was wondering just where Albert was. Albert had half a dozen guys who would shoot Penny if he ordered it. For that matter Albert could say something as simple as,

'Everyone who wants a job tomorrow, attack her now.'

Where was he?

The top third of the dome was brightening. But that only made it easier to see the tendrils of stain, like a circle of teeth, slowly advancing.

Where was Albert?

Quinn led his boats into the marina.

Last time, maybe, he thought. It made his heart want to break.

He had awakened very early in his camp up the coast – his biological clock ran on fisherman time – and seen that the stain would eat the sun.

They had fished for what they could get in the early hours. But the heart was gone from them. The strike was over whether they wanted it or not: their world was dying, and they had bigger problems than the injustice done, or the loyalty they owed, to Cigar.

Albert and three girls were coming down the dock towards him. The three girls each had a backpack. Albert carried the big ledger book he used to keep track of his businesses.

'Why aren't you fishing?' Albert asked.

Quinn wasn't buying that act. 'Where are you going, Albert?'

Albert said nothing. *How rare*, Quinn thought: *Albert speechless.*

'Not really your concern, Quinn,' Albert said finally.

'You're running out.'

Albert sighed. To his three companions he said, 'Go ahead and get in the boat. The Boston Whaler. Yes, that one.' Turning back to Quinn he said, 'It's been good doing business with you. If you want, you can come with us. We have room for one more. You're a good guy.'

'And my crews?'

'Limited resources, Quinn.'

Quinn laughed a little. 'You're a piece of work, aren't you, Albert?'

Albert didn't seem bothered. 'I'm a businessman. It's about making a profit and surviving. It so happens that I've kept everyone alive for months. So I guess I'm sorry if you don't like me, Quinn, but what's coming next isn't about business. What's coming next is craziness. We're going back to the days of starvation. But in the dark this time. Craziness. Madness.'

His eyes glinted when he said that last word. Quinn saw the fear there. Madness. Yes, that would terrify the eternally rational businessman.

'All that happens if I stay,' Albert continued, 'is that someone decides to kill me. I've already come too close to being dead once.'

'Albert, you're a leader. You're an organiser. We're going to need that.'

Albert waved an impatient hand and glanced over to see

that the Boston Whaler was ready. 'Caine's a leader. Sam's a leader. Me?' Albert considered it for a second and shook the idea off. 'No. I'm important, but I'm not a leader. Tell you what, though, Quinn: in my absence you speak for me. If that helps, good for you.'

Albert climbed down into the Boston Whaler. Pug started the engine and Leslie-Ann cast off the ropes. Some of the last gasoline in Perdido Beach sent the boat chugging out of the marina.

'Hey, Quinn!' Albert shouted back. 'Don't come to the island without showing a white flag. I don't want to blow you up!'

Quinn wondered how he would ever reach the island. And how Albert would be able to see a white flag if he did. Unless something changed no one would be seeing anything. It would be a world of universal blindness.

That thought made him think of Cigar. Cigar and his creepy little BB eyes. He had to locate Cigar. Whatever happened, he was still crew.

He heard a surge of sound from the plaza, voices yelling, and one shrill voice screeching. He knew that screech.

He started towards town, then stopped and waited as his fishermen gathered around him. 'Guys, I . . . I, um, don't know what's happening. We may never fish together again. And, you know . . . But I'm thinking it's better if we stick together anyway.'

As an inspirational rallying speech, it was pretty lame. And yet, it worked. He walked towards the sounds of fear and anger with all his people behind him.

Lana kept her hoodie pulled close around her face. She did not want to be recognised by anyone in the crowd. She had come down to town only to see whether Caine would arrange an armed escort for her. She'd found a scene out of some deranged horror novel.

In eerie shadows the crowd of some two hundred kids, armed with spiked baseball bats, crowbars, table legs, chains, knives and axes, dressed in mismatched rags and remnants of costume, stood facing a prancing, fist-shaking, wild-eyed, barefoot lunatic and a handsome boy with a crown stapled to his scalp and his hands trapped in a block of concrete.

Now they were taking up a chant. 'Let him go. Let him go.'

They were chanting for Caine. They were scared to death and now, finally, they really wanted a king. They really wanted anyone who would save them.

'Let him go! Let him go!'

And a second chant: 'We want the king! We want the king!'

Sudden screams from those closest to the steps. Lana could see kids falling back, clawing at their faces, crying out.

Penny had attacked!

'Kill the witch!' a voice bellowed.

A club went flying through the air. It missed Penny. A chunk of concrete, a knife, all missed.

Penny raised her hands over her head and screamed obscenities. A chunk of something hit her arm and drew blood.

The kids who'd been struck by her visions panicked and ran from her, but other kids were shoving forward. It was a melee, a tangle of arms and legs and weapons, shouts, orders; and suddenly from the far side came a wedge of disciplined kids moving forward with arms linked, pushing between the steps and the crowd.

Lana recognised the boy at the centre of that wedge. She laughed in rueful surprise.

'Quinn,' she said to herself. 'Well.'

Penny was staring transfixed at the wound on her arm, but she tore herself away to advance on Quinn. 'You!'

Quinn cried out in agony. There was no way to know what Penny was doing to him, but it must have been awful.

Lana had had enough. There were injured kids. There were about to be more injured kids. Her mission to warn Diana wasn't going to happen.

Lana drew her pistol. 'Get out of my way,' she snapped at two kids blocking her path. She moved quickly, unnoticed, down First Avenue, skirting the crowd from the opposite direction that Quinn had taken.

A panicky riot had broken out at the base of the steps as

Penny wreaked all the damage her sick mind could conjure. Kids were attacking one another, seeing monsters where none existed.

Lana flinched as a crowbar rose high and came down with a sickening crunch.

She made it to the church steps and crossed over from there to town hall. Caine glanced and saw her. Penny did not.

Lana levelled the gun at Penny. 'Stop,' Lana said.

Penny's reddened face grew pale. Whatever visions she was inflicting on the people below her stopped. Kids cried in pain, sobbed from the memories.

'Oh, everyone has to kiss your butt, don't they, Healer.' Penny spit that last word. She made her hands into claws and pawed at the air. Her lips were drawn back in a teeth-baring animal snarl.

'If I shoot you, I won't heal you,' Lana said calmly.

That caught Penny off guard. But she recovered quickly. She put her head down and started to laugh. It began low and rose a few decibels at a time.

Lana's arm burst into flame.

A noose was flung from the ruined church wall. The rope dropped over her head, landed on her shoulders, and tightened around her throat.

The limestone beneath her feet was suddenly a forest of knives all stabbing up at her.

'Yeah,' Lana said. 'That won't work on me. I've gone one-on-one with the gaiaphage. He could teach you a few things. Stop it. Now. Or bang.'

Penny's laugh choked off. She looked hurt. As if someone had said something cruel to her. The visions ceased as suddenly as if someone had switched off a TV.

'I'm kind of opposed to murder,' Lana said. 'But if you don't turn and walk away, I'll blow a hole right where your heart is supposed to be.'

'You can't . . .' Penny said. 'You . . . No.'

'I missed killing a monster once. I've always regretted it,' Lana said. 'But you're a human. Sort of. So you get this chance: walk. Keep walking.'

For what felt like a very long time Penny stood staring at Lana. Not with hatred, but with disbelief. Lana saw her very, very clearly: a head resting atop the sights of her pistol.

She took a step back. Then another. There was a wild look of defiance, but then it died.

Penny spun on her heel and walked quickly away.

Quinn quietly motioned three of his people to follow her.

A dozen or more kids were screaming now for her blood, demanding she be killed.

Lana stuck her gun back in her waistband.

'I don't think Caine is in any condition,' Lana said. Then she raised her voice to be heard. As usual she sounded irritated and impatient. 'So here's the way it is: Quinn is boss. For now. Mess with him, and you mess with me. And I will cut you off from healing. You lose a leg, I will stand by and watch you bleed out. Clear?'

It was apparently clear.

'Good. Now I have work to do. Get out of my way.' She descended into the gore left in Penny's wake. Quinn came to her side.

'Me?' he said.

'For now. Make sure Penny leaves town. Kill her if you want to, because she'll be trouble if she lives.'

Quinn made a face. 'I don't think I'm a guy who kills people.'

Lana smiled her exceedingly rare smile. 'Yeah, I think I figured that out about you, Quinn. Send one of your people to bring Sanjit down here. He has to reach Sam. So find him a gun. Taylor is done for, and we need to be working with Sam, so it's communication the old-fashioned way. Being divided will get us all killed.'

'You've got it.'

Lana's smile died. 'The Darkness is going after Diana. She has to be warned.'

'Diana? Why?'

'Because she has a baby in her belly. And the Darkness needs to be born.'

TWENTY FOUR

14 HOURS 39 MINUTES

DRAKE EMERGED.

He had no idea where he was. It was a cramped, damp place that smelled of oil. He moved his head slightly and felt an impact that would have been pain back in the old days. He had bumped against something steel.

He blinked. The light was very dim. It came from a square in the low ceiling. He realised it was the edge of some kind of hatch. Just inches above him.

With his hand and his tentacle he felt around this tiny space. It took some time to make sense of things. The complex metal object. The square of light. The way the floor seemed to move slightly beneath him. The smell of oil.

He was on a boat.

In the engine room.

Barely room to move.

He grinned. Well, well: clever Brittney. Good job. Somehow she had found a way to sneak aboard one of the boats. Probably not the boat where he'd seen Diana. Could she have pulled that off? Simple metal-mouthed Brittney?

No. But a boat. Definitely a boat.

Nice.

Now what? He still had to get to Diana.

Easier said than done. First, he had to know where he was. He spent a good twenty minutes trying to squirm his body in such a way as to bring his head up against the hatch. He couldn't hold the position for long.

He held himself in place by wedging his hand against the engine block, then used the tip of his tentacle to push gently, gently upwards on the hatch.

It moved up easily enough, A quarter of an inch. A half an inch. And then he could see a long, very narrow slice of the world beyond. A single spoke of a steering wheel. A bucket. Then a foot.

He lowered the hatch as quietly as he had raised it.

Something had bumped against the side of the boat. He heard a muffled voice, a guy.

Then a second male voice that froze his marrow. Sam.

Sam!

Drake heard sounds of someone clambering up the side. Now he could hear the voices more distinctly.

'T'sup, Roger?' Sam said. 'Hey, Justin, hey, Atria. How are you guys holding up?'

The first male voice, presumably 'Roger', whoever that was, said, 'We're fine. Doing fine.'

'Good. Well, I'm just here to hang some lights for you.'

'Sammy suns? So . . .' Roger hesitated. 'Why don't you kids go play? Old people talk here.' The sound of running feet, but no high-pitched voices. Then, 'So it's like that?'

'Well, Roger, we don't know for sure.' Sam sounded weary. Could Drake take him? Right here and now when he was alone, without Brianna or Dekka to add to his power?

No, Drake told himself. He would never get up out of this hatch before Sam started burning him. And his mission was to get Diana, not kill Sam.

'Is it going to be totally dark?' Roger asked in a voice that quavered just a bit.

'Not totally dark,' Sam said reassuringly. 'That's why I'm here. You'll have plenty of light on-board. Is she up or is she asleep?'

They wandered out of earshot at that point, presumably into the cabin. But Drake had heard a female pronoun.

Was it possible? Was Diana on this very boat?

He grinned in the darkness. He would wait and be sure. The opportunity would arise. His faith in the gaiaphage had not failed him yet.

From boat to boat, one after the next, Sam rowed.

At each boat he climbed aboard and crouched to enter whatever cabin they had. In the smaller sailboats or motorboats he installed one or two Sammy suns.

Sammy suns were the long-lasting manifestation of his power. Rather than firing light in a killing beam he could form balls of light, which then burned without heat and hung in the air. They experimented a bit and discovered that the Sammy sun would stay in place relative to the boat when it moved, a rather important consideration.

Some of the boats, like the houseboats, got as many as three or four Sammy suns.

It took a couple of hours to do this. And halfway through Sam realised he was feeling very weary. He'd had this same feeling after battles where he'd had to use his powers. He'd always assumed it was just the depression that followed any fight. Now he was wondering if the use of the power itself had some kind of tiring effect.

Maybe. But it didn't matter. The Sammy suns were reassuring to kids. No one – least of all Sam – could tolerate the idea of being trapped in perpetual darkness. It was inconceivable. It struck terror right down to his core.

The last Sammy suns were for the big houseboat. Five in all, including an especially large one floating beside the front railing.

They would be in the dark. But they would not be totally blind.

'That helps,' Edilio said, welcoming him back.

'For a while,' he said grimly.

'For a while,' he agreed.

He couldn't help but pick up his binoculars and scan the shore. Orc was still out searching. Good. If they were lucky he might find Drake, and Sam would rush to help.

But he wasn't really interested in watching Orc. It was Astrid he searched for.

If she made it to Perdido Beach, what was the earliest she could get back? It had to be before the sky closed. If she was trapped out there in the dark she would have to literally crawl along the road. And not everything needed light to hunt and kill. The darkness might keep Drake at bay, but the coyotes and snakes and zekes . . .

He had to do something. But he didn't know what. It ate out his insides, that not knowing what to do.

'I could hang Sammy suns along the road,' he said.

'Once we have a deal with Albert and Caine,' Edilio agreed. 'But if we do it now, it will just be a beacon enticing all of Perdido Beach to come. We aren't ready for that.'

Sam clenched his mouth shut. He hadn't really expected Edilio to say anything about it. He was just thinking out loud. And he was still mad at Edilio. He needed to be mad at someone, and Edilio was there.

Worse, Edilio did not seem to fear the coming darkness. He

was his usual calm, capable self. Normally that was reassuring. But Sam was having a hard time just taking a full breath. He was exhausted from hanging suns and making all sorts of reassuring noises to his people on the boats.

He didn't believe what he was saying. Astrid was out there somewhere. Darkness was coming. The endgame was being played. And he had no plan.

He had no plan.

Sam looked up. The sun was now beginning to appear as it rose above the edge of the stain. Way, way too high in the sky. But the light was welcome. Welcome and heartbreaking when he contemplated the fact that he might never see it again.

The water sparkled. The white hulls brightened. The village, the little campground, and nearby woods lit up.

Edilio was watching one of the boats through his own binoculars. 'It's Sinder,' he reported. 'She wants permission for her and Jezzie to go ashore and harvest their veggies.'

'Yeah. It makes sense.' He raised his voice to a shout. 'Breeze! Dekka! On deck!' Then in a normal speaking voice to Edilio he said, 'Sinder will need someone watching her back.'

Brianna appeared seconds after the sound of her nickname died. Dekka came up a few moments later.

'It's light enough for you, Breeze,' Sam said.

'Yeah, it's Florida in July,' Brianna said, rolling her eyes at the strange tea-stained light.

'I thought you wanted to go back out,' Sam said tersely.

'Dude. Of course I do. Chill. I was just making a joke.'

'Yeah,' Sam said, teeth still gritted. His jaw hurt. His shoulders were knots of pain. 'Soon as Sinder gets near shore you meet her. Stay on her until she and Jezzie are done.'

'I don't have to sit right on top of them,' Brianna said with faux innocence. 'I mean, I can go in and out, you know? Check on them, run down the road a ways, see what's what . . .'

Before Sam could answer Edilio said, 'We need a strategy, not a lot of people running off in different directions. Astrid's probably in PB by now. If Drake attacks us here, we'll need you, Brianna. But if you run into him without Sam the best you can get is a draw.'

It made perfect logical sense. But it did nothing to address Sam's desperate desire to do. To do. Not to talk, or watch, or worry, but to do.

The mission to grab the missiles had done little to ease his desire for action. Without thinking about it he held his palms up before his face. How long since he had fired the killing light rather than just hanging lights?

He realised Edilio and Dekka were both watching him with solemn expressions. Brianna was smirking. All three of them had read his thoughts.

'Well, we can eat some big-ass radishes, at least,' Sam muttered lamely.

'All this is just coping,' Dekka said. 'None of it is about winning.'

'Drake is here. Somewhere. The gaiaphage is . . . no one knows exactly where,' Edilio said. 'We don't even know what's happening in Perdido Beach. We don't know what Albert is up to. We don't know where Caine stands in all this. We don't know why Taylor hasn't bounced in to tell us what is going on.'

'Yeah, I get it,' Sam said bitterly. 'Astrid's right to try to reach Perdido Beach. And meanwhile we're stuck. Tied down. Flies on one of those sticky strips.'

Sam's palms felt itchy. He squeezed his fists tight.

There was logic. And then there was instinct. Sam's instinct was screaming that he was losing a fight with each passing, passive, patient second.

The rising sun cast deep shadows on Astrid's soul. It was one thing to know it was going to happen. It was a very different thing to see it.

The sky itself was disappearing. This would be the last daylight of the FAYZ.

She looked around, trying to orientate herself. The result was near panic. The road from the lake to Perdido Beach went in a southwesterly direction along the western slope of the Santa Katrina Hills. Then it intersected the highway.

But she'd lost sight of the road. And she'd somehow managed to wander into a gap between two hills.

The Santa Katrinas weren't the biggest hills, though up close they could be imposing. They were dry, of course, without rainfall in the FAYZ. She remembered seeing them from the highway long ago after December rain, when they had suddenly turned green. But now they were just rock and desiccated weeds and stubby, struggling trees.

The road was presumably straight back to the west. But that could be miles, and she might find herself hitting the road no more than a mile or two from Lake Tramonto. That would be humiliating if Sam had sent Brianna out to find her. It would make Astrid's mission to warn Perdido Beach look like the harebrained scheme of an incompetent girl.

Already she'd been delayed. The dawn – such as it was – had come. People in Perdido Beach could see it without any help from her.

Which meant that all she could do now was hope to send a message of solidarity and to offer Sam's services as a light bringer.

Even that relied on speed. She was sure some kids at least would already be on their way out of Perdido Beach.

If she wanted speed, she'd have to go through the hills. If this pass went all the way through in a more or less straight line, then no problem. If it dead-ended against some hill, she'd have to climb, that would be a problem.

Astrid set off at a trot. She was very fit after her months living in the woods and could move at this half-run, half-walk pace for hours so long as she had water.

The hills rose on either side. The one on the right began to seem oppressive, steep and glowering. The peak was exposed rock where some long-ago storm or earthquake had stripped the thin topsoil away. And that exposed rock looked like a grim-faced head.

The trail continued to be pretty easy. Once upon a time there'd been running water, but now the narrow streambed was choked with dried-out weeds.

Astrid saw something move up to her right, up the sheer slope of what she was thinking of as Mount Grimface. She didn't stop, but kept moving, looked and now saw nothing.

'Don't get spooked,' she told herself. That kind of thing had happened a lot in the forest: a noise, a sudden movement, a flash of something or other. And inevitably she'd been afraid it was Drake. Just as inevitably it had been a bird or a squirrel or a skunk.

Now, though, the sense that she was being watched was hard to shake. As if Mount Grimface really was a face and it was watching her and not liking what it saw.

Ahead the path curved away to the left, and Astrid welcomed the chance to move away from the sinister mountain, but at the same time, as she took that curve, she had an almost overpowering sense that whatever had been watching her was now behind her.

And coming closer.

The urge to break into a full-on run was hard to resist. But she couldn't look as if she was fleeing, panicking.

She came around a blind corner and almost ploughed into him.

Astrid stopped. Stared. Screamed.

Screamed so that she forgot to draw her gun until she was already screaming and backing away, and finally out came the shotgun and her fingers fumbled for the trigger. She raised the gun to her shoulder, sighted down the barrel.

She aimed for the eyes. Those awful marble-size eyes in bloody-black sockets.

It was a boy. That fact took a few long beats to penetrate her consciousness. Not some giant monster, a boy. He had strong shoulders and a deep tan. There were cuts on his face, like the claw marks of a wild animal. They seemed fresh. And she saw blood on his fingernails.

His expression was impossible to read – the eyes, those awful chickpea-size eyes – made any emotion impossible to guess.

'Don't move or I'll blow your head off,' Astrid said.

The boy stopped walking. The eyes seemed unable to locate her, looking up and left and everywhere but straight at her.

'Are you real?' the boy asked.

'I'm real. So is this shotgun.' Astrid heard the quaver in her voice, but her grip on the gun was steady and she was keeping it on target. One squeeze of her right index finger and there'd be a loud noise and that horrifying head would explode like a water balloon.

'Are you . . . Are you Astrid?'

She swallowed hard. How did it know her name? 'Who are you?'

'Bradley. But everyone calls me Cigar.'

The gun lowered several inches of its own accord. 'What? Cigar?'

The boy's mouth made a sort of grin. The grin revealed broken and missing teeth.

'I see you,' Cigar said. He stretched out a bloody hand to her, but like a blind person feeling for something he couldn't quite locate.

'Stay back,' she snapped, and the gun went to her shoulder again. 'What happened to you?'

'I . . .' He tried another smile, but it twisted into a grimace and then a terrible groan, a cry of agony that stretched on and on before ending in a wild burst of laughter.

'Listen, Cigar, you need to tell me what happened,' Astrid insisted.

'Penny,' he whispered. 'She showed me things. My hands were . . .' He raised his palms to look at them, but his eyes were elsewhere, and a moan came from deep in his throat.

'Penny did this?' Astrid lowered the gun. Halfway. Then, hesitantly, all the way down. But she did not sling it back over her shoulder. She kept her grip tight and her finger resting on the trigger guard.

'I like candy, see, and I did a bad thing and then the candy was in my arm and then I was eating it and oh, it tasted so good, you know, and Penny gave me more, so I ate it up and it hurt and there was blood, maybe, lots of blood, maybe, maybe.'

The tiny eyes swivelled suddenly to look past Astrid.

'It's the little boy,' Cigar said.

Astrid glanced over her shoulder, just quick, just a glance, almost involuntary because she wasn't ready to lower her guard yet, not ready to turn around. Her head was already turning back towards Cigar when she realised what she had seen.

Seen? Nothing much. A distortion. A twisting of the visual field.

She looked back. Nothing.

Then back to Cigar.

'What was that?'

'The little boy.' Cigar giggled and placed his hand over his mouth like he'd said a dirty word. Then in a low whisper, 'The little boy.'

Astrid's throat was tight. The flesh on her arms rose into goosebumps. 'What little boy, Cigar?'

'He knows you,' Cigar said, very confidential, like he was telling a secret. 'You're screaming yellow hair. Stabby blue eyes. He knows you, he told me.'

Astrid tried to speak and couldn't. Couldn't ask the question. Couldn't accept what the answer might be. But at last, strangled words came from her mouth.

'The little boy. Is his name Pete?'

Cigar reached to touch his own eye, but stopped. He looked for a moment as if he were listening to something, though there was nothing but the sounds of gentle breeze and grating grasshoppers. Then he nodded eagerly and said, 'Little boy says: "Hello, sister."'

OUTSIDE

SERGEANT DARIUS ASHTON was very good with a truck engine. This did not mean he was necessarily good with an air compressor. But his lieutenant said a mechanic was needed at a site around the far side of the dome.

'That's the air base, Lieutenant,' Darius protested. 'They don't have an HVAC mechanic over there?'

'Not one with your security clearance,' the lieutenant said.

'A security clearance for an air conditioner?'

The lieutenant wasn't a bad guy, young but not arrogant. He said, 'Sergeant, I would have thought by now, with your long experience in uniform, you'd know better than to expect everything to make sense.'

Darius couldn't argue with that. He saluted and turned on his heel. A cheerful female driver, a corporal who knew the drive well, was waiting behind the wheel of a Humvee. Darius loaded his tools in the back. The corporal had done a tour in Kabul, something she and Darius had in common, so they talked about that on the long, circuitous drive. And they talked about this supposedly great new Cuban pitcher who had reached the United States on a raft. The Angels were going to sign him.

The drive went up the highway, then on to a series of gravel side roads. There was another way to reach the Evanston Air National Guard base, but it would mean going all the way to I-5, then back south. This path was bumpy and dusty but it was quicker.

Much of the drive was within sight of the bowl. Darius had got used to it. Ten miles high, twenty miles across. It looked like someone had dropped a small, smoothly polished moon down on the Southern California coastline.

But there was no crater, no fracture lines. It hadn't landed; it hadn't exploded; it had just suddenly existed. A gigantic terrarium.

'Been here long?' Darius asked, nodding at the dome.

'Just transferred in last month,' the corporal said. 'I saw it on TV, like everyone else. But it's something in person.'

'It is that.'

'Weird thinking there are kids in there.'

They pulled up at a facility that had obviously been recently built. It had all the usual obsessive military neatness and order. A dozen buildings in ruler-straight rows. A barracks, an officers' quarters, a number of command trailers, a communications building bristling with dishes and antennae.

The base was a hive of activity. Men and women bustling back and forth with very busy expressions on their faces. No one was lounging or grabbing a smoke or chatting on the phone. There was a self-conscious sense of Very Important Stuff Happening.

The facility was ringed with chain link topped with extremely serious-looking razor wire. The gate was guarded by unsmiling military police. IDs were checked against a manifest showing that yes, they were both expected.

One of the MPs accompanied them to one of the trailers. The corporal peeled off and Darius stepped into a blast of air-conditioning.

A sergeant asked him again for his ID. Then he handed Darius a paper to sign. The paper required him to reveal nothing of the purpose of his visit, of the existence of the facility, of the work there, of any of the personnel assigned there.

There was a great deal of official-ese and some decidedly threatening language.

'You understand, Sergeant, that you are governed by this security protocol?'

'Yes, Sergeant. I do.'

'You understand that any violation will result in criminal prosecution?'

The word 'will' had been emphasised, and not subtly.

'I believe I'm getting the message, Sarge.'

The sergeant smiled. 'They keep a very tight lid. Report to building oh-one-four. Your driver will know where it is.'

The driver did.

Building 014 was half a mile from the rest of the camp, which put it a full mile away from the dome wall. It was a vast, hangar-style tin structure. Huge and imposing. It was painted the colour of the surrounding desert.

Darius hefted his tool bag and was met at the door by an MP. One more ID check. Then Darius stepped inside the hangar.

What he saw made him stare. A half dozen trucks filled with dirt. A tower that looked like it had been assembled from leftover bits and pieces of a suspension bridge or maybe the Eiffel Tower.

The MP took him to a civilian in a construction worker's helmet and handed him off. The civilian shook his hand and identified himself as 'Charlie. Just Charlie. Sorry to drag you out here, but our head HVAC mechanic is on paternity leave, and her assistant managed to break an ankle surfing. You're not claustrophobic, are you?'

The question surprised Darius. 'Why?'

'Because we are going deep. The unit we need you to look at is a blower at kilometre six.'

'What's that mean?'

'It means we're going two miles down, my friend. Two clicks

straight down and four clicks south. Kilometre six.'

Darius felt cold. 'That would put you . . . up against the dome. Why . . . I mean, what . . .'

Charlie shrugged and said, 'My friend, the first thing you learn working here is, don't ask questions.'

The elevator ride down seemed endless.

And yet quicker than the narrow-gauge train that carried Darius along an impressive and oppressive tunnel, wide enough to accommodate two rail lines with space on either side. The tunnel was shored up at regular intervals with railroad ties.

Kilometre six turned out to be a cavern bigger than the hangar. The far end was formed by the barrier. Here it was black, not pearly grey.

'It was good luck finding this cave,' Charlie said. 'Would have been a long, hard job carving it out. You know, usually we'd have a hundred guys down here. But as you can probably smell, the air is getting a bit thick.'

'That's why I'm here, right?'

In the cave stood a tall scaffolding tilted at a strange, Leaning Tower of Pisa angle. Darius knew enough about machinery to recognise a drilling platform.

From this spot they were drilling farther still, down below the dome. Not a tunnel for humans. Just a round shaft into which a bomb could be lowered to the lowest point beneath the dome.

Charlie must have seen the look in Darius's eyes. He gripped Darius's arm and pulled him aside. They were alone, but Charlie whispered anyway. 'OK, you're not a fool. You know what's going on here. But you need to know that security watches everyone who comes in or out of this place. I mean, from now on your cell phone will be monitored, and your room may be bugged. Word to the wise.'

Darius nodded.

'What really happened to your HVAC guy?'

Charlie laughed mirthlessly. 'Opened his mouth in a bar. Thirty minutes later the FBI picked him up as he was getting into his car.'

TWENTY FIVE

14 HOURS 2 MINUTES

ASTRID HAD MANAGED to get Cigar to follow her off the path. She worried that someone might come along – if she could get lost en route from the lake to Perdido Beach, so could others.

She found a place beside what had been the stream, hidden by a huge, dying rhododendron bush. She asked Cigar to sit down. She helped to move him into position to do so on a dirt ledge that almost formed a bench.

She sat a few feet away, careful to keep her face towards the grim-faced hill. Even now its shadow bothered her in a way she could not define.

Astrid still felt the relentless tick-tock, tick-tock urging her towards Perdido Beach. But it was possible this was even more important.

And anyway, she couldn't leave. Not with what she had heard from Cigar.

'Bradley. I want this to be easy for you. I'm going to ask you questions. All you have to say is yes or no. OK?'

The tiny eyeballs swerved wildly. But he said, 'OK. Why does he say your hair screams? You're an angel with wings and shiny, shiny, and a long sword with flames and –'

'Just listen, OK?'

He nodded, and revealed a shy grin.

'You did something bad.'

'Yes,' he said solemnly.

'And they punished you by giving you to Penny for a half hour.'

'Half hour.' He giggled and his jaw twisted so hard she thought he might dislocate it. Like he was trying to break his own teeth. 'Not a half hour.'

'They gave you to Penny,' Astrid repeated patiently.

'Sunrise sunset.'

At first Astrid thought he was talking about the eerie sky. Only gradually did the suspicion grow and take shape. 'They put you with Penny for a full day? All day long?'

'Yes,' Cigar said, suddenly calm and sounding quite reasonable.

Astrid did not feel reasonable. What kind of creep would sentence this kid to a day with Penny? No wonder he was insane.

It occurred to her then that he had clawed his own eyes out. The image made her need to throw up. But she couldn't do that. No.

'These new eyes,' Astrid said. 'Are they from Lana?'

'Lana is an angel, too. But it touches her. It tries to take her.'

'Yes, it does,' Astrid said. 'But she's too strong.'

'Mighty!'

Astrid nodded. So he had been driven mad by Penny. And Lana had done what she could. And somehow he had ended up wandering lost out of town, all alone.

Which meant things were very bad in Perdido Beach. Cigar was one of Quinn's fishermen, or had been when last she'd heard. 'You're one of Quinn's fishermen, aren't you?'

'Yay!' Cigar said, and smiled his lunatic grin while his brow furrowed into deep crevices of anxiety. 'Fish. Hah, hah.'

'Now, the little boy . . .'

'Fish! Fish!'

'The little boy,' Astrid persisted. She reached and placed her hand over his. He reacted like he'd been shocked. He yanked his hand back and she feared he might bolt.

'Stay, Cigar. Stay. Quinn would tell you to stay and talk to me.'

'Quinn,' he said and sobbed and finally screamed. 'He came for me. He hit Penny. I couldn't see it but I heard it – Quinn and *bam* and *waaah* and we're going to Lana, "I'll kill you, witch."'

'He's a good guy, Quinn.'

'Yes,' Cigar said.

'He wants you to tell me about the little boy.'

'Little boy? He's next to you.'

Astrid fought the urge to turn and look. No one was beside her. 'I don't see him.'

Cigar nodded as though he knew this, as though it was a given fact. 'He's a little boy. But he's big, too. He can touch the sky.'

Astrid choked out the words, 'Can he?'

'Oh, yes. Little boy is better than an angel, you know; he has the light so bright it shines through you. *Tseeeew!* Right through you.'

'And his name is Petey?'

Cigar was silent. He lowered his head. Again it was as if he was listening. But maybe he was listening only to the terrible nightmare screams in his own head.

Then, with perfect lucidity that was stranger in its way than all his tics and sudden eruptions and weird gestures, Cigar said, 'He was Pete.'

Astrid sobbed.

'That was his body name.'

'Yes,' Astrid said, too paralysed even to wipe away the tears. 'Can I . . . Can he hear me?'

'He can hear . . . anything!' And again the mad cackle, an almost ecstatic sound.

'I'm sorry, Petey,' Astrid said. 'I'm so sorry.'

'Little boy is free now,' Cigar said in a sing-song voice. 'He's playing a game.'

'I know,' Astrid said. 'Petey? You can't play that game. You're hurting people.'

Once again Cigar lowered his head to listen. But even though Astrid waited a long time, he said nothing more.

So in a quiet voice Astrid said, 'Petey. The barrier is turning dark. Can you stop it? Do you have the power to stop it?'

Cigar laughed. 'Little boy is gone.'

And Astrid could feel the truth of it. The sense of something unseen looking at her was gone.

Sanjit did not travel alone. He had intended to, and Lana had said he should, but by the time he got on to the highway heading in the direction of the turn-off to the lake, he was in a gaggle of kids.

People were fleeing Perdido Beach. Sanjit could see at least twenty, arrayed in groups of two or three. The group that had formed around him was a group of three. Two twelve-year-old girls, Keira and Tabitha, and a little boy of maybe three with the very grown-up-sounding name of Mason.

Mason was trying to be a good little soldier, but just a half mile out of town he was already stumbling on very tired legs. The girls were hardier – they'd both put in time working the fields, so they were strong and had the stamina for long hours on the road. But Mason was a little kid hauling a backpack filled with his favourite things – some broken toys, a picture book called *Owl Babies* and a framed picture of his family.

The girls pushed their things, as well as some food and water, in a Ralphs grocery cart with one bad wheel. It rattled as they went. Sanjit knew it would never survive the dirt-and-gravel road that led to the lake.

Mason complicated matters further by insisting on wearing a plastic Iron Man helmet that covered his whole head. He had a small paring knife in a woman's white belt.

Lana had impressed on Sanjit a need for speed when she'd handed him the grubby envelope with the note inside. And he knew he could outpace his three fellow travellers. But somehow, having fallen in with them, he couldn't quite bring himself to do it. Instead he ended up hefting Mason on to his back.

'Are you and Lana, like, together?' Tabitha asked.

'Um . . . Yes. I guess you could say that.'

'I heard she's mean,' Keira offered.

'No,' Sanjit protested. 'She's tough. That's all.'

'You know who's really mean?' Tabitha asked. 'Turk. He pushed me once and I fell down and skinned both my knees.'

'Sorry that –'

'And then I went to see Lana and she told me to go wash off in the ocean and not bother her.' Tabitha lowered her voice and added, 'Only she said it meaner, with a bunch of cusswords.'

Sanjit resisted the grin that wanted to spread across his face. Yep. That would be Lana, all right. 'Maybe she was just busy at the time.'

It was good to have some silly gossip to distract them all. And the two girls seemed to have an endless stream: who liked who; who didn't like who; who might like who.

Sanjit didn't know half the people they were talking about, but it was still better than looking up at the sky and watching the stain grow higher and the ragged circle of light grow smaller.

What were they going to do when the light went out?

As if reading his thoughts, or maybe just noticing his worried expression, Keira said, 'Sam Temple can make lights.'

'With his hands,' Tabitha explained.

'Like lamps.' Then without prompting Keira patted Mason on his Iron Man helmet and said, 'Don't worry, Mase: that's why we're going to the lake.'

At which point Mason began to cry.

Sanjit couldn't blame him. Nothing sounded hollower than a reassurance in this place.

Once he delivered his message to Sam he would have to find his way back to Perdido Beach. Would there be any light at all by then? How was he going to get back to Lana across ten miles of emptiness in the dark?

One thing he was sure of: he would go back.

'I have to poop,' Mason said.

Sanjit let him slide down.

More delay. Less likelihood of any light for the homeward trip.

The sun was already most of the way across the narrowed sky. Sanjit knew he should break away, run for it. He could run the whole way there. He'd deliver his message sooner and he'd get back sooner and . . .

Sanjit saw something moving through the brush off at the limits of his excellent sight. Something low and quick, slinking through brush.

Coyotes.

Lana had offered him a pistol, urged it on him. 'I don't know how to shoot,' he'd said, pushing it back.

'Take it or I'll shoot you with it myself.'

They had kissed after that. Just a hurried kiss in the shadow of the church as Lana moved between injured kids. And he had plastered on his jaunty smile and tossed off a jaunty wave and taken off.

What if he never saw her again?

Mason finished his business. The coyotes were no longer in view. The sun touched the far edge of the remaining sky.

Caine had waited. Patiently, since circumstances had forced patience on him. Lana helped the victims of Penny's assault.

Quinn was running around getting the morning's sparse

catch brought in and cooked up over a fire in the plaza. Caine recognised that as a smart move. The smell of broiled fish and the soothing sound of a bonfire would help keep kids from rushing off.

Well, some kids, at least.

Now Quinn was ready for Caine.

'Get me out of this,' Caine demanded.

Quinn said, 'It's not so easy. You should know: you're the scumbag who invented cementing.'

Caine let that go. He had no choice. For one thing, it was true. For another, he was helpless. And finally, he had wet himself. Hadn't even noticed when it had happened, but somewhere, during one of Penny's vicious nightmare attacks, he had done it and now it smelled.

All of which left him in a vulnerable position.

'We'll have to chip it away a little at a time,' Quinn opined. 'Try swinging a full-size sledgehammer and someone's likely to miss and hit your head or wrists.'

He detailed a couple of the fishermen, Paul and Lucas, to begin the job. They had a small, short-handled sledgehammer and a chisel. That had taken some doing, since both were in use as weapons. The kids who gave them up had to be paid. And no one was taking 'Bertos any more; it was strictly barter.

'Tell me if this hurts,' Paul said, and brought the hammer down on the chisel held by Lucas.

CLANG!

It hurt. The sharp force of the blow translated into a dull pain that Caine felt in the bones of his hands. Not quite as bad as being hit directly by the hammer, but it was close.

He gritted his teeth. 'Keep at it.'

Lana came swaggering over, a lit cigarette dangling from her lips. There were still injured kids crying, but Caine wasn't seeing many serious cases left. Dahra Baidoo was with her, helping tend the wounded. Dahra looked a little weird to Caine's eye, like someone sleepwalking, or a mental patient zoned on meds. But what else was new? Crazy was getting to be the norm. And Dahra had better reason than most – she'd borne the brunt of the bug attack here in town.

Lana stepped beside Dahra, put her hand on Dahra's head, and for a second hugged it against her shoulder. Dahra closed her eyes briefly and looked as if she were about to cry. Then she scrubbed her face with her hands and shook her head almost violently.

Lucas struck a second blow and a three-inch chunk of concrete fell away.

'Caine,' Lana said.

'Yeah, Lana. Want to make some snide crack involving irony and karma?'

Lana shrugged. 'Nah. Too easy.' She knelt down beside Caine and then, feeling weary, sat all the way down, cross-legged.

'Listen, Caine. I sent Sanjit to warn Sam about –'

'About the wave of refugees on their way? He'll figure that out soon enough, won't he? He can make light.' He glared up at the sky, feeling like it was a personal enemy. 'In a couple of hours light will be all anyone cares about.'

'That's not why I sent Sanjit. I was going to go myself before this latest fiasco. I sent him because I think Diana is in danger.'

Caine's heart missed a beat. The reaction surprised him. As did the catch in his throat when he said, as coldly as he could, 'Danger? You mean more than the rest of us?'

CLANG!

All the while Paul and Lucas were chipping away at the concrete. With each hammer fall Caine winced. He wondered if bones were breaking. He wondered how they would get off the last of the cement – the part attached to his flesh. In between the sudden sharp pain there was a constant dull pain and an infuriating itch.

'I can feel its mind sometimes,' Lana said.

He looked sharply at her. 'It?'

CLANG!

'Don't play dumb, Caine.' She touched her hand to his head, where the punctures of the staples still oozed blood. Almost instantly the pain in his head diminished. But nothing helped when the next blow of the hammer and chisel made him feel as if fingers were being broken.

CLANG!

'Ahhh!' he cried.

'You were with it,' Lana said. 'I know you still feel it sometimes.'

Caine scowled. 'No. I don't.'

Lana snorted. 'Uh-huh.'

He wasn't going to argue about it. They both knew the truth. That was something he shared with the Healer: too much up-close-and-personal time with the gaiaphage. And yes, it left scars, and yes, it was sometimes as if the creature could touch the edge of Caine's consciousness.

He closed his eyes and the nightmare came on like a storm-driven wave. It had been all hunger then. The gaiaphage needed the uranium at the power plant. That hunger had been so huge, so frantic, Caine could still feel it as a stifling, heart-throttling, choking feeling.

CLANG!

'AHHHH!' Through grinding teeth he said, 'I don't let the Darkness touch me.'

The chisel was cutting closer now, with more than half the concrete chipped away. Penny hadn't mixed a very good batch, really. No gravel. It was gravel that gave it hardness. He and Drake had learned that.

'Sorry,' Lucas said, not really meaning it.

CLANG!

No, Caine thought, no gentle concern for Caine's well-being. They needed him, but that didn't mean they liked him.

'The sun is setting,' Lana remarked almost without emotion. 'Kids will lose it. They'll set fires. That's the big worry, probably, that they'll finish Zil's work by burning down the rest of the town.'

'If I ever get out of this, I'll stop them,' Caine snarled, biting back a cry of pain as the hammer rose and fell again.

'It's going after Diana,' Lana said. 'It wants the baby. Your baby, Caine.'

'What?'

The hammer waited, suspended. This wasn't exactly a private conversation, and Paul was shocked. He snapped out of it and dropped another awful blow.

CLANG!

'Don't you feel it?' Lana demanded.

'All I feel is my fingers being broken!' Caine yelled.

'I'll fix your fingers,' Lana said impatiently. 'I'm asking you: do you feel it? Can you? Will you let yourself?'

'No!'

'Scared?'

His lips drew back in a snarl. 'You're damned right I'm scared of it. I got away from it. You're saying I should open myself up to it again?'

CLANG!

'I'm not scared of it,' Lana said, and Caine wondered if she really wasn't. 'I hate it. I hate myself for not killing it when I had the chance. I hate it.' Her eyes were dark but hot, like smoldering coals.

'I hate it,' she repeated.

CLANG!

'Oh. Ohhhh!' He was breathing in short gasps. 'I won't . . . What makes you so sure it's going after Diana?'

'I'm not sure. That's why I'm talking to you. Because I thought you might give a damn if that monster is after your kid.'

Caine's hands felt lighter. The concrete block had split. There was a wedge about the size of a double slice of pie hanging from his left hand. His hands were still locked together in a crumbly mass that looked like the stone from which a sculptor might chisel a pair of hands.

Paul and Lucas readjusted their positions, and Caine lifted the hands and carefully, carefully used a piece of concrete to scratch his nose.

'Caine –' Paul said.

'Give me a minute,' Caine said. 'All of you. Give. Me. A. Minute.'

He closed his eyes. Pain in his hands, a deep ache of something – or more than one thing – broken. The pain was terrible.

Worse by far: the humiliation.

He'd been outwitted by Penny. Weakness.

He'd been made to bear the torture he and Drake had invented. Weakness.

He sat here now on the steps of town hall, the steps where not two days earlier he'd ruled as king. He sat there now with piss-smelling pants, made to feel weak and small and cowardly by Lana.

He hadn't been this low since he had walked off defeated into the desert with Pack Leader. Since he had crawled, weeping and desperate, to have his mind messed up by that malevolent, glowing monster.

Lana could let it touch her mind. She was that strong.

He could not. Because he was not.

What did it matter any more? he wondered. It was the end at last. Darkness would fall and the sun would never rise again and they would wander lost in inky blackness until they starved. The smart ones would just walk into the ocean and swim until they drowned.

What did he, Caine, matter? Let alone Diana. Or the . . . whatever. Baby. Kid. Whatever.

He closed his eyes and he could see Diana. Beautiful girl, Diana. Smart. Smart enough to keep pace with him. Smart enough to play her games with him.

They'd been happy, mostly, on the island. Him and Diana. Good days. Then Quinn had come with a message that he was needed to rescue Perdido Beach.

He had come back. Diana had warned him not to. But he had come back. And he had proclaimed himself king. Because kids needed a king. And because after he saved their stupid lives for them he deserved to be that king.

Diana had warned him against that, too.

And no sooner was he in charge than he'd realised it was Albert who was the real boss. And no one really respected Caine. They didn't realise how much he did for them.

Ungrateful.

Now they wanted him, but only because they were all scared of the dark.

'We'll try a smaller hammer now,' Paul said anxiously.

Caine gritted his teeth, anticipating the blow.

CLANG!

'Ahhh!' The chisel had missed. The hardened steel chisel blade skipped and bit into his wrist. Blood poured out over the concrete.

He wanted to cry. Not from the pain but from the sheer awfulness of his life. He needed to use the bathroom. He wouldn't even be able to lower his own pants or wipe himself.

Lana took his wrist. The bleeding slowed.

'You need to let them keep at it,' Lana said. 'It'll be a lot worse in the dark.'

Caine nodded. He had nothing more to say.

He bowed his head and cried.

TWENTY SIX

12 HOURS 40 MINUTES

SINDER WEPT AS she and Jezzie ripped up their vegetables. It was all over. Their hard work, almost done now. This was the final harvest.

Their little dream of helping to make things better for everyone was at an end. And like all failed hopes it seemed stupid now. They'd been idiots to hope. Idiots.

This was the FAYZ. Hope led to a kick in the face.

Idiots.

They filled plastic trash bags with carrots and tomatoes. And cried silently while Brianna stood watch over them, pretending not to notice.

It was hard for Orc to tilt his head back and look up at the sky. His rocky neck just didn't like to bend that way. But he made the effort as the sun, with shocking speed, was swallowed by the western edge of that toothed hole in the sky.

Straight up, over his head: blue sky. The clear blue sky of a

California early afternoon. But below that sky was a blank, black wall. He was only a few hundred feet away from it. He could walk over and touch it if he wanted.

He didn't want to. It was too . . . too something. He didn't have a word for it. Howard would have had a word for it.

Orc was buzzing with a weird kind of energy. He hadn't slept. He had searched through the night, sure that Drake was out here, sure that he could find him. Or if not find him, then at least be here when he showed up.

Then he would rip Drake apart. Rip him into little pieces and eat the pieces and crap them out and bury them in the dirt.

Yeah. For Howard.

No one cared Howard was gone. Sam, Edilio, those guys: they didn't care. Not about Howard. They just cared that something bad was happening. Someone had to care that Howard was dead and gone now. And would never come back.

Orc had to care, that was who. Charles Merriman had to care that his friend Howard was gone.

People didn't know it, but Orc could still cry. They all figured he couldn't . . . No, that wasn't true; they didn't figure anything. They never saw anything but a monster made out of gravel.

He couldn't blame them.

The only one who saw past that was Howard. Maybe Howard used Orc, but that was OK, because Orc used him, too. People did that. Even people who really liked each other. Good friends. Best friends.

Only friends.

Orc was walking a pattern, back and forth. He walked along from almost the dome to as far as the dock was, then maybe a hundred yards farther out, and back and forth, and another hundred yards out. He'd gone all the way to the far end of the lake and back. But something told him Drake wouldn't go all the way around like that.

No, no, not Drake. Orc knew Drake a little from when Drake was running things for Caine back so long ago in Perdido Beach. Back when Drake was just a creep, but a regular human creep.

And he'd known Drake in a way while he and Howard had been his jailer. He'd spent a lot of hours listening to Drake rant and rave.

It was Orc's fault Drake had ever got away.

Drake could be tricky, sure, but he wasn't like Astrid or Jack or one of those real smart kids. He wouldn't have some big plan. He would just hide until he saw a way.

A way to do what? Orc didn't know. Sam and the others hadn't told him anything about it. Just that Drake had killed Howard and let the coyotes eat him. And that he was out loose.

Orc kept his eyes down for the most part. Easier that way. Plus he was looking for something: a footprint, maybe. Coyote prints if he could find them. But even better would be Drake's footprints.

He'd heard all about how you couldn't kill Drake. You could smash him or cut him up into little pieces and he'd still put himself back together.

Well. That might discourage most people. But while a drunken Orc wore out pretty easy, a sober, determined Orc had plenty of time and plenty of energy. He wouldn't mind just taking Drake apart over and over again. And he didn't feel tired. He felt more awake all the time.

Orc was walking in the gloomy shadow of a rock bluff. There were cracks all in those rocks, and he had decided now to check in every one. One by one. Every crack. Under every rock.

Orc froze. Was that . . . Yeah, that was a footprint. Most of a footprint. The ground was hard, and the only reason the print showed at all was that a gopher or whatever it was that dug holes up here had dug out a bit of fresh dirt.

In that dirt was half a footprint. A bare foot, not a shoe.

Orc stared down at it. He placed his own foot beside it. It made the print seem even smaller. It seemed awful small to be from Drake. Drake was a pretty big dude. This was more like a little kid, or a girl.

He could make out three toes: the little ones. The toes pointed down towards the water.

Orc followed the direction with his gaze. Weird, the light

was, weird. The shore of the lake looked strange. Something not right.

Then he was distracted by the sight of Sinder and Jezzie working away in their garden. And there was Brianna, watching him actually, when she should have been watching over Sinder and Jezzie.

He raised a massive arm to wave at Brianna and seconds later she was beside him.

'Hey, Orc. Trade jobs with me. Sam has me babysitting the weepy gardeners there. You could watch them.'

'No.' He shook his head.

Brianna tilted her head, a little like a bird. Orc remembered her, too, from when he first met her and she was just coming down from Coates with Sam. She'd got pretty full of herself since those days.

'You're looking for Drake, right?' Brianna asked. 'A little payback for Howard? I get that. Totally. Howard was your boy.'

'Don't act like you care,' Orc grunted.

'What? Couldn't hear you.'

Orc roared, 'Don't act like you care. No one cared about Howard. No one cares he's dead. Just me.' It was so loud it echoed. Orc snatched up a small boulder and, in violent frustration, threw it.

It flew twenty feet and smashed against the bluff. It set off two things: a small avalanche of pebbles and mid-size stones.

And a sudden rush of panicked coyotes.

Orc stared after them. Brianna's eyes lit up.

She got close to Orc and in a hard whisper said, 'I'll bet those are the coyotes that did the eating. You got a choice: you want me to get them or not?'

Orc swallowed hard. The coyotes were already atop the bluff and in seconds they would be on level ground and running free. He would never catch them.

'Save one for me,' Orc said.

Brianna winked and zoomed away.

Albert had laid the groundwork carefully.

It was very hard for those without Caine-like or Dekka-like powers even to get out of the sea and on to the island. So he'd arranged for Taylor to carry a looped rope out to the island, secure it around a very sturdy tree, and drop the rope over the cliff.

It was right there in plain view. Anyone who went a little way around the western side of the island, past the wrecked yacht, could see it. He'd attached – well, had paid a kid to attach – colourful bits of fabric so that even now, in the eerie brown shadow, the rope was easy to find.

He guided the boat in. There were no waves, just the usual gentle surge. Albert was not a great boat handler, but he'd learned enough, just enough that he could position the boat beside the rope. The rope fell all the way into the water, which meant it was longer – and therefore more expensive – than necessary. But that wasn't really the point. The rope was where he had arranged for it to be.

The loops made it almost like a ladder. A very awkward ladder that had an unfortunate tendency to push away when you tried to stick your feet in the loops. But once you got started you could climb OK, and especially once the end of the rope had been made fast to the chest in the bottom of the boat.

It was a long climb and Albert regretted not having arrived earlier. He shouldn't have waited so long. Another hour or two and he wouldn't have been able to see the ladder, let alone climb it.

He was first up over the lip of the cliff. With a final heave he pushed himself up into the tall grass, rolled out of the way, and, lying on his back, looked up at the sky.

How very strange. Like being inside a soft-boiled egg with the top of the shell chipped away. Sky – normal-seeming sky – but covering only maybe a quarter of the space.

And the growing stain wasn't night. There were no stars. There was nothing at all. Just blackness.

He stood up and helped the others as one by one they reached the top.

The sea spread for miles before splashing against the black

dome. Far away to the south and east was Perdido Beach, lit in sepia, like a crinkly old photo from long ago.

Turning, Albert gazed in quiet satisfaction at the mansion. It was dark, of course. No one was running the generator, which meant Taylor wasn't here.

She was Albert's one concern. Taylor could pop in and out whenever she liked. This would be useful for him – Taylor could let him know what was going on in Perdido Beach and the lake.

On the other hand, Taylor was hard to control. Which was why he'd brought a small sack of combination locks. One would go on the pantry, one on the cover of the generator's switch. Only Albert would know the combination, so only Albert would control the food and the lights. That would chill Taylor's independence a bit.

He ordered the girls to pull up the rope and coil it well back from the cliff's edge. Then he scanned the sea between Perdido Beach and the island. No sign of boats. Which meant most probably no one was coming anytime soon.

But they would. Sitting terrified in the dark, hungry and desperate, kids would see a distant point of light. They would realise it was the island, and that light meant hope.

So just as soon as they had rested a little, had a bite to eat and a look around, Albert would get them busy hauling a couple of the missiles up to the top floor of the mansion. Because whenever that boat came, it, too, would have a light. A single point of light in the darkness.

Albert sighed. He had survived. But he had given up everything. All of Alberco. All he had accomplished. All he had built.

He would miss the challenge of the business.

'Come on, guys,' Albert said. 'Come see our new home.'

Drake was pretty sure Brittney had emerged at least once while he was down in this cramped, oily engine room. But he was back now and Brittney had not moved.

Maybe she was getting smarter.

He listened for Sam's voice. He heard nothing. That didn't prove Sam was gone. But it meant Drake could take a small risk.

With his tentacle arm he edged the hatch up a quarter of an inch.

The light was definitely different. Strange. Like it was shining through a bottle of Coke or something. Unnatural.

Unsettling.

He pushed the hatch just a bit higher. There was a foot. Not moving. Just there, toes in his direction. He shifted. A second foot. Someone was seated right there, just a couple of feet away. Aimed in his direction.

Problem or opportunity?

That was the question.

The hatch came down suddenly, slammed back into place by running feet.

'Hey, you guys, be careful!'

Diana's voice! He'd recognise it anywhere.

'Justin, you're going to break your neck!'

Drake closed his eyes and let the pleasure of it wash over him. She was right there. And from the sound of it there were little kids on board.

Perfect.

Absolutely. Perfect.

Beyond the highway, out in the emptiness at the edge of the desert, Penny stepped on a broken bottle.

It was the bottom of a bottle, the base of what must have been a wine bottle. Green glass. Jagged. A sliver punched up through her calloused sole into the meat of her heel.

'Ahhhh!'

It hurt!

Tears came into Penny's eyes. Blood gushed from her foot, puddling in the sand. She sat down hard and pulled her foot to her and saw the cut. Lana would have to –

Bandages. Band-Aids.

'Owww! Owww!'

Penny started crying aloud. She was hurt and no one would help her. And what would happen to her when it was dark?

It was all so unfair. So unfair. So wrong.

She'd been on top for not even a few minutes. She'd had Caine right where she wanted him, but no one liked her, and all they did was hate on her, and now her foot was hurt and bleeding.

But not as bad as when her legs were broken. Not as bad as that. And she had survived that, hadn't she? She had survived and she had come out on top. She wondered how Caine liked having his hands in a block of cement. If they tried to take it off, they would break his hands like her legs had been broken.

Only Lana would help him, wouldn't she?

She should have taken care of Lana when she had the chance. The Healer might be almost immune to Penny's power, but would she be immune to a gun? Penny should have had Turk kill the Healer. Yeah, that was what she should have done.

The shadows weren't lengthening; the light wasn't really coming from one place. It was like she was down in a well with sun shining up high somewhere directly above, so the light had to bounce down to reach her.

Soon it would be dark.

Then what?

Diana got heavily to her feet just as Justin went tearing past again, full of giddy high spirits and energy.

Atria had wound down. She was in the bow now, reading.

Justin tripped and fell headlong, a projectile aimed right at Diana's giant belly.

But he didn't hit.

The little boy flew forward, mouth open, arms stretching out defensively; then he stopped, yanked back, and hit the deck hard.

Diana was moving towards him, worried, when she saw the tentacle wrapped around his ankle. She froze. It made no sense. The tentacle was coming up from the floor!

No. A hatch.

And in a flash the hatch was thrown back and Drake pushed himself awkwardly up.

Diana shot wild looks in every direction, searching for a weapon. Nothing.

Drake was out of the engine space. Standing on the deck. Grinning at her.

She knew she should scream, but her breath was gone. Her heart was hammering with no rhythm, just thudding wildly in her chest.

Drake lifted the boy off the deck with effortless strength, carried him over the side, and plunged him under the water.

Diana stared at him with horror. How could he be here? How was this possible?

'What. No snarky remark, Diana?'

Diana saw legs kicking below the surface of the water. Drake twisted his tentacle just a bit so that the little boy's face was visible. So that she could see his wide, white eyes. So that she could see that he was screaming away the last of his air, an explosion of suicidal bubbles.

'Let him go,' Diana said, but with no force, because she knew Drake wouldn't listen.

'There's a dinghy tied up. Climb your fine butt down into it, Diana. Once you're in, I let the kid up. Not before. So I'd hurry if I were you.'

Diana sobbed just once, a sudden sharp exhalation.

She could see the fear in the boy's eyes. The pleading.

If she hesitated, he would drown. And Drake would still be here.

Diana rushed to the bow. She climbed over the rail and dropped awkwardly into the boat. 'I'm in!' she cried. 'Let him go.'

Drake sauntered down the length of the sailboat. He kept his whip arm in the water. He was dragging the boy through the water, keeping him submerged.

There was a rush of feet coming from below. Roger emerged on deck, panting. Drake smiled at him.

'I don't believe I've had the pleasure,' he said. Then he lifted Justin up out of the water. The little boy was silent, eyes closed, pale as death.

Roger's expression turned murderous. With a roar he ran at

Drake. Drake swung Justin like a wet wrecking ball and smashed Roger so hard he went over the side.

When he reached the bow he met Diana's tearful gaze. He dumped Justin, like a sack of garbage, in the dinghy.

'I think he's taking a nap,' Drake said, and hopped down into the boat.

Diana knelt over Justin. His eyes were closed. His lips were blue. When she touched his face he felt as cold as death.

Long-lost memories came now. Was it a video they'd shown in some class? In some different world?

It was hard for Diana with her belly to bend over low enough to put her mouth over the little boy's lips. She had to lift his head to her and she was barely strong enough to do it.

She breathed into his mouth. Pause. Breathe again. Pause.

Drake untied the rope and settled in at the oars. He wrapped two feet of his tentacle arm around the right oar.

Breathe. Pause. Breathe.

Pulse, she should check for a pulse. Diana pressed two fingers against the boy's neck.

Drake had started singing. It was the song from the Pirates of the Caribbean ride at Disney World.

Something. A flutter in the little boy's neck.

Breathe. Pause. Breathe.

He coughed. Coughed again and spit up water. Diana pulled him into a sitting position.

'Well, just look at you, Diana: you saved his life,' Drake said. 'You want to keep his life?' He waited as though he actually expected an answer. When she said nothing he went on, 'If you want to keep him alive, you won't open your mean little mouth. One sound from you and I'll drown him like a puppy.'

Already the dinghy was near shore. No more than twenty more pulls of the oars.

Diana shot a glance back at the houseboat. She saw Dekka on the top deck, but she wasn't looking this way. She was looking up at the shrinking sky.

No Sam. No Edilio.

'Yeah, kinda sucks, huh?' Drake said cheerfully. 'Anyway, Dekka couldn't do anything. Not from that distance.'

Diana scanned the onrushing shore. No one.

Wait. Sinder. She was dragging a massive sack of something down the shore. Jezzie was behind her.

Drake saw the hope in her eyes. He winked. 'Oh, don't worry: we'll stop and talk to them. We'll tell them you've decided on a little vacation. Say you're going back to Caine.'

Could Drake be that stupid to believe that anyone would buy that story? To imagine that Sinder and Jezzie would stand calmly discussing things with Whip Hand?

Maybe. Who knew what Drake had been up to? Who could tell how much his psychopathic mind had deteriorated?

He was singing again, more or less in time with the oars.

'What do you want, Drake?' Diana demanded, trying to put on a brave front.

Drake smiled. 'Did I ever thank you for sawing off my arm, Diana? I was mad at the time. But if you hadn't done that for me, I wouldn't be Whip Hand.'

'I should have sawed through your neck.' Diana spat the words.

'Yeah,' he said, meeting her furious, terrified gaze without flinching. 'You should have. You really should have.'

OUTSIDE

SERGEANT DARIUS ASHTON saw the signs that in his absence his quarters had been entered. Nothing most people would notice, but he was by long habit a very organised man. He had a small room in the NCO barracks, no bigger than a walk-in closet, really. The bunk was narrow and the army-issue blanket was so tight you could bounce a quarter off it. The pillow squared just so. And now there was just the slightest indentation where someone had sat on the edge of the bed and then tried to smooth it.

'Pff, that will not cut it,' he said dismissively. 'Not in this man's army.'

He moved next to his footlocker. Yep. They'd been careful, but it had been searched.

The question was, where had they put the bug? They'd surely tap his cell phone – that was a given – and they'd use the phone's GPS to keep track of his location. But had they placed a bug in here as well?

He turned off the tracking feature for his phone. They'd still be able to see what towers his signal reached, but that was a far less accurate way to track him. The GPS would narrow his location to a few feet. Tracking the tower signals would only put them within a mile of his location.

With that done, he turned to searching for a bug. It didn't take long to find it. It was a small room without a lot of options. The bug was in the base of the lamp. Someone had drilled a very tiny hole in the base to allow better reception by a mike no thicker than a piece of angel hair pasta.

Well. OK, then.

So, he would have to be very careful.

He'd already decided to tell Connie. He was under orders. He had signed the secrecy document. But Sergeant Darius Ashton had been in the army long enough to know that the bigger the secret, the more likely it was to be FUBAR.

And this – setting off a nuclear weapon underneath a bunch of kids who were fighting for their lives – that was FUBAR. Not to mention wrong.

If word got out, the American people wouldn't let it happen. He was an American soldier. He obeyed the chain of command from his lieutenant to his captain to the colonel to the general and on up to the president of the United States.

But no American soldier was required – or could ever be legally required – to kill American citizens on American soil. No way. No. That was not what he promised to do when he raised his hand and was sworn in as a soldier.

'I, Darius Lee Ashton, do solemnly swear that I will support and defend the Constitution of the United States against all enemies, foreign and domestic; that I will bear true faith and allegiance to the same; and that I will obey the orders of the president of the United States and the orders of the officers appointed over me, according to regulations and the Uniform Code of Military Justice. So help me God.'

Thing one: defend the Constitution. He was no constitutional law scholar, but he was pretty sure it did not call for nuking a bunch of kids in California.

And the obeying orders part? It said according to the Uniform Code of Military Justice. Which quite definitely did not say that an American soldier should get into the business of killing American kids.

No.

At the same time, Darius was not interested in spending the rest of his life in a windowless cell at Fort Leavenworth. That would be the hard part: to do the right thing and manage not to get caught doing it.

He lay back on his bunk and gave it some thought. Time was short. He was certain of that. There was way too much activity out there. Those boys were in a hurry.

If he left his cell phone here and went out they'd know

he was up to something. They would have to see his cell phone move. Texts, email, all of that would be intercepted. This would have to be old-school. Face-to-face. And if it all went to hell later, he'd have to have left no evidence whatsoever.

He tried to recall everything he knew about Connie Temple. What would she be doing right now? Where would she be? What was today? Thursday? No. It was Friday.

Too early for Connie to be cooking ribs. But not too early for her to be shopping for the Friday-night cookout.

It was a long shot.

But if Connie Temple was cooking ribs then there were only two places she could buy them. Fortunately the Vons grocery and the Fat N' Greezy rib stand were in the same strip centre.

Darius stuck his phone in his pocket. He stopped by a buddy's room on the way out, said he was going to drive down to Vons for some munchies and beer. His buddy told him to pick up some Cheetos. The spicy ones.

It was a twenty-minute drive to Vons. And since it was a straight shot down the highway he was pretty sure he wasn't being followed. They had no reason to suspect him, anyway, and they had lots of other people to watch.

He passed Connie's trailer on the way. Her silver Kia was not in its usual spot.

Unfortunately it was also not in the Vons parking lot.

Darius killed some time filling his tank at the Chevron. He had a good view of the parking lot.

He drove through McDonald's for a coffee.

After that all he could do was wait. An hour he could explain. Two hours? That would be pushing it.

Then he spotted the solution: the movie theatres. Three movies showing, all of them crap, but he'd seen one of them. Perfect. He went to the theatre and bought a ticket using a credit card. He went inside and bought fifteen dollars' worth of popcorn and candy.

As soon as the previews started he ditched the junk food and let himself out through one of the side exits. He was careful to keep his ticket stub.

Outside he almost instantly spotted the silver Kia.

There would be security cameras inside Vons, which was where Connie went. So he moved his own car until it was parked beside Connie's. And waited.

She came out with a cart half-full of plastic bags. She didn't notice him sitting there until she was behind the wheel of her car. Then he rolled down the window.

She did the same.

He looked at her. 'I'm putting my life in your hands, Con,' he said.

'What are you talking about?'

'Life in prison if I get caught and convicted.'

Her brow furrowed. It made her look older. Which was fine with him; he liked a woman who looked like a woman.

'What is it, Darius?'

'They're going to nuke the dome.'

TWENTY SEVEN

11 HOURS 28 MINUTES

THE ARTFUL ROGER shouted from the deck of the sailboat. Edilio heard and knew instantly that something had gone terribly wrong.

Roger was waving furiously, directing Edilio to look towards the shore.

Edilio felt his heart drop into his stomach. A rowboat moved quickly towards the land. Edilio raced downstairs, grabbed Sam's binoculars, and raced back up with Sam and Dekka breathless in his wake.

Edilio jabbed the binoculars into his eye sockets. The boat was inches from shore, scraping along the gravel. There was no mistaking the tentacle arm that jerked Diana rudely up and tossed her on to the ground.

'It's Drake,' Edilio said. 'He's got Diana. And Justin.'

Drake, as if magically hearing his name, turned towards him, raised one of the oars, and waved at Edilio.

Then he smashed the oar down, breaking it in half. Now he

had the jagged wooden stump of it in his tentacle. He pointed it at Justin's throat. The little boy was crying. Edilio could see the tears streaming down his face.

With his hand Drake made a mocking *come and get me* move.

The message was clear. And Edilio had no doubt Drake would do it.

'Where is Breeze?' Sam raged. 'Edilio. Fire a round!'

Edilio didn't hear or at least didn't connect those words with any action. He swivelled to look at Roger. Roger looked like he'd been gutted.

Edilio raised one hand in a fist for Roger to see. So that Roger would know that Edilio understood and had not lost hope.

Sam pulled Edilio's pistol out and fired three rounds into the air.

If Brianna were anywhere close, she would hear and know what it meant.

Drake hurried up the bluff with Diana stumbling ahead and Justin trying pitifully to help her. In seconds they would be out of sight.

Sam cursed Brianna for a reckless, irresponsible idiot. Dekka was already running down the dock. But there was zero chance of her catching Drake, not at this distance.

Sam spun to race after her. He might not catch up, either, but he couldn't just stand there.

'Sam, no!' Edilio snapped.

Sam missed a step, then stopped. He looked at Edilio, puzzled.

'We're scattered. And we can't risk you. You die and the light dies with you.'

'Are you out of your mind? You think I'm going to let Drake come in here and take Diana?'

'Not you, Sam. Dekka, yes. Orc, yes. He's out there, too. And send Jack as well. Anyone but you.'

Sam looked like he'd been punched. Like someone had knocked the wind out of him. He blinked and started to say something and stopped.

'You aren't replaceable, Sam. Figure it out, OK? It's going dark and you make light. So this isn't going to be your battle. Not now. It's on the rest of us to step up.'

Edilio licked his lips and looked miserable. 'Me, too. My place is here. I can't take Drake on. I'd just be another victim.' He glanced back at Roger, who held out his hands in a gesture of incomprehension that Edilio interpreted easily.

Why aren't you going after Justin?

Why are you and Sam standing there doing nothing?

Edilio could see that the whole population was up on deck on the various scattered boats. They'd all heard the shots. They all stared hard at their leaders now, at Sam and Edilio. Some noticed Dekka labouring along the shoreline, trying to reach the place where Drake had come ashore. They pointed at her and then looked back, frowning at Sam and Edilio.

Staring at their suddenly powerless leaders.

Edilio spotted Jack on a motorboat. He was too far away to be able to hear, but Edilio pointed straight at him.

Jack mimed a *who me?* gesture.

Sam emphasised Edilio's order by stabbing his finger unmistakably in the direction of Jack. Then he swept his arm to point at the shore.

Jack reluctantly trudged to the back of the boat and there came the coughing start-up of an outboard engine.

Edilio raised the binoculars again to look at Roger. He was in pain. Helpless.

He forced himself to look away, to follow Jack as he headed to shore, to sweep along the bluff and find Dekka levitating herself over rises.

And there, coming towards her, Orc.

Edilio felt a small breath of hope.

Orc, Jack, and Dekka. Could they do it?

The coyotes trotted with the relentlessness of motion that marked them as successful predators.

Brianna spotted them maybe half a mile away.

'Heh.'

Then beyond them, at the limits of her sight, a second group. The rest of the pack. Or a different pack? It didn't matter, really:

all coyotes were kill-on-sight. In fact, it had got so they were pretty rare.

Take out this nearer pack. Then take a quick look-see for Drake before Sam even noticed she was gone.

One of the coyotes spotted her. The result was a very gratifying panic. She made out four of them. They were tearing away at top speed.

The light was pretty bad. And the terrain was pretty rough. So she couldn't crank it up to anything like full speed. But that was OK: a coyote might break twenty-five, thirty miles per hour. But even Brianna's low gear was twice that.

She ran up beside the nearest of the coyotes. It glanced at her with death in its dumb eyes.

'Yeah,' Brianna said. 'All dogs go to heaven. Coyotes go the other way.'

She swung her machete.

The body took two steps, tripped over the head, and tumbled into the dirt.

Two of the coyotes decided to stand side by side and make a stand. They were panting, tongues lolling, already worn out. One had a ruff matted with dried blood.

'Hey, doggies,' Brianna said.

She danced forward and they snapped at her. But it was no contest. She decapitated one. His mate, the one marked by dried blood that had probably once given life to Howard

Bassem, turned tail and ran and Brianna severed her spine.

'I never liked Howard,' Brianna said to the body. 'But I like you even less.'

She had trouble finding the fourth animal. It had probably decided to cower and hide. In the dim light it was hard to see. Everything was brown on brown, even the air itself, it seemed.

She waited patiently, watching.

But if the coyote waited her out, it could probably get away when the final darkness came.

Anyway, if time was short, she had a more important target. Coyotes were mere accessories: Drake was the main goal.

Brianna took off at the cautious pace of a galloping thoroughbred, pursued by a sense of guilt and worry about what Sam would say if she came back with nothing but three dead coyotes to show for it.

She'd have to get Drake. That would stop Sam's complaining.

Where were the coyotes? Drake had expected them to close in with him as soon as he reached the bluff. They should have been waiting there.

No coyotes.

Not good. They had abandoned him. Which meant they were abandoning his master as well. Like rats deserting a sinking ship.

Not for the first time Drake felt the sharp edge of fear. Maybe the stupid dogs were right to go rogue. Maybe the gaiaphage's power was waning. Maybe he was serving a failing master.

Well, not if Drake succeeded. Then the gaiaphage's gratitude would be even greater.

He had to move fast. Fast! Once night came he would be safe, maybe, but until then . . .

Drake feared two things. One was that Brittney would emerge just when Drake needed to be able to fight.

The second was Brianna.

So far she wasn't in sight. But that was the thing about Brianna: she could show up in a real hurry.

Night would be the end of Brianna's usefulness. Even this weak iced-tea light was dangerous to Swift Girl. But he wouldn't be able to stop worrying about her until true darkness came.

And then there was the problem of finding his way back to the gaiaphage. The coyotes could have done it with smell and their own innate sense of navigation, but he was no coyote.

'Let us go, Drake,' Diana said. 'We're just slowing you down.'

'Then move faster,' he said, and snapped his whip, cutting through her shirt and painting a red stripe on her back. That was nice. That was good. No time to really enjoy it. But yeah, that was good.

She had cried out in pain. That was good, too. But that wasn't his job. No, he had to warn himself: he'd made that error before. He'd let himself be distracted by his own pleasures.

This time he had to come through. He had to deliver Diana to his master.

'You'll move or I'll see if the little kid likes old Whip Hand.'

He heard a noise and glanced over his shoulder, flinching in the expectation of a machete suddenly zooming at him at the speed of a motorcycle.

He should have finished Brianna back at Coates. She had just been an annoying nobody then. He'd barely known she was alive. Now she was his living nightmare. He should have finished her.

Nasty little brat. The memory of her taunts was still a red wound in his psyche. He hated her. Like he hated Diana. And that frosty prig Astrid.

He loved the memory of humiliating Sam, but even now the memory of his triumph over Astrid gave him a warm glow all over. He could hate guys, he could want to destroy them, he could enjoy making them suffer, but it was never as deep and intense as it was with girls. No, girls were special. His hatred for Sam was a cool breeze compared to the seething, hot rage he felt for Diana. And Astrid. And Brianna.

The three of them: so arrogant. So superior.

He reached with his whip and snagged Diana's ankle, tripping her and causing her to land hard on her belly.

It scared him. He could have hurt the baby. The consequences of that he could not bear to think about.

Justin turned and clenched his fists and yelled, 'Leave her alone!'

Drake smirked. Brave little kid. When Brianna came he'd find some way to use him as a shield. See how tough Brianna was when it meant cutting her way past a little kid.

Where was she?

Where was the so-called Breeze?

Diana struggled to her feet. She turned to face him, defiant. 'Why don't you just kill me and get it over with, Drake? It's the closest you'll ever come to pleasure, you sick piece of –'

'*Move!*' he roared.

Diana flinched but did not run. 'Scared, Drake?' She narrowed her eyes. 'Scared of Sam?' She tilted her head to one side, judging him. 'Oh, no, of course not. It's Brianna, isn't it? Of course, a woman-hater like you. What was it with you and females, by the way? Find out your mom was a whore or something?'

The explosion shocked even him. He shrieked in sudden rage, red-hot, bloodlust rage. He flew at her, smashed her with his fist, knocked her to the ground, and stood over her with his whip raised.

'Justin! Run!' Diana screamed as the whip came down.

The little boy yelled, 'No!' But then he broke and ran as hard as his short legs could go.

Drake snapped his tentacle at the boy but missed by inches.

His roar of fury was a pure animal sound. A veil of red came down over his vision.

'Hey!' a voice cried.

Drake had to hear it again before he could even focus his eyes on the source.

Computer Jack bent his knees and leaped what had to be fifty feet. Drake had not witnessed this before. The red mist was receding. He was vaguely aware that Diana was crawling away.

'Hey!' Computer Jack yelled. He landed just a hundred yards away. Justin was running towards him.

The jumping thing: that was a problem. He could move faster than Drake, especially a Drake driving Diana like a reluctant cow through a darkening desert.

Drake walked straight towards Jack. 'Hey, Jack, long time, dude. What are you doing out here?'

'Nothing,' Jack answered defensively.

'Nothing? Just going for a walk, huh?' Drake kept shortening the gap between them.

'Let Diana and Justin go,' Jack said. His voice was shaky. Just then Justin reached him and threw himself at Jack's legs, holding on in terror.

Drake broke into a run. Straight at Jack.

Jack pushed Justin away. The whip tore the air and slashed at Jack's neck. It missed and hit his shoulder instead.

Jack cried out in pain.

Drake never hesitated but swiftly wrapped his tentacle around Jack's neck and squeezed tight. To his amazement Jack just tensed his muscles and resisted all of Drake's strength. It was like trying to choke a tree trunk.

Then Jack snatched at the whip, trying to get hold of it. Drake was too quick, but just barely. He danced back but tripped, took two clumsy backwards steps, and barely kept his feet.

Had Jack attacked right then, right at that moment, he would have had a chance. But Jack was no fighter. He'd grown stronger: not meaner. Drake saw his hesitation and grinned.

He moved instantly back on the attack, whirling his whip arm over his head, slashing and slashing as Jack backed up, backed up, and then again, Drake ran straight at him.

He whipped Jack across the chest. The arm. And then, a sudden vicious cut to Jack's neck.

Blood sprayed from Jack's throat.

He put his hand to his neck, pulled it away, and stared in utter disbelief at a hand not just touched with but drenched in blood.

That throat. It couldn't be choked, but it could be cut.

Justin lay whimpering beside him as Jack sank to his knees in the dirt.

Drake wrapped his whip around the little boy and simply

flung him in the direction of Diana.

Then, leaving Jack on his side bleeding into the dirt, Drake said to Diana, 'All right, that was fun for all of us. Now get moving before I lose my happy mood.'

Orc and Dekka were similar in that neither of them was very fast. Jack had been able to bound ahead. It had been, to Dekka's eyes, a surprisingly brave thing to do. Maybe even reckless. Maybe even a little stupid.

But brave.

She didn't want to like Jack. But Dekka valued one virtue above all others, and Jack had shown it.

Now they found him lying on his side in mud made from his own blood.

'He has a pulse,' Dekka said. She didn't need to feel for it. She could see it.

'Huh,' Orc said. 'Drake.'

'Yeah.' She had her palm pressed against the pumping wound in Jack's neck. 'Tear his shirt off for me.'

Orc easily ripped the T-shirt, like he was tearing tissue paper, and handed it to her. She kept her palm in place but pushed the shirt beneath it, pressing it into the cut.

The blood did not stop flowing.

'Come on, Jack, don't die on me,' Dekka said. To Orc she said, 'It's an artery or something. I can't stop it. What am I supposed to do? It won't stop! You're stronger than I am; push against it!'

Orc did as he was told. He mashed the bloody rag against Jack's throat. The pulsing stopped but the pressure seemed to make Jack's breathing raspy.

Dekka looked around, frantic, like she was expecting to suddenly spot a first-aid kit. 'We need needle and thread. Something.' She cursed furiously. 'We have to get him back to the lake. At least someone there can sew him up. We have to go fast. Right now.'

'What about Drake?' Orc demanded.

'Orc, you have to carry him. I can't keep him from bleeding out. We get him back there. Then we go after Drake.'

'It'll be dark soon.'

'We can't let him die, Orc.'

Orc stared in the direction Drake had gone. For a moment Dekka wondered if he would go off after him. And a part of her – a part she wasn't proud of – wished Jack would just die, because he was probably going to anyway and Drake was going to get away.

'I'll take him,' Orc said. 'You go after Drake. Only don't fight him until I catch up.'

'Believe me, I'll be happy to wait for reinforcements,' she said. And silently realised that by herself she could not possibly beat Drake.

She began trotting after Drake, his footprints – and two other sets – still barely visible in the fading light.

Sanjit was now part of a growing crowd of frightened, hesitant kids. He fumed at the delay. Nothing was going right. He should have reached the lake by now. And darkness, real, serious, *this is it* darkness was coming down fast.

The second coyote pack struck without warning after the noisy, disorganised gaggle had turned off the highway and on to the gravel road that led to the lake.

There were hills to the right, and in the distance to the west a dark line of trees that someone told Sanjit was probably the edge of the Stefano Rey National Park.

The two twelve-year-old girls, Keira and Tabitha, and the boy, Mason, were not the immediate targets. Neither was Sanjit. The coyotes came bounding straight down the road as if sent from the lake. Straight down the road, five of them, bypassed a few larger kids, and suddenly converged on a two-year-old girl.

The first Sanjit knew of it were the screams as the coyotes began their rushing attack. He started running. He drew the pistol Lana had given him but there was no way to get a clear shot. Kids in panic were rushing back towards him. Others scattered left and right, screaming, screaming, calling one another's names.

The lead coyote bit the child's arm. She cried. The coyote

dragged her off her feet and started hauling her off the road. He lost his grip and the child was up and running.

The coyotes, almost casual, formed a semicircle, ready to take her down for good.

'Get out of the way!' Sanjit yelled. 'Get out of the way!'

Screams were general now. Dust kicked up. Slanting tea-coloured light cast lurid shadows of fleeing children and the yellow canines.

A second coyote grabbed the child by her dress and began hauling her away.

Sanjit fired in the air.

The coyotes flinched. A couple trotted away to a safe distance. The one with the little girl in his teeth did not.

Sanjit was just a few feet away now, could see blood, could see the coyote's yellow teeth and intelligent eyes.

He aimed the gun from just a few feet and fired.

BAM!

The coyote let go of the girl and ran off. But not far. Not far at all.

Sanjit reached the girl just as her sister did. The girl was bloody but alive. And screaming, everyone screaming and crying. Kids had their cudgels and blades out, too late, bristling with fearful threat.

The coyotes danced eagerly, a pistol shot away. But Sanjit knew he had no chance of hitting one.

'Get moving!' Sanjit yelled harshly. 'If we're still out here, when night comes we're all dead.'

The group of maybe two dozen kids, all huddling close together, moved down the road as hungry coyote eyes watched and tongues lolled, waiting for fresh meat.

Brianna had been down the road as far as the hills. When she saw kids coming towards Perdido Beach she knew Drake hadn't passed that way.

Which meant he might have retreated towards the air national guard base. So she ran there and looked around. And found nothing.

Which left her baffled. Surely she would have seen him if he were close to the lake. Surely he hadn't come along the road. And he wasn't at the base or anywhere between those three points.

She was tired and frustrated. And worried about Sam yelling at her. Which just sent her off towards Coates, because she couldn't come back empty-handed. She was the Breeze: she was the anti-Drake, at least in her own mind. And if he was out and about, running free, she was the one to find him and take him down.

But she hadn't found him. She had found kids leaving Perdido Beach all babbling about the sky dying, and she'd found that rabbits were proliferating near Coates, and she'd found a dropped jar of Nutella on the line between the lake and the air base and had promptly eaten it.

But no Drake.

The sky was so weird. The light so wrong. That blank blackness all around, rising from the horizon to make a new, jagged horizon, it was all wrong.

And if it really did turn dark and stay dark? Then what? Then what for the Breeze? She would be stumbling around in the dark like everyone else. She would go from being important to being just another girl.

Sam wouldn't even need her. He wouldn't ask her to meetings. She wouldn't be his go-to person. The mighty Brianna. Swift Girl. The most dangerous person in the FAYZ after Sam and Caine.

She had to get some altitude; that was it. Get the larger view while there was still a view to get.

She raced towards the Santa Katrina Hills. She blew right past two sets of footprints, registered them belatedly, then raced back to find them again.

They were quite clear. A pair of boots. And a pair of sneakers. Both leading from the hills in the general direction of Perdido Beach. Neither was big enough to be Drake. And he wouldn't be heading that way.

Brianna glanced anxiously at the sky. She couldn't stay out here. And she couldn't go back to Sam with empty hands. It would be the end of her. She had disobeyed orders before, but now to be such a failure, nothing but a few dead coyotes . . . and a failure when her powers might be almost useless . . .

She was nothing if she was not the Breeze.

She raced to the top of the nearest hill, a scraped-bald thing maybe two thousand feet tall. She could make out the lake, shimmering strangely in the unnatural light. Turning the other way she could see the ocean. The road was hidden from view.

What to do?

Then she saw what looked like a person walking. To the north. It was hard to be sure because of the light and the narrowness of the gap between two hills. But she thought she saw a single person moving.

Brianna said a prayer that it might be Drake. She had a plan for dealing with him. A plan that would make Sam proud. She was going to slice and dice him and use her speed to spread the parts all around the FAYZ.

Hah! See if Drake could put himself back together then.

It would be great. If.

TWENTY EIGHT

10 HOURS 54 MINUTES

DIANA'S LEGS ACHED. Her bare feet were bloody. Justin was trying to help her but there was no way to ease the pain of bare soles on sharp stone.

Anytime she slowed or stumbled Drake would snap his whip, and the pain of that was so much worse.

She couldn't imagine that she would make it to the gaiaphage alive.

Diana knew that was the objective. Drake had taken to gloating about it. She'd had plenty of opportunity to think of snide remarks. But each one came at the cost of another slice in her flesh. Or worse yet, Justin's. So she stumbled along in silence.

'Don't know what he wants with you,' Drake said, not for the first time, 'but whatever he leaves is mine. That's all I know. Make some of your witty remarks to the gaiaphage. Hah. Try that.'

He was still looking over his shoulder constantly. Diana had come to think of it as Breezanoia – a terrible fear of Brianna.

'She can come zooming up all she wants,' Drake said. 'See if she can cut me without cutting the brat. See if she can do that.'

Drake was spiralling down almost as fast as Diana herself. His fear was palpable. And not just fear of Brianna. The dying of the light scared him, too.

'Gotta get there before dark,' he muttered more than once.

Diana realised that once absolute night fell Drake would be as lost as anyone. And then how would he keep control of Diana and Justin?

No comfort. They could get away from Drake. Maybe. And then what?

Diana's hand went to her stomach. The baby kicked.

The baby. The three-bar baby. The baby was what he wanted, of course. Diana had no doubt about that. The dark creature wanted her baby.

When she could take her mind off the agony in her feet and legs and back, when she could suspend for a brief few seconds the crushing fear that bore down on her, Diana tried to understand. What did it want with her baby?

Why was this happening?

She missed her step, stumbled, and landed hard on her knees. She cried out in pain, and then screamed as the lash landed across her back.

In a rage she flew at him. Her fists punched and her

fingernails tore but he was far too quick. He punched her in the face. It was not a slap. It was a full, hard punch. Her head swam and she saw stars.

Just like a cartoon, she thought. Then she fell straight back.

When she came to she found Justin next to her, holding on to her and crying.

Brittney was seated a few feet away.

The circle of blue sky was the colour of new denim, and smaller, noticeably smaller than it had been. The sky was a black, featureless bowl.

'You're pregnant, aren't you?' Brittney asked almost shyly.

It took Diana a few moments to make sense of things. Drake was not here. Drake couldn't be here so long as Brittney was.

Whip Hand was not here.

Diana climbed quickly to her feet. 'Come on, Justin, we're out of here.'

'I found some rocks,' Brittney said. She held up a good-size rock in each hand. 'I can hit you with them.'

Diana laughed in her face. 'Bring it, zombie freak. You're not the only one who can find a rock.'

'Yes, that's true,' Brittney said. 'But it won't hurt me when you hit me. And you can't kill me.' Then, as an afterthought she added, 'Anyway, I'm not a zombie. I don't eat people.'

'Why are you doing this, Brittney? You were the one fighting us at the power plant. You were on Sam's side. Or don't you remember that?'

'I remember,' she said.

Diana's mind was turning at top speed. If she told Justin to run back towards the lake, how far would he get before the darkness closed in? Which was worse? To wander alone in the dark until he fell off a cliff or was scented by a coyote or wandered into a zeke field or . . . or . . . or . . .

'Then what happened to you? Why are you helping Drake? You should be fighting him every time you get the chance.'

She smiled and Diana saw the broken wire sticking out of her braces. 'I can't ever fight Drake, you know. We're never together.'

'Exactly. So whenever he's gone you can –'

'I'm not doing this for Drake,' Brittney said earnestly. 'I'm doing this for my lord.'

'Your . . . Your what? Your what? You think God wants you to be doing this? Did you go stupid on top of being undead?'

'We each must serve,' Brittney recited, like a lesson she'd learned a long time ago.

'And you think Jesus wants you to do this? This? Threaten a pregnant girl with a rock? That's your religious theory? Jesus wants you to help a sadistic mental case to turn me over to a monster? I must have missed that part of the Bible. Is that part of the Sermon on the Mount?'

Brittney looked at her, very serious, and waited until Diana had run out of breath, if not scorn.

'That was the old God, Diana. That God was before. He doesn't live in the FAYZ.'

Diana felt like choking the girl. She wondered if she could stun Brittney long enough to get away. Surely a big rock would at least stun her.

But unfortunately everyone knew the story of what had happened when Brianna fought Drake. She had sliced him up like a butcher with a hog. And yet, he had survived. The same would be true of Brittney. And Diana didn't have a machete.

'God is everywhere,' Diana said. 'You were a church girl; you must know that.'

Brittney's eyes were bright, eager, as she leaned forward. 'No. No. I don't have to follow an invisible god any more. I can see him! I can touch him! I know where he lives, and what he looks like. No more little children's stories. He wants you. That's why we came for you.' She made a chiding face. 'You should be excited.'

'You know what? I'm ready for Drake to come back. He's evil, but at least he's not an idiot.'

Diana stood up. So did Brittney.

'Justin,' Diana said.

'Yes?'

'See the place where the hills end? The lake is just past that. Start running.'

'Are you coming?' Justin cried.

'Right behind you. Now, *run*!'

Brittney didn't come after Diana, although Diana swung on her again. Brittney ran after Justin.

She caught him easily. Diana tried to grab Brittney, but a pregnant girl running in the sand . . .

Brittney hugged Justin to her with one arm. In her free hand she held a sharp rock very close to Justin's chattering, fearful mouth. It was a heartbreaking parody of maternal protectiveness.

Diana remembered again who Brittney had once been. The brave, decent girl who refused to disappoint Sam and Edilio.

It was Diana, along with Caine and Drake, who had made this Brittney. Them and, of course, the Darkness. What a fatal little group they had proved to be. Look at the damage they had done, her and Caine and Drake. And the gaiaphage.

Now here they were on their way to a reunion. And Caine's role would be played by his son or daughter.

She had wanted so badly to escape it all. For that briefest moment she believed she had changed Caine. And that was when they had created the baby inside her.

'Keep walking,' Brittney said, actually stroking Justin's face with the stone. 'Please.'

* * *

It was not Drake. The distant figure Brianna had seen was not Drake. It was Dekka. And Brianna had raced up within shouting distance with her machete out before she realised.

She skidded to a halt.

Dekka was covered in blood from hand to elbow, with sprays of it across her face.

'Where have you been?' Dekka demanded without so much as a hello.

Brianna sheathed her machete and decided against answering. 'What's with the blood?'

'It's your boyfriend's,' Dekka grated.

'My what?'

'Jack. He went after Drake by himself. Drake cut his throat.'

Brianna stared at her. 'Are you nuts? Jack went after Drake? Jack doesn't do things like that.'

'He does when there's no other choice,' Dekka said.

Dekka kept looking past her. Brianna kept doing the same. The world was ending, Jack was hurt, maybe dying, maybe dead already, and they were being awkward.

'Drake has Diana and Justin. He's heading towards the mineshaft, towards the gaiaphage.'

Brianna shook her head, feeling like she was missing something. 'Who is Justin?'

'Where were you? You were supposed to be within earshot. Sam shot off some rounds and no Brianna.'

'I was looking for Drake,' Brianna said defensively.

Dekka glared pure fury at her. 'You don't love Jack. You don't even care about him, do you? You haven't even asked how he is.'

Brianna actually took a step back. 'Why are you hating on me?'

Dekka's jaw actually dropped. It would have been almost funny, if it wasn't Dekka. 'Are you that clueless? How do you not understand how irresponsible you are? Right now Orc is running back to the lake with his hands barely holding Jack's blood in. And Drake is probably whipping Diana across the desert.'

Brianna shook her head violently. 'That's not my fault! That's not on me! I was out looking for Drake.'

Suddenly Dekka's bloody fist was flying straight for Brianna's nose. Brianna easily sidestepped and Dekka stumbled forward.

Brianna was too astonished to hit back.

Dekka wasn't finished. She actually kicked at Brianna. This unbalanced her completely and she fell heavily on her side.

Suddenly Brianna found herself in a column of floating sand. She tried to run but there was no solid ground beneath her. Gravity was suspended.

That did it. Brianna yanked out her sawed-off shotgun and levelled it at Dekka. 'Put me down or I'll shoot you!'

Dekka had got to her feet. 'You would do it, too, wouldn't

you?' She waved her hand angrily and Brianna dropped two feet back to earth.

'Do you ever think about anything besides yourself?' Dekka yelled. To Brianna's amazement there were tears in Dekka's eyes. She wiped them away so violently it was like she was slapping herself. She left a smear of blood, like red paint.

'Hey, I'm sorry or whatever,' Brianna said hotly. 'What do you want me to say? I hope Jack's OK. And I'll kill Drake if I get the chance. What do you want from me?'

Dekka's face was an ugly mask of emotion, unreadable to Brianna. Aside from it being obvious that Dekka was mad about something.

'Four months and you haven't even said anything to me,' Dekka said.

'I've talked to you,' Brianna said. But she looked away as she said it, suddenly even more uncomfortable. She could deal with anger. Need was something different.

'I told you –' Dekka began before her voice choked off. She took a few seconds to master it. Then, unable to meet Brianna's eyes, she said, 'I thought I was done for. I mean, I don't scare easy. The pain . . .' That stopped her again; then she shook her head angrily, like she was pushing through it. 'It was bad, that's all. And I was dying. I should have died. But I didn't want to die without telling you.'

'Yeah, whatever,' Brianna said, shifting from side to side and just about unable to resist the desire to go tearing off at a hundred miles an hour.

'I told you I loved you.'

'Uh-huh.'

'And you said nothing. Nothing. For four months.'

Brianna shrugged. 'Look, OK, look.' She swallowed hard. 'Look, besides me you're the bravest, toughest chick in the FAYZ,' Brianna said. 'I mean, I always thought we were like sisters, you know? Like badass sisters.'

Dekka's eyes, so hot and furious, went blank. For a long time she just looked at nothing. At the space beside Brianna. Finally Dekka sighed. 'Like sisters.'

'Yeah, but like rocking-the-tough-chick-thing sisters.'

'But . . . You don't . . .'

This was a Dekka Brianna wasn't prepared for. She looked smaller. She looked like a big rag doll with half the stuffing gone. Darkness was coming on fast now. Shadows were deeper, and the shadows were just shadows of other shadows.

Dekka squared her shoulders. Seemed to be arguing with herself. Finally: 'You're not gay. You don't like girls.'

Brianna frowned. 'I don't think so.'

'Do you like boys?' Dekka asked, her voice strained.

Brianna shrugged. Every part of this made her uncomfortable. 'I don't know, jeez. I made out with Jack a couple of times. But that's because I was bored.'

'Bored.'

'Yeah. And it didn't help that much.'

'You're not in love with Jack?'

Brianna barked out a surprised laugh. 'Jack? Computer Jack? I mean, I like him OK. He's nice. I mean, he's sweet. And if I'm reading a book I don't understand he can always explain stuff. He's smart. But he's not –' And there she stopped herself.

To Brianna's surprise that drew an incredulous laugh from Dekka. 'This is you, isn't it? The real you.'

Brianna squinted. What kind of question was that?

'All this time . . .' Dekka didn't finish the thought. 'Why didn't you just tell me?'

'What?'

Dekka balled her fists up. 'I swear to God I'm going to kill you if you keep playing dumb!'

'I like boys, OK? I think. I guess. Probably. I mean, I'm just thirteen! Jeez! I know it's the FAYZ and all, but I'm really just . . . a kid.'

Brianna blushed. Why had she said that? She wasn't a kid. She was the Breeze. She was the most dangerous person . . . OK, third most dangerous person . . . not a kid, though. Not like a little kid.

Well, she was fast, but she couldn't snatch words back. Jack probably dying. The light going out. Maybe it was just OK to say stuff.

A sharp intake of breath from Dekka. 'You are, aren't you?' Dekka said softly. 'I forget.' She repeated it sadly. 'I forget.'

'I mean, it's like, you know, I have a crush on Sam or whatever, like every other girl – well, except you, I guess – but it's not like that. It's like . . . you know . . .' She tapered off lamely. Then added, 'I just like being the Breeze. With a capital "B".'

All the anger was gone from Dekka. 'I forget, Brianna. I mean, I see you do stuff that's so crazy brave . . . And I see how Sam depends on you. How everyone does. And I see you run into a fight with Drake and, wow, I mean, I look at you and you're, like, everything I ever wanted in a girlfriend. And I forget you're still just a kid.'

'I'm not that young,' Brianna said, now really wishing she could take some of it back.

Dekka sighed a deep, long sigh.

'I mean, maybe in a couple of years,' Brianna said, definitely feeling like she was coming out on the worse end of this conversation.

Dekka laughed. 'No, Brianna. No. A crush on Sam? Making out with Jack? Nope. Nope. I was letting my own . . . I was seeing what I wanted to see. That's what I was doing. I wasn't seeing you.'

'But you and me. We're cool?'

Dekka was crying again, but this time she wiped the tears away with a laugh. 'Breeze, how could we not be cool?

We are definitely the badass sisters.'

'What do we do now? I can't run very fast in the dark.'

'Yep. But we still go after Drake. He's got Diana, and we can't leave her to him. He hates women, you know.'

'Yeah. I did notice that about him.' Brianna felt energy flowing through her again. The tiredness, the frustration, they were gone. And the coming darkness? Well, she could still swing a very, very fast machete. 'The boy hates chicks, right? Let's go give him a good reason to.'

Astrid walked holding Cigar's hand. Sometimes it would freak him out and he'd be convinced she was going to eat him. His mind was gone. Or if not gone forever, then gone for now. Gone until he somehow got help.

But he could see what she could not. He could see her brother. She had sensed it from the start when she had seen the coyote with the human face. Not stupid, but ignorant, heedless. Something or someone with staggering power and no idea how to use it.

Little Pete was an unseen, almighty god who played thoughtless games with the helpless creatures in the FAYZ.

Maybe the stain was his, too.

Maybe he was the one shutting down the light.

Well, it would figure, wouldn't it? Sooner or later the game had to end.

She walked on tired feet towards Perdido Beach, knowing now that it was a hopeless effort.

They were all mere humans, after all. And the closest thing they had to a god was a reckless, indifferent child.

TWENTY NINE

10 HOURS 35 MINUTES

'THAT'S THE BEST I can do,' Roger said. The lower half of his face and the front of his shirt were covered with blood. The deck was smeared with it.

Sam looked down at Jack, covered with a blanket. They couldn't move him. They couldn't really do much for him unless they found a way to bring Lana to him.

Roger had started with green thread. At first that was all anyone could find. That was what he had used to sew up the artery or vein or whatever it was that lay slit and exposed by the angry slash in Jack's neck.

The outer part of the wound was sewn up with white thread, though formerly white was more like it. It was red now.

They had smeared a little of their precious stock of Neosporin on the wound and covered it with a bandage torn from an old flag. Jack's neck was red, white, and blue, though the bandage was soaking through with seeping blood as well.

Roger was the unofficial nurse. Mostly because he seemed

nice and was good with kids. He had taken on the job of sewing up Jack's neck.

He'd said it was like trying to sew a piece of pasta. A piece of pasta that pulsed and sprayed blood.

'Thanks, Roger,' Sam said. 'You absolutely stepped up, dude.'

'He's so pale,' Roger said. 'Like a piece of chalk.'

Sam had nothing to say about that. Lana could save Jack. But she was far away, and soon there would be almost no way to even contact her.

Where was that little bimbo Taylor? They needed her.

He had stopped being mad at Brianna, because now he was just too worried about her. If she was out there running around after Drake, Sam would kill her. Hug her first. Then kill her.

This couldn't be. It just couldn't. Poor Jack, who had maybe not always been the most stand-up guy in the world, but who had never had a mean bone in his geeky body. And Breeze missing. And Diana. Howard dead. Orc heading back into the fray.

And Astrid.

It was all coming apart in his hands. He was watching his whole world bleed out like Jack.

'We've got Astrid, Dekka, Diana – and I hope Brianna – all out there in the desert with Drake,' Sam said. 'Orc's on his way back out. And in an hour they'll all be in absolute darkness.'

'And Justin,' Roger said, making a point of it.

'And Justin,' Sam agreed.

Edilio wiped his face with his hand, a sign of nervousness in the usually impassive Honduran.

Suddenly Sam remembered the first time he'd run into Edilio after the coming of the FAYZ. It had been up at Clifftop. Edilio had been trying to dig under the barrier. Practical, even then.

'Look,' Sam pressed. 'People here have lights. It's not much, but they have something; they can at least see. What chance do those kids out there in the desert have?'

'Drake's probably reached the mineshaft by now,' Edilio said.

'No,' Roger said sharply. 'No. Don't do that. Don't just write Justin off like that.'

Sam saw shame on Edilio's face. 'I'm sorry, babe; you know I love that little guy. I didn't mean it like that.'

Edilio reached for Roger, then, with a darting sideways glance at Sam, stopped himself.

Roger had made an identical move, and also stopped after an abashed glance at Sam.

Sam stood very still, and for a few very awkward seconds no one spoke.

Finally Sam said, 'Edilio, I have to go after them.'

'We can't risk you, Sam. What if you're killed? What if

there's no more light, and you're it; you're the only thing between us and total darkness?'

'Then we're all dead anyway, Edilio.' Sam spread his hands in a helpless gesture. 'We barely stay alive in this place as it is. In total darkness? A few Sammy suns won't save us.'

'Look, we have to keep people calm. That's what's most important.'

It was a job that suddenly got a lot harder as a gaggle of a dozen kids came pelting madly down the slope past the Pit.

'Help us! Help! Help us!'

The coyotes knew their prey were getting close to safety. That was Sanjit's conclusion as he watched them begin closing in.

The crowd on the road had grown. Kids had huddled closer together as the darkness deepened. Kids who had started out later ran till they were falling down, desperate to catch up.

Those who had begun with a lead began to doubt the wisdom of being out front. So front and back had joined middle and now they were a mob of thirty kids, spilling off the road, moving as a cluster, walking as fast as they could, crying, whining, complaining loudly, demanding . . . Demanding of whom, Sanjit couldn't guess.

This was officially a fiasco, he knew. One of those efforts that was doomed from the start. His little mission to tell Sam what was happening in Perdido Beach, to hand him Lana's request for lights in Perdido Beach, all a waste of time.

Too late. And unnecessary, anyway, since the crowd of refugees would have got the same point across.

A stupid, wasted effort.

He didn't blame Lana for sending him. It never occurred to him to blame her. He was head over heels, lost, lost, lost in love with her. But she would agree – if he ever saw her again – that it had not worked out very well.

He could barely see a hundred feet to either side of the road. The gloom that had been weirdly tea coloured had now deepened and shifted in the spectrum. The air itself seemed a dark blue. There was an element of opacity to the light that remained. Like it was foggy, but of course it wasn't.

A hundred feet was enough to see the coyote pack. Their lolling tongues. Their intelligent, hyper-alert yellow eyes. The way their ears stood up and swivelled to each new sound.

As soon as it was dark they would come. Unless the kids reached the lake before that happened. Sanjit could read anxiety in their avid expressions and the way they paced back and forth.

'Everyone just stay together and keep moving,' he urged.

Somehow he was in charge. Maybe it was that he was the only one with a gun. Others had the usual assortment of weapons, but his was the only gun.

Or maybe it was his association with the revered Lana. Or the fact that he was among the three oldest kids.

Sanjit sighed. He missed Choo. He missed all his brothers and sisters, but especially Choo. Choo was the pessimistic one, which allowed Sanjit to be the perky optimist.

One of the coyotes had had enough and started trotting purposefully towards the crowd of kids.

'Don't do it!' Sanjit yelled, and aimed the pistol. Zero chance of hitting the animal from here, in this light, with his total lack of skill. But the coyote stopped and looked at him. More curious than afraid.

Sanjit knew the animal was sizing the situation up. In the maths of a coyote the smart move was to kill as many as the pack could. Meat didn't have to be fresh for them; they could drag the bodies away at their leisure and eat for weeks.

Then the coyote spoke. The voice was a shock: guttural, slurred like a shovel dragged through wet gravel. 'Give us the small ones.'

'I will absolutely shoot you!' Sanjit said, and walked forward, holding the gun with both hands, self-consciously emulating a hundred TV cop shows.

'Give us three,' the coyote said without the slightest evidence of fear.

Sanjit said something rude and defiant.

But someone else yelled, 'It's better than all of us getting eaten!'

'Don't be stupid,' Sanjit snapped. 'They just know we're

close to the lake. Trying to distract us so –' The horrible reality of his own words came to him.

Too late.

He spun and shouted, 'Look out!' Three of the coyotes, unobserved as the people all fixated on Pack Leader, attacked the rearmost kids.

There were screams of pain and terror. Screams that made Sanjit feel as if his own flesh were being torn.

Sanjit ran towards the back, but this was the signal for Pack Leader and two others to attack the front.

Everyone bolted, kids knocking one another down, stepping on one another, being knocked down in turn to cries and screams and pleas and the awful growls of the coyotes as they went after slow, defenceless children.

Sanjit fired. *BLAM! BLAM! BLAM!*

If the coyotes even noticed, they gave no sign.

He saw Mason going down beneath two growling beasts. The older girls were already far up the road. Keira turned, stared, her mouth wide in horror, and ran away.

Sanjit jumped in the air and landed with both feet on one of the coyotes. The animal rolled away and was on its feet again while Sanjit was still absorbing the landing. A kid or a coyote, he didn't see which, knocked him down and a coyote was on him in a heartbeat, fangs snapping in his face.

BLAM!

The coyote's right eye exploded outward and the beast collapsed atop Sanjit.

Two coyotes were fighting over Mason, like dogs fighting over a toy. Dead. Dead by now, dead.

He aimed, but badly, hands shaking, chest heaving.

BLAM!

One of the coyotes ran off with a child's leg in its mouth.

Kids from the front, other kids from the back were being torn at by the coyotes. And the crowd, the herd – because that's what they were now, a terrified herd no different from antelope panicked by a lion attack – ran as fast as they could.

There was nothing Sanjit could do.

Pack Leader stood with his legs braced wide. Something awful was in his jaws. He stared at Sanjit and growled.

Sanjit ran.

Diana glanced up at the sky. It was a habit now. A fearful habit.

It was a sphincter at the top of a black bowl. A fitting commentary on the FAYZ, Diana thought. A giant sphincter.

Justin held on to her as they walked, and she to him.

Which is worse? she wondered. *To reach the mineshaft before darkness falls? Or not?*

She had dragged her feet and stalled every step of the way on the theory that whatever the gaiaphage wanted, she was for the opposite. But then Drake reemerged and any slight delay meant pain.

He drove them forward with his whip. Like some ancient slave master. Like some long-ago Egyptian beating a Hebrew, or a not-so-long-ago overseer whipping a black slave.

But she saw that he, too, glanced up at the sky. He, too, was afraid of the coming darkness.

They had reached the ghost town. There wasn't much to it any more. Some sticks and boards. Suggestions of places where a saloon and a hotel and a stable might once have been. There was a better-maintained building set apart from the others, and it was from this building, through a creaky door, that Brianna stepped.

Diana almost fainted with relief.

'Hey, guys,' Brianna said. 'Out for a walk?'

'You,' Drake hissed.

'Weren't you expecting me?' she asked. She made an embarrassed face. 'Wasn't I invited?'

Drake snapped his whip and wrapped it around Justin. He jerked the terrified boy through the air and held him over his head.

'Move and I smash his brains out,' Drake said.

'And then what?' Brianna asked in a silky whisper.

'Then Diana.'

'Yeah, I don't think so, Drake Worm Hand; I don't think

you brought her all this way to kill her.' Then, to Diana: 'What do you think, Diana? Has he told you what he wants?'

She was stalling. Diana knew it, but did Drake? And if someone as headlong and impetuous as Brianna was stalling for time it meant she had an ally. Someone obviously slower than herself.

'It's my baby he wants,' Diana said.

Brianna made a fake-astonished face. 'Is that true, Drake? Is it because you love babies?'

Drake shot a look up the path that led from town up the hill and to the mineshaft. He was only a few hundred yards away from the opening. He would be confident about finding his way that far in the dark. But he couldn't be sure that Brianna would care about Justin. Even slowed down by darkness, Brianna could probably outrun him and cut him up.

'If you trip in the dark, Brianna, it'll be all over for you. Trip at a hundred miles an hour, hit a rock? It'll kill you. If it doesn't, I will.'

He still held Justin aloft.

'Let me down,' the boy cried pitifully. 'Please let me down. I'm scared up here.'

'Hear that, Brianna? He's scared. He's scared I might let him down too fast. Ouchie.'

Brianna nodded like she was considering this. Stalling. She took a deep breath and blew it out slowly. Stalling.

Diana saw her eyes dart to her right. Who was coming? Who was she waiting for? Brianna must have passed them on her way here. She must have chosen not to take Drake on alone and instead moved to block his path while reinforcement was on its way.

That indicated someone a bit wiser than her. Sam. Or maybe Dekka. Not Orc. Sam or Dekka, they were the only two who could help Brianna in a fight with Drake and be smart enough and carry enough influence to convince her to wait like this.

Diana dared to hope. If it was Dekka she could stop Justin from falling. If it was Sam maybe, at long last, he would rid the universe of Whip Hand.

There came a sound.

Coming from the gloom on the ghost town's long-forgotten main street.

Diana saw the wicked smile of triumph on Brianna's face.

Brianna drew her machete.

And from the darkness walked – limped – a small, barefoot girl in a sundress.

OUTSIDE

'PROFESSOR STANEVICH?'

'Yes.' The voice was clipped. Annoyed. Heavily accented. 'Who are you? This is a private number.'

'Professor Stanevich, listen to me, please,' Connie Temple begged. 'Please. We appeared on CNN together once. You probably don't remember. I'm one of the family members.'

A pause on the other end. She was at an ancient, graffiti-tagged pay phone outside a gas station minimart in Arroyo Grande. She couldn't use her own cell phone for fear of betraying Darius. She hadn't used Stanevich's office phone for fear that it, too, might be tapped.

'How did you get this number?' Stanevich asked again.

'The internet can be very useful. Please listen to me. I have information. I need you to explain something to me.'

Stanevich sighed heavily into the phone. 'I am with my children at the Dave and the Buster. It is very noisy.' Another sigh, and sure enough, Connie could hear the sounds of video games and clattering dishes. 'Tell me your information.'

'The person who gave me this information is in very serious trouble if it gets back to him. The army has dug a secret tunnel; it's on the eastern edge of the dome. It's very deep. And security is very, very tight.'

'They are presumably drilling to see the extent of this recent change in the energy signature –'

'No, Professor, with all due respect. There are nuclear response teams here. And the tunnel they've drilled is thirty-two inches in diameter.'

Nothing but the sounds of Dave & Buster's.

Connie pressed on. 'They don't need a shaft that size to send down a probe or a camera. And my source says there is a rail descending.'

Still no response. Then, when she was sure he'd decided to hang up: 'What you are suggesting is impossible.'

'It's not impossible, and you know it. You're one of the people who warned that breaching the dome might be dangerous. You're one of the reasons people are so scared of this thing.' Connie held her breath. Had she pushed too far?

'I was discussing various theoretical possibilities,' Stanevich huffed. 'I am not responsible for the nonsense from the media.'

'Professor. I want you to discuss the theoretical possibilities of this. Of a nuclear weapon . . . Please. If it will release the children, then that's one thing. But –'

'Of course it will not release the children.' He snorted a laugh into her ear. 'It will do one of two things. Neither of them involves peacefully releasing the children inside.'

'The two things. What are they?' A highway patrol car pulled in and she gripped the phone hard. The car slid into a parking place. The patrolman looked at her. Recognising her from TV?

'It depends,' Stanevich equivocated. 'There are two theories of the so-called J waves. I won't bore you with the details – you wouldn't understand anyway.'

The patrolman got out. Stretched. Locked his car and went into the minimart.

'A nuclear device would release a great deal of energy. Which might overload the dome, might blow it up. Think of it as a hair dryer, let us say, yes, a hair dryer that runs on one-hundred-and-ten-volt electricity. And suddenly it is plugged into ten thousand volts.'

He sounded as detached as if he was lecturing a room full of undergraduates. Pleased with his hair dryer analogy.

'It would be blown apart. Combust.'

'Yes,' Connie said tersely. 'Wouldn't that also blow up everything nearby?'

'Oh, certainly,' Stanevich said. 'Not the device itself, you understand, not if it is buried deep. But a twenty-mile-wide sphere that suddenly overloads? It would likely obliterate everything inside. And perhaps, depending on various factors, destroy an area around the dome.'

Connie's stomach was in her throat. 'You said two possibilities.'

'Ah,' Stanevich said. 'The other is more interesting. It may be that the barrier is not overloaded. It may be that it can convert the energy. It may take the sudden release of energy and essentially store it. Soak it up like an incredibly efficient battery. Or, let us say, a sponge.' He made a dissatisfied sound. 'It's not a perfect analogy. No, far from it. Ah, here it is: the barrier's energy signature is changing, yes? Weakening. So imagine a starving man who at last gets a good, healthy meal.'

'If this happens, the absorbing thing. What does that do to the barrier? Maybe it makes it easier to get through.'

'Or it strengthens it,' Stanevich said. 'Alters it in ways we cannot yet predict. It will be fascinating, though. More than one PhD dissertation will result.'

Connie hung up the phone. She walked quickly to her car.

Her head was buzzing. Stanevich was as much of an ass as when he'd been on CNN with her. But now his willingness to speculate was welcome, even if the details were horrifying.

There was time to stop this. She would make a public stink. She just had to figure out how to do it. Talk to the media, surely, but how to best bring pressure on the army and the government to stop this reckless madness?

She drove up 101 and practically ran into a column of army vehicles coming towards her. Trucks. Flatbeds loaded with trailers.

Two miles from Perdido Beach she saw the flashing lights of police cars. A roadblock. They were diverting traffic off the highway, on to a side road, and sending it back south.

Connie pulled on to the shoulder and stopped, breathing hard. Of course they saw her. She couldn't outrun them; the CHP would pull her over and wonder why she had run, and then there would be explanations demanded.

She pulled up to the roadblock. Highway patrol and army MPs were running the roadblock together. She knew the MPs.

She leaned out of the window. 'Hey, what's up?'

'Mrs Temple,' the corporal said, 'there's been a bad chemical spill up the road. A truck carrying nerve agent.'

Connie stared into the young face of the corporal. 'That's your story?'

'Ma'am?'

'This road's been closed for almost a year. And your story is that some trucker carrying deadly chemicals did what? Took a wrong turn and crashed?'

The MP's lieutenant stepped up. 'Mrs Temple, it's for your own safety. We're pulling everything back until we figure out how to contain the spill.'

Connie laughed. This was their cover story? Was she supposed to believe them? It would be a strain to even pretend to believe them.

'Just take the side road here,' the lieutenant said, and pointed with a sort of karate-chop hand. Then, in a voice that was at once compassionate and hard, he added, 'It's not optional, ma'am. You know the Oceano County Airport? That's the rendezvous. I'm sure the soldiers there will fill you in on all the details.'

THIRTY

10 HOURS 27 MINUTES

SAM LEAPED FROM the top deck straight down on to the dock and raced towards the onrushing refugees.

None too gently he pushed them aside and ran on through, up past the Pit, up to the gravel road, up to where he could hear snarling and a gun being fired.

Sanjit ploughed into him and for second Sam didn't know who he was. He held him out at arm's length, said, 'Stay out of the way,' and took off for the scene of slaughter.

That he was too late was apparent. The coyotes weren't killing at this point; they were feeding and dismembering.

He raised his palms and a beam of searingly intense green-white light shot forth. The beam caught part of a body and the head of a coyote. The coyote's head ballooned like a time-lapse video of a burning marshmallow.

Sam swept the beam up the road to where coyotes were already racing away, dragging bodies or pieces of bodies along through the dirt. He caught a second coyote in the hindquarters, which erupted in flame. The coyote howled in pain, fell, tried to keep running with just its two front legs, and lay down on its side to die.

The rest were out of range by then, some even abandoning their meat.

Sanjit came running up to stop beside a heaving, panting Sam.

A boy, maybe twelve, unrecognisable but alive and crying pitiably, lay in two pieces in a bush off the road.

Sam took a deep breath, marched to him, took careful aim, and burned a neat hole in the side of his head. Then he widened his beam and played it over the corpse until there was nothing but ashes.

He shot an angry look at Sanjit. 'Anything you have to say about that?'

Sanjit shook his head. He couldn't form a complete thought. Sam wondered if he'd be sick. He wondered if he himself would be.

'If it was me . . .' Sanjit began, and ran out of words.

That blunted Sam's anger. But only a little. This was his fault. It was his job to protect . . . Why hadn't he sent Brianna off months ago to exterminate the last coyotes? Why hadn't he thought to send a patrol up the road to meet the inevitable refugees?

He now faced the task of cremating the rest of the dead.

There was no way he could let brothers and sisters and friends see what the coyotes had left behind. These mangled slabs of meat could not be what loved ones carried with them in memory for the rest of their lives.

'Why are you here?' Sam demanded as he began his grisly work. 'Did you bring these kids here?'

'Lana sent me.'

'Explain.' He didn't know Sanjit well. Just knew that he had pulled off something close to a miracle in flying a helicopter from the island to Perdido Beach.

'Bad stuff in Perdido Beach,' Sanjit began. 'Penny somehow managed to cement Caine. They're going to try to free him, but last I saw Caine he was crying and having his cemented hands beaten on with a hammer.'

Sam's reaction surprised him: his first feeling was worry, and even outrage, on Caine's behalf.

Caine had been an enemy from the start. Caine was responsible for battle after bloody battle. He had come close to killing Sam on more than one occasion. Maybe, Sam reflected, he was reacting to the fact that Caine was, after all, his brother.

But no. No, it was that Caine was strong. And however much of a power-mad jerk he was, Caine would have tried to keep some kind of order. He would have – probably – worked to avoid panic. Always for his own reasons, but still . . .

'So, Albert's in charge,' Sam said thoughtfully, and burned a foot resting almost comically upright.

'Albert bailed,' Sanjit said. 'Quinn talked to him as he was heading to the island with three girls.'

This was worse news than the incapacitation of Caine. A lot worse. There were three major powers in the FAYZ: Albert, Caine, and Sam. Three people whose combination of power and authority and skills might have kept things together for a few days or a week until . . . until some kind of miracle happened.

Albert, Caine, and Sam. That was the foundation of the stability and peace of the last four months.

'Did you see Astrid?' Sam asked.

'Astrid? No. I don't even know if I would recognise her; I've only seen her once, months ago.'

'She went to warn you guys about the stain. And offer my . . . my light-hanging services.'

'Well, I guess I'm relieved that I'm not the only one off on a wild-goose chase.'

Sam looked sharply at him. There was some steel in this kid. He had been the last one to run from the coyotes. And judging by the fat pistol in his hand and the discarded weapons lying along the road, he'd been the only one to really give them a fight.

And he hadn't quibbled when Sam did the hard but merciful thing.

'Sanjit, right?' Sam said. He held out his hand.

Sanjit took it. 'I know who you are, Sam. Everyone does.'

'Well, you're with us for now.' He jerked his head up at the sky.

'I have a family,' Sanjit said. 'I have to get back.'

'Brave is good,' Sam said. 'Stupid is another thing. Those coyotes don't need light to find you. You're a friend of Lana's, right?'

Sanjit nodded. 'Yeah. We live at Clifftop with her.'

'The Healer has you living with her?' he asked incredulously. 'I'm learning all kinds of things today.'

'I guess she's my girlfriend,' Sanjit said.

Sam fired at what looked like a chunk of hamburger wearing a part of a T-shirt.

'If you're with Lana, then your family is as safe as anyone. You getting killed won't help them. You're with us now. Just one thing: talk freely to Edilio, but no one else. Clear? If kids hear that Albert has bailed . . .' He shook his head. 'I thought better of Albert than that.'

It left a bad taste in his mouth, Albert running away. No doubt it made good business sense. But the word 'treason' was on the tip of his tongue.

Backstabber.

Coward.

Astrid was on her way to offer an alliance with a beaten and humiliated 'king' and a cowardly 'businessman'.

He shoved away the image of the coyotes finding her before she could reach town. There were thoughts too painful to allow.

He had to think, and think clearly, not let his mind be seized and paralysed by lurid images of Astrid brought down in some lonely place by coyotes, or zekes, or Drake.

He squeezed his eyes shut.

'Are you OK?' Sanjit asked.

'OK?' Sam shook his head. 'Nope. I'm not. The guys I was counting on to be with me aren't. It was already hopeless. Now?'

'Lana's still there,' Sanjit said. 'And Quinn.'

'Quinn?' Sam frowned. 'What's he got to do with anything?'

'Lana put him in charge. He's got his people with him.'

Sam nodded, distracted. He was seeing a chessboard in his mind. Most of the pieces he might have played, the powers that might have helped, his bishops and knights and rooks, were all down or missing. Dekka, Brianna, Jack, Albert, possibly Caine, all down or missing. His steady knight, Edilio, would have to watch over the lake. Which left Sam with pawns.

On the other side Drake. Maybe Penny. The coyotes.

And the opposing king, the gaiaphage, who was so well protected he might be impossible to reach, let alone destroy.

'What was that TV show?' Sam asked, rubbing his face to clear away the smoke of burning bodies. 'The one where they vote you off the island?'

'*Survivor?*'

'Yeah. "Outwit, Outplay, Outlast." Right?'

'I guess,' Sanjit said doubtfully.

'Outwitted and outplayed. That's me, Sanjit. You just joined the losing team. I've got nothing left. And pretty soon? I'll be blind.'

'No. Not you, Sam. You're the only one who won't be.'

'Sammy suns?' Sam laughed derisively. 'They might as well be candles.'

'In the land of the blind the one-eyed man is king,' Sanjit said.

'In the dark the one guy with a candle is an easy target,' Sam countered.

One thing was crystal clear to Sam: his job was not to sit here and protect his charges at the lake. That was a losing move. That was him waiting for the enemy to gather its forces to come for him. Maybe he'd been outwitted and outplayed. He had not yet been outlasted.

Without another word to Sanjit he headed back to the lake.

Diana saw Penny and her knees gave way. She sat down hard in the dirt. She couldn't breathe.

No, she mouthed soundlessly.

Penny looked at Drake first. At his terrible tentacle. At the little boy suspended in the air. She glanced curiously at

Brianna, like she wasn't quite sure who she was.

Then she looked at Diana, and her eyes widened with pleasure. Her smile started small and grew and grew and became a laugh of pure delight. She clapped her hands together.

'Too good,' Penny said. 'Too, too good.'

Diana's mind had stopped working. Thoughts would not form. Reactions would not take shape. Fear took her. A low keening sound came from deep in her throat.

This was no longer about pain: terror was here.

Drake shot a look at Penny. 'Who are you?'

'I'm Penny,' she said. 'You used to push me out of your way back at Coates. I was nobody to you.'

'You have a beef with me?' Drake asked, just a little worried.

Penny smiled. 'Oh, you were just a jerk, Drake. Nothing special. Whereas Diana . . .' She laughed her demented, delighted laugh. 'I absolutely love Diana. She took such good care of me on the island.'

'Leave me alone,' Diana heard herself beg, like hearing someone else, not like the words were coming from her, because she had no words in her brain; she could see what was coming; she knew what was coming.

God save me, Diana begged, *God save me, save me, save me.*

'How's the baby, Diana?' Penny asked, her voice slithering, her eyes bright. 'Do you want a boy or a girl?'

And suddenly the baby woke up, and its claws came out like

the claws of a tiger, and its insect face with sabre mandibles ripped at her insides, tearing through the flesh of her belly, tearing out of her, a wild animal, nothing human there, but no, that wasn't true; it had Caine's face, his face but smeared across a soulless ant-face and the claws and the pain, and she screamed and screamed.

Diana was facedown in the dirt. Penny's bare feet – one of them crusted with bloody mud – were in front of her.

There was no monster baby.

Her belly had not been torn open.

Diana cried into the dirt.

'Cool, huh?' Penny said.

'What did you do to her?' It was Drake, fascinated.

'Oh, she just saw something. She saw her baby as a monster. And she saw it rip her apart from the inside. Felt it, too,' Penny said.

'You're a freak?' Drake asked.

Penny laughed. 'The freakiest of the freaks.'

'Don't hurt the baby,' Drake warned. He tossed Justin aside, ready to take this interloper on if necessary. The boy landed hard but without breaking anything.

Penny was not intimidated by Whip Hand. 'What's in there?' She indicated the narrow path leading up to the mineshaft.

Drake didn't answer. His whip was ready to slash at her. But he hesitated, unsure if she was friend or foe.

'I've felt it since I got close,' Penny said, looking past Drake up at the path. 'I was just wandering. Going nowhere. And then, little by little, I realised I was going somewhere.' She said this in a sing-song voice. 'I was going here.' Then, like a person waking out of a dream, she said, 'It's that thing Caine went to, isn't it? The Darkness. The thing that gave you that whip hand.'

Drake said, 'Would you like me to introduce you?'

'Yes. I would,' Penny said very seriously.

Diana had stolen tear-distorted glances at Brianna, who seemed content to let this go on, so long as it ate up more time. Now Brianna spoke. 'I don't think you two are going anywhere.'

She flew at Drake.

But Diana had been there at times when Brianna moved at top speed. When she moved at top speed you didn't see her arms or legs; you didn't see her draw her deadly machete. Diana saw those things now and knew that the Breeze had slowed.

But she was still fast.

The machete swung and Drake's whip was cut in half. Five feet of flesh-coloured tentacle lay in the dirt like a dead python.

Brianna spun, came back around fast, but with her eyes carefully down on the ground, cautious, distracted, and suddenly she cried out, skidded, leaped across something Diana could not see.

Penny had struck!

Drake picked up his severed tentacle and pushed the two

stump ends together. He looked less furious than peevish. The injury was at worst a temporary inconvenience.

Brianna was jumping around like a crazy person, leaping from place to place, focused like mad on every move, arms windmilling for balance.

'What is she doing?' Drake asked.

Penny laughed. 'Trying not to fall into the lava. And her friend, Dekka? The one she was expecting to show up? She's out there somewhere . . .' She jerked her head back towards the night-dark desert. 'Trying to get her little brain back to reality.'

Diana saw wary concern on Drake's face. It was beginning to occur to him that perhaps Penny might be more than he could handle. 'Let's go. The gaiaphage is waiting.'

'Do you think I'm cute?' Penny asked him.

Drake froze, stood stock-still, and now the look on his face was more than just wary.

'Yeah,' Drake said. 'Yeah. You're cute.'

His tentacle had grown back, the stumps melding quickly together, smoothing as if he was made out of clay and an invisible hand was pinching the edges together, then rolling the whole thing like a Play-Doh snake. He raised the whip high and snapped it in front of Diana's face.

'Now move,' he said.

Diana watched Brianna, still leaping desperately, trapped in some illusion of danger.

And she saw the little boy, Justin, crawl ahead of her into the darkness.

Dekka lay sobbing in the darkness. She could barely see her hands in front of her face.

She didn't know what had happened to her. Just that in an instant she had been frozen, completely immobile. Paralysed.

She'd been covered in a translucent white goo, like clay or Silly Putty. And it had coated every single inch of her body. It had pushed its way into her ears. Like invisible fingers were poking it in there, filling her right up to the eardrums.

So that she could hear nothing but the beating of her own heart.

So that she could hear the gristle in her neck as she squirmed helplessly.

The white putty was pushed into her nose. So deep, up into her sinuses. She had to breathe through her mouth, but as soon as she opened her mouth the white stuff filled her mouth and pushed its way into the space between her teeth and her cheeks, under her tongue, then down her throat. She gagged but it didn't matter; the stuff filled her mouth and throat and she could feel it cold and dense and heavy in her lungs.

She screamed but no sound came out.

In some panic-free corner of her mind, some small remnant of Dekka knew this wasn't real. It couldn't be real. She knew it was Penny who had done this, who had filled her mind with this vision.

But she could not breathe. Could. Not.

She was buried alive in it, buried alive, and her brain screamed in a way that her body no longer could.

Had to be an illusion. Had to be a trick. But did it really? Was she so sure it wasn't real in this nightmare world?

She couldn't breathe, but she realised too that she wasn't dying. Her heart still beat. She was covered and filled with the white stuff, and she should be dying but she wasn't.

Then she felt the white stuff harden. It wasn't putty any more but fast-drying clay. Already her teeth bit on something as hard as porcelain.

Then the bugs were inside of her.

The bugs.

Not real, she knew that in some tiny, cowering corner of her mind; couldn't be real, the bugs had been eliminated. They'd been made non-existent. So there was no way they could be inside her again, no way they could be swarming through her guts and no Sam to cut them out and let them out; she was trapped inside this porcelain tomb and they were inside her again.

She screamed and screamed and screamed.

Suddenly, all of it was gone.

She was on dirt. Air was in her nose. Her eyes opened.

A girl had stood there and said, ‘That’s a new one for me. Did you like it?’

And Dekka, trembling like a leaf ready to fall, said nothing. Just breathed. Breathed.

‘Don’t come after me,’ Penny had said.

And Dekka had not.

THIRTY ONE

10 HOURS 4 MINUTES

'**RING** THE BELL,' Sam said.

Edilio nodded at Roger, who ran off to ring the bell atop the marina office.

'What are you going to do?' Edilio asked.

'Why didn't you tell me you were gay?' Sam demanded.

Edilio looked like he'd been punched. But he recovered quickly, to go to an expression that was half-wary, half-embarrassed. 'You got enough stuff to deal with.'

'That's not something I have to "deal with", Edilio. My girlfriend lost, the world ending, having to go out there after Drake, that's stuff I have to deal with. Me finding out you've got someone to care about like that? How is that something I have to deal with?'

'I don't know, I just . . . I mean, it took me a while to kind of figure it out. You know.'

'Does everyone except me know?' Sam asked. He realised this was a stupid concern; this was hardly the time to worry about seeming out of touch. But no one had been closer to him than Edilio, almost from the first day. It bothered him to think everyone knew something he didn't. It hurt his feelings.

'No, man,' Edilio reassured him. 'No. And it's not about me being, you know, ashamed or whatever. It's that . . . look, I have a lot of responsibility. I have to have people trust me. And some kids are still going to call me a faggot or whatever.'

'Seriously? We're about to be plunged into eternal darkness and you think those kids out there are going to worry about who you like?'

Edilio didn't answer. And Sam had the feeling maybe Edilio knew more than he did on the subject. He let it go.

'I gotta tell you the truth, man,' Sam said, shaking his head slowly, side to side, as he spoke. 'I don't see a way out of this. I don't even see the starting point for a way out of this. I don't expect us to survive this.'

Edilio nodded. Like he knew this. Like he was ready for it to be said.

'So in case this is it, Edilio, in case I go out there and don't come back, I want to say thank you. You've been a brother to me. My true brother.' Sam carefully avoided looking at Edilio.

'Yeah, well, we're not done for yet,' Edilio said gruffly. Then, more pointedly, 'So you're going?'

'Everything you said before is right,' Sam said. 'We can't afford me getting killed. Not in the short run. But once I turn on some lights we're still done for if we don't find a way to turn this around. We can't grow crops or fish or survive living in the dark. Next thing that happens is people will start setting fires. Perdido Beach will burn all the way down next time. The forest will burn. Everything. Kids won't live in the dark.'

He was interrupted by the loud ringing of the bell. When it was finished he said, 'I'm not the only one scared of the dark, Edilio. Anyway, this is just part of something bigger. Something is happening. I don't know what, but something big and . . . and final. So, yeah, short-term I'm important. But if I want to be important long-term, I need to go out there and find a way.'

'You going to talk to everyone?' Edilio asked.

'Yeah.'

Barely visible in the darkness, mere shadows on the water, the boats rocked and drifted lazily. The Sammy suns shining through portholes were the only light. Bodies could be seen only when they passed before one of those lights.

'Then make sure you tell them the truth.'

'Toto!' Sam yelled down. 'Get up here.'

When Toto was on deck Sam lit a Sammy sun just over his head. Like a gloomy spotlight. It revealed him, Edilio, and Toto.

'Toto's here so you know I'm telling you what I believe is true,' Sam shouted to be heard across the water. 'First: I don't think we have to worry about Drake here at the lake. He's gone – for now, at least.'

Toto said, 'He believes it,' but in a whisper.

'Speak up,' Edilio said.

'He believes it!'

'So you're all coming back ashore. We have kids who've come here from Perdido Beach. They've lost people on the way here, and we're going to take them in and care for them.'

Some grumbling and a couple of defiant, shouted questions came out of the dark.

'Because good people help people who need to be helped. That's why,' Sam yelled back. 'Listen. Things are bad in Perdido Beach. It seems Caine is out of business. And so is Albert.'

'He believes it!'

'So that's bad. Astrid is . . .' Emotion clenched his throat but he pushed forward. He had nothing to hide, he realised. It wasn't like anyone didn't know he was worried about her. 'She's out there in the dark somewhere. And so are Brianna and Dekka and Orc. Jack, well, we don't know if he'll make it.'

'True,' Toto said. Then, louder, 'True!'

'Drake has Diana and Justin, who is just a little kid, and we don't know for sure what Drake is up to. Whatever it is, I believe it's connected to this stain that is blotting out the light.'

Toto just nodded and no one seemed to care.

Sam looked up. The stain was no longer blotting out the light. It had finished its work. The small circle of darkening blue had turned flat black.

'So, I don't have some big plan. I just don't.' He repeated it, feeling amazed that it was true. 'I have a reputation as the guy who comes up with a way out of trouble. Well, I don't have that now.'

Someone was crying, loudly enough to be heard. Someone else shushed him.

'That's OK. Cry if you want to cry, because I feel like crying with you.'

'Yes,' Toto said.

'You can be sad and you can be scared. But we built this place and kept ourselves going by hanging in there together. Right?'

No one answered.

'Right?' Sam demanded more insistently.

'Damn right,' a voice called back.

'So we hang together still. Edilio is here. You listen to Edilio.'

'But you're the leader!' a different voice cried, and others seconded it. 'We need you! Sam!'

Sam looked down, not pleased, really, but maybe a little gratified. At the same time, though, he was beginning to realise something. It took a few moments to form coherently in his mind. He had to check it against what he knew, because at first it seemed wrong.

Finally he said, 'No. No. I'm a lousy leader.'

There was a pause before Toto said, 'He believes it.'

Sam laughed, amazed that he really did believe it. 'No, I'm a lousy leader,' he repeated. 'Look, I mean well. And I have powers. But it's Albert who kept people fed and alive. And up here it's Edilio who really runs things. Even Quinn, he's a better leader than me. Me? I get pissed off when you need me, and then I pout when you don't. No. Edilio's a leader. I . . . I don't know what I am, except for being the guy who can make light shoot out of his hands.'

He stepped back, out of the direct glow of the Sammy sun, baffled by the unexpected turn his speech had taken. He had meant to tell everyone to stick together and be disciplined. He had ended up feeling like a fool, taking a momentous occasion to just make an idiot of himself.

Edilio spoke up. He had a softer voice. And still had a trace of his Honduran accent. 'I know what Sam is. Maybe, like he said, he's not a great leader. But he's a great fighter. He's our warrior; that's what he is. Our soldier. So what he's going to do, Sam, what he's going to do is go out there into the dark and fight our enemies. Try to keep us safe.'

'He believes it,' Toto said unnecessarily.

'Yeah,' Sam whispered. He looked down at his hands, palms up. 'Yeah,' he said louder. Then, still to himself: 'Well, I'll be damned. I'm not the leader. I'm the soldier.' He laughed and looked at Edilio, his face nothing but shadows in the light of the Sammy sun. 'It takes me a while to figure things out, doesn't it?'

Edilio grinned. 'Do me a favour. When you find Astrid,

repeat that to her, word for word, the part about how it takes you a while. Then remember her exact reaction and tell me.'

Then, serious again, Edilio said, 'I'll take care of these people here, Sam. Go find our friends. And if you run into Drake, kill that son of a bitch.'

The sky closed.

Darkness. Absolute, total darkness.

Astrid heard her own breathing.

She heard Cigar's hesitant footsteps. Slowing. Stopping.

'We aren't far from Perdido Beach,' Astrid said.

How strange what absolute black did to the sound of words. To the sound of her own heart.

'We have to try to remember the direction. Otherwise we'll start walking in circles.'

I will not panic, she told herself. I will not let the fear paralyse me.

She reached for Cigar. Her hand touched nothing.

'We should hold hands,' Astrid said. 'So we don't get separated.'

'You have claws,' Cigar said. 'They have poison needles in them.'

'No, no, that's not real. That's a trick your mind is playing on you.'

'The little boy is here,' Cigar said.

'How do you know?' Astrid moved closer to the source of his voice. She thought she was quite close to him. She tried to call on other senses. Could she hear his heartbeat? Could she feel his body warmth?

'I see him. Can't you see him?'

'I can't see anything.'

She should have brought something to use as a torch. Something she could burn. Of course, showing light out here in the open would make her visible to people and things she didn't want seeing her.

It was just that the pressure of the dark – and that was how it felt, like pressure, like it wasn't an absence of light, but like it was black felt or something hung in drapes all around her – was hemming her in. Like it was a physical obstruction.

Nothing had changed except that light had been subtracted. Every object was exactly where it had been before. But that wasn't how it felt.

'The little boy is looking at you,' Cigar said.

Astrid felt a chill.

'Is he talking?'

'No. He likes quiet.'

'Yes. He always did,' Astrid said. 'And darkness. He liked the dark. It soothed him.'

Had Petey made all of this happen? Just to get his blessed silence and peace?

'Petey?' she said.

It felt ridiculous. She was talking to someone she couldn't see. Someone who probably wasn't there. Someone who, if he existed at all, was not human, not anything physical or tangible.

The irony made her laugh out loud. She'd just given up talking to one perhaps unreal spiritual entity. Now here she was doing it again.

'He doesn't like when you laugh,' Cigar said, shushing her.

'Too bad,' Astrid said.

That brought silence. She could hear Cigar breathing, so she knew he was still there. She didn't know whether he was still looking at Petey. Or something that was supposed to be Petey.

'He was in my head,' Cigar whispered. 'I felt him. He went inside me. But he left.'

'Are you saying he took you over?'

'I let him,' Cigar said. 'I wanted him to make me be like I used to be. But he couldn't.'

'Where is he now?'

'He's gone now,' Cigar said sadly.

Astrid sighed. 'Yeah. Just like a god, never there when you need one.'

She listened hard. And smelled the air. She had an impression, barely an impression, that she could tell in which direction the ocean lay.

But she also knew that the land between where she was and

the ocean was largely fertile fields seething with zekes. Zekes that had probably not been fed in some time.

There were fields between her and the highway, but once she got to the highway she would be able to follow it towards town. Even in the dark she could stay on a concrete highway.

Sam wanted to follow the road from the lake down to the highway, because that was where Astrid would be. Most likely. Despite none of the refugees having seen her on their way from Perdido Beach to the lake.

But finding Astrid was not the right move. Not yet. She would slow him down, even if he found her. And she wasn't a soldier. She wasn't Dekka or Brianna or even Orc. They could help him win a fight; Astrid could not.

But oh, Lord, how he wanted her now. Not to make love but just to have her there in the darkness beside him. To hear her voice. That above all. The sound of her voice was the sound of sanity, and he was entering the valley of shadow. Walking into pure, absolute darkness.

He walked until he was out of the faint circle of light cast by the numerous Sammy suns of the lake. Then he hung a new light, taking solace from the sphere as it grew in his hands.

But the light reached only a few feet. Turning back as he walked on, he could see it. But it cast only a faint light, a light whose photons seemed to tire easily.

Into the darkness. Step. Step.

Something was squeezing his heart.

His teeth would fragment if he bit down any harder.

'It's just the same as it was,' he told himself. 'Same but darker.'

Nothing changes when the light goes out, Sam. His mother had said that a thousand times. *See? Click. Light on. Click. Light off. The same bed, the same dresser, the same laundry you've strewn all over the floor . . .*

Not the point, that younger Sam had thought. *The threat knows I'm helpless in the dark. So that's not the same.*

It's not the same if the threat can see and I can't.

It's not the same if the threat knows it doesn't have to hide, but can make its move.

Useless to pretend the darkness isn't any different.

It's different.

Did something bad happen to you in the dark, Sam? They always wanted to know. Because they assumed all fear must come from a thing or a place. An event. Cause and effect. Like fear was part of an algebra equation.

No, no, no, so not getting the point of fear. Because fear wasn't about what made sense. Fear was about possibilities. Not things that happened. Things that might.

Things that might . . . Threats that might be there. Murderers. Madmen. Monsters. Standing just a few inches from him, able to see him, but his eyes useless. The threats, they could laugh silently at him. They could hold their knives, guns, claws right in his face and he wouldn't be able to see.

The threat could be. Right. Here.

His legs already ached from tension. He glanced back at the lake. He had been climbing and it was below him now, a sad collection of stars like a dim, distant galaxy. So very far away.

He couldn't look back for long because the possibilities were all around him now.

The light of day showed you the limits of possibility. But walk through the dark, the absolute, total darkness, and the possibilities were limitless.

He hung a Sammy sun. He didn't want to leave it behind. It was light that revealed stones. A stick. A dried-out bush.

It was almost better not to bother. Seeing anything just made the darkness seem darker. But the lights were also a sort of bread-crumb trail, like Hansel and Gretel. He would be able to find his way home.

Hopefully as well, he'd be able to see whether he was veering left or right.

But the lights had one other effect: they would be seen by whatever else was out here.

In the land of the blind the one-eyed man is king. But in the darkness the one man holding a candle is a target.

Sam walked on into the dark.

* * *

Quinn had brought everyone into the plaza with grilled fish. The fire still burned, but lower and lower.

Lana had healed all who needed it.

For now there was quiet.

Kids had broken into Albert's place and come back with some of his hoard of flashlights and batteries. Quinn had quickly confiscated them. They were worth far more than gold, far more even than food.

Some of Quinn's crew were using the light of a single flashlight and a number of crowbars to tear apart the pews in the church and bring them out to keep the fire going.

No one was leaving. Not yet.

The orange-red glow cast a faint, flickering wash of colour on the limestone of the town hall, on the long-abandoned McDonald's, on the broken fountain. On grim young faces.

But the streets leading away simply disappeared. The rest of the town was invisible. The ocean, occasionally faintly audible over the sound of snapping wood and muted conversation, might as well be a myth.

The sky was black. Featureless.

All of the FAYZ was just this bonfire now.

Close to the fire sat Caine. People left plenty of room for him. He smelled. And he still cried out in pain as a new pair of kids – the third pair – chipped away at his hands by firelight.

They were down to the small stuff now. The very painful, small strokes that often drew blood.

Every now and then Lana would come by to heal a cut or two so that the blood didn't render the concrete too slippery for the chisel.

Quinn was there at the moment when a firm blow separated Caine's hands so that they were no longer attached to each other.

'The palms first,' Caine ordered, still somehow commanding, despite everything.

They used needle-nose pliers to pry pieces off. Skin came away, too. Each time they asked him if it was OK, and each time he gritted his teeth and said, 'Do it!'

His hands were being skinned. Piece by piece.

Quinn could barely stand to watch it. But he had to admit one thing: Caine might be a thug, an egomaniac, a killer, but he was no coward.

Lana pulled Quinn aside a little way, into the dark beyond the reach of firelight. Down Alameda Avenue until Quinn could see nothing. Not even the hand in front of his face. 'I wanted you to see just how dark it is,' she said.

She was inches from him. He could see nothing.

'Yeah. It's dark.'

'Do you have a plan?'

Quinn sighed. 'For total darkness? No, Lana. No plan.'

'They'll burn buildings if the fire goes out.'

'We can keep the bonfire going for a while. We'll feed the whole town in, piece by piece if we have to. And we have water. Little Pete's cloud is still producing. It's the food.'

They both had too many memories of hunger. Silence.

'We're bringing all the food in. From storage at the Ralphs, from Albert's compound. People didn't have much in their homes. Add it all up and we've got maybe two days' short rations. Then it starts.'

'Starvation.'

'Yeah.' He didn't know what the point of this conversation was. 'Do you have a plan?'

'It won't take two days, Quinn. You feel what this darkness does to you? The way it closes in around you? All of a sudden kids realise they're in this big fishbowl. Fear of the dark, fear of being closed in. Most will be OK for a while, but it's not about "most". It's about the weakest links. The kids who are already about as messed up as they can be.'

'Anyone goes nuts we'll deal with him,' Quinn said.

'And Caine?'

Quinn said, 'You're the one who put me in charge, Lana. I hope you didn't think I had some magic answer.'

A third breathing sound could be heard. 'Hi, Patrick. Good boy.'

Quinn heard her fumbling around in the dark, looking for his ruff, finding it, then scratching it vigorously.

'They'll start going crazy,' Lana said. 'Absolutely crazy. When that happens . . . ask Caine for help.'

'What's he going to do?' Quinn asked.

'Whatever it takes to keep people under control.'

'Wait a minute. Whoa.' He had an instinct to grab her arm. But he didn't know where her arm was. 'Are you telling me to turn Caine loose on anyone who gets out of line?'

'Can you stop some bunch of kids if they decide to steal the food for themselves? Or go nuts and start burning things?'

'Lana. Why does it matter?' he asked. He felt the energy draining from him. She had asked him to take over. Now she was telling him to use Caine like a weapon. For what? 'What does anything matter, Lana? Can you tell me that? Why should I hurt some kid for losing his mind when anyone could lose their mind?'

Lana said nothing. She said nothing for so long Quinn began to wonder if she had left silently. Then, in a voice so low it didn't even sound like her: 'In the dark like this I can feel it. So much closer. It's more real to me than you are because I can see it. I see it in my head. There's nothing else to see, so I see it.'

'You're not telling me why I should hurt anyone, Lana.'

'It's alive. And it's scared. It's so scared. Like it's dying. Like that kind of scared. I see . . . I see images that don't really mean anything. It's not really reaching for me any more. It doesn't have time to reach for me any more. It's the baby it wants. All its hopes are on the baby.'

'Diana's baby?'

'It doesn't have the baby yet, Quinn. Which means it's not over yet. Even here in the dark, with all of us so scared. It's not over. Believe that, OK? Believe that it's not over.'

'It's not over,' Quinn said, feeling and probably sounding puzzled.

'Those kids back there, if they start to panic they'll hurt themselves. I won't be able to find them and help them, so they'll die. And see, that's what I'm not going to let him do. The gaiaphage, I mean. I can't kill him, I can't keep him from getting the baby. What I can do, and what you can do, too, Quinn, is keep as many of us alive as possible, for as long as possible. Maybe because it's the right thing to do. But also . . . also . . .' He felt her touch his chest, fumble from there to find his shoulder, then down to take his hand and hold it with a surprisingly strong grip. 'Also because I'm not letting him win. He wants us all dead and gone, because as long as we live, we're a threat. Well, no. No. We're not going to give up.'

She let go of his hand.

'It's the only way I have left to fight him, Quinn. By not dying, and by not letting any of those kids back there die.'

THIRTY TWO

8 HOURS 58 MINUTES

PENNY HAD NEVER felt like this before. She'd never experienced a sense of awe. Never even known what people were talking about when they went on and on about some sunset or the sweep of stars in a clear night sky.

But now she was feeling something.

She couldn't see. It was as black as if her eyes had been gouged out. (A thought that made her smile at memories of Cigar.) And yet she knew where she was going.

Her cut foot no longer mattered. When she stubbed her toe on a rock it didn't matter. That she had to feel her way along the narrow path with her hands out like a blind person; it didn't matter, none of it, because she could feel . . . feel something so great, so, so magnificent.

She'd never been here before, but it was a homecoming anyway.

She laughed out loud.

'You can feel it, can't you?'

Penny was startled by the voice. It was coming from where Drake had been but it was a girl's voice. Of course: Brittney.

'I feel it,' Penny confirmed. 'I feel it.'

'When you get closer you'll hear his voice inside you,' Brittney said. 'And it's not some dream or something; it's real. And then, when you get all the way down to the bottom, then you can actually touch him.'

Penny thought that sounded weird. Not that she had a big problem with weird. But Brittney was not Drake. Drake she could respect. The whip hand – and even more, the will to use it – made Drake powerful.

And attractive, too, as she remembered from former days. She hadn't ever paid that much attention to him back then because Caine was the one for her. Caine had the dark good looks and the brain – so smart. Drake had been a very different boy: like a shark. He looked like a shark, with dead eyes and a hungry mouth.

Well, she'd been wrong about Caine. Caine was totally under the thumb of that witch Diana. Drake, though, he sure didn't love Diana. In fact, he hated her. He hated her as much as Penny did.

Maybe Drake was better-looking after all. Anyway, good luck to Diana trying to steal him away like she had Caine.

Brittney was bringing up the rear. Then Penny. Diana and

Justin stumbled and wept and fell down in front, feeling their clumsy way along.

Unfortunately Penny could not sustain the illusion that had terrified Brianna from this distance. It would have faded by now. Which meant Brianna was free to come after them.

Penny grinned in the dark. Good luck catching them. Let Brianna come back in range again. Her speed was useless now. She was nothing now. The Breeze? Hah. If she came within range Penny would make her run, run real fast, run until her legs broke. Hah!

'He'll speak to me; he'll speak to you,' Brittney said in that lilting voice. 'He'll tell us what to do.'

'Shut up,' Penny snapped.

'No,' Brittney chided in a voice dripping with sincerity. 'We mustn't fight amongst ourselves.'

'We mustn't?' Penny mocked her. 'Shut up until Drake comes back.' Then, not happy with the silence from Brittney, silence that sounded like disapproval, Penny said, 'I don't take orders from anyone. Not you. Not Drake. Not even the whatever you call it.' But she licked her lips nervously as she said it.

'The gaiaphage,' Brittney said. She laughed, not cruelly, but with a knowing condescension. 'You'll see.'

Penny was already 'seeing'. Not that she could see anything, not even a finger held right up to her eye, but she could feel the power of it. They had reached the entrance to the mineshaft. The darkness, already absolute, was now tight around them.

It was easier to find their way, just to feel for the timbers along the side. But harder to breathe.

A low moan escaped from Diana.

Penny had a fleeting impulse to give her something to be scared of. But that was the problem: fear was the very air they were breathing now.

'There are some hard places,' Brittney warned. 'There's a big, big drop. It will break your legs all up if you fall.'

Penny shook her head, a gesture no one could see. 'No way. No way. Done that, not doing it again.'

Brittney's voice was silky. 'You could always leave.'

'You think I . . .' Penny had to struggle to take the next breath. 'You think I won't?'

'You won't,' Brittney said. 'You're going to the place you always wanted to be.'

'No one tells me –' Penny snarled. But the defiance died in mid-sentence. She tried again. 'No one . . .'

'Careful,' Brittney said smugly. 'This next section is all jumbled-up rock. You'll have to crawl over it.' Then, in that weird prophetic voice she got from time to time, she said, 'Crawl on our knees, on our knees we crawl to our lord.'

Brianna was breathing hard without moving.

The darkness, it was her kryptonite. Couldn't use super-speed when you couldn't see where you were going.

So dark. It was actually worse than the images Penny had put in her head. Those had been cool in a way. This, though, this was just nothing.

Just nothing nothing nothingness.

Well, not total nothing, now that she thought about it. When she held the machete up in front of her face there was the tangy smell of steel. She drew her shotgun and there was the feel of the short stock and the smell of gunpowder residue.

She could imagine the muzzle flash. It would be loud.

Bright, too.

Now there was a thought. She had what? Twelve rounds?

Yeah. Interesting.

There were sounds, too. She could hear them all up the path. Probably at the mineshaft entrance by now.

Brianna could feel the dark presence of the gaiaphage. She wasn't immune to that dark weight on her soul. But she wasn't paralysed by it. She felt the gaiaphage, but it didn't frighten her. It was like a warning, like a terrible deep voice saying, 'Stay away, stay away!' But Brianna didn't scare worth a damn. She heard the warning; she felt the malice behind it; she knew it wasn't a fake or a joke; she knew it represented a force of great power and deep evil.

But Brianna wasn't wired the way most people were. She'd

known that about herself – and about other people – for some time. Since even before the FAYZ, but much more now since she had become the Breeze.

She remembered once when she was young. How old was she then? Maybe three? Her and some older kids, that boy and his stupid sister who used to live three houses down. And they said, 'We're going to sneak into the old restaurant that burned up.'

It was a big old Italian restaurant. It looked half-normal from the outside except there was yellow police tape across the charred front door.

The two kids, she had no idea what their names were, tried to get little Brianna to be spooked. 'Oh, look, that's where some guy burned up. His ghost is probably haunting this place. Boo!'

She hadn't been scared. Actually she'd been disappointed when she realised there was no ghost.

Then came the rats. There must have been two dozen of them, at least. They came scurrying out like they were being chased, rushing from the burned-out kitchen into the smoke-stinking dining room where the three kids were and the Olafsons – that was their name, Jane and Todd Olafson – those two had screamed and run for it. The girl, Jane, had tripped and cut her knee pretty badly.

But Brianna had not run. She'd stood her ground with her talking Woody doll in one hand. She remembered one of the rats had stopped and cocked its rat face to look at her. Like it couldn't believe she wasn't running. Like it wanted to say, 'Hey, kid, I'm a huge rat: why aren't you running?'

And she had wanted to say, 'Because you're just a stupid rat.'

She felt her way step by step now. Way too slow for a normal person, let alone the Breeze.

'Oh, I feel you, old dark and scary,' she muttered. 'But you're just a stupid rat.'

Sam could look back and see a string of ten lights behind him. The line they made wobbled a bit but it was basically straight. Of course, he could no longer see the lake or its firefly lights.

He wondered about all the others out in this terrible darkness. Some maybe had flashlights going slowly dim. Some might have built fires. But many were just walking into darkness. Scared. But not stopping.

Walking into darkness.

His feet were going up a hill. He allowed it. Maybe he would see something from higher up. It was strange. He wished Astrid was here to talk to about how strange it was to move like this, blind, feeling a hill but not seeing it, not knowing was he near the top or not even close?

Everything was about feel now. He felt the slope with his ankles rather than seeing it with his eyes. He felt it in his forward lean. When the angle increased he was caught by surprise and stumbled. But then it would lessen and that, too, would catch him by surprise.

He hung a Sammy sun. It took him a while to make sense of his immediate surroundings. For one thing, there was an old rusted beer can.

For another he was less than six feet from what might be a sheer drop. It might have killed him if he'd gone off. Then again, maybe it was only a two-foot drop. Or six. He stood at the edge and listened hard. He could almost hear the emptiness of that space. It sounded big. It felt huge. And maybe he could develop those senses someday. But not now, not right now at the edge of a one- or ten- or hundred-foot drop.

He picked up the rusted beer can and dropped it over the edge.

It fell for perhaps a full second before it hit something.

And then it fell some more.

Stopped.

Sam breathed and the sound of his own breath seemed dramatic in the darkness.

He was going to have to backtrack down this hill. Or risk taking a long fall. He turned carefully, slowly, a one-eighty. He was pretty sure that the lake was blocked from view by the bulk of the hill. But he wasn't absolutely sure. A single point of light appeared. It was as small as a star, much dimmer, and orange, not white.

A single distant point of barely visible light. Probably a bonfire in Perdido Beach. Or out in the desert. Or even out on the island. Or maybe it was just his imagination.

The sight of it wrung a sigh from Sam. It didn't make the dark less dark; it made the dark seem vast. Endless. The tiny point of light served only to emphasise the totality of the darkness.

Sam started back down the hill. It took all his willpower to turn left when he reached the lowest light on the hill and move towards the ghost town.

Or where he thought, hoped, pretended the ghost town might be.

'Aaaahhh, aaaaahhh, aaaahhhh.'

Dekka cried into the dirt. A despairing sound. She cried and gasped in air mixed with dirt and cried again.

Penny had taken her most terrible fear – that the bugs could return – and she had doubled it. Dekka would rather die than endure it. Rather die a thousand times. She would beg for death before she would live through it again.

She heard someone crying and then screaming and then babbling, all three mixed up together, all of it coming from her own mouth.

Trapped and eaten alive.

Eaten from the inside out, forever, no end, trapped inside

seamless white stone, alabaster, a tomb that went inside her, immobilised her so that she couldn't even lash out, couldn't move as they ate her insides . . .

Never let it happen again.

Never.

Would kill herself first.

She clutched dirt in her hands, squeezed it like she was holding on to reality. The dirt ran through her fingers and she gathered more and again it got away and she grabbed at more and more, needing something to hold on to, and something to hurt. Needing to feel her body move and not be in that terrible, blank white-stone prison.

She was just a girl. Just some girl. Just this girl with the stupid name of Dekka. She had fought enough. And what for? For emptiness. For loneliness. All of it came to here. To this nothing. To clutching at sand and jibbering like a crazy person, beaten.

Die here, Dekka. It's OK if you do. It's OK to just lie here in the dark and let your eyelids close, because there's nothing more to see, Dekka; do you hear me? Do you, Dekka? Because there's nothing for you but fear. And death is better because death is the end of fear, isn't it?

Quiet. Peace.

It wouldn't be suicide. That was was the thing you could never do, right? Never kill yourself. But let yourself go? Where was the sin in that?

You want me to explain how I could wish for that, God? Tell you what, hit the rewind button and play the last hour . . . no, no, the last, what's it been, almost a year?

Not even enough. Come on, God, you want to see, right? Have a good laugh. See what you did to me. Make me brave and then break me. Make me strong and leave me weeping in the dirt.

Make me love and then . . . and then . . .

Just kill me, OK? I give up. Here I am. You can see in the dark, right, God? Don't you have night-vision goggles? You know, the ones that make everything green and glowing? Well, strap them on and take a good long look at what you did.

See? See me here facedown in the dirt?

Can you hear me?

Can you smell me? Because when the fear had me I made a mess all over myself. Fear does that, you know.

So, I beg of thee, all right? Oh, most high Lord: kill me. Do I have to beg? Is that it? You get off on that? OK. I beg you to kill me.

'I don't want to kill you.'

Dekka laughed. In her fevered mind she thought for a second there she'd heard an actual voice. The voice of God.

She waited, silent.

Something was there. She could sense it. Something close.

'Is that you, Dekka? It sounds like you.'

Dekka said nothing. The voice was familiar. It probably did not belong to God.

'I was out here. I heard you crying and yelling and praying and all,' Orc said.

'Yeah,' Dekka said. Her lips were coated with dirt. Her nose was blocked by it. Her body was damp with sweat.

She couldn't think of anything else to say.

'Like you was wanting to die.'

He couldn't see that she was facedown in the dirt. He couldn't see that she was finished. Beaten.

'You can't kill yourself,' Orc said.

'I can't . . .' Dekka began, but then she couldn't form any more words without spitting the dirt out of her mouth.

'If you kill yourself, you go to hell.'

Dekka snorted, a derisive sound, as she spit dirt. 'You believe in hell?'

Dekka waited while he thought it out. And suddenly she wanted to hear the answer. Like it mattered.

'No,' Orc said at last. 'Because we're all children of God. So he wouldn't do that. It was just a story he made up.'

Despite herself Dekka was listening. It was hard not to. Talking nonsense was better than remembering. 'A story?'

'Yeah, because he knew our lives would be really bad sometimes. Like maybe we'd be turned into a monster and then our best friend would get killed. So he made up this story about hell, so we could always say, 'Well, it could be worse. It could be hell.' And then we'd keep going.'

Dekka had no answer to that. He had completely baffled her. And she was almost angry at him, because baffled was a different thing from despairing. Baffled meant she was still . . . involved.

'What are you doing out here, Orc?'

'I'm going to kill Drake. If I find him.'

Dekka sighed. She stuck out her hand and eventually encountered a gravelly leg. 'Give me a hand up. I'm a little shaky.'

His massive hands found her and propped her up. Her legs almost gave way. She was drained, empty, weak.

But not dead.

'Are you OK?'

'No,' she said.

'Me neither,' Orc said.

'I'm . . .' Dekka stared into the darkness, not even sure she was looking in his direction. She paused until a sob subsided. 'I'm afraid I won't ever be me again.'

'Yeah, I get that, too,' Orc said. He sighed a huge sigh, like he'd walked a million miles and was just so weary. 'Some of it is stuff I did. Some of it is stuff that just happened. Like the coyotes eating on me. And then, you know, what happened after that. I never wanted to remember that. But none of it goes away, not even when you're really drunk or whatever. It's all still there.'

'Even in the dark,' Dekka said. 'Especially in the dark.'

'Which way should we go?' Orc asked.

'I doubt it matters much,' Dekka said. 'Start moving. I'll follow the sound of your footsteps.'

'Aaaahhh,' Cigar screeched. His hand in Astrid's squeezed with incredible strength.

It was not the first time he'd suddenly cried out. It was a fairly regular thing for him. But in this case there were other sounds. A rush of wind, a stink like rotting meat, and then a snarl.

Cigar was torn away from Astrid.

She instinctively dropped into a crouch. A coyote missed its attack as a result and rather than closing its jaws around her leg just ploughed into her with enough force to knock her on her back.

She fumbled in the dark for her shotgun, felt something metallic, not sure which way it was pointing, fumbled, and was brushed aside by a rushing coyote, fur over muscles.

They could hunt in the dark, but the close-in killing work was harder without sight.

Astrid rolled over, flat, stretching her arm, trying to find the shotgun. One finger touched metal.

Cigar was screaming now in that despairing, beaten voice of his. And the snarling was intensifying. The coyotes were frustrated, too, it seemed, unable to pinpoint their prey, snapping blindly where their ears and nose told them the prey would be.

Astrid rolled towards the gun and now she was on top of it, feeling with trembling fingers, searching for – yes! She had the grip. She pushed it forward, probably filling the barrel with sand, probably jamming the trigger. She tried to tell where Cigar was, rolled once more, pulling the shotgun on top of her, and fired.

The explosion was shocking. A jet of light so much bigger than it had ever seemed before.

In the split-second flash Astrid saw at least three coyotes, and Cigar mobbed by them, and a fourth just a few feet away, lips back in a snarl, all of it freeze-framed for the duration of the flash.

The noise was awesome.

She pushed herself to one knee, aimed at the place where the fourth coyote had been standing, and pulled the trigger again. Nothing! She'd forgotten to jack another round in. She did it, aimed shakily at blank space, and fired again.

BOOM!

This time she was expecting the flash and saw that the coyote she'd aimed at was no longer there. Cigar was no longer mobbed by the beasts. His terrible, white marble eyes stared.

Something had happened to the coyotes. They had exploded.

The flash wasn't enough to show more. Just that their insides were where their outsides had been.

Silence.

Darkness.

Cigar panting. Astrid, too.

The smell of coyote guts and gunpowder.

It was a while before Astrid could master her voice. Before she could reassemble her shattered thoughts into something like coherence.

'Is the little boy here?' Astrid asked.

'Yes,' Cigar said.

'What did he do?'

'He touched them. Is it . . . Is it real?' Cigar asked tentatively.

'Yes,' Astrid said. 'I think it's real.'

She stood with her smoking shotgun in her hands and looked at nothing. She was shaking all over. Like it was cold. Like the darkness was made of wet wool wrapped all around her.

'Petey. Talk to me.'

'He can't,' Cigar said.

Silence.

'He says it will hurt you,' Cigar said.

'Hurt me? Why doesn't it hurt you?'

Cigar laughed, but it wasn't a joyful sound. 'I'm already hurt. In my head.'

Astrid took a breath and licked her lips. 'Does he mean it will make me . . .' She searched for a word that wouldn't hurt Cigar.

Cigar himself was beyond worrying about euphemisms.

'Crazy?' He said. 'My brain is already crazy. He doesn't know how to do it. Maybe it would make you crazy.'

Astrid's fingers ached, she was clutching the gun so hard. There was nothing else to hold on to. Her heart beat so loud she was sure Cigar must hear it. She shivered.

Anything else. Not that. Not madness.

She could get all the answers she needed by way of Cigar. Except that Cigar was coherent for only snatches of time before he spiraled down into lunatic rantings and shrieks.

'No,' Astrid said. 'Not taking the risk. No. Let's get going.'

Like she knew which way to go. She'd been following Cigar, who had been following – or so he said – Little Pete.

Panic. It tickled her, teased her. There was something smothering about the darkness. Like it was thick and hard to breathe.

The darkness was so absolute. She could walk in circles and never know it. She could walk into a zeke field and not know it until the worms were inside her.

'Just turn the damned lights on, Petey!' she yelled.

Her words seemed to barely penetrate the blackness.

'Just fix it! You're the one who did this. Fix it!'

Silence.

Cigar started moaning and giggling again, talking about Red Vines and how good candy tasted.

She had a vision of herself back at the lake, lying in the

bunk with Sam. She had loved touching his muscles. What an embarrassing, juvenile thing. Like the girls she despised, always mooning over some rock star, some movie star, some guy with hard abs and yet, and yet, hadn't that been her all along?

She recalled with intimate detail having her hand on his biceps when he flexed to pick her up and the way the muscle had just doubled in size and become hard as if it were carved out of oak. He'd lifted her up like she weighed nothing. And set her down again, so gently, with her hands sliding to his chest to balance and . . .

And now, she was here. With a ghost and a lunatic. In the dark.

Why?

Risk your sanity and maybe know something. But maybe not. Maybe just be destroyed. And what would she know then, if Petey scrambled her mind?

Scrambled brain, full of things she needed to know, but wouldn't really know if her brain was twisted in the learning.

'Fix it! Fix it!' she screamed at the dark.

'My leg, it's not my leg; it's a stick, a stick with nails poking through,' Cigar moaned.

A dark, terrible urge to turn the shotgun around and end Cigar's misery had Astrid breathing hard and clenching her jaw. No. No, she'd already played Abraham to Petey's Isaac, not that ever again. She would not allow herself to take an innocent life, not ever again.

Innocent, a derisive voice in her head taunted. *Innocent? Astrid Ellison, prosecutor and jury and executioner.*

There's nothing innocent about Petey, the voice teased. *He built this. All of it. He made this universe. He's the creator and it is all his fault.*

'Let's go,' Astrid said. 'Give me your hand, Cigar.' She shouldered the shotgun. She felt around in the dark until she found Cigar, and then fumbled some more before she had his hand. 'Get up.'

He got up.

'Which way?' Cigar asked.

Astrid laughed. 'I have a joke for you, Cigar. Reason and madness go for a walk in a dark room, looking for an exit.'

Cigar laughed like it had been funny.

'You even know what the punch line is, you poor crazy boy?'

'No,' Cigar admitted.

'Me neither. How about we just walk until we can't walk any more?'

OUTSIDE

CONNIE TEMPLE SAT sipping coffee at a booth in Denny's. Across from her sat a reporter named Elizabeth Han. Han was young and pretty but also smart. She had interviewed Connie several times before. She reported for the *Huffington Post* and had been on the Perdido Beach Anomaly story from the start.

'They're setting off a nuclear device?'

'The so-called chemical spill is a trick. They just want everyone away from the dome. They must have deliberately left it for the last minute so it would seem like a real emergency.'

Han spread her hands wide. 'A nuclear explosion, even underground, will show up on seismographs all over the world.'

Connie nodded. 'I know. But –' At that moment Abana Baidoo came into the restaurant, walked past the hostess, and slid into the booth beside Connie. Connie had called her but told her nothing. Quickly, and without revealing Darius's name, she backed the story up to the start.

'Are they out of their minds?' Abana demanded. 'Are they insane?'

'Just scared,' Connie said. 'It's human nature: they don't want to just wait, feeling powerless. They want to do something. They want to make something happen.'

'We all want to make something happen,' Abana snapped. Then she put a reassuring hand on Connie's arm. 'We're all worn-out with worry. We're all sick of not knowing.'

Elizabeth Han barked out a laugh. 'They can't do this without approval from very high up. I mean, all the way up.' She shook her head thoughtfully. 'They know something. Or at least they suspect something. This president doesn't go off half-cocked.'

'We have to stop it from happening,' Connie insisted.

'We still don't have any idea what caused this,' the reporter said. 'But whatever it is, it rewrote the laws of nature to create that sphere. They didn't just decide this overnight; there must have been a plan in place for a long time. They wanted this as an option. So why suddenly, now, use that option?'

'The dome is changing,' Connie said. 'They briefed us. There's some change in the energy signature or whatever.' She looked at her friend. 'Abana. They don't want our kids coming out. That's why. They think the barrier is weakening. They don't want our kids coming out.'

'They don't want whatever made this coming out,' Abana

said. 'I can't believe they're targeting our kids. It's whatever made this happen.'

Connie hung her head, aware that she was bringing conversation to a halt, aware that Abana and Elizabeth were exchanging worried glances.

'OK,' Connie said, wrapping both hands around the ceramic coffee mug and refusing to look at either woman. 'What's happened inside . . . I mean, the kids who have developed powers . . . I never shared this, and I'm so sorry. But with Sam . . .' She bit her lip. She looked up sharply, her jaw set. 'Sam and Caine. Their powers developed before the anomaly. I saw them both. I knew what was happening. The, whatever they are, the mutations, they came before the barrier. Which means something caused them besides the barrier.'

Elizabeth Han was thumbing frantically into her iPhone, taking notes, even as she said, 'Why would this scare the government any more than –' She frowned and looked up. 'They think the dome is the cause of the mutations.'

Connie nodded. 'If that's the way it is, then when the dome comes down the mutations will stop. But if it's the other way around, if the mutations came before the barrier, then maybe they caused the barrier. Which means this isn't all just some freak of nature, some quantum flux or whatever, or even an intrusion from a parallel universe, all those theories. This means there's something or someone inside that dome with unbelievable power.'

Elizabeth Han looked grim as she went back to taking notes. 'You have to give me the name of the person who told you about the nuke. I need to source this.'

Out of the corner of her eye Connie saw Abana pull back. A cold distance opened between them for the first time since the anomaly had begun. Connie had lied to her. All this time, as they had suffered together, Connie Temple had been holding something back.

And now, Connie knew, Abana was wondering if somehow her friend could have kept this from happening.

'I can't give you his name,' Connie said.

'Then I can't run the story.'

Abana stood up abruptly. She banged the table hard and rattled the cups. 'I'm stopping this. I'm calling the parents, the families. I'm going to get around that roadblock, and if they want to blow up my child, they'll have to blow me up, too.'

Connie watched her go.

'What do you want me to do?' the reporter asked Connie, angry and frustrated. 'You won't tell me who gave you this information; what am I supposed to do?'

'I promised.'

'Your son –'

'Darius Ashton!' Connie said through gritted teeth. Then,

quieter, more calmly, but hating herself, she repeated, 'Sergeant Darius Ashton. I have his number. But if you leak his name he'll end up in prison.'

'If I don't get this out, and right now, it sounds like all those kids inside may die. What's your choice?'

'Sergeant Ashton? Sergeant Darius Ashton?'

He froze. The voice, coming from behind him, was unfamiliar. But the tone, the repetition of his name, that told him all he needed to know.

He forced a pleasant smile and turned to see a man and a woman, neither smiling, both holding badges so he could read them.

His cell phone rang.

'I'm Ashton,' he said. Then, 'Excuse me.' He held the phone to his ear.

The FBI agents seemed momentarily uncertain as to whether they should or could stop him taking the call.

Darius held up a finger to signal *just a minute.* He listened for a while.

He was, he knew, destroying himself. With two FBI agents watching he was going to commit what might as well be suicide.

'Yes,' he said into the phone. 'What she told you is one hundred per cent true.'

The FBI agents took his phone then.

THIRTY THREE

7 HOURS 1 MINUTE

DIANA CRAWLED AND fell. She was cut and bruised in so many places she couldn't even begin to keep track. Her palms, her knees, her shins, her ankles, the soles of her feet, all ripped and torn. And the cuts from Drake's whip were on her back, shoulders, the back of her thighs, her bottom.

But she felt little of the pain now. That pain was something far away. Something that happened to a real person who was not her. Some shell she'd once inhabited, maybe, but not her, not this person, because this person, this Diana, felt something so much more awful.

It was inside her.

The baby. It was inside her and pushing and kicking.

And it was growing. She felt her belly grow each time she reached to hold it. Bigger and bigger, like someone was filling a water balloon from a hose and didn't have the sense to stop, didn't know that it would burst if you just kept making it –

A spasm went through her, seizing her insides, drawing

on every ounce of her strength and concentrating it in that one spasm.

Contraction.

The word came to her from the depths of memory.

Contraction.

Was her stomach really growing? Was the impatience of the baby inside her real, or was it Penny playing some game with her reality?

She felt the gaiaphage's dark mind. She felt the fear that squeezed the air from her lungs. And more horrible still, she felt that evil mind's eagerness. It strained to hurry her on. It reached for her from the depths. Like a little kid impatient for the ice cream. Give me, give me!

But worse by far was the echo that came from the baby.

The baby felt the force of the gaiaphage's will. She knew it. It would be his.

How long had she crawled like this? How many times had Drake grabbed her roughly with his whip hand and lowered her down some sheer drop to cling with torn fingernails to the rock wall?

And blind. Always blind. A darkness so total it reached into her memory and blotted the sun from the pictures there.

Then, at long last, a glow. At first it seemed like it must be a hallucination. She had accepted that light was gone forever, and now here was a faint, sickly glow.

'Go!' Drake urged her. 'It's straight and level now. Go!'

She stumbled forward. Her belly was impossibly big, the flesh stretched like a drum. And the next contraction now racked her, a vice inside her that tightened so hard it seemed it must break her very bones.

It was hot and airless. She was bathed in sweat, her hair sticking to her neck.

The glow brightened. It stuck to the floor and walls of the cave. It revealed the contours of rock, the stalagmites rising from the floor, the tumbled piles of broken stone like waterfalls rendered with a child's blocks.

And then, beneath her bare feet, the electric zap of the barrier, forcing her to climb for safety up on to pieces of the gaiaphage itself.

She could feel the gaiaphage move under her, like stepping on a million ants, all packed tight together; the cells of the monster seethed and vibrated.

Drake cavorted across the chamber, snapping the air with his whip, shouting, 'I did it! I did it! I brought you Diana! I, Drake Merwin, I did it! Whip Hand! Whip! Hand!'

Justin. Where was he? Diana realised she hadn't seen him in a long time.

Where was he? She looked around, frantic, amazed to have eyes to see with. Her vision blurred green. No Justin.

Penny caught the frantic look. Her face was grim. She, too,

now realised they'd lost the little boy somewhere along the bloody miles leading them here.

Penny, too, had not fared well. She was almost as battered, bruised, and bloodied as Diana. The trip down a jet-black tunnel had not been good to her. At some point she must have hit her head very hard, because a gash in her scalp bled down into one eye.

But Penny had already lost interest in Justin. Now she looked with narrow, jealous eyes at Drake in all his joy. Drake was ignoring her. He hadn't introduced her. 'Gaiaphage, meet Penny. Penny, gaiaphage. I know you two will get along.'

The image would have made Diana laugh if not for a contraction that forced her to her knees.

It was in that position that Diana felt a sudden wetness. It was warm and ran down her inner thighs.

'Impossible,' she wept.

But she knew in her heart, and had known for some time, that this baby was no normal child. Already it was a three bar, an infant with powers not yet defined.

The child of an evil father and a mother who had tried, had wanted to . . . but somehow had failed.

Repentance had not saved her. Burning tears had not been enough to wash away the stain.

The water that had gushed from inside her had not washed away the stain.

Diana Ladris, beaten and scourged and crying out to heaven for forgiveness, would still be the mother of a monster.

Brianna had a little roasted pigeon in her backpack. She had a more than healthy appetite, and she liked to always keep food handy. A history of starvation did that to people: made them nervous about food.

Now she tore a piece of the pigeon breast away from the bone, felt through the meat with dirty fingers for any fragment of bone or cartilage. Then she found the little boy's hand and put the meat into it.

'Eat that. It'll make you feel a little better.'

They were deep inside the mineshaft. She'd almost laid into Justin with her machete before realising he was sniffling, not snarling.

Now what, though? She could walk him out to the mineshaft entrance, but what difference did it make? It was dark in here, and it was dark out there. Although at least out there that oppression of the soul that came with proximity to the gaiaphage might be lessened.

'What can you tell me, kid? Did you see the thing?'

'I can't see anything,' he sniffed. But he was cried out. More like shell-shocked, that was how he sounded. Brianna felt an unaccustomed stab of sympathy. Poor kid. How was it right that this kind of stuff happened to a little kid?

How was he ever going to forget it?

He'd forget when he was dead, Brianna thought harshly, and that wouldn't be too long from now, most likely.

Then, surprisingly, Justin said, 'There's a really long drop.'

'Up ahead, you mean?'

'That's where they forgot about me.'

'Yeah? Right on, kid, that helps me to know that.'

'Are you going to save Diana?'

'Kind of more thinking about killing Drake. But if that means I save Diana, I can live with that.' She tore off another piece of her precious pigeon meat and gave it to him. What did it matter? This was a suicide mission. She wasn't coming back. She wouldn't need much to eat.

Not a happy thought.

'The lady. Diana. I think her baby is going to come out.'

'Well, that would make everything just about perfect,' Brianna said with a sigh. 'Kid. I have to keep going. You understand? You can keep heading back to the entrance. Or you can just sit tight right here and wait for me.'

'Are you coming back?'

Brianna gave a short laugh. 'I doubt it. But that's me, little dude. I'm the Breeze. And the Breeze doesn't stop. If you get out of this somehow, and you get out of the whole FAYZ and get back home to your mom and dad and everyone out in the world, you tell people that, OK? Maybe find my family some –'

Her voice choked. She could feel tears in her eyes. Wow, where had that come from? She shook her head angrily, pushed her hair back, and said, 'I'm just saying: you tell people the Breeze never wimped out. The Breeze never gave up. Will you do that?'

'Yes, ma'am.'

'Ma'am,' Brianna echoed in an ironic tone. 'Anyway. Later, OK?'

She began to make her way down the tunnel. She had worked out a way to move a little faster than a normal person might. She used her machete, twirling it ahead of her in a variety of different patterns to avoid getting too bored – figure eight, a five-pointed star, a six-way star. She could swing the machete maybe two, three times as fast as a regular person. Nowhere near her usual speed, but one had to adapt.

When the machete struck something, she slowed down until she found an open way. It was like a blind person using a cane, but so much more badass.

From time to time she would feel for a rock and throw it ahead, listening for something that might be, as Justin had called it, 'a really long drop'.

She was very much against really long drops.

She tossed a pebble finally and did not hear it clatter on stone. 'Ah. I believe we have the long drop.' She edged forward until, sure enough, she could sense a gap in the floor.

She crept to the edge of it on hands and knees. She positioned herself in a way to see straight downward. 'Eyes open, don't flinch,' she told herself.

She aimed the shotgun down into the hole and pulled the trigger.

Shotguns were never exactly quiet. But in the confines of the mineshaft it was like a bomb going off.

The muzzle flash stabbed thirty feet down, painting an indelible image of stone walls, a ledge perhaps twenty feet straight down.

The echo of the blast went on for some time. It sounded a bit like when a jet broke the sound barrier. Most likely Drake would hear, unless this shaft went down even farther than she imagined.

Brianna smiled. 'That's right, Drakey boy: I'm still coming.'

Two explosions. Two stabs of light.

No way to know how far away they were. The sound said a long way. The light seemed nearer. Impossible to tell.

It could be anyone. Brianna. Astrid. Or just any number of armed kids who might be lost in the darkness.

'Definitely a gun,' Sam said to no one. How weird that gunfire was almost reassuring.

He did not believe it had come from the same direction as the mineshaft. It was to the right. More like in a line to where he thought Perdido Beach might be. Which was not his objective. He wasn't on a mission to find and rescue Astrid, if that was her. He was on a mission to –

'Too bad,' he snapped, again talking defiantly to no one.

If it was Astrid, and if she was in a fight, then having whoever she was fighting – maybe even Drake – see a line of Sammy suns approaching would give everything away. If it was Astrid – and he'd already convinced himself it was – he needed to move fast. He wouldn't just have to walk tentatively into the dark, lighting his path back to home with a row of lights. He would have to run straight into darkness.

Sam fixed in his mind's eye the direction the flashes had come from. He began to trot, lifting each step high to avoid tripping. He made it surprisingly far before something hard caught his foot and he slammed facedown into the dirt.

'That's one,' he said. Stood up, and started running again.

It was insanity, of course. Running blind. Running with his eyes closed. Running with absolutely no idea where his foot would land, running when maybe there was a wall or a branch or a wild animal just right there. Right there an inch from his nose.

That was his choice: to inch his way cautiously, try to avoid falling, but never get anywhere. Or to run, and maybe get somewhere, but maybe just run right off a cliff.

Yeah, that's life, he thought, and as the wry smile formed he ploughed into a bush that tripped him, tangled him, and threatened not to let him escape.

Finally he rolled free, stood up, and started running again, picking thorns out of his palms and arms as he went.

All his life Sam had feared the darkness. As a kid he'd lain in his bed at night, tensed against the assault of the unseen but well-imagined threat. But now in this ultimate darkness, it seemed to him that fear of the dark was fear of himself. Not a fear of what might be 'out there', but a fear of how he would react to what was out there. He had spent hundreds, maybe thousands of hours in his life imagining how he would cope with whatever terrible thing his imagination had conjured up. It used to shame him, that incessant hero fantasy, that endless mental war-gaming for threats that never materialised. An endless series of scenarios in which Sam did not panic. Sam did not run away. Sam did not cry.

Because that, more than any monster, was what Sam had feared: that he was weak and cowardly. He had a terrible fear of being afraid.

And the only solution was to refuse to be afraid.

Easier said than done when the darkness was absolute, and nothing was foreseen, and there really were genuine, actual, terrible monsters lying in wait.

No night-light now. No Sammy sun. Just darkness so total it negated the very idea of sight.

Having thought about his fear did not lessen it. But continuing to run straight ahead did.

'So just don't cry,' Sam said.

'I miss Howard,' Orc said. Dekka wasn't exactly talkative. In fact, she'd barely said a word. Normally Orc didn't talk all that much, either, but it wasn't like there was anything to see. Or anything else to do.

Orc was walking in front with Dekka just behind him, following the sounds of his steps. The nice thing about being the way he was, Orc reflected, was that it was pretty hard for anything to trip him.

Most things he just ploughed right through. And if it was a bush or a bumpy place or whatever, he could warn Dekka.

In some ways it was a pleasant stroll. Nothing to see, hah, hah. But it wasn't too hot or too cold. The only real problem was that they didn't know where they were going.

'Sorry about Howard,' Dekka said, too late. 'I know you were friends.'

'No one liked Howard.'

Dekka didn't choose to disagree.

'Everyone just saw him as this guy who sold drugs and booze and all. But he was different sometimes.' Orc crushed a tin can under one foot and with his next step flattened the earth over what felt like a gopher hole.

'He liked me anyway,' Orc said.

Nothing from Dekka.

'You have lots of friends, so you probably don't understand why Howard –'

'I don't have a lot of friends,' Dekka interrupted. Her voice was still shaky. Whatever had happened to her back there, it must have been pretty bad. Because as far as Orc was concerned Dekka was a hard, hard girl. Howard always said that about her. Sometimes he would call Dekka names. Probably because Dekka had this way of looking at Howard, like her face would be down, but her eyes would be on him, like they were watching him through her own eyebrows kind of. And from that direction all you saw were these cornrows and her broad forehead and those hard eyes.

'Sam,' Orc said.

'Yeah.' Dekka's voice softened. 'Sam.'

'Edilio.'

'We work together. We're not really friends. How about you and Sinder? She likes you OK.'

The idea surprised Orc. 'She's nice to me,' he admitted. He thought it over a little more. 'She's pretty, too.'

'I wasn't saying she liked you that way.'

'Oh. No. I knew that,' Orc said, feeling as if he'd be blushing if he had more than a few inches of skin left. 'That's not what I was talking about. No.' He forced a laugh. 'That kind of stuff, that's not for me. Not a lot of girls are interested in someone like me.' He didn't want it to sound like he was feeling sorry for himself, but it probably did.

'Yeah, well, it turns out there aren't a lot of girls interested in me, either,' Dekka said.

'You mean boys.'

'No. I mean girls.'

Orc missed a step, he was so shocked. 'You're one of those lesbos?'

'I'm a lesbian. And I'm not one of those anything in this place; it looks like I'm the only one of those.'

This was making Orc feel very uncomfortable. Lesbo was just a name to call some ugly girl back when he'd been at school. He hadn't really thought much about it. And now he had to think about it.

Then a thought occurred to him. 'Hey, so you're like me.'

'What?'

'An only. Like me. I'm the only one like me,' Orc said.

He heard a derisive snort from Dekka. It was an annoyed sound, not a happy laugh. But it was the best she'd come up with so far.

'Yeah,' Orc went on. 'You and me, we're onlies is what we are. The only person made out of rocks and the only lesbo.'

'Lesbian,' Dekka corrected. But she didn't sound that mad.

Something smacked Orc's head and poked at his eyes. 'Careful. There's a tree. Grab my waist and I'll go around it.'

Lana was right. It wasn't long before trouble started. Quinn stopped a kid who had taken a burning stick from the fire and was heading towards his home.

'I just want to get my stuff.'

'No fire outside the plaza,' Quinn said. 'Sorry, man, but we don't want another Zil thing with the whole town going up in flames.'

'Then give me a flashlight.'

'We don't have any to –'

'Then mind your own business. You're just a stupid fisherman.'

Quinn had grabbed the torch. The kid tried to rip it away, but he, unlike Quinn, had not spent months with his hands gripping an oar.

Quinn wrested the torch away easily. 'You can go where you want. But not with fire.'

He'd escorted the kid back to the plaza just in time to see two torches heading away on the far side of the plaza.

Quinn cursed and sent some of his people after them. But the fishing crews were exhausted. They'd been chopping wood and dragging it and sawing it and distributing food and organising a slit trench.

Lana had been right. She was looking at him now, not saying it, but knowing he was coming to the same conclusion.

'Caine,' Quinn said. 'Do you have it back?'

Caine had disappeared for a while. Later Quinn realised he'd walked down to the ocean and washed himself up. His clothing was wet but more or less clean. His hair was slicked back, and the scars of the staples Penny had driven into his head had been healed by Lana.

His hands – the backs, at least – were still covered in anywhere from an eighth of an inch to half an inch of cement. He had a hard time articulating his fingers. But his palms were mostly clean.

He looked grey, even by firelight. He looked like a much older person, like he had gone straight from handsome teenager to weary, beaten old man.

But when he stood he held himself with some dignity.

Caine turned towards the steps. The church had been emptied of anything that would burn. The last of the roof had come down with a sequence of crashes that sent dust billowing out to spark the bonfire. Now the tired crews were tearing handrails and old wooden office chairs, framed pictures and broken-up desks out of the town hall building.

Caine focused on the largest fragment, most of a desk. He extended his hand, palm out.

The desk rose from the ground.

It sailed through the air over upturned faces. Caine set it gently atop the burning pile.

Quinn braced himself for an announcement by Caine that he was back. That he was in charge. That he was still king. And the sad reality was that Quinn would have welcomed it: being in charge of all this was more than he wanted to handle.

'Let me know what else I can do,' Caine said quietly. Then he sat down, cross-legged, and stared into the fire.

Lana sauntered over. 'Have to admit: the guy has a genius for doing the wrong thing. We actually need him to be the bad guy, and suddenly he's Mr Meek and Mild.'

Quinn was too tired to think of some clever retort. His shoulders sagged. He let his head drop down. 'I wish I knew how long we had to keep it together.'

'Until we can't,' Lana said.

The panic started then. There was no cause that Quinn could see. Suddenly kids on the far side of the fire were shouting and some were squealing. Maybe nothing more than a rat passing through.

But those beside them didn't know what it was and the panic spread lightning-quick.

Lana cursed and started running. Quinn was right behind her. But the panic came to meet them, kids suddenly screaming without knowing why, running, circling back to the fire, getting spooked and running again, knocking one another over, yelling.

Sanjit's sister, Peace, knocked into Quinn. He grabbed her shoulders and yelled, 'What is it?'

She had no answer, just shook her head and pulled away.

A kid ran into the darkness. His clothing was on fire; the flames streamed behind him as he fled screaming. Dahra Baidoo tackled him like a football player and rolled him over to kill the flames.

Other kids grabbed torches and formed into knots and paranoid clusters, back-to-back like ancient warriors surrounded by foes.

And then to Quinn's utter horror a girl ran straight into the fire. She was screaming, 'Mommy! Mommy!'

He leaped to cut her off, but he was too late. The heat drove him back as he cried, 'No! No! No!'

Then, as if grabbed by a divine hand, the girl came flying back out of the fire. She was rolled across the ground. It was rough but effective. The fire that had just caught on to her shorts went out.

Quinn turned, grateful, to Caine. But Caine did not look at him. Quinn heard Lana shouting at kids, telling them to stop acting like idiots, to calm down.

Some listened. Others did not. More than one lit torch went off into the darkness. Quinn wondered how long it would be before he started seeing fires throughout this poor, beaten town.

Lana came storming back, furious, practically spitting with rage. 'No one even knows what it was. Some idiot yelled something and off they went. Like cattle. I hate people.'

'Do we go after the ones that got away?' Quinn wondered aloud.

But Lana wasn't ready for a calm discussion. 'I really, sometimes, really just hate them all.'

She threw herself down on the steps. Quinn noticed a slight smile on Caine's lips. Caine favoured him with a curious look. 'Question for you, Quinn: how long would you have stayed on strike?'

'What?'

'Well, seemed to me like you were ready to have all these people go hungry over Cigar.'

Quinn rested his fists on his sides. 'How long would you have defended Penny?'

Caine made a small laugh. 'Being in charge. It's not easy, is it?'

'I haven't tortured anyone, Caine. I haven't turned anyone over to some psycho girl who'll drive them insane.'

Caine sagged a little at that. He looked away. 'Yeah, well . . . You pretty much had me beat, Quinn. Albert was already thinking about how he'd get rid of me, not whether.'

'Albert had his escape plans ready.'

Caine's eyes glinted in the firelight. 'We'll see. I liked that island. Never should have left. Diana told me not to. There are other boats. Just maybe I'll pay old Albert a visit one of these days.'

'You should do that,' Quinn said. He was remembering the sight of those tiny eyes like beans in the blackened sockets of Cigar's head. Let Caine go after the island. It might be good to see whether those missiles Albert claimed to have would work.

But Caine seemed already to have lost interest in Quinn's anger. 'More likely we're all dead soon,' he said.

'Yeah,' Quinn agreed.

'I would have liked to see Diana again. No baby now.'

'Are you relieved?' Lana asked harshly.

Caine thought it over for so long it seemed he'd forgotten the question. Then at last, 'No. Just kind of sad.'

THIRTY FOUR

5 HOURS 12 MINUTES

WAS THAT LIGHT?

Astrid opened her eyes wide. Stared.

Yes. An orange glow. A fire.

A fire!

'Cigar, I think I see town. I think I see a fire.'

'I see it, too. Like devils dancing!'

They walked forward eagerly. Astrid registered the fact that the ground beneath her boots was no longer flat and hard and occasionally interrupted by some unnamed weed, but had become bumpier, dry clods of dirt that tripped her as they rose and formed rows and from those rows rose neatly ordered plants.

What she noticed was the light.

And then Cigar's screams.

But Cigar screamed a lot, so Astrid kept walking and ignored his mad shrieks that something was in his feet.

Then it all came together and Astrid knew. She felt

something pushing at the leather of her boot.

'Zekes!' she cried, and stumbled back, fell down, jumped up like the ground was electrified, crawled, stood, ran back, back until the ground was hard and flat again.

She fumbled in the dark, fingers searching for and then finding the whipping worm, its head already through the leather and touching her flesh, and she got her hands around it even though it fought, and she pulled at it with all her strength and it came free and whipped around, quick as a cobra, and sank its nasty, tooth-ringed mouth into her arm, but she had the tail and yelled, '*No! No!*' and then it was away from her.

She had thrown it. Somewhere.

Cigar cried pitiably.

And then, so much more terrible, laughed and laughed in the dark.

Astrid with shaking hands grabbed the shotgun and fired it once.

She saw the edge of the field.

She saw Cigar frozen in a twisting fall.

He was in the field.

She heard the greedy mouths burrowing into him. A sound like hungry dogs eating.

'Petey! *Petey!* Help him!'

Cigar said, 'Oh,' in a small, disappointed voice.

And the only sound in the darkness was the relentless feeding of the worms.

She sat there listening, no choice but to hear. Tears flowed. She sat with her knees together, head in twisting hands, crying.

How much time passed until the worm sounds were finished she couldn't know. The stink . . . that remained.

She was alone now. Completely and absolutely alone in a darkness that seemed almost like a living thing, as if she had been swallowed whole and was now in the belly of some indifferent beast.

'All right, Petey,' Astrid said at last. 'No choice, huh, brother? The crazy behind door number one, or the crazy behind door number two. Show me what you have to show me, Peter.'

She saw him. Not him, not like there was light, but something, like the darkness had warped around itself. A suggestion of a shape. A little boy.

'Are you there?' she asked.

Something cold, like someone had slid an icicle through her scalp and through her skull and pushed it deep inside her brain. No pain. Just a terrible cold.

'Petey?' she whispered.

Peter Ellison did not move. He stayed very, very still. His hand touched her on the head, but only just, just barely, and he stayed very still.

The avatar that was his sister had within it an amazing complexity of lines and designs, signs inside of mazes inside of maps that were part of planets and . . .

He pulled himself back. Inside her was a game of such beautiful complexity.

This was what it was to be the girl with the yellow hair and the stabbing blue eyes. It took his breath away. Or would have if he had breath and body.

He mustn't play with those complex swirls and patterns. Each time he had tried he'd broken the avatar and it had come apart. He couldn't break this one.

It's me. Petey, he said.

The avatar shuddered. Patterns twisted around his touch, feeling for him like tiny light-snakes.

'Can you fix it, Petey? The FAYZ. Can you make it stop?'

He could hear her voice. It came straight up through the avatar, words of light floating to him.

He wondered. Could he fix it? Could he undo the great and terrible thing he had done?

He felt the answer as a sort of regret. He reached for the power, the thing that had made him able to create this place. But there was nothing there.

It was in my body, he said. *The power.*

'You can't end it?'

No.

No, sister Astrid, I can't.

I'm sorry.

'Can you bring the light back?'

He pulled away. Her questions made him feel bad inside.

'No. Don't go away,' she said.

He had memories of how much her voice had hurt when he was the old Pete. When he had a body, with a brain all wired crazily so that things were always too loud, even colours.

He stopped moving away. He resisted an urge to reach inside that mesmerising avatar and take its sadness away. But no, his fingers were too clumsy. He knew that now. The girl named Taylor, he had tried to make her better, and he had torn the avatar to shreds.

'Petey. What is the Darkness doing?'

Pete considered. He hadn't looked at that thing lately. He could see him, a green glow, tendrils like a writhing octopus reaching out through the placeless place where Pete now lived.

The Darkness was weak. His power, spread all through the barrier, was weakening. He was the thing Pete had used to create the barrier. In that panic moment with the terrible loud sounds and the fear on all the faces, when Pete had screamed inside his own head and reached out with his power he'd stretched the Darkness into that barrier.

Now it was weakening. Soon it would break and crack.

Dying.

'The Darkness, the gaiaphage, it's dying?'

It wants to be reborn.

'Petey. What happens if it is reborn?'

He didn't know. He was out of words. He opened his mind to her. He showed sister Astrid images of the great sphere he had built, the barrier that had pushed all the rules and laws away, the barrier made of the gaiaphage, that had become the egg for its rebirth, the numbers all twisted together, fourteen, and the twisting, screaming distortion when anything passed through from one universe to the other, and now sister Astrid was screaming and holding her head; he could see it in the avatar, funny screaming, like words that popped and exploded around him and –

He pulled away.

He was hurting her.

He'd done it. With his clumsy fingers and his stupid, stupid stupidness, he had hurt her.

Her avatar twirled away like a snowflake in a storm.

Petey fled.

THIRTY FIVE

4 HOURS 56 MINUTES

'OH, GOD, IT'S coming!' Diana screamed.

She was sweating, straining, on her back with her legs spread wide, knees up. The contractions were just minutes apart now, but they lasted so long it was as if she had no rest in between, just a chance to gasp some super-heated fetid air.

She had no more energy for crying. Her body had taken control. It was doing what it was supposed to do five months from now. She was not ready. The baby was not ready. But the enormous swell of her belly said different. It said the time was now.

Now!

Who was there to help her in this? No one. Drake stared in horrified fascination. Penny curled her lip with contempt. Neither of them interfered or spoke, because it was clear, clear to anyone with a heart or brain, that the only other thing in the room that cared about the baby was the pulsing green monster.

Diana felt its hungry will.

Doom for her baby.

She had known there would be pain. And while it was bad, it was not as bad as the stroke of Drake's whip.

It was not the pain that made her cry out, but the despair, the certain knowledge that she would never be the baby's mother. That she would fail even at this. The deadening reality that she was unforgiven, still an exile from the human race, that she still bore the mark of her evil deeds.

The taste of human flesh.

She had been so hungry. So close to death.

I've said I'm sorry, I repented, I begged for forgiveness; what do you want from me? Why won't you help this baby?

Penny moved closer, careful of her damaged, bloody feet. She leaned down to look at Diana's straining face.

'She's praying,' Penny said. She laughed. 'Should I give her a god to pray to? I can make her see whatever –'

Through a veil of bloody tears Diana saw Penny reel back. Like a marionette she slammed hard, face-first into a wall.

Drake laughed. 'Stupid chick. If the gaiaphage wants something, he'll let you know. Otherwise it's best not to spend a lot of time down here thinking about how powerful you are. There's only one god down here, and it's not Diana's, and it sure isn't you, Penny.'

Diana tried to remember what she had read in the pregnancy

books. But she'd barely glanced at the sections having to do with birth. Birth was months away, not now!

Contraction. Oh, oh, a hard one. On and on.

Breathe. Breathe.

Another.

'Ahhhh!' she cried out, earning a jeer from Drake. But even as he laughed he was changing. Bright metal wire crossed his exposed teeth.

Hold on, hold on, Diana told herself. Don't think. Just wait for –

Another contraction, like her guts were being squeezed hard by a gigantic fist.

And then Brittney was there, kneeling between Diana's legs.

'I see its head. The top of its head.'

'I have to – Have to – Have to –' Diana gasped. Then, 'Push!' she yelled, urging herself on.

A sudden motion. Something very fast. Brittney's head rolled off her neck. It landed on Diana's belly and then rolled heavily to one side.

BLAM!

Penny's left arm took a partial hit. A chunk the size of a small steak was vaporized, leaving a divot in her shoulder, a divot that sprayed blood.

Brianna's face appeared, looking down at Diana. 'We're out of here!'

'I can't . . . can't . . . oh, oh, aaaaahhhhhh!'

'You're doing this right now?' Brianna asked, incredulous and offended. 'It has to be right now?'

Diana grabbed Brianna's shirt in an iron grip. 'Save my baby. Forget about me. Save my baby!'

Sam found her, not by sight but by sound. By her weeping and her giggling.

He hung lights, more than one, illuminating a patch the size of a suburban lawn. He saw Astrid, crumpled and unaware.

He saw a skeleton just a dozen feet away, still seething with zekes.

Sam knelt sat down wordlessly beside Astrid. He put his arm around her shoulder.

At first it was as if he wasn't there. Like she didn't notice him. Then, with a sudden, loud sob, she buried her face in his neck.

The tenor of her sounds changed. The wild flights of giggling stopped. So did the keening, heartbroken wail. Now she just cried.

Sam sat there perfectly still, saying nothing, and let her tears run down his neck.

The warrior who had gone out from the lake to save his people by slaying the evil one was now just a boy sitting in the dirt with his fingers in a mane of blond hair.

He stared at nothing. Expected nothing. Planned nothing. Just sat.

Brianna picked up Brittney's head. It was surprisingly heavy. She threw it as hard as she could down the tunnel.

Brittney's body got up, swayed a little, and seemed as if it was ready to go after its head, so Brianna shot it in the leg at close range. The loss of one bloodless leg caused the whole body to topple over.

Penny was obviously in shock, staring at the terrible wound that was draining her life away, squirt, squirt, squirt.

Got to finish her off, Brianna told herself. But she hesitated. Penny was a human being. Not much of one, but an actual human being. Whereas the Drake/Brittney thing, well, whatever it was, it wasn't human, because humans pretty much never stood up and tried to walk away after their heads were chopped off.

Brianna jacked a round into the chamber and aimed at Penny.

Then the gun blew apart in her hands. Exploded!

Brianna dropped it, but even as she let go she realised it was a trick. An illusion of Penny's making.

The girl was spraying blood like a Super Soaker and still able to mess with Brianna's head.

Brianna bent down to get the shotgun, determined to ignore

any further interference, but Diana gave a huge cry of pain, and suddenly there was a head sticking almost all the way out of a place on Diana that Brianna had never wanted to see.

'Yaa-aahh-ah!' Brianna said. 'Oh, this is wrong.'

But it just kept coming out as Diana grunted like an animal, and if Brianna didn't get down there and do the right thing, the baby was going to land on the floor, on a rock.

Brianna snatched up her shotgun, snapped off a quick, poorly aimed, one-handed shot in the general direction of Penny – *BLAM!* – and cupped her hands beneath the emerging head.

'It's got a snake around its neck!' Brianna cried.

Diana sat up – amazing that she could even think about sitting up – and yelled, 'It's the umbilical cord. It's around the neck. It'll choke!'

'Oh, man, I hate slimy stuff,' Brianna moaned. She pushed the baby's head back a little, which wasn't easy, because it was really ready to come out, and yelled, 'Ewww!' a couple of times as she stretched and wrestled the umbilical cord over the baby's head, freeing it.

And now in a rush the baby came out. It spilled out with liquid sounds and a hideous translucent sac attached and a pulsating snakelike thing leading to its belly button.

Diana shuddered.

'I am so never doing this,' Brianna said fervently. She shot a look to see if Penny was dead or alive and couldn't see her at all.

The Brittney body was gone as well, no doubt crawling off to look for its head.

'You have to cut the cord,' Diana said.

'The what?'

'The cord.' Diana gasped. 'The snake thing.'

'Ah. The snake thing.'

Brianna took her machete in hand, raised it up, and chopped through the umbilical cord. 'It's bleeding!'

'Tie it off!'

Brianna tore a strip from the waist of her T-shirt, twisted it to make it easier to handle, and tied it around the six-inch stump of the umbilical cord. 'Oh, man, oh, it's all slimy.'

Brianna worked her hands beneath the baby. It was slimy on its back, too. Then she looked down and saw something that made her smile.

'Hey. It's a girl,' Brianna said.

'Take her,' Diana cried.

'She's breathing,' Brianna said. 'Isn't she supposed to cry? In a movie it cries.'

She frowned at the baby. Its eyes were closed. Something strange about it. The baby wasn't crying. She seemed perfectly calm. As if this was all no big thing, being born.

'Take her away from here!' Diana yelled. Her voice was coming from far away.

Brianna lifted the little girl up and oh! Her eyes opened. Little blue eyes. But that couldn't be, could it?

Brianna stared into those eyes. Just stared. And the tiny little girl stared back, eyes focused so clearly, not the squinty little eyes of a newborn baby but the eyes of a wise child.

'What?' Brianna asked. Because it almost sounded like the baby was saying something. She wanted Brianna to take her over and lay her down in that crib.

Well, of course, who wouldn't want to lie down in that nice, white crib?

There was a siren going off here at the hospital, an insistent screech that Brianna just ignored. As she laid the baby down and . . .

But wait. No. That wasn't a siren.

It was a voice.

Run. Run. Ruuuun! the siren said.

But now Brianna's breath was short; she was choking because the baby wanted to be put down in that nice crib with the green sheets.

Green? Hadn't they been white?

Green was a nice colour, too.

Brianna was so incredibly weary holding the baby. She must have weighed a million pounds. So tired, and the green sheets, and – *Ruuuun! Ruuun! Nooooo!*

Brianna blinked. She gulped air.

She looked down and saw the baby lying on rock covered with a sickly green that looked up close like a billion tiny ants.

The green swarmed up on to the baby's chubby little legs and arms.

'No, Brianna! Noooo!' Diana cried.

Brianna, paralysed with horror at what she had just done, watched as the seething green mass flowed on to the baby's arms and legs and belly and then poured like water into her nostrils and mouth.

Penny, holding a rag to the bloody hole in her shoulder, staggered back, laughed, and suddenly collapsed to the ground.

'What did I do?' Brianna cried.

A noise. She spun, ducked, and barely avoided the whip.

She snatched up her shotgun – *BLAM!* – fired into Drake's belly. He smiled his shark grin.

Too much. Too much!

Brianna ran.

OUTSIDE

ABANA BAIDOO WAS shaking as she reached her car outside Denny's. She could barely take a breath.

No. No way she was letting this happen. But if she was going to stop it she had to focus. And not focus on how angry she was at Connie Temple.

Liar!

She pulled out her iPhone and, despite her fumbling, shaking fingers, found the mailing list of families.

First, email.

Everyone! Emergency! They are blowing up the dome. I have solid proof that they are blowing up the dome. All families immediately call your senators and congressmen and the media. Do it now. And if you are close to the area come! The chemical spill story is a lie! Don't let them stop you!!!!!

Then text. The same message, but shorter.

Nuclear explosive is being used to blow up the anomaly. Call everyone! This is not a joke or a mistake!!!

Then, without delay, she opened her Twitter app.

#PerdidoFamilies. Nuclear explosion planned. Not joke or mistake. Help now. Come if u can!

Facebook app, same message, but a little longer.

There. Too late for anyone to cover up now.

Connie was coming from the restaurant at a run. She raced to her own car, hopped in, started it, and pulled up, tyres squealing beside Abana. Abana rolled down her window.

'Hate me later, Abana,' Connie said. 'Follow me now. I think I know a dirt road.'

Connie didn't wait but took off, laying rubber across the parking lot.

'Hell, yeah,' Abana said, and drove with one hand as the tweets and messages started pinging her phone.

THIRTY SIX

4 HOURS 21 MINUTES

'HE CAN'T CONTROL it,' Astrid said. The first words she'd spoken in what felt to Sam like an eternity.

He'd become aware after a while that she had stopped crying. But she had not pulled away then. And for a long time afterward he wondered if she was asleep. He'd determined that if she was sleeping he'd let her go right on doing so.

He knew Edilio and all the rest were expecting him to solve something, everything. He recalled the high of realising he wasn't the leader, carrying everything on his shoulders. He remembered the liberation of believing that his role was as warrior. The great and powerful warrior and that was all. And he was that. Yes: he was. He had the power in his hands, and he knew he had the strength and courage and violence to use that power.

But he was also, at least as much, the boy who loved Astrid Ellison. Right now he was powerless to put that part of himself aside. He couldn't have left her side when she was like this, ever, not if Drake had shown up and challenged him to one-on-one combat to the death.

He was a warrior. But he was also this. Whatever this was.

'Who?' he asked.

'Petey. Pete. It doesn't feel right to call him Petey now. He's changed.'

'Astrid, Petey's dead.'

She sighed and pulled away. He stretched his arm and got pins and needles in payment. His arm was asleep.

'I let him in. In my head,' Astrid said.

'His memory?'

'No, Sam. And I'm not crazy. I was pretty close there, though, and then you came. And I turned it all to you. How weak, huh? I'm embarrassed at how lame it is. But I was on the edge. It messed me up. Twisted my thoughts into . . . Well, messed me up, that's all I can say. Words are coming hard to me right now. I feel like I'm bruised in my brain. Again: sorry that's not more coherent.'

He had let her ramble on, but he wasn't making any sense of it. Now that she mentioned feeling crazy he wondered if she had, well, become . . . stressed.

Almost as if she could read his thoughts, Astrid laughed softly and said, 'No, Sam. I'm fine. I cried it out. Sorry. I know crying freaks boys out.'

'You don't cry much.'

'I don't cry ever,' Astrid said with some of her usual snap.

'Well, rarely.'

'It's Pete. He's . . . I don't know what he is.' There was a marvelling quality to her words, the exalted sound of Astrid discovering something new. 'There's some kind of space, some kind of reality that exists here in the FAYZ. He's like a spirit. His body is gone. He's outside. Not in his old brain. Like a data pattern or something, like he's digital. Yes, I know I'm babbling. It's not something I understand. It's like a slippery thought, and Pete can't explain it.'

'OK,' Sam said. He couldn't think of anything better to say.

'Here's the thing I remember clearly: the gaiaphage, Sam. I understand it now. I know what happened.'

For the next half an hour she explained. It began in a rambling way, but, Astrid being Astrid, the thoughts grew clearer, the explanations more crisp, and by the end she was getting annoyed with him for failing to immediately grasp some details.

Nothing was more reassuring to him than an impatient, condescending Astrid.

'OK. The gaiaphage is part of the barrier,' Sam summarised. 'And the barrier is part of the gaiaphage. He's the building material Pete used to create the barrier. And now the gaiaphage is running out of energy. Starving for energy. So the barrier is failing – going dark, then maybe breaking open. That's good news, then. In fact, that's great news.'

'Yes,' Astrid said. 'It would be the best possible news. Unless somehow the gaiaphage escapes the barrier.'

'But how is he or it or whatever going to do that?'

'I don't know, but I can guess. Listen, Sam, when the gaiaphage gave Drake that disgusting whip arm he needed Lana's powers to do it. Ever since then he's tried to lure her back. And all the while, too, he tried to entice Pete. Now that Pete has lost most of his power, he can interfere with what he sees as data patterns – people and animals – but he can't just perform miracles like he could. Somehow Pete's power was a function of his body. Like Lana's power is part of her body.'

'The baby,' Sam said. 'The gaiaphage wants the baby. We guessed that much, but didn't really know why.'

'Diana can read power levels,' Astrid said. 'Did she ever . . .'

Sam nodded. 'She said the baby is a three bar. As a fetus. Who knows what it will be when it's born. Or as it grows. Diana's only, like, four or five months along. I should know exactly, but I forget. When she would talk about it I would kind of, you know.' He made a shivering move, like it all gave him the creeps.

Astrid shook her head in disbelief. 'Really. That's the part of all this that makes you squirm: pregnancy.'

'She made me touch her, you know, stomach. And she talked about her, um, her things.' He pointed at his chest and whispered, 'Nipples.'

'Yeah,' Astrid said dryly. 'I could see where that would be devastating.'

At that Sam had no choice but to go to her, put his arms around her, and kiss her. Because now she was one hundred per cent Astrid again.

'So now what?' Astrid asked a few minutes later.

'Drake's had plenty of time to get Diana to the mineshaft. Going in there after them is a job for an army, not just me alone,' Sam said, thinking out loud. 'In any case, however bad it is for Diana, they won't kill her until they have the baby, and that won't happen for months.'

'That must mean the gaiaphage has months before the barrier cracks. How do we survive that long?'

Sam shrugged. 'That, I don't know. Yet. But if we're going after that thing in the mineshaft, we'll need help. Brianna, if she's still alive. Dekka, Taylor, Orc. And Caine. Especially Caine. If he'll help.'

'So we go to Perdido Beach?'

'Slowly. Carefully. Yeah. And we'll leave a trail of lights for anyone else needing a safe path. I need to get my troops back together. Then we worry about going after the gaiaphage.'

After a while Drake lifted the baby up with his whip hand. He was gentle. He knew what the baby was. Who it was.

He laid it down just as gently on Diana's belly.

'Feed it,' he ordered.

Diana shook her head.

Yeah, Drake thought with a smirk, all the snark has been beaten right out of that girl. Still, he'd have loved to make her beg . . . But no. The will of the gaiaphage was clear in his mind. The baby body must be nurtured, protected. That baby now was the gaiaphage. Drake's god. And he would follow it. He would obey it.

Even though the baby itself was a girl.

That was a shame. It would have been cooler if it was a dude's body. But OK, what was a body but a tool or a weapon?

Drake gave Diana the baby. Diana closed her eyes, squeezing out a tear.

The baby latched on and nursed.

Now, at irresistible urging from the gaiaphage, Drake went to Penny. She was white as a ghost. She was shivering like she was cold, although it was hot as always down here.

She was lying in a pool of her own blood.

Fine with Drake. She was too full of herself. Way too impressed by her own power. The gaiaphage didn't need her.

But a voice in his head made him turn around. The baby was sitting up on Diana's belly. Sitting up. Looking at Drake.

Drake knew nothing about babies, but that wasn't right. He

knew that much. This was definitely not right. Babies still covered with slime weren't supposed to be sitting up and making eye contact.

Then, to his even greater shock, the baby seemed to be trying to speak. No sounds came out, but he knew without question what the gaiaphage wanted.

'Yeah,' Drake said, annoyed but submissive.

He curled his tentacle arm around Penny. She was small, not hard to carry. So he brought her, shivering and muttering incoherently, to the baby gaiaphage.

Drake set her down and the baby toppled over. It would have been comical in another time and place. The baby's giant head was too big for the body to support it very well.

So it toppled, but then, with surprising speed, it was on all fours. It crawled the few inches to Penny.

It reached out a pudgy hand and touched the grisly wound.

Penny gasped, a sound that might have been either pain or pleasure.

Drake felt a stab of jealousy, thinking the gaiaphage might give Penny the gift of a whip hand. But no, all it did was to heal the wound.

The baby healed the shotgun-destroyed flesh in seconds.

And then the baby crawled back to her mother and nursed.

Brianna had not expected to return to Justin. But there he was, breathing softly in the pitch-black. And here she was, a mess of cuts and bruises, but alive.

'It's me, kid,' she said wearily.

'Did you rescue her?'

'No. I didn't. I couldn't pull it off. It was a fight I couldn't win. Not by myself. Besides . . .' She stopped herself, unwilling to explain about the baby. And about the overwhelming urge to place the baby on the gaiaphage.

'I need to find Sam,' Brianna said. 'Which is pretty hard in the dark.'

'Take me, too, OK?'

'Yeah. Of course, little dude, what am I going to do, leave you here?' Actually the thought had occurred to Brianna. She was already slowed to a crawl by the dark. With Justin she'd be moving at whatever it was that was slower than a crawl.

They began feeling their way, inch by bruising inch, towards the mineshaft entrance. In her imagination, with her boundless optimism, Brianna still hoped that when they emerged they would find the world magically restored. Sun shining. Light everywhere.

But when, after a terribly long time, Brianna finally felt clearer, cleaner air on her face, she knew her hope had been futile.

The trip was from narrow darkness to wide-open darkness. She was still blind. And still slow.

* * *

The bonfire in the plaza was much smaller now. They'd realised that it had to be if they were going to keep it burning. Even with Caine's sullen help, ripping flammable materials out of buildings and carrying them to the fire was not easy. So now the bonfire was more like a campfire. And the light of it barely cast a glow on the first circle of kids. Most sat in darkness, staring at the fire, unable even to see the person sitting beside them.

In the dark fights broke out. And there was nothing Quinn could do but yell at them.

One fight went from curses to sickening thuds of some blunt weapon on flesh and bone.

A few seconds later someone – no one knew who – dashed forward to grab a burning chair leg and ran off into the night.

The first home fire had flared in the west end of town. It sent sparks a hundred feet into the air, and Quinn was certain it would spread. It didn't seem to, at least not quickly, but the greater glow did draw some of the people to it. They could be heard jostling and calling out to one another as they felt their way to it like moths drawn to a lightbulb.

'I wish I knew whether Sanjit was safe,' Lana said.

'I was just thinking about Edilio for some reason,' Quinn said. 'Somehow I always feel like if Edilio's still standing, we're not totally beaten yet.' He laughed. 'Weird, I guess, because I didn't used to like him. I used to call him a wetback. Not the worst thing I ever did, I guess, but I wish I could take it back.'

Caine was resting beside them, having used his power to noisily rip some wooden doors off houses and then carry them back to feed the fire.

'It's stupid to waste time worrying about what you did,' Caine said. 'It's not going to matter.'

'Your brother, Sam, he worries about it all the time,' Quinn said. He winced, thinking maybe that was violating a confidence. But weren't they past all that? Past everything, in fact? Wasn't this maybe the last peaceful conversation before the end?

'Does he?' Caine asked. 'Idiot.'

So much for peaceful conversation. Caine was returning to form. Soon he'd grow tired of pretending to get along. Of course, for now he still liked the fire, as they all did. No wonder ancient man had worshiped fire. On a dark night surrounded by lions or hyenas or whatever, it must have seemed like it was more than just burning twigs.

'I'm hungry!' a voice cried out of the dark.

Quinn ignored it. It wasn't the first such cry. It wouldn't be the last. Not by a long shot.

Lana had been quiet for a long time. Quinn asked her whether she was OK. No answer. So he let it go. But a few minutes later Patrick came nosing against Quinn, and so he said, 'Lana, I think Patrick's starting to wonder about dinner, too.'

And again she didn't answer. So Quinn leaned past his former king and saw Lana staring, eyes wide, into the fire.

He reached past Caine and shook her.

'What?' she snapped. Like someone awakened from a dream.

'Are you OK?'

Lana shook her head, a frown deepening the black and orange lines of her face. 'None of us are OK. It's free. Oh, my God, it finally did it.'

'What are you ranting about?' Caine snapped, irritated.

'The gaiaphage. It's coming.'

Quinn saw Caine snap his mouth shut. He saw Caine's eyes widen. His jaw clenched hard.

'I can feel it,' Lana said.

'Probably just –' Quinn started to say something reassuring, but Caine cut him off.

'She's right.' He shared a strange, frightened look with Lana. 'It's changed.'

'It's coming,' Lana said. 'It's coming!'

Quinn saw then what he never expected to see in this life: sheer terror in Lana's eyes.

THIRTY SEVEN

4 HOURS 6 MINUTES

THE BABY TRIED to walk. But it failed. It toppled over, legs still too weak, coordination lacking. But it wasn't supposed to try. It shouldn't even be born, let alone attempting to stand up.

'I'll carry it,' Drake announced.

'No,' Penny said. 'You may need your whip hand free. I will carry it. My powers don't need me to use my hands.'

Diana could see that Drake was not happy. Not happy at all with Penny. He'd have been happier to see her die. Drake was now trapped with females he couldn't just beat on or intimidate.

'What do we do with her?' Penny pointed at Diana with utter contempt, curling her lips at Diana's dishevelled appearance. The torn clothing barely put back together. The stains. The wounds. The weakness.

Drake's dark discontent grew darker still. 'The gaiaphage says she has to live.'

Penny snorted. 'Why? Is the gaiaphage getting sentimental now that it has a girl's body?'

'Shut up,' Drake snapped. 'It's just a body. It's a weapon the master uses. He's still he. He's still what he always was.'

'Uh-huh.' Penny smirked.

Drake squatted down in front of Diana. 'You're a mess. You look like roadkill. You even stink. You're sickening.'

'So kill me,' Diana said, meaning it. Willing him to do it. 'Do it, Drake. Big man. Do it.'

Drake sighed theatrically. 'Babies need milk. And you're the cow, Diana. Moo.'

That made him laugh, and Penny, after a hesitation during which Diana saw contempt for Drake in her eyes, joined in. More terrible by far, the baby girl, Diana's baby, grinned as well, a weird smile revealing pink gums and no teeth.

'Let's go, cow,' Drake said.

'Are you a moron?' Diana said. 'I just had a baby. I can't –'

They hit her then, both of them, competing to see who could force her to her feet. Drake's whip hand, Penny's sick visions. Diana was on her feet, woozy, feeling she should vomit except that her stomach was empty.

The greenish glow of the gaiaphage – because not all of the lurid green had flowed on to or into the baby – had faded so that there was almost no light. Within a few feet they found themselves in total blackness.

Diana recalled that there were places where she might throw herself down a crevasse and end her hellish life. If Drake didn't stop her.

No, not Drake now; now it was Brittney. The sound of her breathing was different from his. Were the emergences coming faster? She dared to hope that Drake was weakening. She dared to hope that he and Penny would go after each other.

Diana relaxed a little. Brittney was as much a tool of the gaiaphage as was Drake, but she lacked Drake's own personal hate-fuelled insanity.

She also, unfortunately, had less knowledge of the path. And she did not intimidate Penny.

'You know what would be creepy, Diana?' Penny asked. 'If you were pregnant again. Only this time with, let's say, a belly full of rats! Hungry rats!'

Diana felt her belly swelling, felt the hundreds of –

'No,' Brittney said calmly. 'No. She's our lord's mother.'

The illusion, barely begun, ended abruptly.

'Shut up, Brittney,' Penny said. 'Maybe I listen to Drake, but I don't listen to you. You're nobody.'

Brittney didn't argue. She just said, 'She gave birth to our lord.'

Penny must have tripped over a rock, because she went sprawling with the baby in her arms. She ploughed into Diana, almost but not quite knocking Diana over.

The baby hit solid rock with a sickening thud.

From the darkness a thin wail of baby fury. It was the first time the baby had cried. It cried just like any baby.

Diana felt her heart respond. And her body, as her breasts leaked milk.

She felt in the dark and touched the baby's arm. She fumbled the baby to her and cradled it. It latched on and again began to suck vigorously.

In that first contact Diana had read the baby's power level. A four bar now. The equal of Caine or Sam.

A four bar. And still just a baby!

'Our lady should carry our lord,' Brittney said.

'Are you mental?' Penny was disbelieving. 'Are you that stupid? You think this is Jesus in the manger and she's Mary, you dumb metal-mouthed hick?'

'I will walk in front,' Brittney announced. 'I will make straight the way of the lord.'

Diana looked down at the baby. She could see its cheek. Impossible. Nothing could be seen in this absolute darkness.

And yet, she did see the baby's cheek. And her squeezed-shut eyes. And her little rosebud mouth holding on. And then her fat little arm, and her tiny fist pressed into her mother's breast.

'She glows!' Brittney said. 'Our lord gives us her light!'

'That's it, I've tried to put up with your –'

'Hush!' Brittney put up a hand, amazingly visible in the

glow that came from the baby. 'She speaks to me. We must go forth . . .'

'Go forth,' Penny echoed with cutting sarcasm. 'Hallelujah. Drake's a psycho but at least he's not a moron.'

'We must go to the barrier and prepare for our rebirth.'

Diana heard all this, but her thoughts were all for the baby at her breast. It was, after all, her baby. The gaiaphage might be inside it, might take over its thoughts and use it. But something in there was still her daughter. Hers and Caine's.

And if terrible things awaited this little girl, whose fault was that? The guilt lay on Diana and Caine.

Diana had no right to reject Gaia.

The name came to her as if she'd known it all along. It made her sad. It would have been so much better if she could have named her baby Sally or Chloe or Melissa. But none of those would have been the right name.

Gaia.

Gaia's eyes opened. She squinted blue eyes at Diana.

'Yeah,' Diana said. 'I'm your mommy.'

'It's a trail of lights,' Dekka said. 'Wow. I can see my hands.'

She stepped close to the Sammy sun and checked her body for marks. Penny's vision had been powerful. Even now it was almost impossible to believe it was just an illusion. But her skin was unmarked.

'Most of them go that way.'

Orc pointed, and Dekka could actually see him. Not well, of course. Each small pebble that made up his body was surrounded by blackest shadows. His eyes were down inside deep wells. The small patch of human skin around his mouth and part of one cheek looked as grey-green as every other part of him.

But he was real, not just a sound and a resistance at the fingertips.

'Yeah. But what does that mean if more go one way?' She could see perhaps half a dozen of the suns spreading out to the right. Just four to the left. 'I mean, they could be blocked. And it's not like they show up all that well anyway. If we had a compass . . . I mean, Orc, we don't even know which way is which. We don't know if Sam is moving right or left from this point.'

'I have an idea. But it's probably stupid,' Orc said.

'Stupid ideas are all we've got. So what is it?'

'Well, can't you see better if you're up high?'

Dekka said, 'Yes, as a matter of fact. And that's not stupid at all. In fact, I don't know why I didn't think of it.'

Orc shrugged his massive shoulders. 'You're having a bad day.'

This was such an understatement, and yet so kind in a way, that Dekka had to laugh. 'You could say that. So, Orc, you want to fly a little?'

'Me?'

'Why not you? There're some rocks over there. Better than dirt, because when I switch off gravity the dirt tends to float up and get in your eyes.'

They moved to a rock outcropping. Orc stood stiff, like he was on display and wanted to look right. Dekka did her thing and Orc rose. At ten feet he let out a huge, delighted guffaw.

'Hah! This is fun!'

At thirty feet she could no longer see him at all. 'What do you see, Orc?'

'Fire,' he said. 'And I think the Sammy suns are going that way.'

'I'm bringing you down now.'

When he was back on terra firma Dekka said, 'The fire. What did it look like?'

'Like it was two or maybe three different fires, but all close together.'

'Perdido Beach?'

'Maybe,' he said reluctantly.

'OK, so we follow the Sammy suns towards town.'

But Orc hesitated. 'You can do that, Dekka. But me, I set out to find Drake and kill him.'

'Orc, you must know we can't look for anything. Not in this pitch-black. It could take us forever to just accidentally run into Drake.'

He nodded, but he wasn't really agreeing. 'I don't mind the dark as much you do, Dekka. In the dark I don't have to be like I am. You know? People can't see me. Anyway, there'll likely be some booze back there in town. So I'm just going to go on in the dark. It's probably better for me.'

He held out his oversize paw and Dekka felt strangely moved taking it. 'Thanks, big guy. You saved me, you know.'

'Nah.'

'No, listen to me, Orc. I know you have some bad stuff on your conscience.'

He nodded and muttered, 'But I've been forgave of that. I prayed and I was forgave.' Then he added, 'But that don't mean it doesn't weigh me down.'

'That's what I'm saying, Orc. When all that weighs you down, you remember that you saved me. OK?'

He didn't look too sure of that. But he may have smiled. It was hard to tell. And then he went galumphing off into the dark.

Dekka followed the lights leading left.

'There's a light out there. Down the highway. It just appeared!' Lana said.

'A Sammy sun!' Quinn said. The sense of relief was amazing. Sam was coming.

He felt like he might well faint from the sheer release of tension.

Quinn, Lana, and Caine – with Patrick as well – had snuck away from the dying campfire, leaving some of Quinn's people in nominal charge. Not that anyone was able any more to do more than yell, 'Knock it off!'

Torches were spreading through Perdido Beach, little knots of kids looking for food, water, beloved toys, or just a bed.

Now Sammy suns were blossoming like radioactive flowers on the highway.

Patrick barked once, announcing himself, and took off down the highway.

'Hail the conquering hero,' Caine muttered. 'Mr Sunshine.'

After ten minutes a new Sammy sun appeared, perhaps no more than a hundred feet away, and they walked towards it, still moving carefully. The highway was littered with debris up to and including entire trucks.

Then Quinn could make out two forms dimly outlined.

The two groups came together and Sam illuminated the scene.

'Quinn, Lana,' Sam said. One hand was scratching Patrick's ruff. 'Caine.'

'Hey, brother. How's it going? Some weird weather we're having, huh?' Caine said.

'What happened to your hands?' Sam asked.

Caine raised his hands, still patched with concrete. 'Oh, this? It's nothing. I just need a little lotion.'

'Astrid?' Lana said. 'You're back?'

'About time,' Quinn said under his breath.

'Well, then, it's a happy ending,' Caine said savagely. 'I love a happy ending.'

Quinn was about to say something to Caine, something along the lines of, 'Shut up'. But he stopped himself. Caine was a power-mad tool, but he'd been through hell this day. Sarcasm wasn't the worst thing he was capable of.

'You here to turn on some lights?' Lana asked. 'Because as good as that would be, we have bigger problems. The gaiaphage is coming.'

'How?' Astrid asked sharply. 'Everyone says the gaiaphage is a green encrustation in the bottom of a mineshaft.'

'I don't know how,' Lana said, a little evasively. 'It just is. That's why we're standing out here. We weren't waiting for you. We're waiting for it.'

'I won't ask how you know,' Astrid said.

'Yeah?' Lana shot back. 'Well, here's my question, Astrid: why aren't you arguing more? I tell you this is happening and you just meekly accept it? You know something.'

'Oh, Astrid? She knows everything,' Caine said.

'It has Diana,' Astrid said. She tilted her head and considered Caine. 'And your baby, Caine. At least, Diana says it's yours.'

'Yeah,' Caine said. He seemed about to say something more, but stopped himself and just muttered, 'Yeah. A baby.'

'Wait,' Lana interrupted. 'Sanjit. Did . . .'

'Barely,' Sam said. 'But as far as I know he's safe at the lake. I got your message. Too late. And Astrid was bringing a message to you as well.'

'Funny how things fall apart when the lights go out,' Quinn said. 'Lots of plans, and nothing works.'

'The gaiaphage is looking for a body,' Astrid said. 'It needs a physical body. The barrier is dead. It's going to crack open. It's finally going to be over. But when that happens the gaiaphage is going to try to get out.'

'And you know this because of your amazing geniusness?' Caine said, smirking. 'You know what time this is all supposed to happen? Because I have to say, I'm ready to get out of this place. Can't happen soon enough for me. I've been really craving some ice cream.'

'I don't know when. It could be months. Your son or daughter isn't due for –'

'Stop that!' Caine snarled, abandoning his snarky pose. 'Don't play that game with me, Astrid. What do you think I'm going to do? Suddenly become a different person just because I had sex with Diana?'

'You got her pregnant,' Astrid said quite calmly. 'I thought maybe that fact might make you consider something besides yourself.'

'Oh, it does, Astrid,' he said with savage sarcasm. 'It makes me want to go toss the football around in the backyard. Maybe barbecue some steaks. Real daddy kind of stuff. Only slight problem is this darn darkness.'

A flame leaped into the air not far from the road. They heard the agitated voices of young children.

'Thanks, that's better,' Caine yelled over his shoulder. 'So Lana says the gaiaphage is coming, and you guys say it's got Diana – by the way, great job protecting her, Sam – and I should be taking parenting classes, plus, oh, by the way, the barrier is coming down. Someday. Probably after we've all starved to death.'

All the while Sam had been watching Caine like a specimen under a microscope. Trying to figure him out. 'You going to fight or not?'

'Who, me?' Caine laughed. 'What's the matter with you, Sam? Genius girl says the barrier is going to come down. And you want to run out and get killed before that happens? Let the barrier crack open like an egg. If the gaiaphage wants to walk on out I say we wish him well, wait until he's a ways down the road, and then leave ourselves.'

'Taking Diana and your . . . and the baby,' Sam said.

'You hear what Albert did? Did you?' Caine tried to point in the direction of the ocean and the island, but it drew attention to his still-encrusted hand, so he dropped it to his side. 'As soon as Albert realised what was happening he caught a boat and ran for the island. And the best part? He's been planning it for a long time. He bribed Taylor. He apparently got hold of some missiles – who knows how he pulled that off; he's Albert – and moved them out there, too.'

Quinn saw Sam's jaw clench hard at that.

'Now,' Caine went on, 'Albert's sitting out there eating cheese and crackers and laughing his butt off at fools like us.'

Sam ignored, or at least pretended to ignore, all of that. He said, 'Look, Caine. I don't know where Brianna is, or Dekka, or Orc. Jack is maybe dead by now. Anyway, he won't be coming to the fight. So maybe I can take down Drake myself, and maybe not. But I don't even know what it means to say the gaiaphage is coming. Coming how? Coming as what? With what kind of power? I don't even know if –'

Quinn held up his hand and Sam stopped. 'Penny,' Quinn said. 'We followed her until she crossed the highway. She's out there somewhere, too. Out there in the dark.'

'There's no reason to think she would run into Drake,' Lana said, but she sounded worried.

'Now, there,' Caine said, holding up his crusted index finger, 'there's someone I'll fight. Show me Penny and I'll kill her for you. I'll kill her twice.'

The conversation died. And they stood there in silence, the five of them and one dog, underneath a weak mockery of a light.

Quinn said, 'Everyone saw you, Caine. Dragging that cement

bowl around. Hunched over like a monkey walking on its knuckles. That crown stapled into your scalp. You got beat. King Caine, and all you could do was be Penny's little monkey. Kids will be laughing about that for a long time. Yeah. If the barrier comes down, you'll be hearing stories about that on TV. Internet jokes about it.' Quinn watched Caine's hands warily. He was hoping someone would stop Caine before he struck and threw Quinn against and through the nearest wall.

Caine turned with menacing slowness to Quinn. Quinn felt the heat of his malevolence. Humiliation was dangerous stuff to play around with.

'What do you think your story will look like, Caine? Always swaggering around, playing all bad and tough. You did one right thing, Caine: you went out, helped Brianna, and you fought those bugs back, and that's why the people said, "yeah, he can be our king."'

'I helped Brianna?' Caine snapped. 'She helped me.'

'All that, though, that gets wiped out, because the end of the story is how Penny humiliated you –'

'Enough, all right?' Caine said sharply.

'What people remember is the end of the story. And if the barrier comes down, the end of the story will be how you cried and crapped yourself and danced like a trained monkey for Penny.'

There was no way to know whether Caine was as pale as he

seemed by the light of the Sammy sun. His eyes were narrow, and his lips were drawn back, almost like a wolf baring its teeth. His face was right in Quinn's.

He kept his gaze on Quinn but spoke to Sam. 'Your loser friend here must have grown a pair, Sam.'

'Seems like,' Sam said, sounding amazed.

Then Caine spoke to Quinn. 'Tell you what, Quinn, since you're so worried about my . . . legacy. Is that the right word, Astrid? Since you're worried about my legacy, Quinn, I'll go out Drake-hunting with my brother there, if . . .'

'If what?' Quinn asked.

'If you come with us,' Caine said with a cruel smile. 'You've been a pain in my ass, fisherman. It's because of you I had a beef with Penny in the first place. So it's real dark out there, and most likely Drake, and maybe even our old friend Penny, are out there. Not to mention Mr Nasty himself.'

Quinn couldn't stop himself glancing out towards the utter darkness within which he knew monsters hid.

'He's a fisherman,' Sam said. 'He doesn't even have a weapon.'

Caine laughed. 'Have you been to Perdido Beach? It's a nice little town. Not much food, no entertainment, plenty of weapons. Weapons are the one thing we do have. And he'll need one.'

'I don't even know how to shoot,' Quinn protested.

FEAR

Caine laughed cruelly. 'It's not for you to shoot Drake or Penny, let alone the Darkness, if he's actually coming,' he mocked. 'It's for you to stick in your mouth and pull the trigger if any one of them gets hold of you.'

THIRTY EIGHT

18 MINUTES

AFTER HOURS AND hours of total darkness, the soft glow of her baby's skin allowed Diana to walk with more confidence. She was a light in the darkness.

Gaia. Her baby.

She felt still the horror at seeing the green pixels, that swarm that was the gaiaphage, enter her daughter's nose and mouth. She would never, ever be able to block that out.

So many things she would never be able to forget.

But against it all was this person. This soft, chubby little girl, who looked up at her with eyes so absurdly blue and so unnaturally aware.

She seemed to grow heavier even as Diana carried her down through the ghost town beneath the mineshaft. Soon Gaia would not need to nurse. Already Diana could feel tiny teeth biting.

And then what would Gaia do with her mother?

'Doesn't matter,' Diana whispered. 'It doesn't matter. She's mine.'

Brittney walked beside her, peering in eagerly to see Gaia's face. Brittney wore the expression of an ecstatic believer. Diana knew that if Gaia somehow spoke and told Brittney to leap off a cliff, Brittney would do it.

But Gaia spoke through Diana now.

She spoke through her mother.

Diana could feel her baby's mind probing inside her own. Not the mind of a baby, true, but not quite the cold violence of the gaiaphage, either. The two were becoming one: Gaia and the Darkness. The two were growing together, and the resulting entity might be more than or less than, but definitely not equal to, either the baby or the monster.

Just one thing, though, that Diana couldn't dismiss from her thoughts. Just one thing. The way Gaia reached into Diana's memory and opened it up as if she was thumbing through a picture book. Like she was looking for something. Something the baby sensed must be there.

Not rustling around blindly, but looking for something.

Diana had no defences against Gaia. She could hide nothing from her. Diana could only watch as her memories unfolded to reveal pictures of things past. And of people.

Gaia was studying the people Diana knew. Now Brianna. Now Edilio. Now Duck and Albert and Mary.

Not Panda. No.

Caine. Gaia lingered long on pictures of Caine. A first

meeting at Coates. The many flirtations. The teasing. The way Diana had made him want her. The dark ambition she had seen in him. The first time he had revealed his power to her.

The terrible things they had done. Battles.

Murder.

Yes, but don't look any further; all that I confess, Gaia, my daughter, but enough. Enough. Please don't.

The smell. That was what the baby found first. The aroma of roasted human flesh.

Diana's eyes filled with tears.

'What's the matter?' Brittney asked.

The baby tasted what Diana had tasted.

The baby felt her stomach gratefully receive the meat that had been a boy named Panda.

Yes, Diana said to the mind within her own, *I'm a monster, and so are you, little Gaia. But your mommy loves you.*

'There's a string of lights up there,' Penny said. 'They look like Christmas lights.'

Yes, go there, Gaia said inside Diana's thoughts.

'Go to the lights,' Diana said without even thinking about it. 'Then follow them to the left.'

'Shut your mouth, cow,' Penny said. 'You don't give orders.'

Gaia kicked against Diana's enfolding arms. She pushed herself up so that she could see over Diana's shoulder. She looked at Penny.

The baby pushed her clenched fist over Diana's shoulder, opened her hand, and Penny screamed.

Diana stopped. She watched and listened. And did it fill her with a brutal sort of joy to see Penny writhe in terror and pain? Yes. As it pleased her daughter to cause that terror.

Gaia laughed a baby's innocent, gurgling laugh.

Penny's scream seemed to last a very long time. Long enough that Drake emerged from where Brittney had been.

When at last Penny stopped, and just sat on her meagre haunches, staring, staring in horror at the baby, Drake said, 'So, the baby has game.' He unwrapped his whip from around his waist and said, 'Don't think that means I can't do what I want with you, Diana.'

Diana met his dead gaze. It occurred to her for the first time that she felt better. Much better. She had just gone through hell, but she felt . . . fine. She inventoried her body, checking in with her whipped back, her bruises, her murderously stretched belly, her torn parts.

She was fine.

Gaia had healed her.

'Actually, Drake,' Diana said, 'I think it means you'd better watch very carefully what you do or say to me.'

Gaia, once more cradled in her mother's arms, grinned a two-toothed grin.

* * *

'Something coming down the highway,' Sam said.

'It's a light,' Astrid said.

'A light called Darkness,' Lana said in a faraway voice.

'It's following the Sammy suns. Straight for us,' Caine said. He wasn't snarking or snarling any more. Sam saw the same look on his face and Lana's. They both knew, deep down in their souls, what was coming.

Lana went to Caine and put a hand on his arm. Just making contact. Caine didn't shake her off.

It was a weird bond they shared: memories of the gaiaphage. Memories of its painful touch deep inside their minds. Scars left on their souls.

'"Fear is the mind-killer,"' Lana said, reciting from memory. '"Fear is the little-death that brings total obliteration. I will face my fear. I . . ." I can't remember the rest. From a book I read a long time ago.'

To almost no one's surprise, Astrid said, '*Dune*, by Frank Herbert. "I must not fear. Fear is the mind-killer. Fear is the little-death that brings total obliteration. I will face my fear. I will permit it to pass over me and through me. And when it has gone past I will turn the inner eye to see its path. Where the fear has gone there will be nothing."'

She and Lana together spoke the last phrase of the incantation. '"Only I will remain."'

There was a collective sigh that was almost a sob.

Sam pulled Astrid to him and they kissed. Then Sam pushed her away and said, 'I love you. All my heart. Forever. But get the hell out of here, because I can't be watching out for you.'

'I know,' Astrid said. 'And I love you, too.'

Lana took a furious, defiant look down the highway. Sam knew what was in her heart.

'Lana. What you've got won't kill him. What you've got may save a bunch of others. Go. Now.'

Then it was just the three of them, Sam, Caine, and Quinn, watching the dim light advance. Seeing now that it was three indistinct shapes. It was as if the one in the middle was carrying a Sammy sun of a different hue. Sam couldn't make out faces. But he was sure he saw a tentacle twisting, twisting.

'Three of them,' Caine said. 'That means most likely Penny is one of them.' Caine took a deep breath. 'Get outta here, Quinn.'

Quinn said, 'No. I don't think I will.'

'Hey. I'm letting you off the hook, fisherman, OK? I'm being a good guy. You can go tell everyone the last thing I said was, 'Just get out of here, Quinn, and try to stay alive.'

'Quinn,' Sam said. 'You've got nothing to prove, man.'

They had found Quinn a pistol. A revolver. It had three bullets.

'I'm in this,' Quinn said shakily.

'You have a plan, Sammy boy?' Caine asked.

'Yeah.' He extinguished the nearest Sammy sun, plunging

them into darkness. The next one back was a hundred yards down the road. 'Quinn, you start walking backwards towards the last light. They won't have any depth perception, no more than we do in this light. They'll keep coming towards you. Caine, you drop left; I drop right; we hit them when they're fifty feet out. Hopefully before Penny can find a target.'

'Great plan,' Caine said a little sarcastically. But he melted into the darkness on the left-hand side of the road.

'Quinn. My friend. What Caine said before. Save one bullet.' With that Sam plunged into the deep, enveloping darkness.

He watched Quinn begin to walk backwards. It would mean Quinn was in darkness until he neared the next Sammy sun back. If Drake had seen them at all, he probably hadn't been able to tell how many there were. But he would eventually be able to see Quinn. At that point he would fixate, anxious to take whoever it was standing in his way.

There might be an opportunity there. A few confused seconds where Caine and Sam could strike unexpectedly. If they were fast and lucky they could take out at least one of the three and reduce the odds.

Who was that third person?

Drake. Penny. And someone – or something – glowing like an old headlight.

Whoever it is, he told himself, first go for Penny.

Penny was the one to fear.

* * *

'Dada,' Gaia said.

Diana stared down at her bright, glowing child. She was already the size of a two-year-old. There were teeth in her mouth. There was hair – dark like her parents' – on her head. Her movements were already deliberate and controlled, no more wild lack of coordination. Diana wondered if she could already walk.

'Did you say "Dada"?'

Gaia was looking fixedly at the dark off to the right. Straight ahead a lone figure stood beneath the light of a Sammy sun. Beyond him at least two fires could be seen, one fairly close and dramatic.

Gaia was in her head again, not straining to use her child mouth, but reaching straight into Diana's memories. Pictures of Caine. And suddenly it was clear.

'It's an ambush!' Diana said.

'Shut the –' Drake said, and was hurled bodily on to his back with such sudden force that he skidded clear out of sight.

A beam of terrible green light shot from the other direction.

Penny had reacted faster to Diana's warning. She was already moving to hide behind Diana when the light split the night. Half of Penny's hair frizzled and burned, leaving a terrible smell.

A roar from the dark behind them and Drake was rushing

forward, his terrible whip at the ready, searching for a target. Light sliced deep into his side. He spun and fell. But even as he fell the burn was healing.

Diana saw Sam rush from the darkness. He yelled, 'Diana, get down!' and fired at the spot where Drake had been a split second earlier.

Suddenly, revealed by the flash of light from Sam's palms: Caine.

It had been four months since she had seen him. Just a little longer since together they had made Gaia.

Their eyes met. Caine froze. He stared at Diana. A look of pain creased his brow.

That moment's hesitation was too long.

Caine reeled back, slapping at his body with hands weirdly encrusted on their backs. Slapping and yelling, and then Sam was yelling, 'It's Penny, it's just Penny, Caine!'

Caine seemed to get control of himself, though barely, and for only a moment as he raised his hands and, with a wild sweep of both hands, flung Penny into the dark.

It was a mistake. An invisible Penny was even more dangerous.

Sam saw it and swept his killing beam around in a semicircle, searching for her. A flash of Penny, running. But when the beam pursued her, burning up the shrubbery, turning sand to bubbling glass, she wasn't there.

Penny was not there. Astrid was.

Astrid in flames. Running, screaming towards Sam. Her skin was crisping. There was a smell of burned meat. Her blonde hair was like a single flame and the edges of that fire ate at her forehead and cheeks.

'Astrid!' Sam cried, and ran to her. He was already whipping off his shirt to smother the flames when she suddenly ballooned, like a marshmallow dropped into a fire. She swelled and her skin turned charcoal and her eyes were just smears and . . .

The vision was gone.

Sam was in the dark. Panting. Staring.

He turned and saw the glow of the child in Diana's arms. They were marching calmly towards Quinn.

Caine? Where was he?

Sam heard the sound of a whip. He ran towards that sound, but now the darkness had closed in and he had to toss Sammy suns profligately in order to see.

'Quinn! Run! Get out of there!' Sam yelled.

He watched as Quinn started to make a brave show of it, then he realised it wasn't so much brave as stupid.

It was several minutes before Sam found Caine. He was breathing, but just now returning to consciousness. There was a livid red mark around Caine's throat.

He sat up, then accepted Sam's extended hand.

'Drake?'

Caine nodded and rubbed his neck. 'But it was Penny who distracted me. You?'

'Penny,' Sam confirmed.

'OK, next time we have to take Penny out before we do anything else,' Caine said.

The little procession – Drake, Penny, and Diana, with a baby in her arms – kept walking on down the road.

'So she had the baby,' Sam said. 'Congratulations?'

'We lost the element of surprise,' Caine said. 'They'll be ready.'

As if to make the point, Drake, now even with the next Sammy sun, turned to look back at them, laughed, and snapped his whip. The laugh carried. So did the crack.

'Why didn't they finish us?' Sam wondered.

'If I tell you something crazy, will you just accept it?'

'It's the FAYZ.'

'It was the baby. The baby stopped Drake. I was choking and he was behind me so I couldn't get at him. Anyway, as good a hold as he had on me, if I'd thrown him or pushed him I'd have ripped my own head off. I saw the baby. Looked right at me. And Drake let me go.'

Sam wasn't sure if he believed it or not. But the days of doubting a story just because it sounded crazy were over.

'They're heading for the barrier.'

'Maybe it really will open?'

'Maybe,' Sam said. 'But they're going through town. Tearing up your people, King Caine.'

A scream reached their ears.

'Well, I guess we'd better give Quinn a good story,' Caine said dryly. 'My legacy and all.'

'Penny first,' Sam said, and started running.

THIRTY NINE

3 MINUTES

GAIA LAUGHED AND Diana couldn't help laughing, too. They'd passed a burning house with kids lurking as near as they could get to the light without burning.

Penny had done something to make them run into the burning house.

Diana was horrified until Gaia laughed. And then Diana couldn't help but laugh, too. It was funny, in a way.

Gaia had a sense of humour. How amazing to see it in an infant. Diana credited herself, her genes. Gaia had got that from her mommy.

Down the street, and the light that shone from Gaia was enough to draw people like moths to the flame. They would come creeping or cavorting, needing that light, needing it after so long in the hopeless pitch-black.

They came, and when they did Drake would whip them until they ran away again, or danced just out of his range.

Gaia laughed and clapped her hands. Amazing how fast

she learned.

The barrier would be broken and Diana and her baby girl would be free. They could go to the zoo. Or what was that place kids went for pizza and games? Chuck E. Cheese's! Yes, they could play the games and eat pizza. And watch TV in . . . They would find a house. Who could stop them, really? With Drake and Penny as their servants. Hah! Servants.

Who could stand against them? They had brushed Caine and Sam aside like they were nothing.

And Gaia had yet to even reveal the extent of her own power.

Diana wanted to laugh aloud and dance around with her baby. But even as the high of joy washed through her, Diana felt the falseness of it. The strained edginess of it. She wanted to shout for joy and scream for joy and then stab the baby, her baby, her beloved little daughter, stab her with a knife. For joy.

Gaia was looking at her. Her eyes held her. Diana couldn't look away. They cut right through her and saw the truth. Gaia could see the fear inside Diana, the fear of Gaia.

Gaia laughed and clapped her hands and her blue eyes shone and Diana felt weak inside, and sick, and all the suffering her body had been through all felt as if it was still there and only concealed from view. She was hollow. An empty nothingness tottering along on stick-figure legs that would snap and collapse.

Screams of burning children pursued Diana as she held her baby close and looked fearfully into its glittering eyes.

OUTSIDE

THERE WAS NO way the suspension on Connie's car was built for this road. The Camry kept bottoming out with a sound like chain saws ripping through steel.

But the time for hesitation was over. Now was the time for her to behave like a mother. A mother whose child – whose children – were in danger.

In the rearview mirror she saw Abana keeping pace. Her SUV was doing a little better. Fine: if they survived this day they could drive home in that.

If Abana ever talked to her again.

The road came perilously close to the highway when they were just half a mile from the barrier. The dust trail they were putting up would be obvious.

Sure enough, as the awful blank monstrosity that was the Perdido Beach Anomaly filled the entire field of view, Connie heard a helicopter overhead.

A loudspeaker blared, audible even over the *chop-chop-*

chop of the rotors.

'You are in a dangerous, restricted area. Turn around immediately.'

This was repeated several times before the helicopter sped ahead, pivoted neatly, and began to land in the road a quarter mile away.

In the rearview mirror Connie saw Abana's SUV take a sharp, bouncing, crazy veer into the rough terrain. She was angling towards the highway where it met the barrier. It would lead straight through the remains of the hastily moved camp.

There were still a few trailers there. Still a satellite dish array. Dumpsters. Porta Pottis.

Connie swore to herself, apologised to her car, and veered after Abana.

It was no longer a case of the car just bottoming out. Now the car was flying and crashing, flying and crashing. Each impact jarred Connie's bones. She hit the ceiling so many times she quickly lost count. The steering wheel tore itself from her grip.

Then suddenly she was on tarmac, blistering through the remains of the camp.

The helicopter was after them again and it blew overhead.

It executed a daring, almost suicidal manoeuvre, and landed way too hard in the final feet of pavement before the intimidating wall of the barrier.

Two soldiers jumped out, MPs with guns drawn.

Then a third soldier.

Abana slammed on her brakes.

Connie did not stop. She aimed the battered, disintegrating car at the helicopter and stood on the accelerator.

The Camry hit the helicopter's skids. The air bag exploded in her face. The seat belt jerked back against her. She heard something snap. She felt a jolt of pain.

She jumped out of the car, stumbled over the twisted metal remains of the skid, saw that the rotor had ploughed into concrete and stuck fast.

And Connie ran, staggered, realised she'd broken her collarbone, ran on towards the barrier. If she could reach it, if they couldn't stop her, couldn't drag her away, then she could stop it all from happening.

One of the soldiers snagged Abana as she ran, but Connie dodged, and only as she ran past him, only when he called out, 'Connie! No!' did she realise that the third soldier was Darius.

She reached the barrier.

Reached it. Stopped. Stared at it, at the eternal grey wall.

Darius was behind her, breathless. 'Connie. It's too late. It's too late, babe. Something's happened to the device.'

She turned on him, somehow believing he was reproaching her, too emotional to understand what he was saying. 'I'm sorry,' she cried. 'It's my boys in there. It's my babies!'

He took her in his arms, squeezed her tight, and said, 'They tried to stop the countdown. It worked, the message got out, and they tried to stop it.'

'What?'

Abana came running up then. The MPs had given up holding her back. The soldiers wore identically strained expressions. Neither seemed interested in the two women any more.

'Listen to me,' Darius said. 'They can't stop it. It's this place. Something went wrong and they can't stop the countdown.'

At last his words penetrated.

'How long?' Connie asked.

Darius looked at the MPs. And now Connie understood the passive, strained look on their faces. 'One minute and ten seconds,' the larger of the two MPs, a lieutenant, said. And he knelt on the pavement, folded his hands, and prayed.

FORTY

2 MINUTES

SAM WAS TORN between spreading light with abandon and being seen coming, or going without light and moving much more slowly. He chose a compromise. He tossed off Sammy suns at a run as he and Caine made their way to the beach, and then along the beach until they were hidden from view beneath the cliffs.

The ocean had a faint, very faint phosphorescence that seemed almost bright. It could be seen not as particular waves or even ripples, but as a fuzzy mass that was only dark as opposed to utterly black.

'Here,' Sam said, hanging a sun. He pointed at the forbidding wall of stone to their left. 'The climb isn't too bad.'

'You don't need to climb.'

Sam felt himself lifted off his feet. He rose through the air with the cliff face just within reach. In the eerie light, the rock face looked like the blades of broken knives.

Sam scrambled to get from Caine's grip on to solid ground.

Did he dare hang a light? No. Too near the highway. He could sense – at least, he hoped he could – Clifftop off to his right. If he was where he thought he was, he could easily cross the driveway, the access road, a sand berm, and then descend at the point where the highway ran into the barrier.

Caine landed beside him.

'You going to light up?'

'No. Let's try for surprise number two.'

They stumbled across rough ground, tripping, falling, silencing their curses.

They were just beside the sand berm, a sand wind-barrier that ran within fifty feet of the road, when they heard a crack. It was like a peal of thunder, but with no lightning.

It seemed to go on forever and ever.

'It begins,' a strange, childlike, but beautiful voice said. 'The egg cracks! Soon! Soon!'

'She speaks!' Diana cried.

'We're getting out,' Drake cried. 'It's opening!'

'Now,' Sam hissed.

He and Caine motored up the side of the sand. As soon as Caine could see his target he swept his hands down and literally threw himself into the air. The swoosh gave him away, and Penny saw him in an instant.

Sam aimed carefully, but Diana moved between him and Penny. Calm, fluid, as if she'd known he was there.

'Get her!' Caine screamed in despair as a horrific vision left him plummeting, screaming, to the ground.

Sam ran straight for them. He fired once, hitting Drake full in the face. It didn't kill him, but it would keep him from talking for a while.

He shouldered Diana roughly aside, seeing tiny blue eyes follow him.

Penny spun.

Sam fired wildly.

Penny's left leg caught fire. She screeched and ran in panic, spreading the flames to her clothing.

'No, Sam!' Diana cried.

An unimaginably powerful force threw Sam spinning into the air. It was like someone had set a bomb off under him. And then he stopped spinning. He stopped falling back to earth.

He looked down and saw the baby looking up at him and laughing and clapping her hands. The infant seemed luminous, lighting the whole scene with an unnatural glow. Then the baby took her chubby little fingers and made a motion like she was stretching dough.

Sam felt his body pulling in opposite directions. It squeezed the air from his lungs. It was as if two giant hands had each taken a rough grip on him and were tearing him apart.

He heard his bones cracking.

Felt the sharp pain of ribs separating from cartilage.

The baby was bringing him closer now. Like she wanted to see better. Like she wanted to be sprayed with his very blood as he was ripped in –

Diana stumbled forward. She ploughed into her child and both fell, but without hitting the ground.

Sam fell to earth. But he, too, did not quite smash on to the concrete.

Dekka!

She was panting like she'd just run a marathon. She stood in the middle of the road, glaring furiously, hands raised. She looked, Sam thought, like she'd taken a trip to hell. But she had shown excellent timing.

Sam did not hesitate. As soon as his feet touched the ground he jumped up, ignoring the bone-shattering pain in his body.

Penny had dropped and rolled, the fire was out, but her skin was the colour and texture of a well-glazed ham.

Sam ran to where she lay gasping with pain, real pain, no illusion, and straddled her and aimed his hands down at her.

'You're too dangerous to live,' Sam said.

His own flesh suddenly caught fire, but he was too close, too ready. He was already there and all he had to do now was to think and –

– and a chunk of pavement, a slab of concrete two feet across and shedding the dirt from which it had been ripped, smashed down on Penny's head with such force that the ground bounced beneath Sam's feet.

Her body ceased moving instantly. Like a switch had been thrown.

Caine stood over her, breathing hard. 'Payback,' he snarled. He kicked the slab of cement for emphasis.

Drake's melted face had begun to repair itself, but he still looked like a microwaved action figure. His whip, however, was in perfect working order.

He struck and Sam cried out in pain.

Caine raised the rock he'd used to kill Penny and readied it to smash down on Drake.

'No, Daddy,' said Gaia.

OUTSIDE

'IT BLOWS UP and kills us all,' Connie said quietly, weirdly calm. 'Or it does . . . something else.'

Abana took her hand. The two of them.

And other vehicles were coming down the highway. Not police, there were no sirens. The police and soldiers had been withdrawn to a safe distance.

These were a handful of private cars and vans. Parents. Friends. People who had got the emails and tweets and were rushing to stop what could not now be stopped.

Connie and Abana looked at each other. A look full of fear and sadness and guilt: they had brought these people here to die.

Connie looked at the MPs. The chopper pilot, a woman with blonde hair and captain's bars, had joined them after roundly cursing the damage to her craft.

'I'm sorry,' Connie whispered. 'I'm sorry I did this to you.'

She heard a cracking sound. Like slow-motion thunder, or

like a world-size eggshell breaking open. Everyone fell silent and listened. It went on for a long time.

'It's opening,' Abana whispered. 'The barrier, it's cracking open!'

Too late, Connie thought. *Too late.*

Connie went to Darius and they waited, side by side, for the end.

FORTY ONE

15 SECONDS

THE BABY. IT was no longer in Diana's arms. It stood. All on its own, a glowing, naked two-year-old, by all appearances.

Caine flew back. He was pressed against the barrier, in full contact, yelling at the pain, then barely making a sound at all as the pressure grew stronger, relentless.

Sam could see him being squashed; he could quite literally see Caine's body flatten as if a truck were pushing against him, squashing him like a bug against the barrier.

'Make her stop!' Sam yelled at Diana.

'I . . .' Diana looked stricken. Like she was coming out of a nightmare into a worse reality.

'She's killing him!'

'Don't,' Diana said weakly. 'Don't kill your father.'

But there was a determined look on the child's face. Her cherub lips drew back in a weird snarl.

Sam raised his hands, palms out.

'Get back, Diana,' Sam said.

Diana did not move.

Sam glanced at Caine. A bug against a windshield.

Sam fired. Twin beams of murderous light hit the child dead centre.

And the entire world exploded in blinding light.

Caine slid to the ground. Diana reeled back, covering her face. Drake used his tentacle to shield his eyes.

Sam was blinded by it. It was not the light of his hands. It was not the light of the baby.

Sunlight.

Sunlight!

Brilliant, blazing, Southern California midday sunlight.

No sound. No warning. One second the world was black, with only the pitiful light of a few Sammy suns. And the next instant it was as if they were staring into the sun itself.

Sam squeezed open one eye. What he saw was impossible. There were people. Adults. Four, no five, six adults.

A wrecked helicopter.

A Carl's, Jr. The same flash of the world outside Sam had seen for only a millisecond once before. But now the vision lingered.

The barrier was gone!

Drake cried out in a sort of ecstatic fear. He ran straight for freedom, his whip swishing at his side.

Caine, groggy, injured, stood up.

But something was wrong about it. Caine was leaning on something, propping himself up, then pulling his hand sharply away.

From the barrier.

Drake hit the wall. He ran with his whip hand lashing straight into something unyielding but invisible.

The adults, the women, the soldiers, all stared, mouths open.

They were seeing!

Seeing Diana screaming.

Seeing Drake lashing viciously in every direction with his whip.

Seeing the brutally pulverised head and face of a young girl named Penny driven half into the pavement.

Seeing a little girl, a toddler, untouched, unharmed by Sam's now-extinguished light.

Faces everywhere. They pressed closer; they tried to walk, but Sam could see them touching, then jumping back from the barrier.

The barrier was still there. But now it was transparent.

Sam's heart seemed to stop. One face suddenly came into focus.

His mother.

His mother mouthing some unhearable words and looking at him as Sam aimed his palms towards the defenceless little girl.

He couldn't stop. He had stopped once before. No: he couldn't stop.

Sam's light burned.

His mother's face, all the faces, all of them screaming soundlessly. *No! Noooo!*

The little girl's hair caught fire. It flamed magnificently, for she had her mother's lush, dark hair.

Sam fired again and the little girl's flesh burned at last.

But all the while the girl, the gaiaphage, its face turned away from onlookers, stared at Sam in undiminished fury. The blue eyes never looked away. Her angelic mouth leered in a knowing grin even as it burned.

Until at last, the gaiaphage was a pillar of flame, all features obscured.

Sam stopped firing.

The baby, the child, the monster, the devil, turned and ran back down the highway.

Diana, her face a twisted mask, ran after her.

Drake, eyes hollow and vacant, horrified, turned and ran, lashing impotently at nothing.

Sam and Caine were left standing side by side, bruised and battered, to stare over Penny's sickening corpse, at the face of their mother.

LATER

A HELICOPTER HAD arrived overhead. It was decorated with the logo of a news station out of Santa Barbara. It made no sound, of course – the dome was still impervious to noise – but Astrid could see faces in the cockpit, and could guess at the telephoto camera lens aimed down at them.

The helicopter's view was slightly hampered now by the fact that outside, out there beyond that diamond-hard, glass-clear barrier, it was raining. The drops splatted on the dome and then ran down in streams.

Along the inside of the barrier, on both sides of the highway, kids stood as close as they could get to the outside. Three or four dozen kids had come so far, rushing from Perdido Beach. At first all they saw were the soldiers and the state cops who had raced up with lights flashing, the helicopter, and a handful of parents.

But more parents were arriving in cars and SUVs from their new homes in Arroyo Grande, Santa Maria, and Orcutt. The parents who had found new places to live farther away, in Santa Barbara or Los Angeles, would take a while longer to get here.

Some of the parents were holding up signs.

Where is Charlie?

Where is Bette?

We love you! With the ink bleeding from the rain.

We miss you!

Are you OK?

There wasn't much paper left in the FAYZ, and kids had come at a run, not even waiting to grab anything. But some found pieces of wallboard or tattered windblown scraps of cardboard, and used bits of gravel to write back.

I love you, too.

Tell my mom I'm OK!

Help us.

And all of this was watched by the TV camera on the helicopter, and the people, the adults – parents and cops and gawkers. Half a dozen smartphones were snapping pictures and shooting video. Astrid knew that more, many, many more, would come.

There were boats beginning to appear on the ocean outside the dome. And they, too, stared with binoculars and telephoto lenses.

An old couple came running from a motorhome, scribbling as they ran. Their sign read, *Can you check on our cat, Ariel?*

No one would answer that, because the cats had all been eaten.

Where is my daughter? And a name.

Where is my son? And a name.

And whose job was it, Astrid wondered bitterly, to write the answers? Dead. Dead. Died of carnivorous worms. Died of a coyote attack.

Murdered in a fight over a bag of chips.

Dead of suicide.

Dead because she was playing with matches and we don't exactly have a fire department.

Killed because it was the only way we could deal with him.

How did one explain to all those watching eyes what life was like inside the FAYZ?

Then a familiar car that almost rear-ended a parked police cruiser. A man jumped out. A woman moved slowly, unsteady. Astrid's mother and father came to the barrier. Her father was holding her mother up, as though she might collapse.

The sight of them tore Astrid apart. The adults and older teens who had been in the FAYZ area when Petey had performed his mad miracle had obviously made it out. How many thousands of hours had Astrid spent trying to figure it out, trying to walk through each possible outcome? Parents dead; parents alive; parents all off in some parallel universe; parents with all memory rewritten; parents erased from past as well as present.

Now they were back, crying, waving, staring, carrying loads of emotional baggage and demanding explanations that most kids – Astrid included – could not somehow reduce to a few words scratched on a piece of plaster, or gouged with a nail on a piece of wood.

Where is Petey?

Astrid's mother held that sign. She'd written it with a Magic Marker on the side of a canvas bag, because now the rain was too intense to allow for paper.

Astrid stared at it for a long time. And in the end she could manage no answer better than a shrug and a shake of her head.

I don't know where Petey is.

I don't even know *what* Petey is.

Sam was beside her, not touching her, not with so many eyes watching. She wanted to lean against him. She wanted to close her eyes and, when she opened them again, be with him up at the lake.

Desperate months had gone by when all Astrid had wanted was to be out of this place and back in her old life as her parents' loving daughter. Now she could barely stand to look at them. Now she sought desperately for an excuse to leave. They were strangers. And she knew, as Sam had always known, that they would in the end be accusers.

They were a stab in her heart when she just could not take any more, when she just could not start to feel any more. Too much. She couldn't switch suddenly from one despair to a different despair.

Dekka stood with arms crossed behind Sam, almost as if she were hiding. Quinn and Lana stood a little apart, just marvelling at the sight of the outside world, but having as yet no faces to connect with.

'We're monkeys in a zoo,' Sam said.

'No,' Astrid said. 'People like monkeys. Look at the way they look at us. Imagine what they're seeing.'

'I've been picturing it since the beginning.'

Astrid nodded. 'Yeah.'

'You want to know what they see? What my mother sees? A boy who fired light from his hands and tried to incinerate a baby,' Sam said harshly. 'They saw me burn a child. No explanation will ever change that.'

'We look like savages. Filthy and starved, dressed like street people,' Astrid said. 'Weapons everywhere. A girl lying dead with a rock crushing her brains.' She looked at her mother and oh, there was no avoiding her mother's look of . . . of what? Not joy. Not relief.

Horror.

Distance.

Both sides, parents and children, now saw the huge gulf that had opened up between them. Astrid's father seemed small. Her mother looked old. They both were like ancient photographs of themselves, not like real people. Not as real as her memories of them.

Astrid felt as if their eyes were looking through her, searching for a memory of their daughter. Like they didn't want to see her, but some girl she had long since ceased to be.

Brianna came zooming up, a welcome distraction that caused silent faces on the other side to form round circles with their mouths: Ooh. Ahh. And hands to point and cameras to swivel. Brianna gave a little salute and a wave.

'She's ready for her close-up,' Dekka said dryly.

'Is it bright in here, or is it just me?' Brianna said. Then she drew her machete, whirled it at ten times human speed, stopped, sheathed it again, and executed a little bow to the baffled and appalled onlookers. 'Yes. Yes: I will play myself in the movie. The Breeze is way beyond special effects.'

Astrid breathed for what felt like the first time in a long while. She was thankful Brianna had broken at least some of the tension.

'By the way, back to business: they're headed into the desert,' Brianna announced to Sam. 'A happy little crew, Mom and daughter and Uncle Whip Hand. I got a little too close and that baby nearly buried me under about a ton of rock. That is one bad baby.'

Brianna nodded, satisfied. 'That can be my tag line. "That is one bad baby."'

'No, no,' Dekka said. 'Just: no.'

Astrid smiled, and her mother thought it was meant for her and smiled back.

'I saw someone recording it,' Sam said. 'Me burning that . . . that creature. You know what they'll see? You know what people out there will think?'

Astrid knew he was jumping out of his skin. She could see – anyone could see – the look of horror on Connie Temple's face every time she looked at her son.

'Son', singular, for Caine had taken one long look at his mother, turned, and walked away, back to town.

'You've been afraid of this for a long time, Sam,' Astrid said in a low voice. 'You've been afraid of being judged.'

Sam nodded. He looked down at the ground, then at Astrid. She had expected to see sadness there. Maybe guilt. She almost cried out with relief when she saw the eyes of the boy who had never backed down. She saw the eyes of the boy who had first stepped forward to fight Orc and later Caine and Drake and Penny.

She saw Sam Temple. *Her* Sam Temple.

'Well,' Sam said, 'I guess they'll think what they want to think.'

'It's getting dark out there,' Dekka said. 'When night comes, we'd better get Penny out of there. Bury her. Everyone who shows up stares at –'

Dekka fell silent, because Sam was moving. He walked purposefully to the spot where Penny's body lay, her head crushed beneath a rock, like some grotesque parody of the Wicked Witch of the East.

Cameras tracked Sam's movement.

Eyes – many of them hostile, condemning – traced his every step.

Sam looked straight at the cameras. Then he looked at his mother. Astrid held her breath.

Then Sam systematically, thoroughly, incinerated Penny's body. Until nothing but ash was left.

Connie Temple stood still as a statue, refusing to look away.

When Sam was finished, he nodded once at his mother, turned his back, and walked back to Astrid. 'She will not be buried in the plaza with good kids who died for no good reason. If we're looking for people to bury, we'll find what's left of Cigar and Taylor.'

Lana shook her head just slightly. 'I can't say for sure that Taylor is dead. Or that she's alive.'

Sam nodded. 'That's the kind of thing all those people out there are going to have a hard time understanding. But anyway, there they are, and you know what? We still have kids to feed and a monster to kill.' He reached his hand towards Astrid. 'You ready to go?'

Astrid looked past him, over his shoulder, to her mother's

worry-etched face. Then she took Sam's hand.

'There's a lot to do,' Sam said to the kids within earshot. His back was turned to the outside. 'A lot to do, a lot to work out, and this war is a long way from over. They will be back.' He jerked his head towards the north, where Gaia had fled.

'Quinn,' Sam said. 'You want to be in charge of business down here in Perdido Beach? Take over Albert's job? I think Caine would agree.'

'Absolutely not,' Quinn said. 'No. Nooo. No.'

Sam looked a little taken aback. 'No? Well, I guess they'll work something out. Caine and Lana and Edilio and Astrid.'

'I hope they do,' Quinn said fervently. He gave Sam a friendly punch on the shoulder. 'Thanks for saving our butts. Again. But me? Dude: I am going fishing.'

Astrid felt she should look back at her parents. Explain that she had to leave. Make some excuse. Stay there to reassure them.

But something fundamental had changed, like a shift in the magnetic poles or a rearranging of the laws of physics. Because she no longer belonged with them. She was no longer theirs.

She was *his.*

And he was *hers.*

And this was their world.

WWW.EGMONT.CO.UK/GONE

WWW.THEFAYZ.CO.UK

THE FAYZ

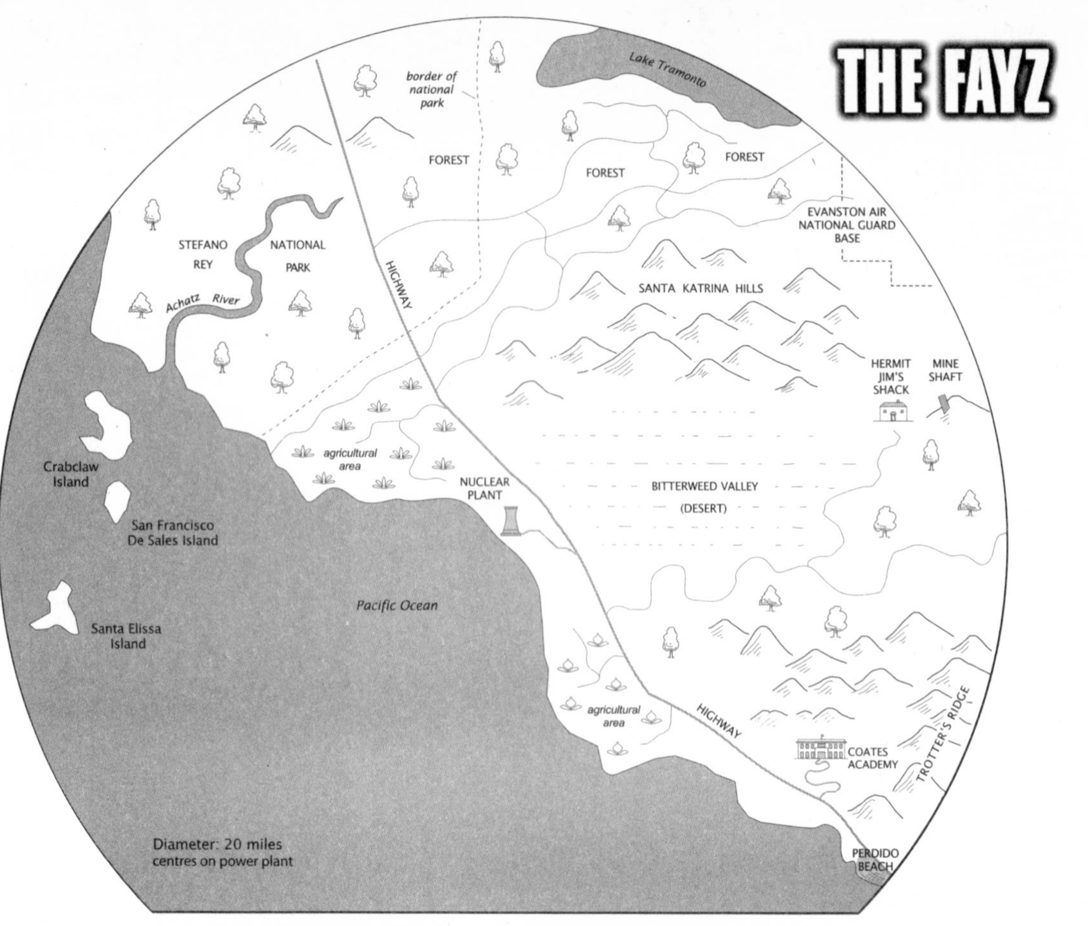

Lake Tramonto
border of national park
FOREST
FOREST
FOREST
EVANSTON AIR NATIONAL GUARD BASE
STEFANO REY
NATIONAL PARK
Achatz River
HIGHWAY
SANTA KATRINA HILLS
HERMIT JIM'S SHACK
MINE SHAFT
agricultural area
NUCLEAR PLANT
BITTERWEED VALLEY
(DESERT)
Crabclaw Island
San Francisco De Sales Island
Pacific Ocean
Santa Elissa Island
agricultural area
HIGHWAY
COATES ACADEMY
TROTTER'S RIDGE
PERDIDO BEACH
Diameter: 20 miles
centres on power plant

Legend

- A — hardware and day care
- B — burned apartment building
- C — church
- D — town hall
- E — Quinn's square
- F — Astrid's house
- G — Sam's house
- H — McDonald's
- I — Bully Row
- J — firehouse
- K — school

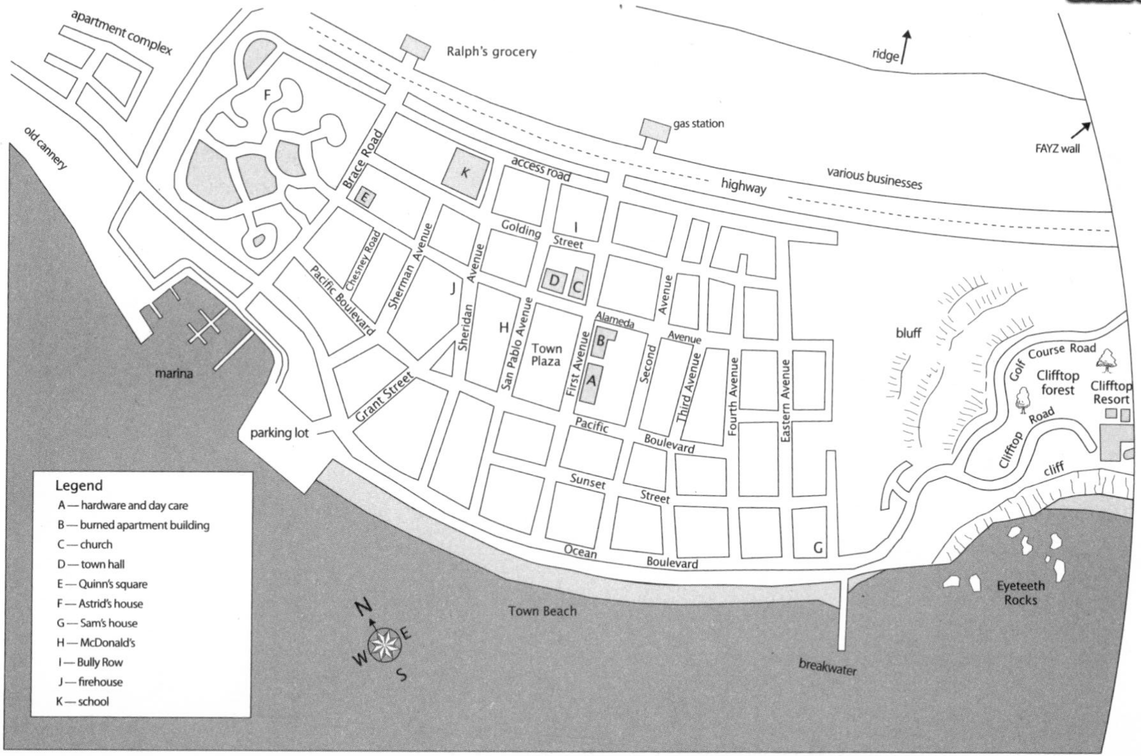

THE STORY CONCLUDES IN

LIGHT

Coming in 2013

Turn over for a sneak preview of the astonishing new series from Michael Grant

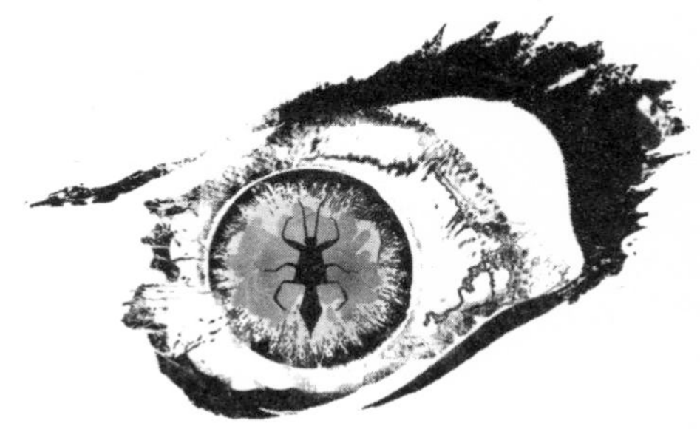

BZRK

ONE

A girl sat just three chairs down from Noah talking to her hand. To the back of her hand, actually, as she spread her fingers wide. Her fingertips were painted alternately red and gold, but not with fingernail polish, and not strictly on the fingernails. Rather, it looked as if she had used a can of spray paint.

She explained to the back of her hand that she was 'Perfectly all right. Perfectly all right.'

Noah thought she might have been pretty, but it was hard to really assess her face or body when his glance was drawn so irresistibly to the rope burn around her neck.

She started screaming when the orderlies came for her. They had to lift her up bodily, one on each rigid arm. Her mother, or perhaps older sister, stood with her hand over her mouth, wept and echoed the girl's own speech.

'It'll be all right,' said the sane one.

'I'm perfectly all right!' cried the crazy one.

The girl kicked her chair across the floor, and shot Noah a savage look from eyes edged red.

Noah Cotton. Sixteen years old. He had brown hair that defaulted to bed head without any effort on his part. His lips were full and downturned just a little, as if prepared for sadness. The nose was strong and sharp, a damned-near-perfect nose. But of course it was those blue eyes that drew you in. Where had he gotten eyes that blue? They looked unnatural. Like someone wearing tinted contact lenses. And Noah would turn those bright, unnatural blue eyes on you, and you wouldn't know whether you were looking into profound depths or maybe just into a very crazy place.

Well, if the answer was, 'a very crazy place,' then he would fit in perfectly with his location, which was the waiting room in the central hall of The Brick.

This place weighed down on him. Maybe it was the history. In the eighteenth century it had been called the Lord Japheth LeMay Asylum for the Incurably Mad. By the mid-nineteenth century that had been softened a bit to become the East London Asylum for the Insane.

Today it was officially called the East London Hospital for the Treatment of Serious Mental Illness.

But no one called it that, at least not outside the facility itself. Out in the world it was called The Brick.

It was a redbrick architectural monstrosity that had grown – metastasized, maybe – over the course of more than two hundred years. It wasn't all brick. Some of the towers and wings were stone. Some outbuildings were flaking, painted plaster over ancient half-timbered walls. But the massive hall, with its fraternal twin towers, the Bishop and the Rook – one tall and pointed, the other squat and intimidating – were all in soot-encrusted red brick.

Noah was doing his best not to feel the echoes of the mad girl's cries, but the waiting room was about as schizophrenic as many of the patients: ancient oil paintings, a vaguely off-kilter black-and-white tile floor, yellow walls that were probably someone's idea of cheerful, and furniture from a rummage sale. Then, to top it all off, there was the chandelier, which had to have been plundered from some gaudy palace during a long-ago colonial war. It cast a light that was excellent at creating shadows, so that even the space under the chairs looked as if it might be the dark lair of tiny monsters.

Noah was here to visit his brother, Alex. His much older brother, Alex. Age twenty-five, ex-army veteran of Afghanistan, Royal Highland Fusiliers. (Motto: *Nemo Me Impugn Lacessit* – No One Assails Me with Impunity. Or the alternative version – Do Not Fuck with Us or We Will Hurt You.) Shoulders you could break a cinder block on, disciplined, up every morning to run ten kilometers in whatever weather London had on offer.

Alex Cotton, who had earned the Conspicuous Gallantry Cross for basically having balls so big he had taken out three

Hajis in a machine-gun nest while literally carrying a wounded comrade on his back.

And now . . .

Noah's name was called. An attendant, a swaggering thug with fat legs, a Taser in one pocket and a leather-covered sap sticking out of the other, led the way. Past office doorways. Through a reinforced glass and steel security doorway.

Through a second security door.

Past the control center where bored guards watched flickering screens and discussed sports with their feet up.

Through a third door. This one had to be buzzed open by an attendant on the other side.

And here the screams and wails and sudden shrill, rising cries and gut-wrenching sobs began. The sounds leaked through steel doors of individual rooms: cells, in reality.

Noah didn't want to feel those screams inside himself, but he wasn't armored, he wasn't impervious. Each wild trill of mad laughter made him flinch as if he was being whipped.

A nurse and two scruffy attendants were making their way from door to door. One of the attendants pushed a squeaky cart loaded with little plastic cups, each designated with a code number and containing no fewer than half a dozen and sometimes a baker's dozen brightly colored pills.

The pill crew came to a door, knocked, warned the inmate to stand back, waited, then unlocked and opened the door. One attendant – no, let's cut the bull, they were guards, turnkeys, screws, but not attendants – went inside with the nurse while the remaining guard stood ready with a Taser.

Noah reached Alex's cell. Number ninety-one.

'Don't worry, he's shackled,' the guard said. 'Just don't try to touch him. He don't like people touching him.' The guard grinned ruefully and shook his head in a way that suggested Noah knew what he meant.

The door opened on a room five feet wide, eight feet deep. The only furnishing was a steel bunk. Fat steel bolts fixed the cot to the cracked tile floor. There was a radio on a high shelf, too high for a person to reach. The BBC was on, soft, some politician being grilled.

Alex Cotton sat on the edge of the bunk. His wrists were handcuffed to steel rings on either end. The effect was to stretch his arms out and limit his ability to move anything but his head.

The ghost of Alex Cotton turned hollow, vacant eyes on his little brother.

Noah couldn't speak for a moment. Because what he wanted to say was, 'This is the wrong room. That's not my brother.'

Then a low growl that at first sounded as if it might be coming from the radio. An animal sound. Alex Cotton's mouth snapped suddenly, like a shark missing the bait.

'Alex,' Noah said. 'It's me. It's just me, Noah.'

The guttural sound again. Alex's eyes suddenly focused.

Stared at Noah, shook his head as if the vision caused him pain.

Noah made just the slightest move to touch his brother's strained arm. Alex yanked his whole body as far away as he could, which was no more than a few inches. He strained so hard that the handcuffs drew blood.

Noah backed away, held up his hands reassuringly.

'Told you, don't try and touch him, he'll start in screaming about his little spiders and shit,' the guard said.

'Alex, it's just me. It's Noah.'

'Nano nano nano nano,' Alex said in a singsong voice, and then giggled. He wiggled his fingertips like he was acting something out.

'Nano? What is that, Alex?' He whispered it, speaking as he would to a frightened child. Gentle.

'Heh heh heh, no. No. No no no nano nano nano. No.'

Noah waited until he was done. He refused to look away. This was his brother. What was left of his brother.

'Alex, no one can figure this out. No one can figure out what happened to you. You know what I mean, to have you end up here.'

Explain your craziness, crazy man. Tell me what happened to my brother.

'Nano, macro, nano, macro,' Alex muttered.

'He says that a lot,' the guard offered. 'Mostly nano.'

'Is this from the war?' Noah asked, ignoring the guard. He

wanted an explanation. None of the doctors had been very convincing. Everyone said it was probably the war, but Alex had been examined for posttraumatic stress when he came home, and everything had seemed fine with him. He and Noah had taken in some sports, gone on a road trip to the Cornish coast for the beach and for some girl Alex knew. His brother had been a little distracted, but that was all. Distracted.

The guard hadn't answered.

'I mean, is it memories and all that?' Noah pressed. 'Is that what he goes on about? Afghanistan?'

To his surprise, it was Alex who answered.

'Haji?' Alex laughed a crooked-mouth laugh, like half his face was paralyzed. 'Not Haji. Bug Man,' Alex said. 'The Buuug Man. One, two, three. All dead. Poof!'

'That's pretty good for him,' the guard opined approvingly.

And for a few seconds it almost seemed as if the crazy had cleared away. Like Alex was straining to make his mouth say words. His voice went down into a whisper. He nodded, like he was saying, *Pay attention to this; this is important.*

This. Is. Important.

Then he said, 'Berserk.'

Alex nodded, satisfied with himself, then kept nodding harder and harder, until his whole body was vibrating almost like some kind of seizure. The shackles rattled the bed. The whole cell seemed to vibrate in sympathy.

'Berserk!' Alex said, louder now and louder still until he was shouting it.

'Berserk! Berserk!'

'Jesus,' Noah said, hating himself for reacting, for letting his horror show.

'Once he starts on this, it's over for the day,' the guard said wearily. He grabbed Noah's arm, not unkindly. 'Goes on for hours with this berserk shite of his.'

'Berserk! Berserk!'

Noah let himself be led from the cell.

'Berserk!'

When he heard the door locked behind him, he felt a wave of sickness and relief. But it didn't stop the sound of his mad brother's cries, which followed him down the hallway, drilling holes into Noah's reeling mind.

'Berserk!'

'BERSERK!'

Michael Grant has always been fast paced. He's lived in almost 50 different homes in 14 US states, and moved in with his wife, Katherine Applegate, after knowing her for less than 24 hours. His long list of previous occupations includes cartoonist, waiter, law librarian, bowling alley mechanic, restaurant reviewer, documentary film producer and political media consultant.

Michael and Katherine have co-authored more than 150 books, including the massive hit series *Animorphs*, which has sold more than 35 million copies. Working solo, Michael is the author of the *New York Times* bestselling series *GONE* and the groundbreaking transmedia trilogy *BZRK*.

Michael, Katherine and their two children live in the San Francisco Bay Area, not far from Silicon Valley. Michael can be contacted on Twitter (@thefayz), Facebook (authormichaelgrant), and via good, old-fashioned email (Michael@themichaelgrant.com).

EGMONT PRESS: ETHICAL PUBLISHING

Egmont Press is about turning writers into successful authors and children into passionate readers – producing books that enrich and entertain. As a responsible children's publisher, we go even further, considering the world in which our consumers are growing up.

Safety First
Naturally, all of our books meet legal safety requirements. But we go further than this; every book with play value is tested to the highest standards – if it fails, it's back to the drawing-board.

Made Fairly
We are working to ensure that the workers involved in our supply chain – the people that make our books – are treated with fairness and respect.

Responsible Forestry
We are committed to ensuring all our papers come from environmentally and socially responsible forest sources.

For more information, please visit our website at www.egmont.co.uk/ethical

Egmont is passionate about helping to preserve the world's remaining ancient forests. We only use paper from legal and sustainable forest sources, so we know where every single tree comes from that goes into every paper that makes up every book.

This book is made from paper certified by the Forestry Stewardship Council (FSC®), an organisation dedicated to promoting responsible management of forest resources. For more information on the FSC, please visit **www.fsc.org**. To learn more about Egmont's sustainable paper policy, please visit **www.egmont.co.uk/ethical**.